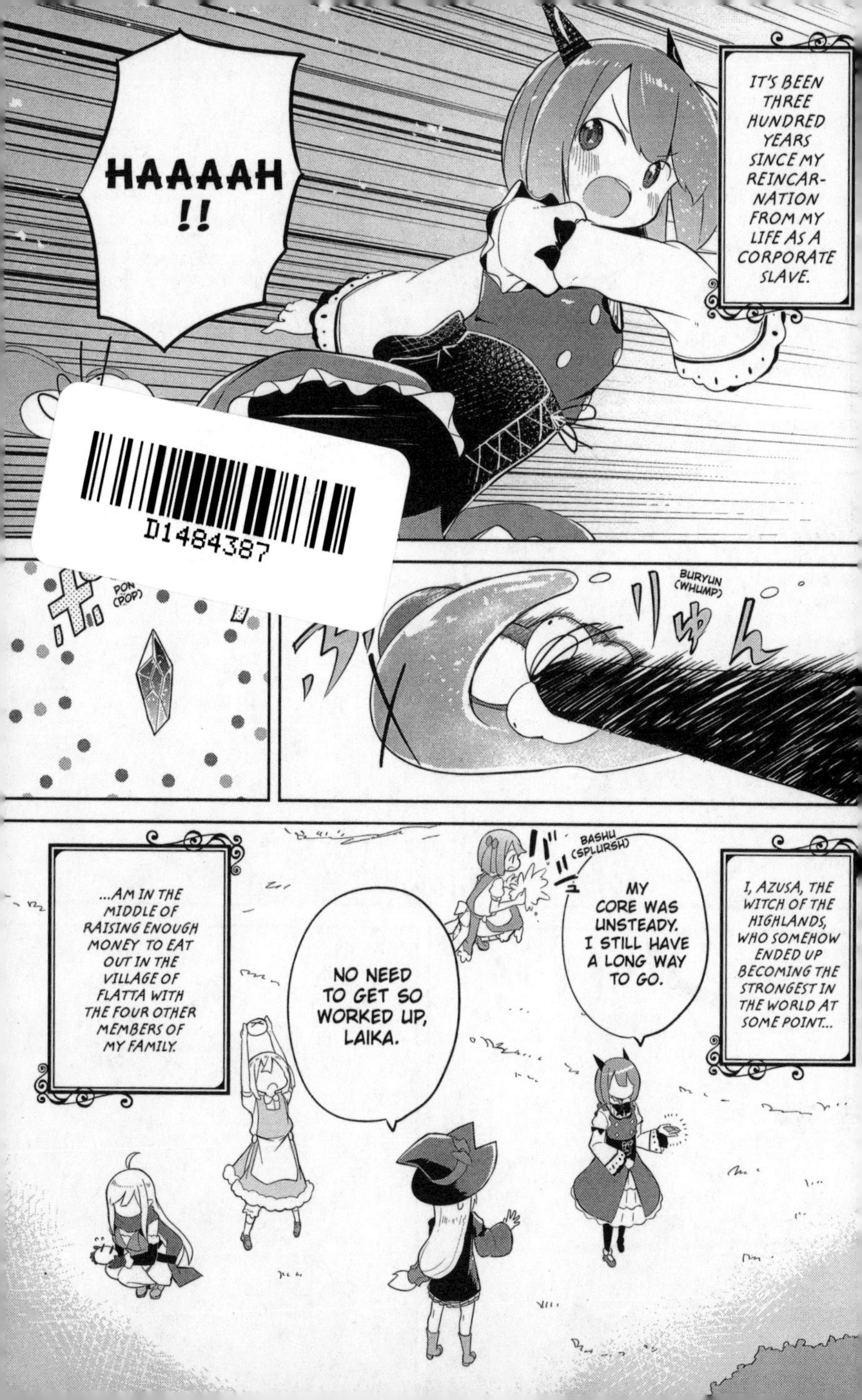
IT'S BEEN THREE HUNDRED YEARS SINCE MY REINCARNATION FROM MY LIFE AS A CORPORATE SLAVE.
HAAAAH!!
BURYUN (WHUMP)
PON (POP)
I, AZUSA, THE WITCH OF THE HIGHLANDS, WHO SOMEHOW ENDED UP BECOMING THE STRONGEST IN THE WORLD AT SOME POINT...
BASHU (SPLURSH)
MY CORE WAS UNSTEADY. I STILL HAVE A LONG WAY TO GO.
NO NEED TO GET SO WORKED UP, LAIKA.
...AM IN THE MIDDLE OF RAISING ENOUGH MONEY TO EAT OUT IN THE VILLAGE OF FLATTA WITH THE FOUR OTHER MEMBERS OF MY FAMILY.

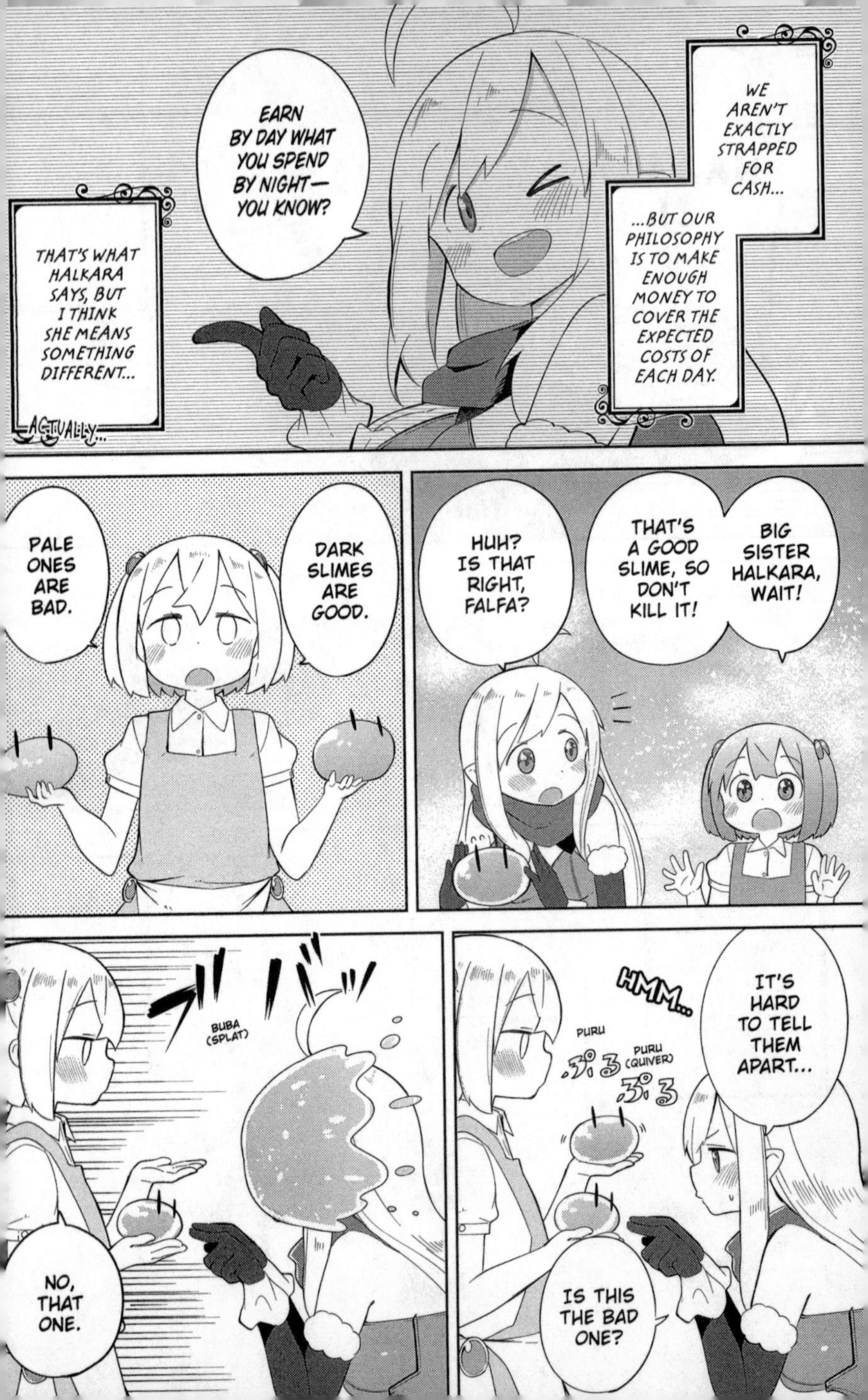
WE AREN'T EXACTLY STRAPPED FOR CASH...
...BUT OUR PHILOSOPHY IS TO MAKE ENOUGH MONEY TO COVER THE EXPECTED COSTS OF EACH DAY.
EARN BY DAY WHAT YOU SPEND BY NIGHT—YOU KNOW?
THAT'S WHAT HALKARA SAYS, BUT I THINK SHE MEANS SOMETHING DIFFERENT...
ACTUALLY...
BIG SISTER HALKARA, WAIT!
THAT'S A GOOD SLIME, SO DON'T KILL IT!
HUH? IS THAT RIGHT, FALFA?
DARK SLIMES ARE GOOD.
PALE ONES ARE BAD.
IT'S HARD TO TELL THEM APART...
HMM...
PURU
PURU (QUIVER)
IS THIS THE BAD ONE?
BUBA (SPLAT)
NO, THAT ONE.

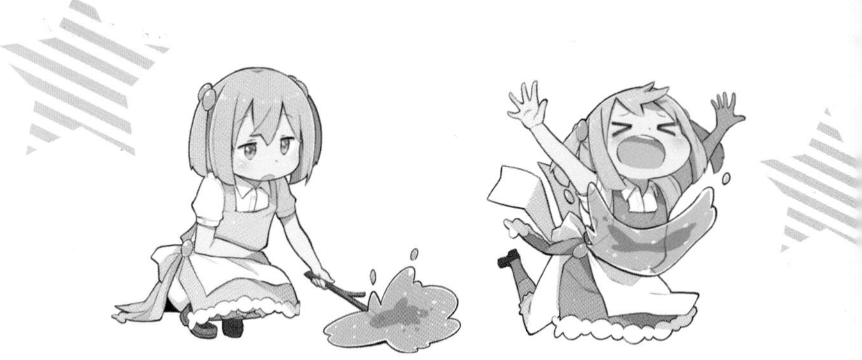

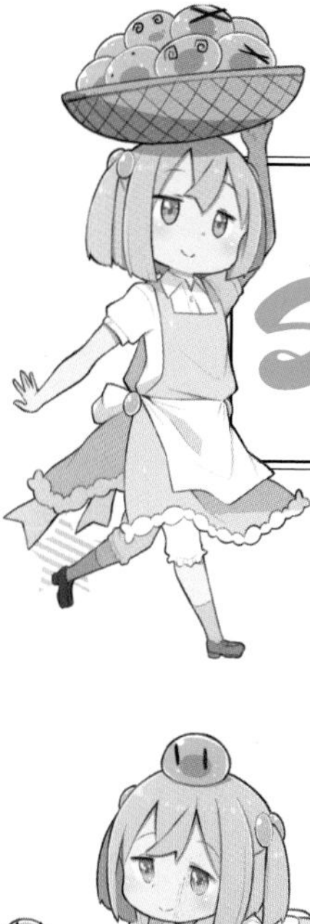

I've Been Killing Slimes for 300 Years and Maxed Out My Level

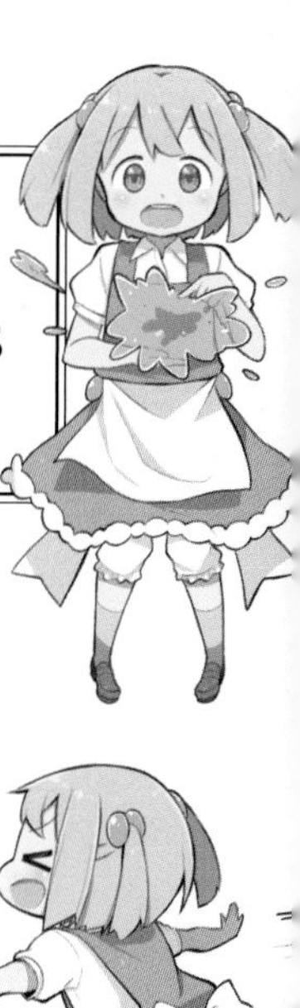

3

Original Story **Kisetsu Morita**
Art **Yusuke Shiba**
Character Design **Benio**

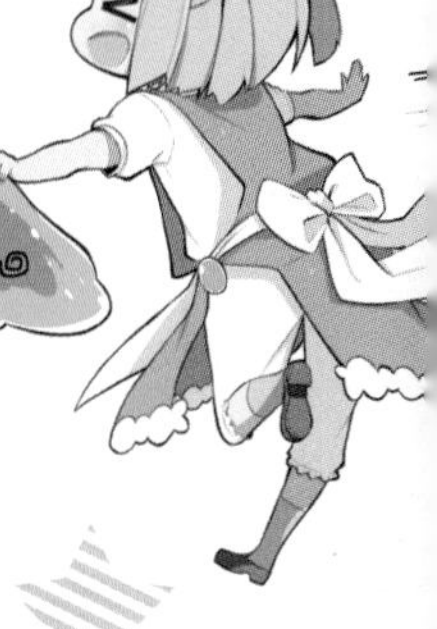

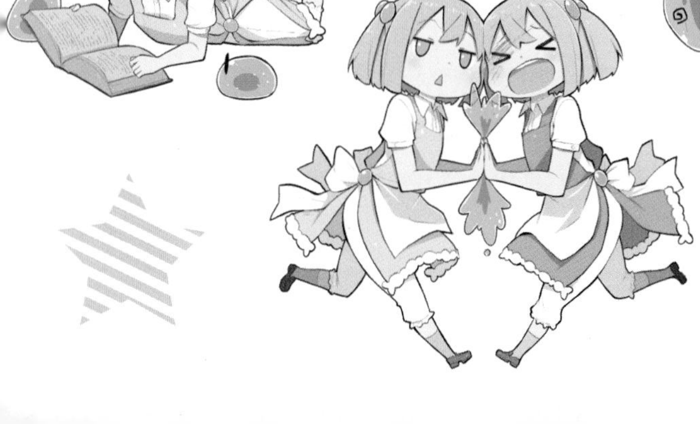

Contents

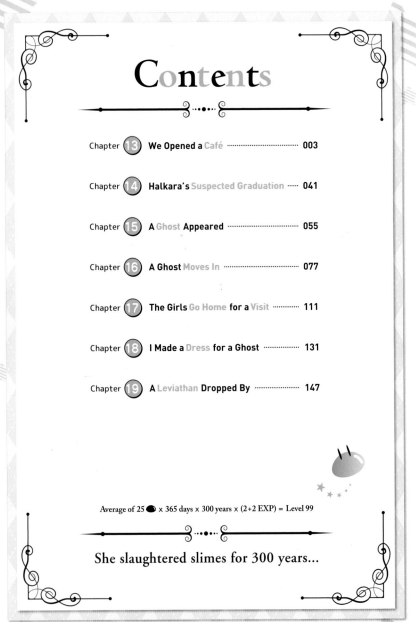

Chapter 13 **We Opened a** Café ·· **003**

Chapter 14 **Halkara's** Suspected Graduation ······ **041**

Chapter 15 **A** Ghost **Appeared** ·· **055**

Chapter 16 **A Ghost** Moves In ·· **077**

Chapter 17 **The Girls** Go Home **for a** Visit ··········· **111**

Chapter 18 **I Made a** Dress **for a Ghost** ················· **131**

Chapter 19 **A** Leviathan **Dropped By** ···················· **147**

Average of 25 ● x 365 days x 300 years x (2+2 EXP) = Level 99

She slaughtered slimes for 300 years...

CHAPTER 13
We Opened a Café

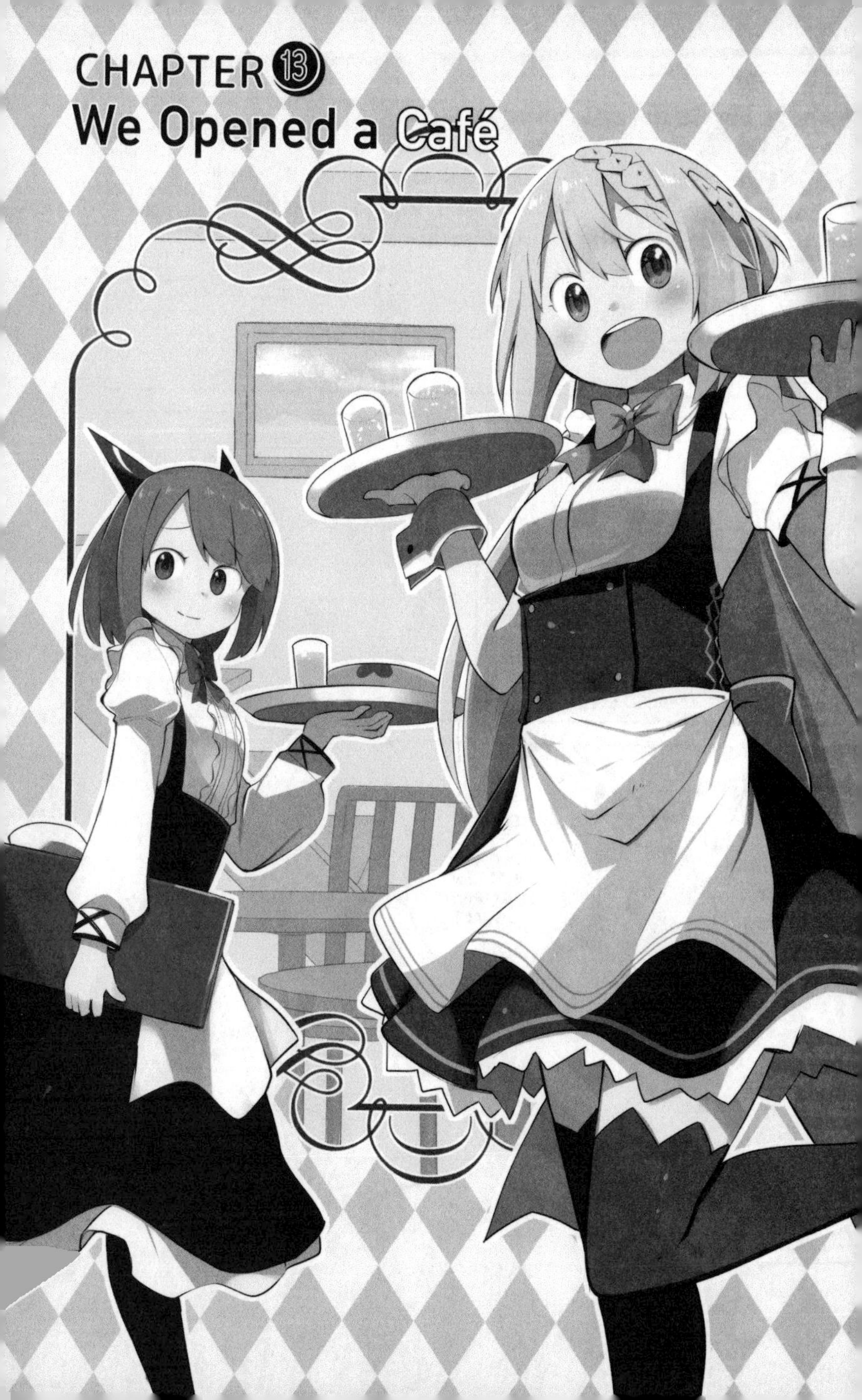

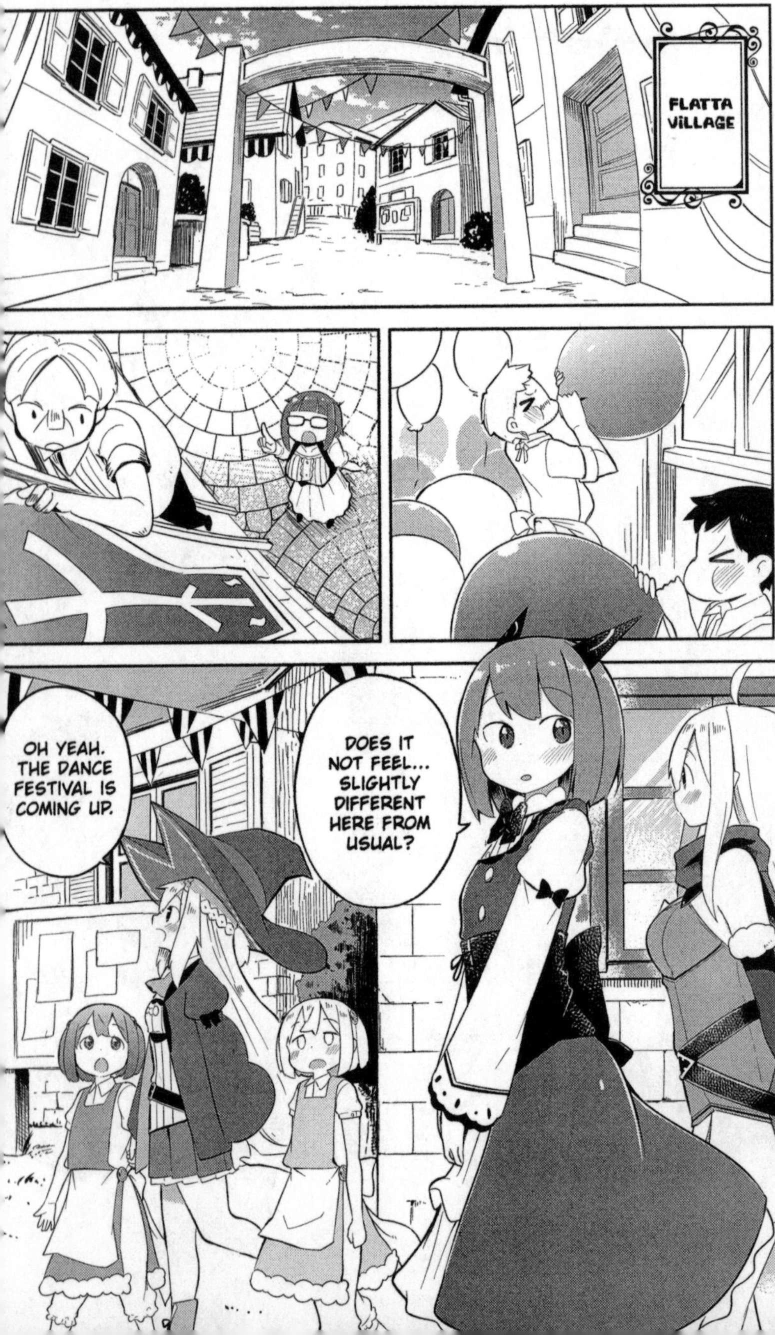
FLATTA VILLAGE
DOES IT NOT FEEL... SLIGHTLY DIFFERENT HERE FROM USUAL?
OH YEAH. THE DANCE FESTIVAL IS COMING UP.

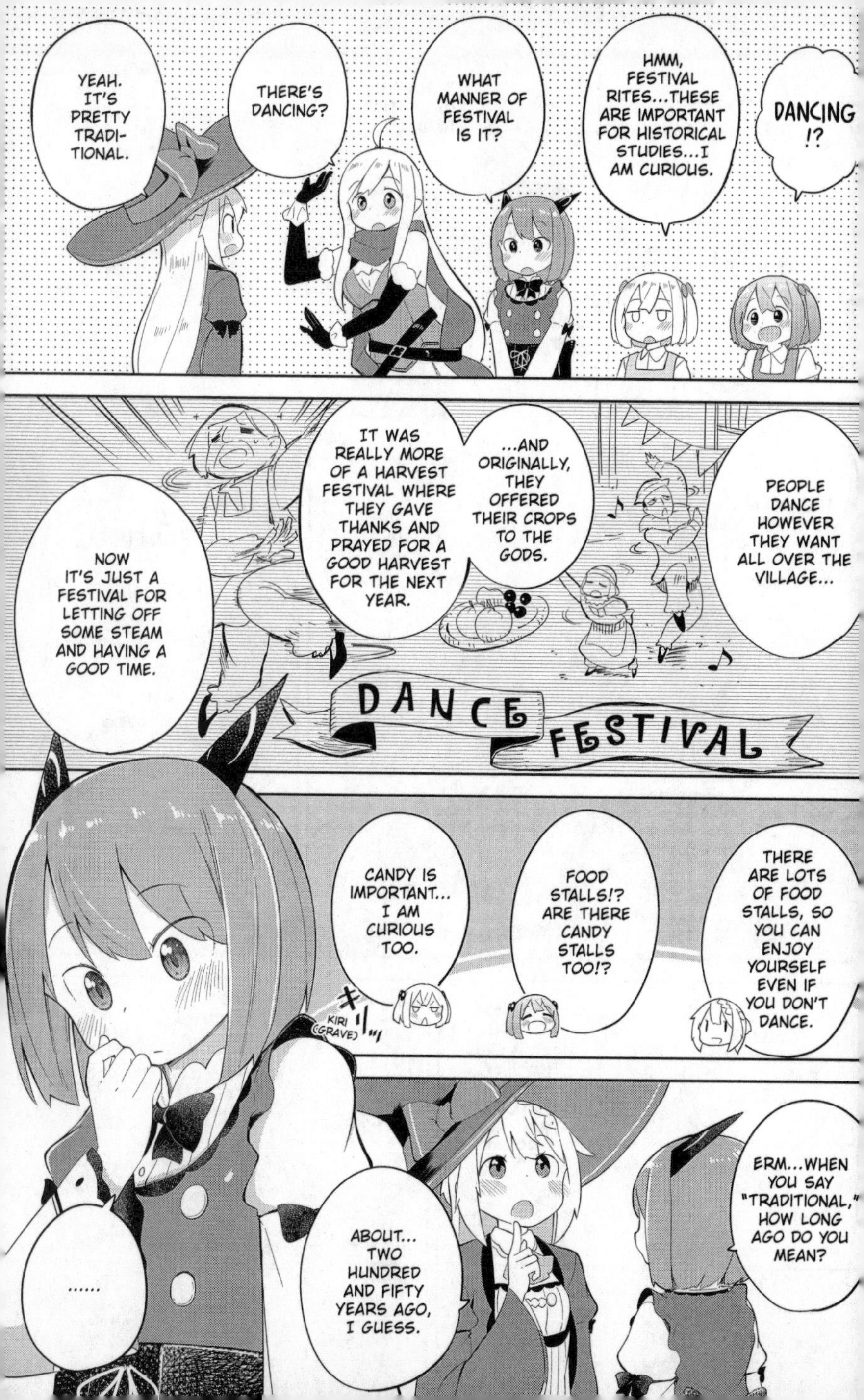
DANCING !?
HMM, FESTIVAL RITES...THESE ARE IMPORTANT FOR HISTORICAL STUDIES...I AM CURIOUS.
WHAT MANNER OF FESTIVAL IS IT?
THERE'S DANCING?
YEAH. IT'S PRETTY TRADI-TIONAL.
PEOPLE DANCE HOWEVER THEY WANT ALL OVER THE VILLAGE...
...AND ORIGINALLY, THEY OFFERED THEIR CROPS TO THE GODS.
IT WAS REALLY MORE OF A HARVEST FESTIVAL WHERE THEY GAVE THANKS AND PRAYED FOR A GOOD HARVEST FOR THE NEXT YEAR.
NOW IT'S JUST A FESTIVAL FOR LETTING OFF SOME STEAM AND HAVING A GOOD TIME.
DANCE FESTIVAL
THERE ARE LOTS OF FOOD STALLS, SO YOU CAN ENJOY YOURSELF EVEN IF YOU DON'T DANCE.
FOOD STALLS!? ARE THERE CANDY STALLS TOO!?
CANDY IS IMPORTANT... I AM CURIOUS TOO.
KIRI (GRAVE)
ERM...WHEN YOU SAY "TRADITIONAL," HOW LONG AGO DO YOU MEAN?
ABOUT... TWO HUNDRED AND FIFTY YEARS AGO, I GUESS.
......

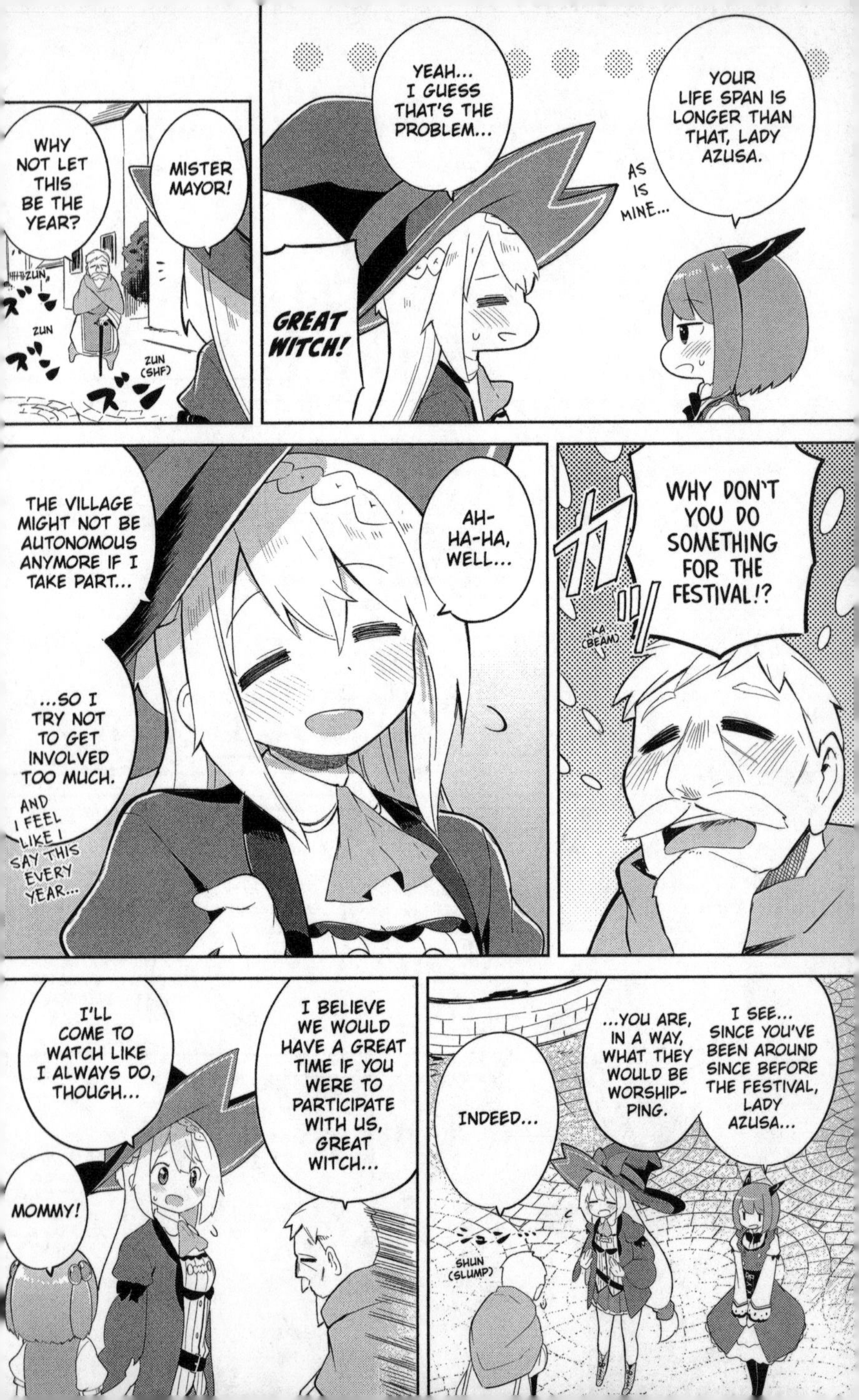
YOUR LIFE SPAN IS LONGER THAN THAT, LADY AZUSA.
AS IS MINE...
YEAH... I GUESS THAT'S THE PROBLEM...
GREAT WITCH!
MISTER MAYOR!
WHY NOT LET THIS BE THE YEAR?
ZUN
ZUN
ZUN (SHF)
WHY DON'T YOU DO SOMETHING FOR THE FESTIVAL!?
KA (BEAM)
AH-HA-HA, WELL...
THE VILLAGE MIGHT NOT BE AUTONOMOUS ANYMORE IF I TAKE PART...
...SO I TRY NOT TO GET INVOLVED TOO MUCH.
AND I FEEL LIKE I SAY THIS EVERY YEAR...
I SEE... SINCE YOU'VE BEEN AROUND SINCE BEFORE THE FESTIVAL, LADY AZUSA...
...YOU ARE, IN A WAY, WHAT THEY WOULD BE WORSHIP-PING.
INDEED...
SHUN (SLUMP)
I BELIEVE WE WOULD HAVE A GREAT TIME IF YOU WERE TO PARTICIPATE WITH US, GREAT WITCH...
I'LL COME TO WATCH LIKE I ALWAYS DO, THOUGH...
MOMMY!

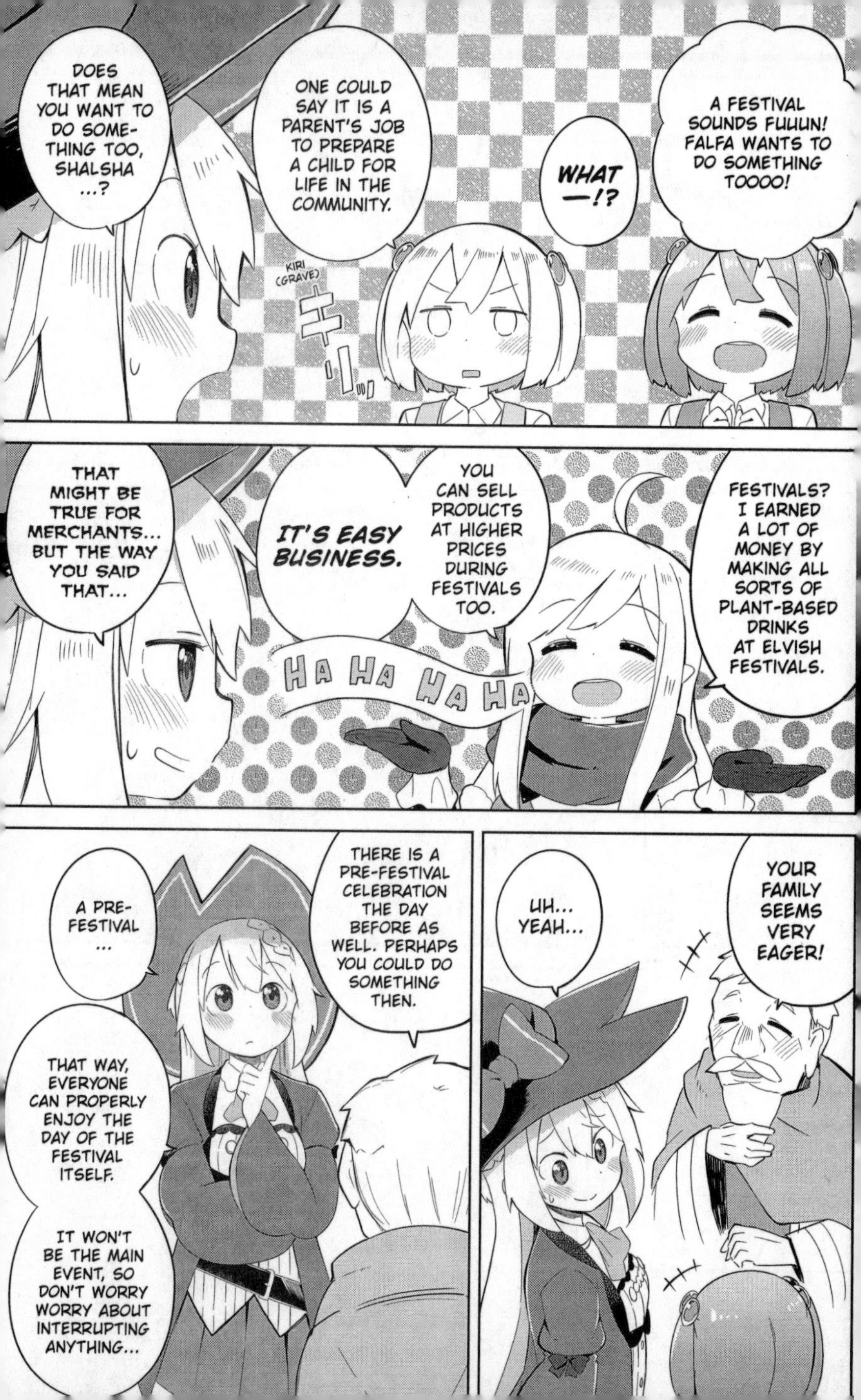
A FESTIVAL SOUNDS FUUUN! FALFA WANTS TO DO SOMETHING TOOOO!
WHAT—!?
ONE COULD SAY IT IS A PARENT'S JOB TO PREPARE A CHILD FOR LIFE IN THE COMMUNITY.
KIRI (GRAVE)
DOES THAT MEAN YOU WANT TO DO SOMETHING TOO, SHALSHA...?
FESTIVALS? I EARNED A LOT OF MONEY BY MAKING ALL SORTS OF PLANT-BASED DRINKS AT ELVISH FESTIVALS.
YOU CAN SELL PRODUCTS AT HIGHER PRICES DURING FESTIVALS TOO.
IT'S EASY BUSINESS.
HA HA HA HA
THAT MIGHT BE TRUE FOR MERCHANTS... BUT THE WAY YOU SAID THAT...
YOUR FAMILY SEEMS VERY EAGER!
UH... YEAH...
THERE IS A PRE-FESTIVAL CELEBRATION THE DAY BEFORE AS WELL. PERHAPS YOU COULD DO SOMETHING THEN.
A PRE-FESTIVAL...
THAT WAY, EVERYONE CAN PROPERLY ENJOY THE DAY OF THE FESTIVAL ITSELF.
IT WON'T BE THE MAIN EVENT, SO DON'T WORRY ABOUT INTERRUPTING ANYTHING...

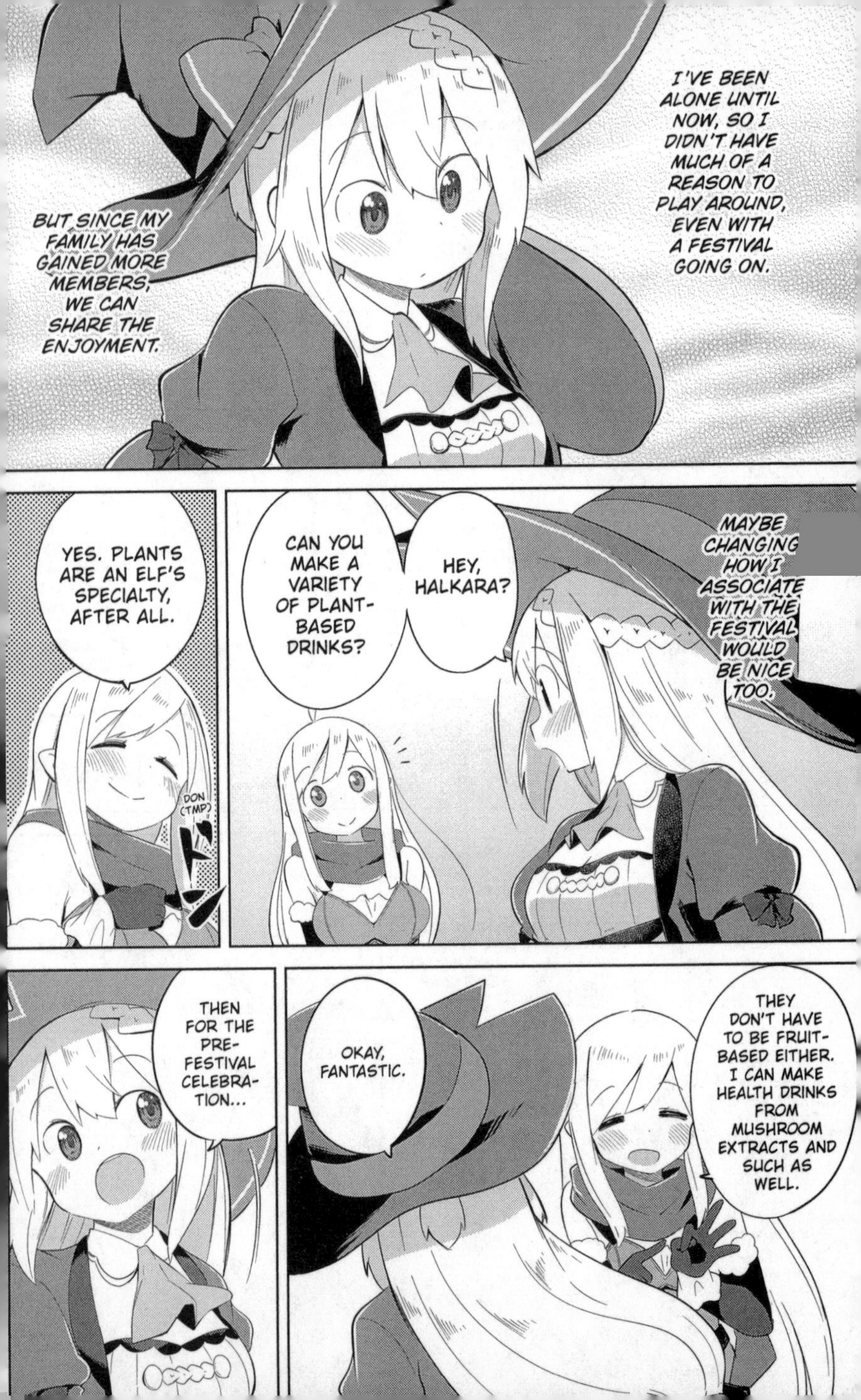
I'VE BEEN ALONE UNTIL NOW, SO I DIDN'T HAVE MUCH OF A REASON TO PLAY AROUND, EVEN WITH A FESTIVAL GOING ON.
BUT SINCE MY FAMILY HAS GAINED MORE MEMBERS, WE CAN SHARE THE ENJOYMENT.
MAYBE CHANGING HOW I ASSOCIATE WITH THE FESTIVAL WOULD BE NICE TOO.
HEY, HALKARA?
CAN YOU MAKE A VARIETY OF PLANT-BASED DRINKS?
YES. PLANTS ARE AN ELF'S SPECIALTY, AFTER ALL.
DON (TMP)
THEY DON'T HAVE TO BE FRUIT-BASED EITHER. I CAN MAKE HEALTH DRINKS FROM MUSHROOM EXTRACTS AND SUCH AS WELL.
OKAY, FANTASTIC.
THEN FOR THE PRE-FESTIVAL CELEBRATION...

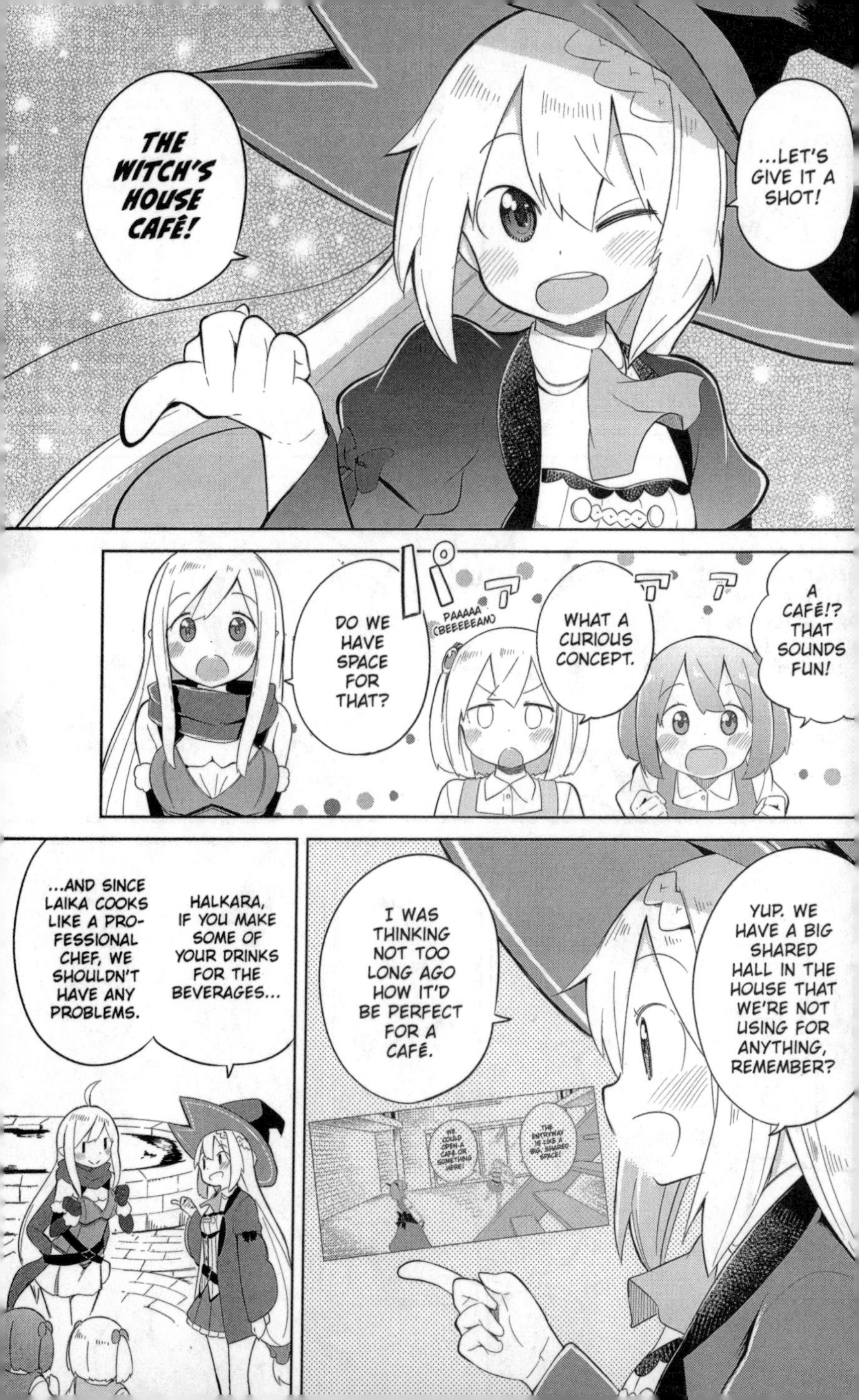
...LET'S GIVE IT A SHOT!
THE WITCH'S HOUSE CAFÉ!
A CAFÉ!? THAT SOUNDS FUN!
WHAT A CURIOUS CONCEPT.
PAAAAA (BEEEEEAM)
DO WE HAVE SPACE FOR THAT?
YUP. WE HAVE A BIG SHARED HALL IN THE HOUSE THAT WE'RE NOT USING FOR ANYTHING, REMEMBER?
I WAS THINKING NOT TOO LONG AGO HOW IT'D BE PERFECT FOR A CAFÉ.
THE ENTRYWAY IS LIKE A BIG, SHARED SPACE!
WE COULD OPEN A CAFÉ OR SOMETHING HERE!
HALKARA, IF YOU MAKE SOME OF YOUR DRINKS FOR THE BEVERAGES...
...AND SINCE LAIKA COOKS LIKE A PRO-FESSIONAL CHEF, WE SHOULDN'T HAVE ANY PROBLEMS.

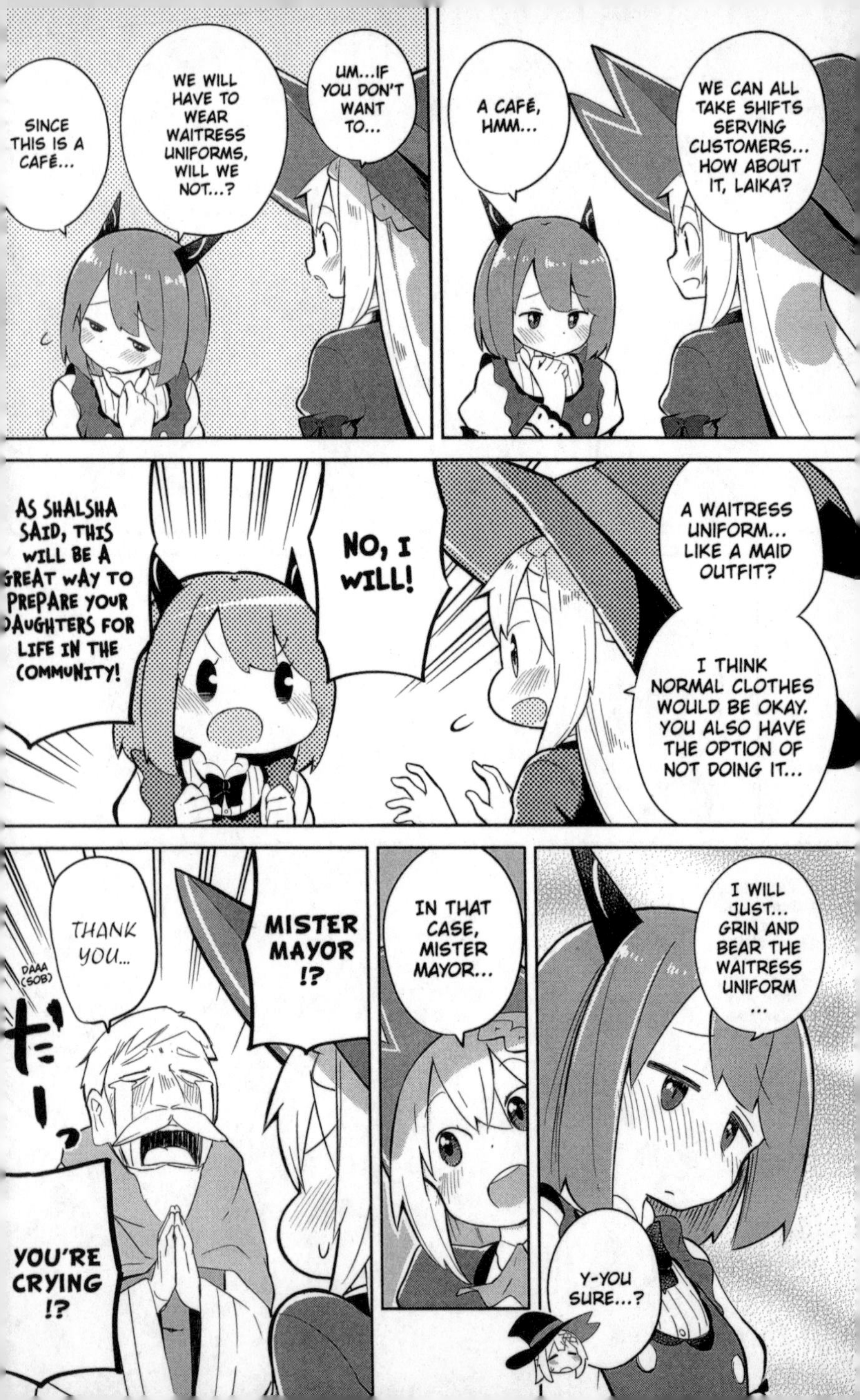

WE CAN ALL TAKE SHIFTS SERVING CUSTOMERS... HOW ABOUT IT, LAIKA?
A CAFÉ, HMM...
UM...IF YOU DON'T WANT TO...
WE WILL HAVE TO WEAR WAITRESS UNIFORMS, WILL WE NOT...?
SINCE THIS IS A CAFÉ...
A WAITRESS UNIFORM... LIKE A MAID OUTFIT?
I THINK NORMAL CLOTHES WOULD BE OKAY. YOU ALSO HAVE THE OPTION OF NOT DOING IT...
NO, I WILL!
AS SHALSHA SAID, THIS WILL BE A GREAT WAY TO PREPARE YOUR DAUGHTERS FOR LIFE IN THE COMMUNITY!
I WILL JUST... GRIN AND BEAR THE WAITRESS UNIFORM ...
Y-YOU SURE...?
IN THAT CASE, MISTER MAYOR...
MISTER MAYOR !?
THANK YOU...
DAAA (SOB)
だーっ
YOU'RE CRYING !?

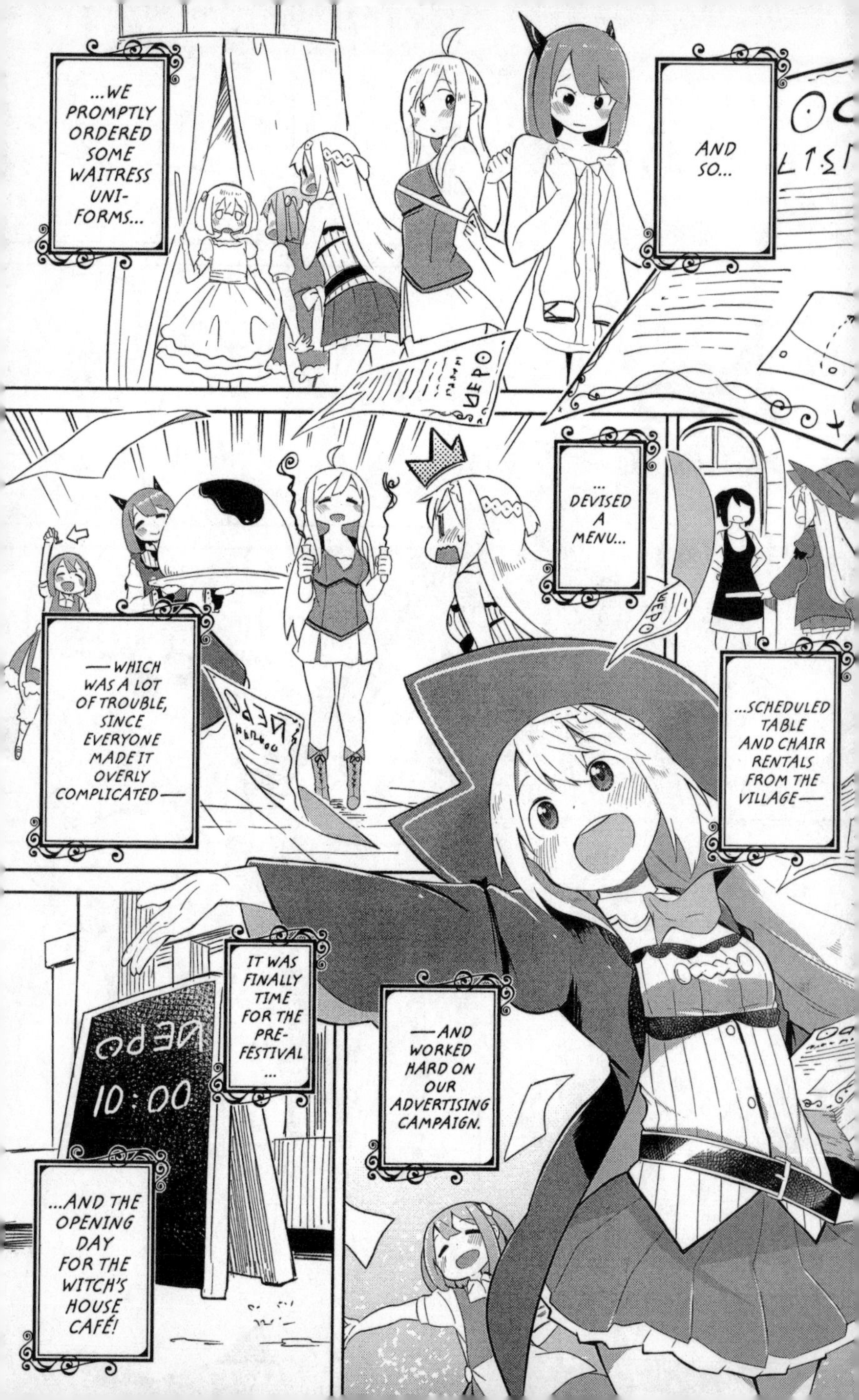
AND SO...
...WE PROMPTLY ORDERED SOME WAITRESS UNI-FORMS...
...DEVISED A MENU...
—WHICH WAS A LOT OF TROUBLE, SINCE EVERYONE MADE IT OVERLY COMPLICATED—
...SCHEDULED TABLE AND CHAIR RENTALS FROM THE VILLAGE—
—AND WORKED HARD ON OUR ADVERTISING CAMPAIGN.
IT WAS FINALLY TIME FOR THE PRE-FESTIVAL...
...AND THE OPENING DAY FOR THE WITCH'S HOUSE CAFÉ!
10:00

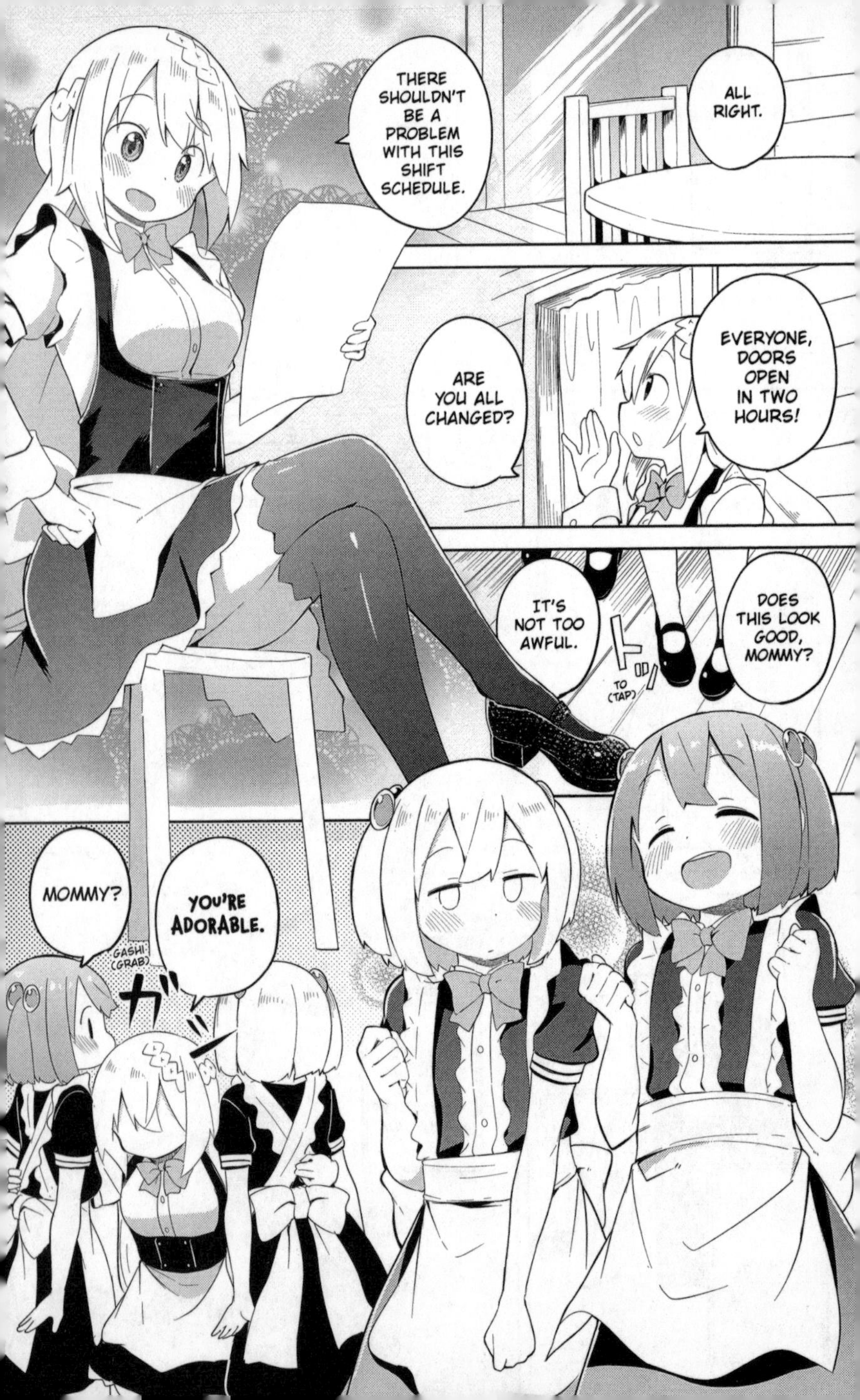
ALL RIGHT.
EVERYONE, DOORS OPEN IN TWO HOURS!
ARE YOU ALL CHANGED?
DOES THIS LOOK GOOD, MOMMY?
TO (TAP)
IT'S NOT TOO AWFUL.
THERE SHOULDN'T BE A PROBLEM WITH THIS SHIFT SCHEDULE.
YOU'RE ADORABLE.
GASHI (GRAB)
MOMMY?

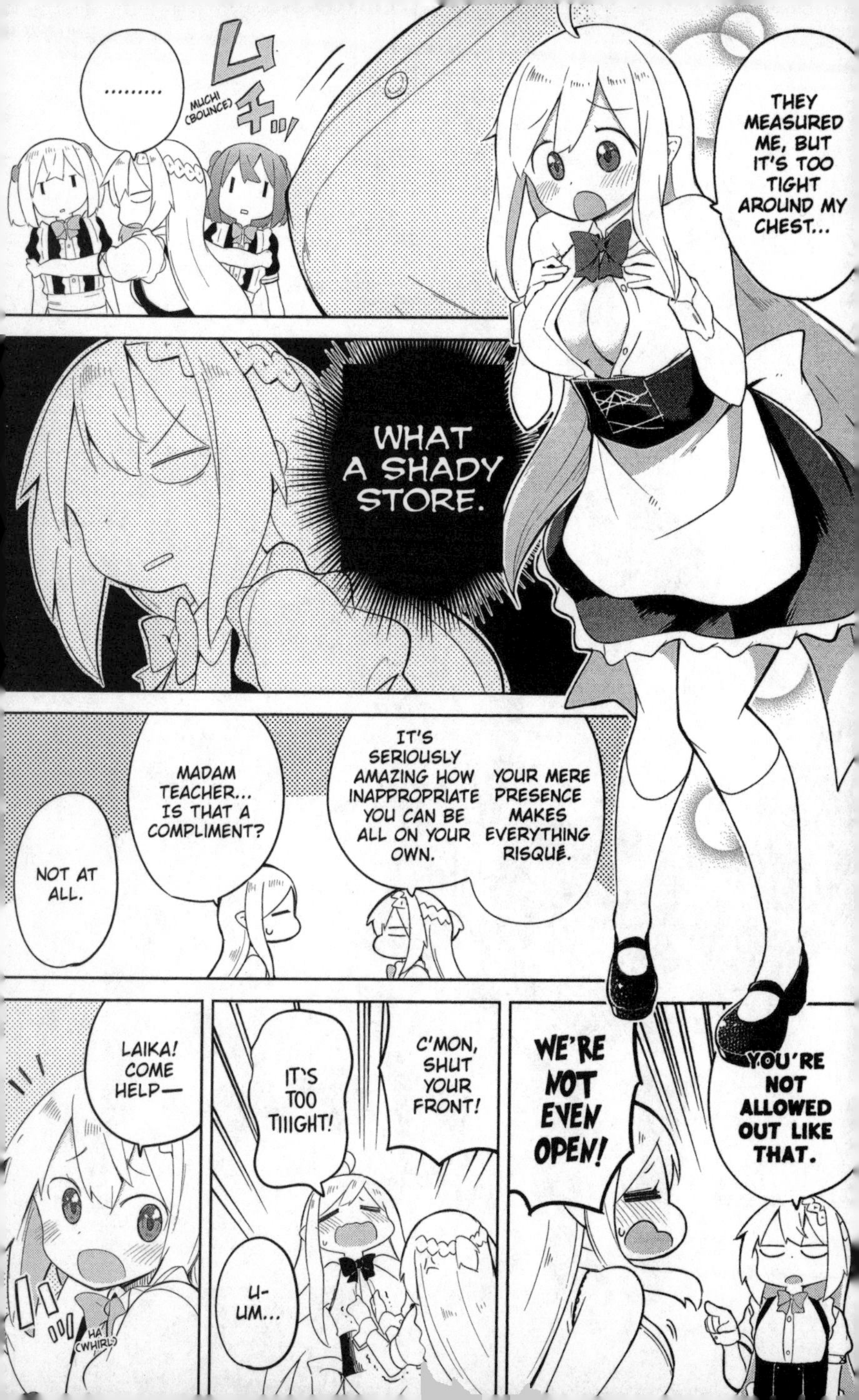
THEY MEASURED ME, BUT IT'S TOO TIGHT AROUND MY CHEST...
MUCHI (BOUNCE)
....
WHAT A SHADY STORE.
YOUR MERE PRESENCE MAKES EVERYTHING RISQUÉ.
IT'S SERIOUSLY AMAZING HOW INAPPROPRIATE YOU CAN BE ALL ON YOUR OWN.
MADAM TEACHER... IS THAT A COMPLIMENT?
NOT AT ALL.
YOU'RE NOT ALLOWED OUT LIKE THAT.
WE'RE NOT EVEN OPEN!
C'MON, SHUT YOUR FRONT!
IT'S TOO TIIIGHT!
U-UM...
LAIKA! COME HELP—
HA (WHIRL)

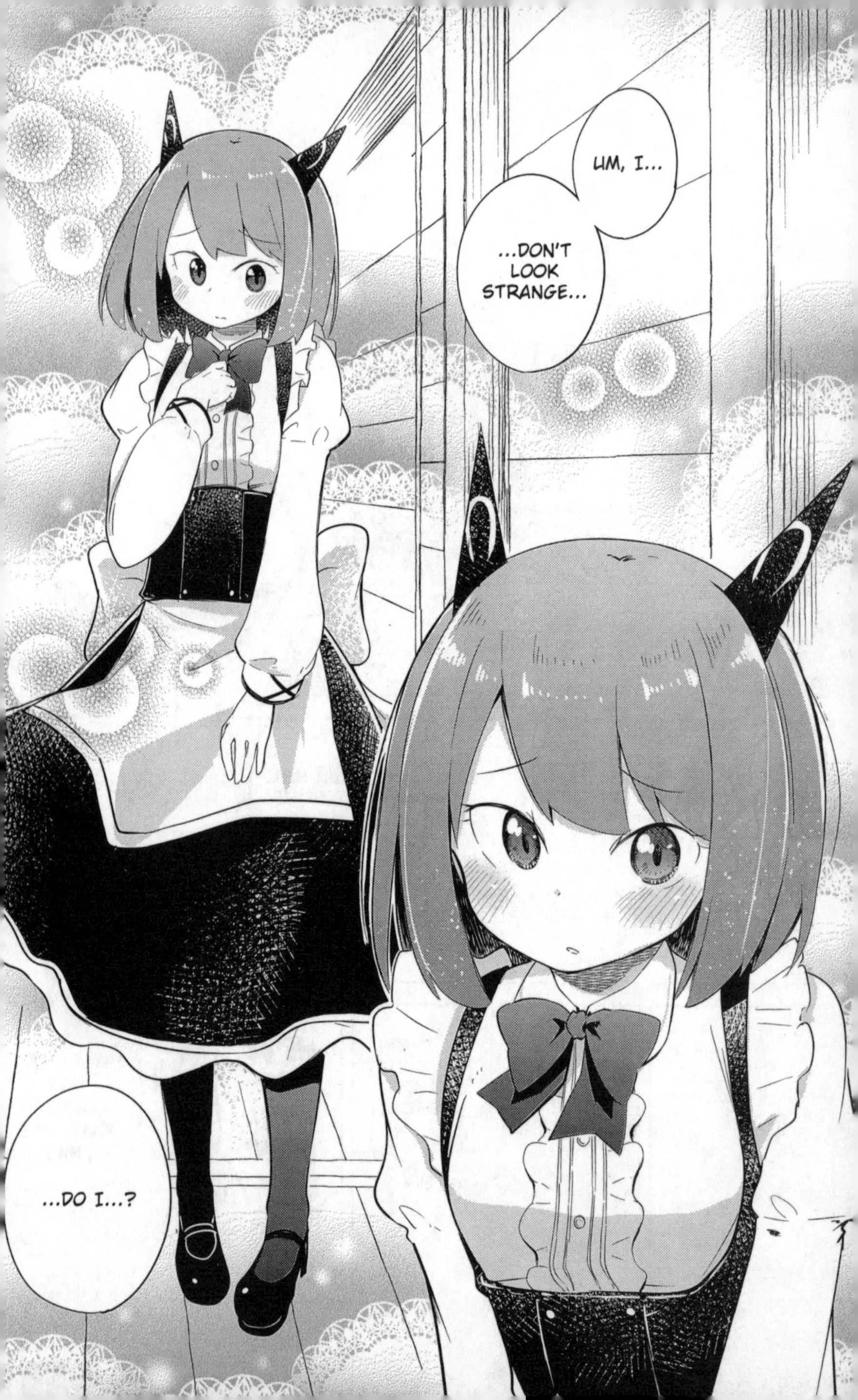
UM, I...
...DON'T LOOK STRANGE...
...DO I...?

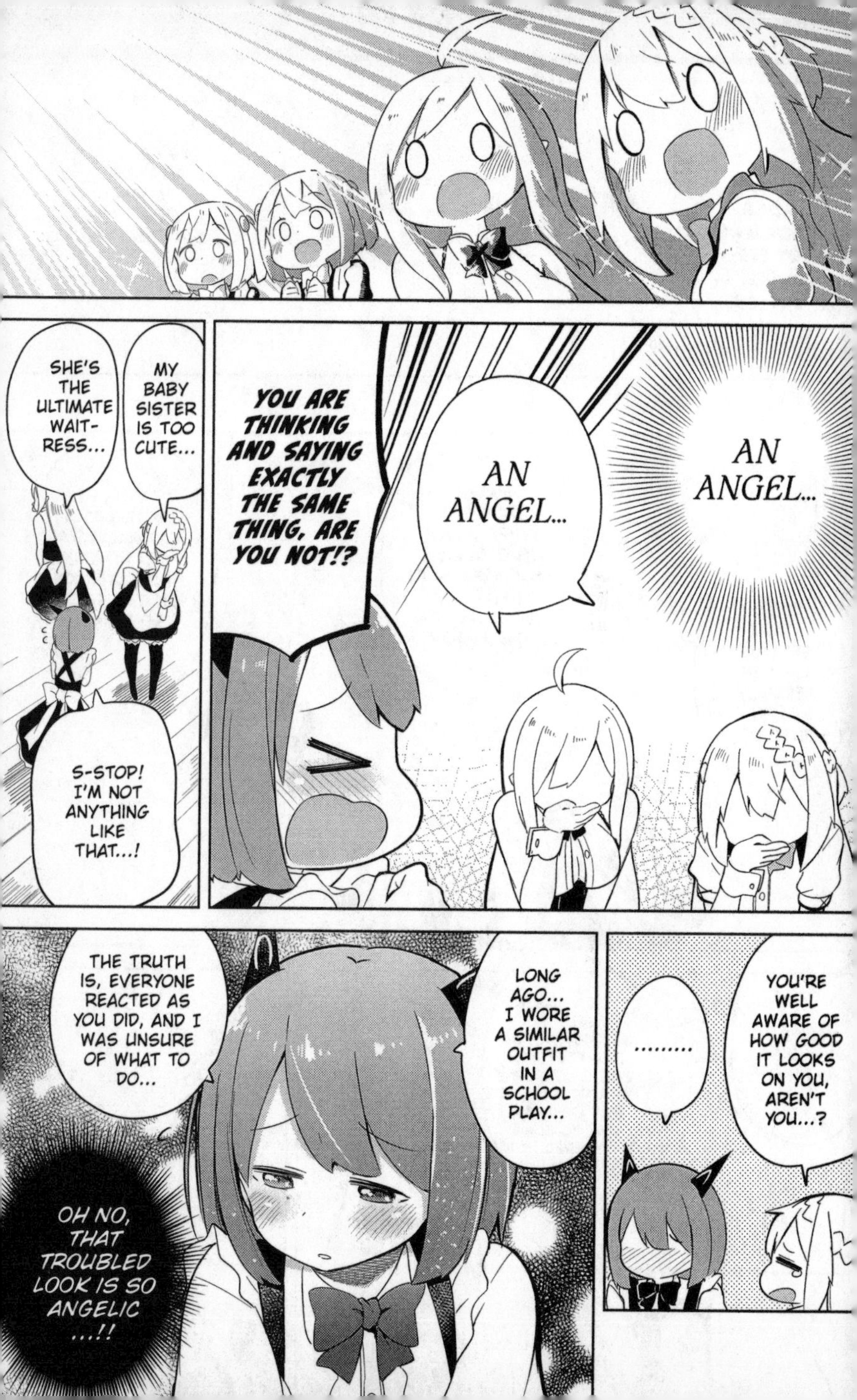
AN ANGEL...
AN ANGEL...
YOU ARE THINKING AND SAYING EXACTLY THE SAME THING, ARE YOU NOT!?
MY BABY SISTER IS TOO CUTE...
SHE'S THE ULTIMATE WAIT-RESS...
S-STOP! I'M NOT ANYTHING LIKE THAT...!
YOU'RE WELL AWARE OF HOW GOOD IT LOOKS ON YOU, AREN'T YOU...?
....
LONG AGO... I WORE A SIMILAR OUTFIT IN A SCHOOL PLAY...
THE TRUTH IS, EVERYONE REACTED AS YOU DID, AND I WAS UNSURE OF WHAT TO DO...
OH NO, THAT TROUBLED LOOK IS SO ANGELIC ...!!

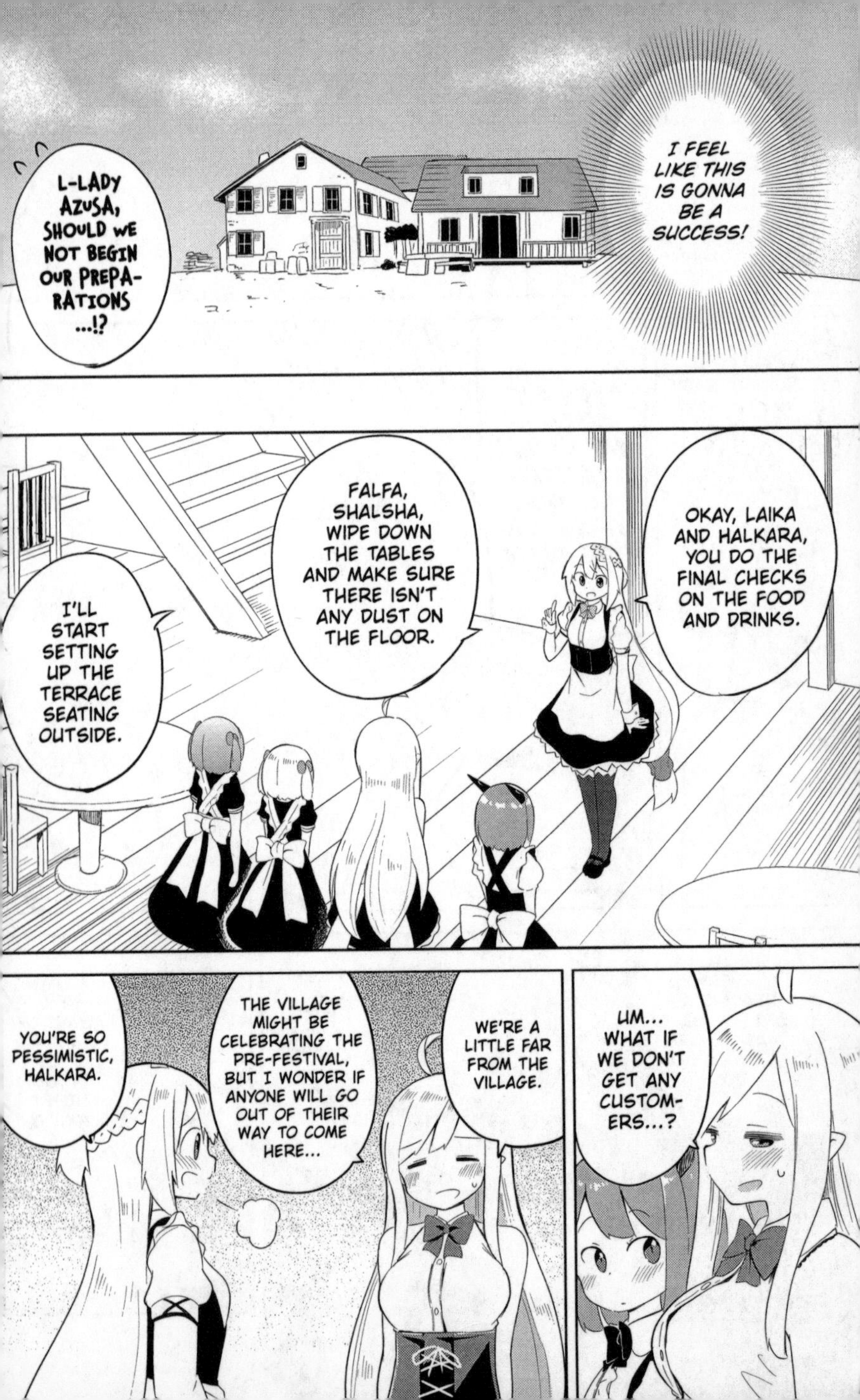
I FEEL LIKE THIS IS GONNA BE A SUCCESS!
L-LADY AZUSA, SHOULD WE NOT BEGIN OUR PREPARATIONS ...!?
OKAY, LAIKA AND HALKARA, YOU DO THE FINAL CHECKS ON THE FOOD AND DRINKS.
FALFA, SHALSHA, WIPE DOWN THE TABLES AND MAKE SURE THERE ISN'T ANY DUST ON THE FLOOR.
I'LL START SETTING UP THE TERRACE SEATING OUTSIDE.
UM... WHAT IF WE DON'T GET ANY CUSTOMERS...?
WE'RE A LITTLE FAR FROM THE VILLAGE.
THE VILLAGE MIGHT BE CELEBRATING THE PRE-FESTIVAL, BUT I WONDER IF ANYONE WILL GO OUT OF THEIR WAY TO COME HERE...
YOU'RE SO PESSIMISTIC, HALKARA.

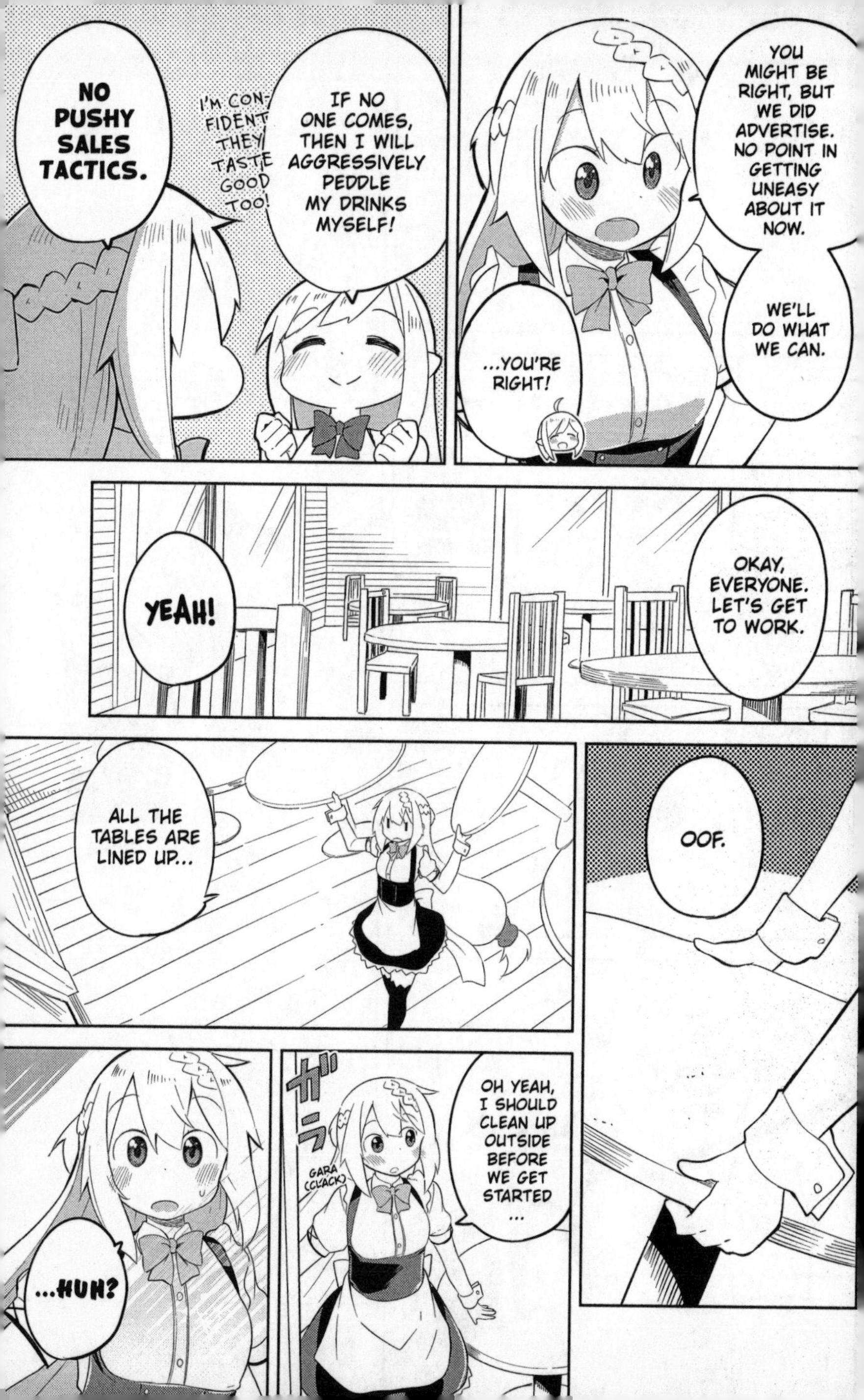
YOU MIGHT BE RIGHT, BUT WE DID ADVERTISE. NO POINT IN GETTING UNEASY ABOUT IT NOW.
WE'LL DO WHAT WE CAN.
...YOU'RE RIGHT!
IF NO ONE COMES, THEN I WILL AGGRESSIVELY PEDDLE MY DRINKS MYSELF!
I'M CONFIDENT THEY TASTE GOOD TOO!
NO PUSHY SALES TACTICS.
OKAY, EVERYONE. LET'S GET TO WORK.
YEAH!
OOF.
ALL THE TABLES ARE LINED UP...
GARA (CLACK)
OH YEAH, I SHOULD CLEAN UP OUTSIDE BEFORE WE GET STARTED ...
...HUH?

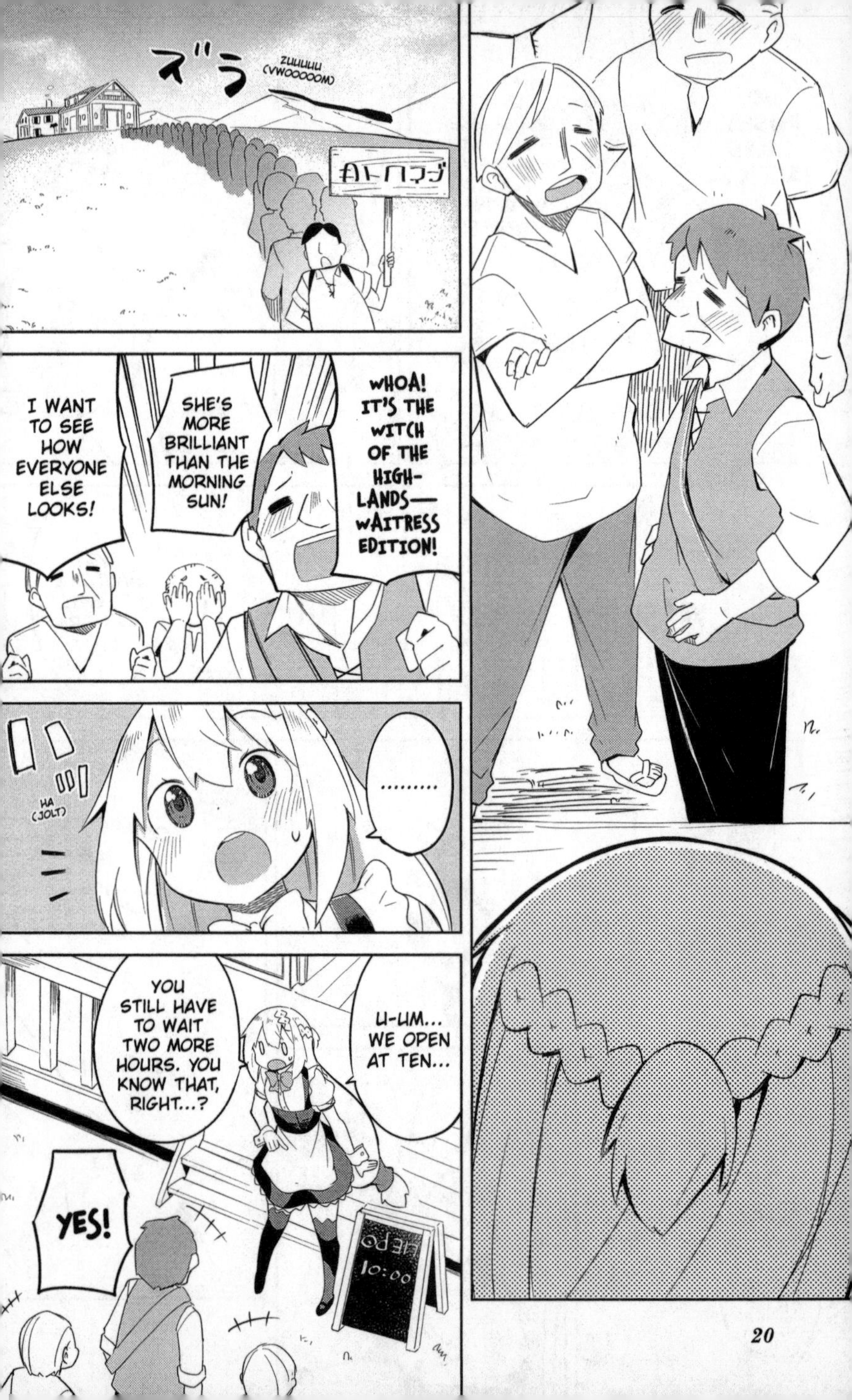
ズう
ZUUUUUU (VWOOOOOM)
WHOA! IT'S THE WITCH OF THE HIGHLANDS— WAITRESS EDITION!
SHE'S MORE BRILLIANT THAN THE MORNING SUN!
I WANT TO SEE HOW EVERYONE ELSE LOOKS!
HA (JOLT)
....
U-UM... WE OPEN AT TEN...
YOU STILL HAVE TO WAIT TWO MORE HOURS. YOU KNOW THAT, RIGHT...?
YES!
10:00

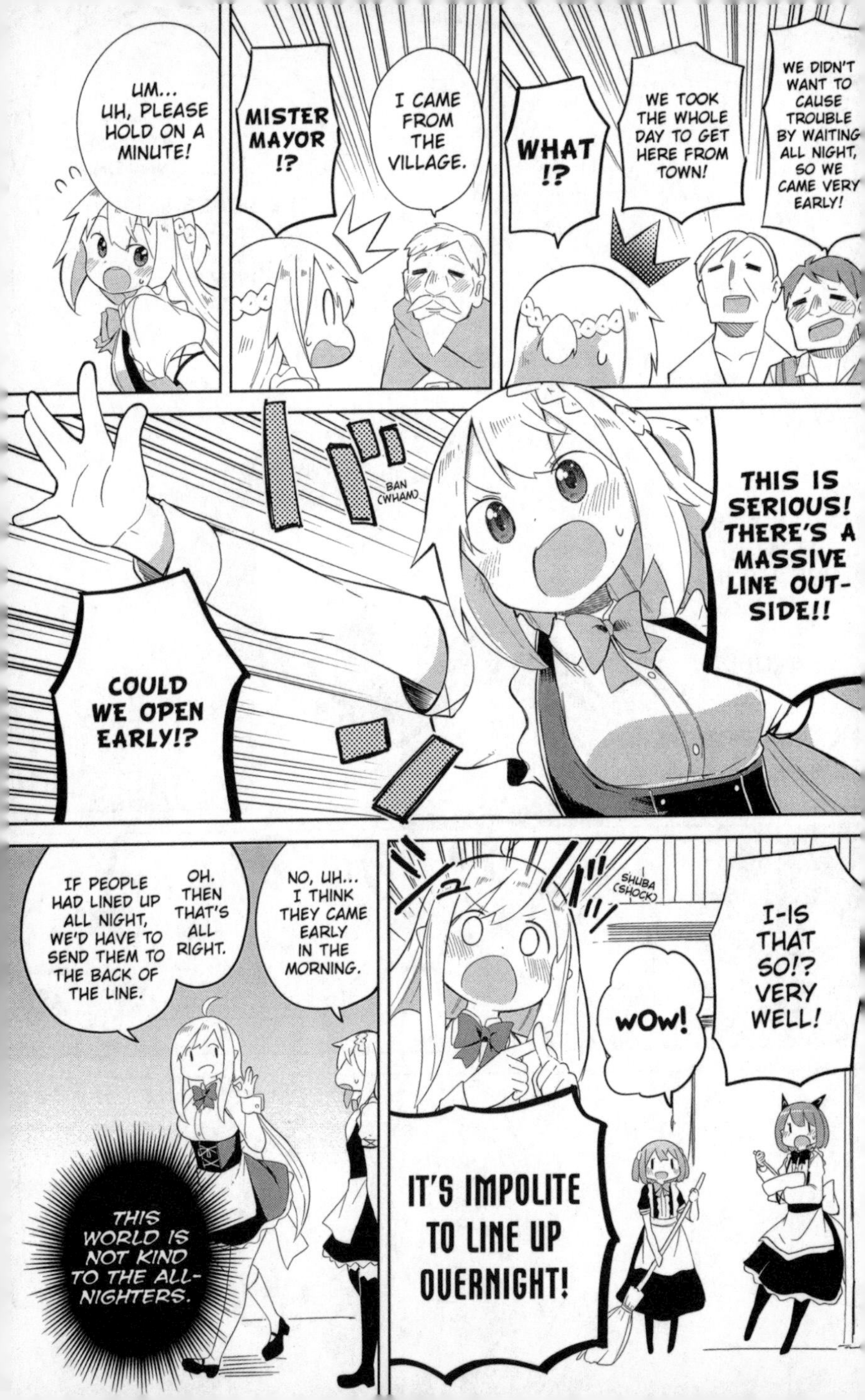
WE DIDN'T WANT TO CAUSE TROUBLE BY WAITING ALL NIGHT, SO WE CAME VERY EARLY!
WE TOOK THE WHOLE DAY TO GET HERE FROM TOWN!
WHAT!?
I CAME FROM THE VILLAGE.
MISTER MAYOR!?
UM... UH, PLEASE HOLD ON A MINUTE!
THIS IS SERIOUS! THERE'S A MASSIVE LINE OUT-SIDE!!
BAN (WHAM)
COULD WE OPEN EARLY!?
I-IS THAT SO!? VERY WELL!
SHUBA (SHOCK)
WOW!
IT'S IMPOLITE TO LINE UP OVERNIGHT!
NO, UH... I THINK THEY CAME EARLY IN THE MORNING.
OH. THEN THAT'S ALL RIGHT.
IF PEOPLE HAD LINED UP ALL NIGHT, WE'D HAVE TO SEND THEM TO THE BACK OF THE LINE.
THIS WORLD IS NOT KIND TO THE ALL-NIGHTERS.

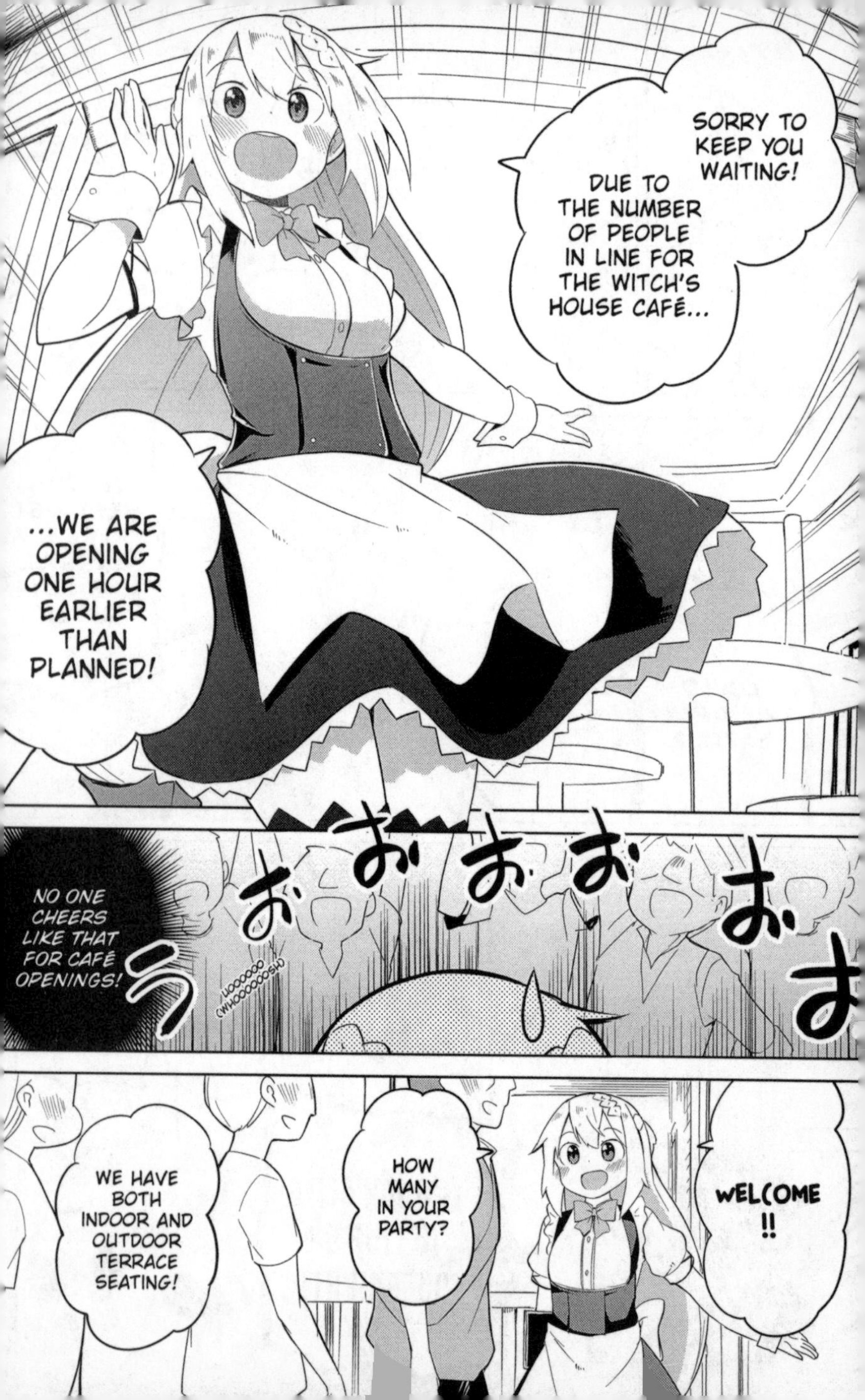
SORRY TO KEEP YOU WAITING!
DUE TO THE NUMBER OF PEOPLE IN LINE FOR THE WITCH'S HOUSE CAFÉ...
...WE ARE OPENING ONE HOUR EARLIER THAN PLANNED!
おおおおおおう
WOOOOOOO (WHOOOOOOOSH)
NO ONE CHEERS LIKE THAT FOR CAFÉ OPENINGS!
WELCOME!!
HOW MANY IN YOUR PARTY?
WE HAVE BOTH INDOOR AND OUTDOOR TERRACE SEATING!

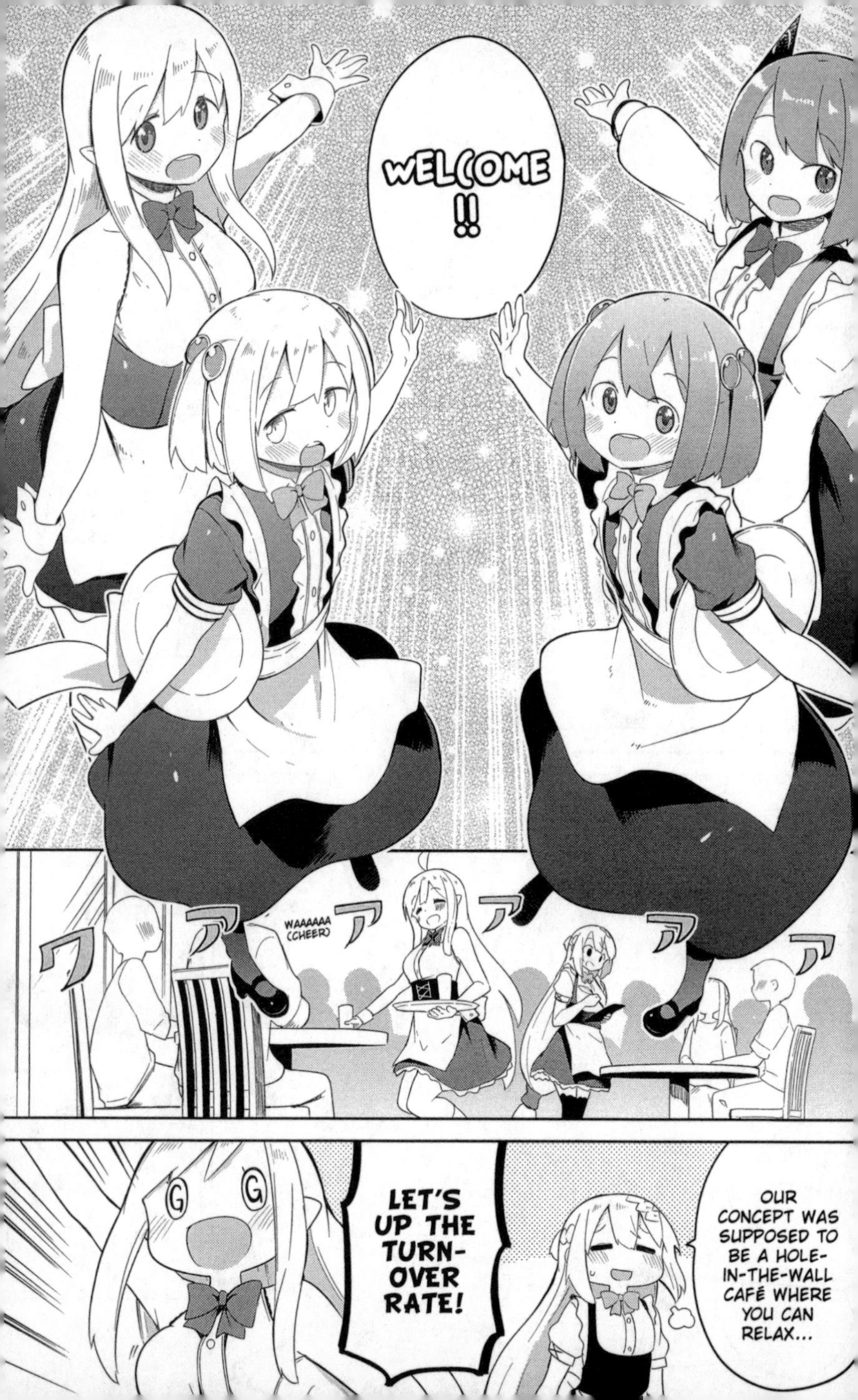
WELCOME !!
WAAAAAA (CHEER)
OUR CONCEPT WAS SUPPOSED TO BE A HOLE-IN-THE-WALL CAFÉ WHERE YOU CAN RELAX...
LET'S UP THE TURN-OVER RATE!

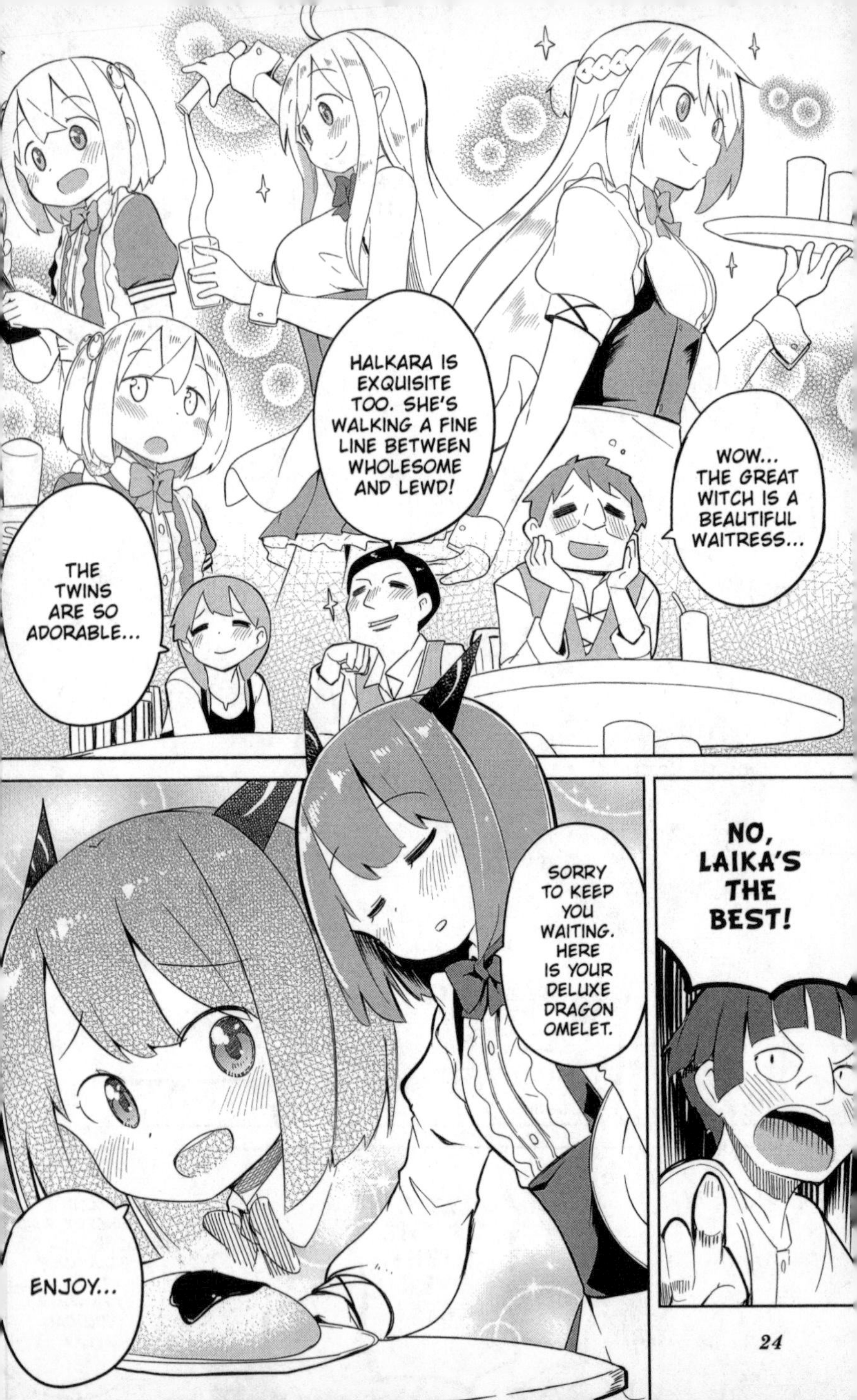
WOW... THE GREAT WITCH IS A BEAUTIFUL WAITRESS...
HALKARA IS EXQUISITE TOO. SHE'S WALKING A FINE LINE BETWEEN WHOLESOME AND LEWD!
THE TWINS ARE SO ADORABLE...
NO, LAIKA'S THE BEST!
SORRY TO KEEP YOU WAITING. HERE IS YOUR DELUXE DRAGON OMELET.
ENJOY...

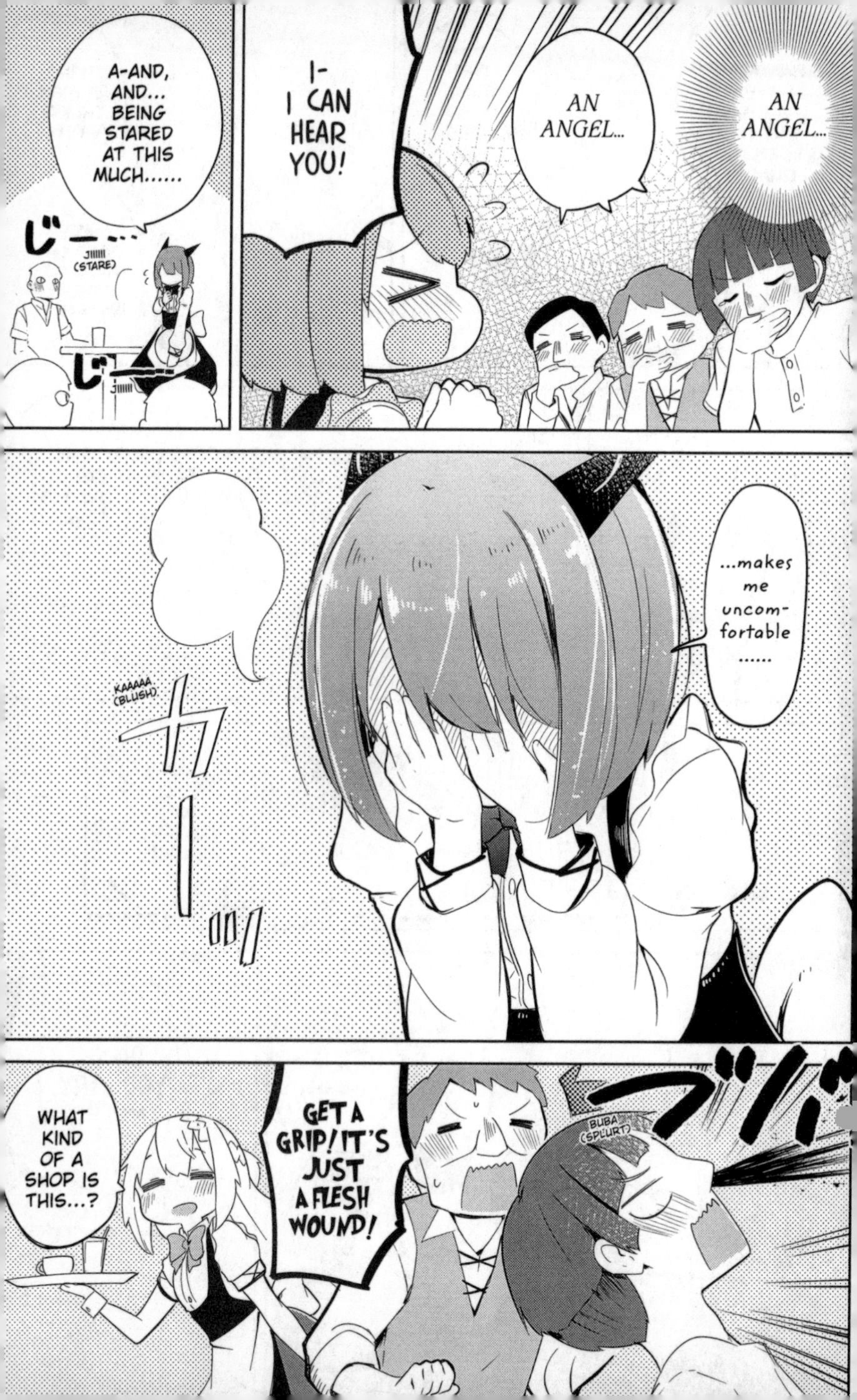
AN ANGEL...
AN ANGEL...
I- I CAN HEAR YOU!
A-AND, AND... BEING STARED AT THIS MUCH......
JIIIII (STARE)
...makes me uncom- fortable ......
KAAAAA (BLUSH)
BUBA (SPLURT)
GET A GRIP! IT'S JUST A FLESH WOUND!
WHAT KIND OF A SHOP IS THIS...?

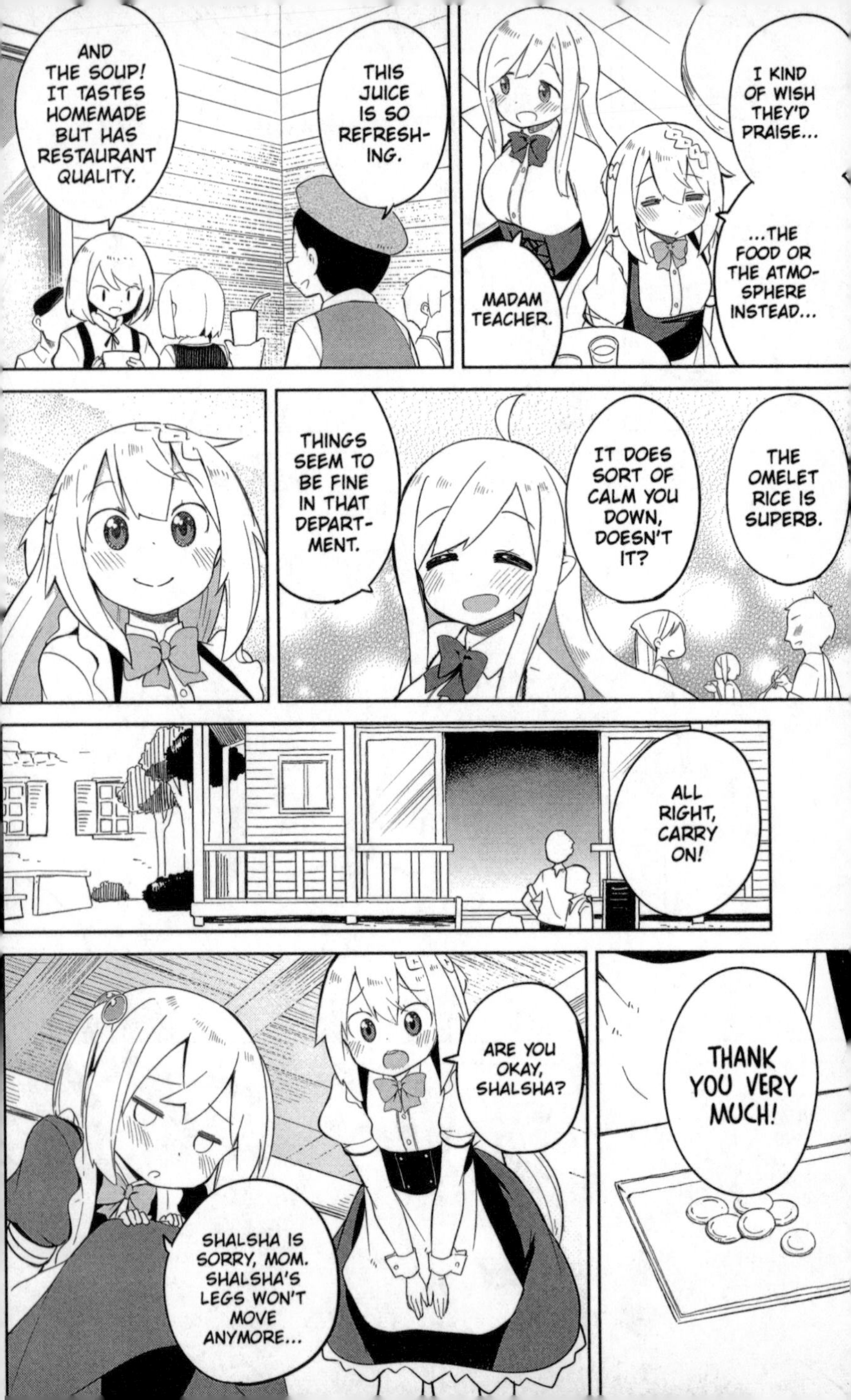
I KIND OF WISH THEY'D PRAISE...
...THE FOOD OR THE ATMOSPHERE INSTEAD...
MADAM TEACHER.
THIS JUICE IS SO REFRESHING.
AND THE SOUP! IT TASTES HOMEMADE BUT HAS RESTAURANT QUALITY.
THE OMELET RICE IS SUPERB.
IT DOES SORT OF CALM YOU DOWN, DOESN'T IT?
THINGS SEEM TO BE FINE IN THAT DEPARTMENT.
ALL RIGHT, CARRY ON!
THANK YOU VERY MUCH!
ARE YOU OKAY, SHALSHA?
SHALSHA IS SORRY, MOM. SHALSHA'S LEGS WON'T MOVE ANYMORE...

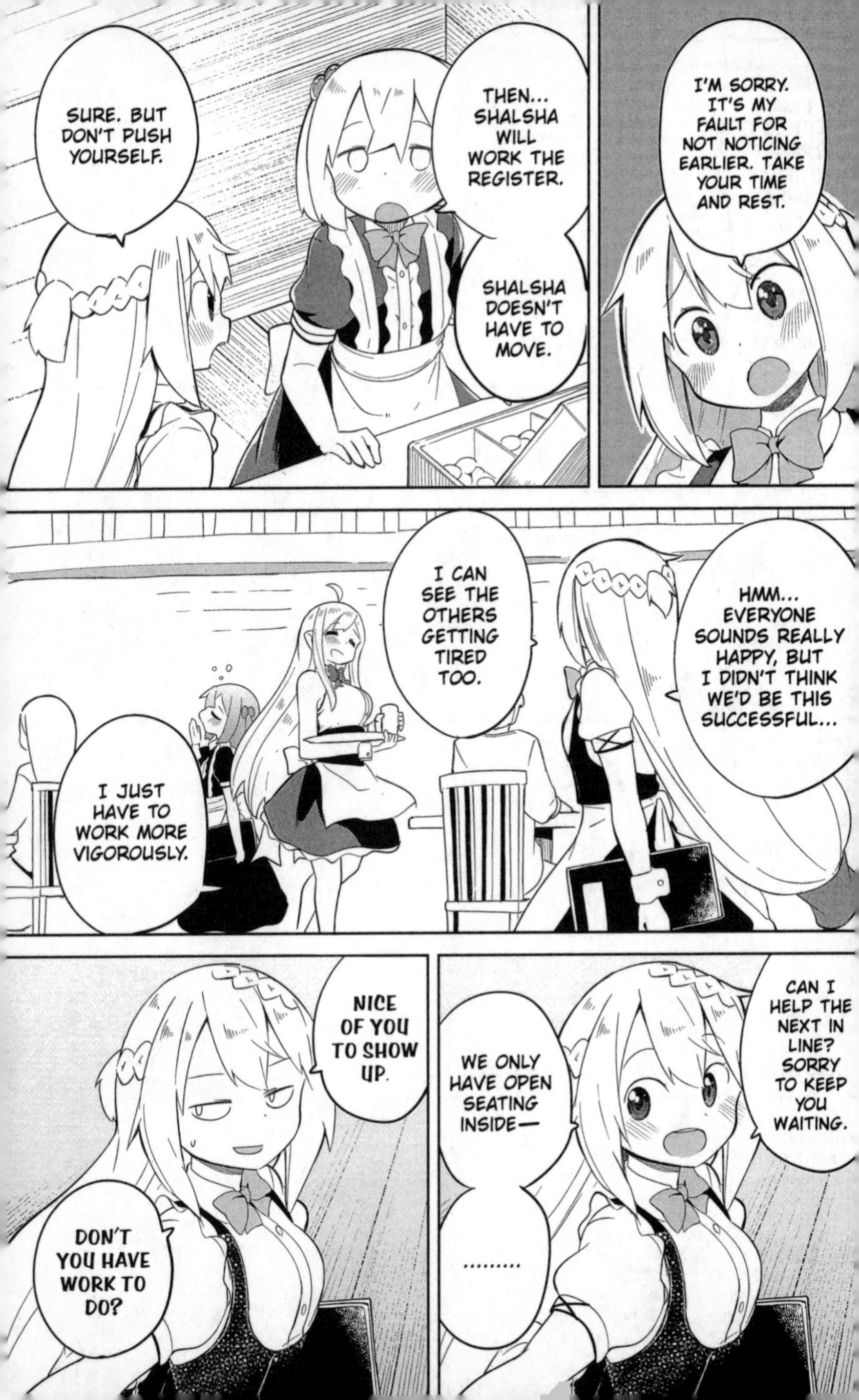
I'M SORRY. IT'S MY FAULT FOR NOT NOTICING EARLIER. TAKE YOUR TIME AND REST.
THEN... SHALSHA WILL WORK THE REGISTER.
SHALSHA DOESN'T HAVE TO MOVE.
SURE. BUT DON'T PUSH YOURSELF.
HMM... EVERYONE SOUNDS REALLY HAPPY, BUT I DIDN'T THINK WE'D BE THIS SUCCESSFUL...
I CAN SEE THE OTHERS GETTING TIRED TOO.
I JUST HAVE TO WORK MORE VIGOROUSLY.
CAN I HELP THE NEXT IN LINE? SORRY TO KEEP YOU WAITING.
WE ONLY HAVE OPEN SEATING INSIDE—
....
NICE OF YOU TO SHOW UP.
DON'T YOU HAVE WORK TO DO?

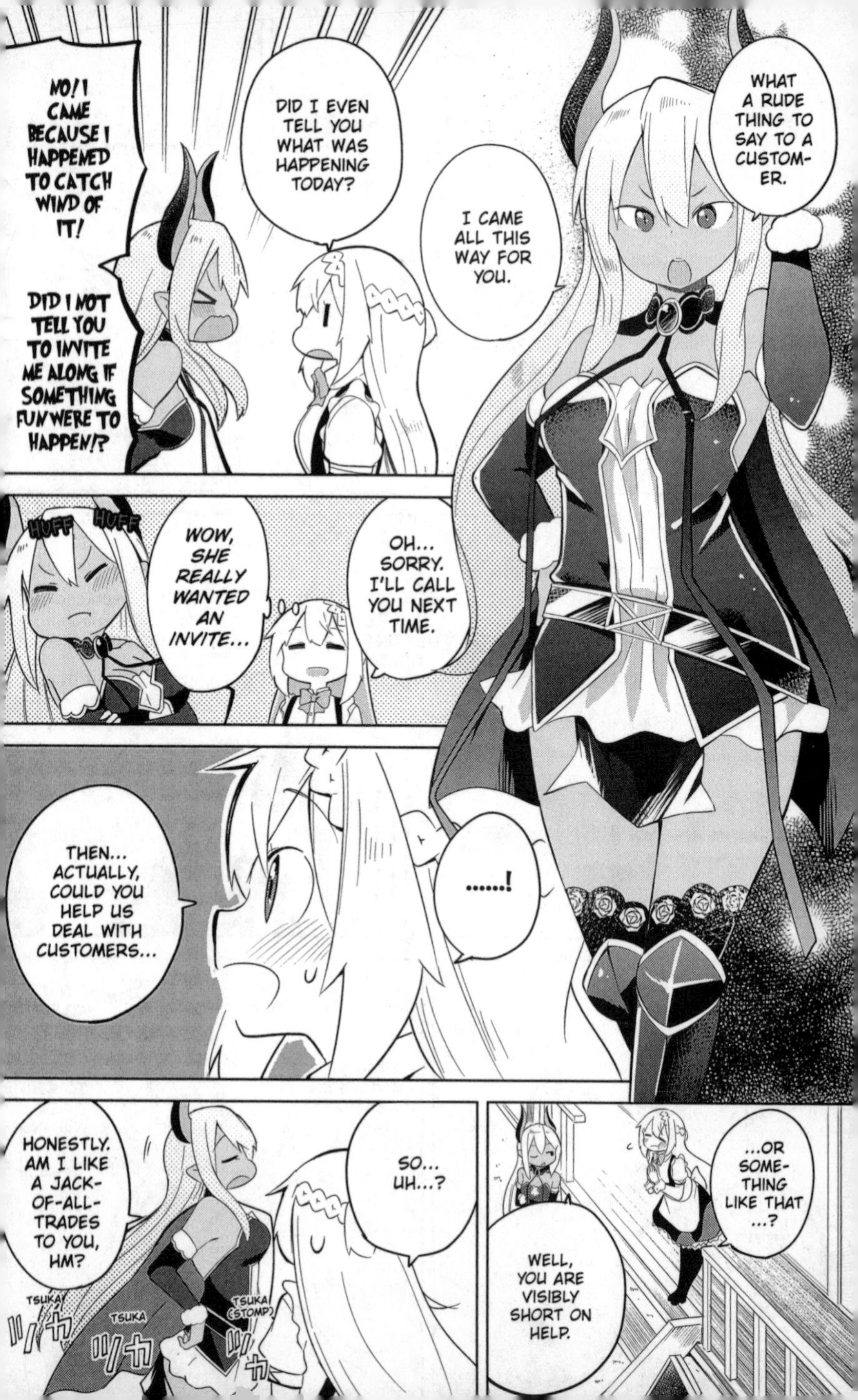
WHAT A RUDE THING TO SAY TO A CUSTOMER.
I CAME ALL THIS WAY FOR YOU.
DID I EVEN TELL YOU WHAT WAS HAPPENING TODAY?
NO! I CAME BECAUSE I HAPPENED TO CATCH WIND OF IT!
DID I NOT TELL YOU TO INVITE ME ALONG IF SOMETHING FUN WERE TO HAPPEN!?
OH... SORRY. I'LL CALL YOU NEXT TIME.
WOW, SHE REALLY WANTED AN INVITE...
HUFF HUFF
......!
THEN... ACTUALLY, COULD YOU HELP US DEAL WITH CUSTOMERS...
...OR SOMETHING LIKE THAT...?
WELL, YOU ARE VISIBLY SHORT ON HELP.
SO... UH...?
HONESTLY. AM I LIKE A JACK-OF-ALL-TRADES TO YOU, HM?
TSUKA (STOMP)
TSUKA
TSUKA

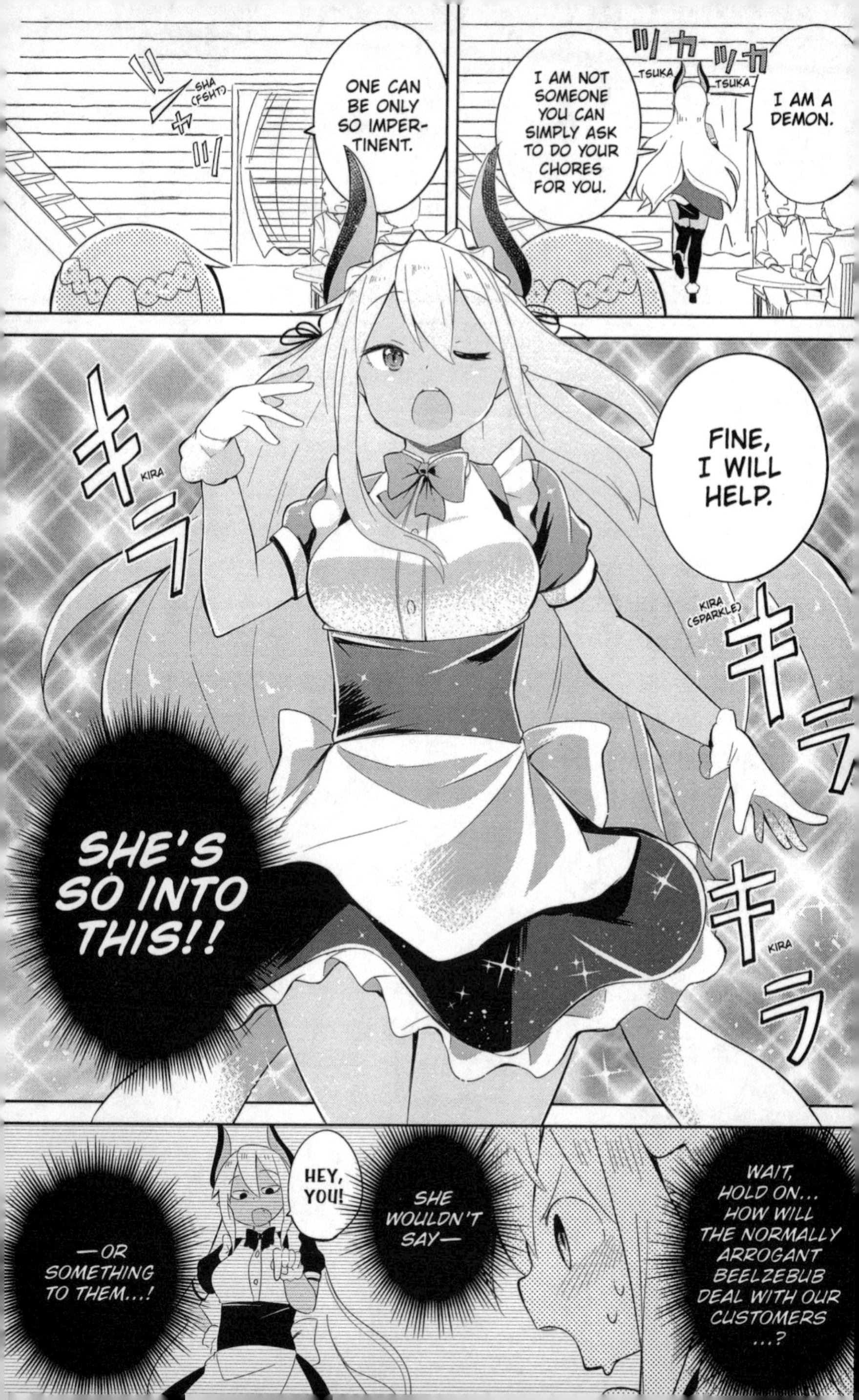
TSUKA
TSUKA
I AM A DEMON.
I AM NOT SOMEONE YOU CAN SIMPLY ASK TO DO YOUR CHORES FOR YOU.
ONE CAN BE ONLY SO IMPER-TINENT.
SHA (FSHT)
FINE, I WILL HELP.
KIRA (SPARKLE)
KIRA
KIRA
SHE'S SO INTO THIS!!
WAIT, HOLD ON... HOW WILL THE NORMALLY ARROGANT BEELZEBUB DEAL WITH OUR CUSTOMERS...?
SHE WOULDN'T SAY—
HEY, YOU!
—OR SOMETHING TO THEM...!

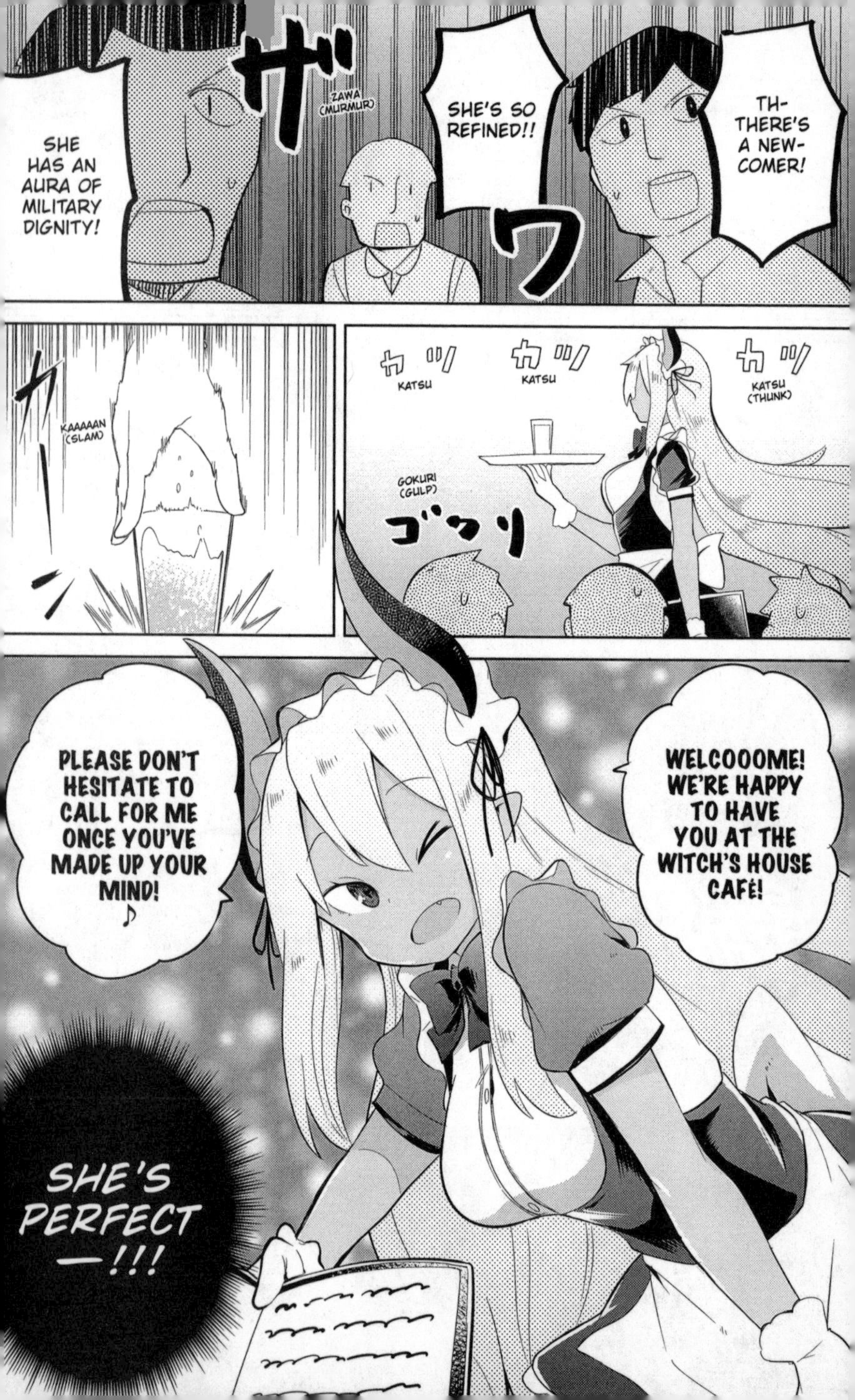

TH- THERE'S A NEW-COMER!
ザワ
ZAWA (MURMUR)
SHE'S SO REFINED!!
SHE HAS AN AURA OF MILITARY DIGNITY!
カツ
KATSU (THUNK)
カツ
KATSU
カツ
KATSU
ゴクリ
GOKURI (GULP)
KAAAAAN (SLAM)
WELCOOOME! WE'RE HAPPY TO HAVE YOU AT THE WITCH'S HOUSE CAFÉ!
PLEASE DON'T HESITATE TO CALL FOR ME ONCE YOU'VE MADE UP YOUR MIND! ♪
SHE'S PERFECT—!!!

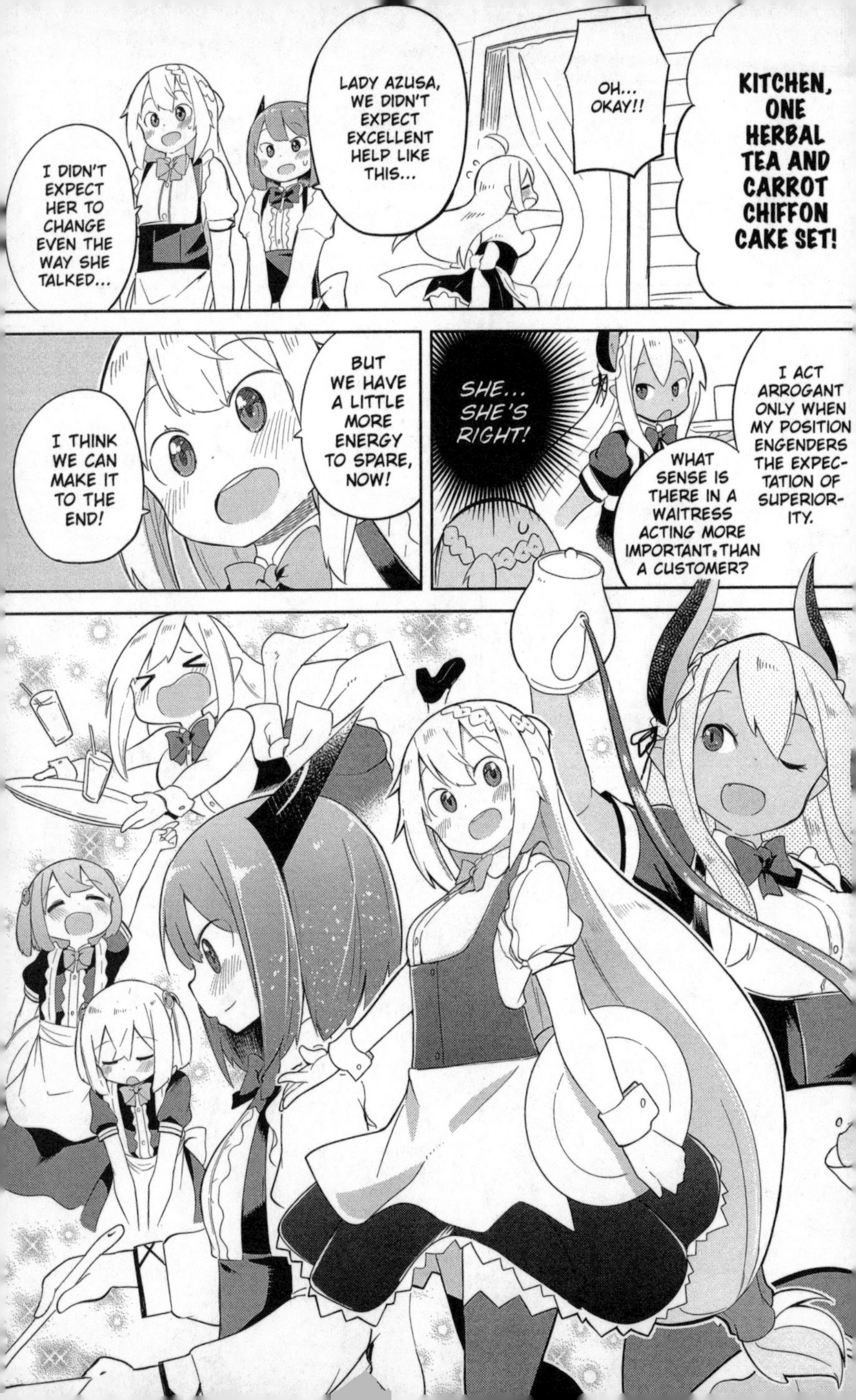
KITCHEN, ONE HERBAL TEA AND CARROT CHIFFON CAKE SET!
OH... OKAY!!
LADY AZUSA, WE DIDN'T EXPECT EXCELLENT HELP LIKE THIS...
I DIDN'T EXPECT HER TO CHANGE EVEN THE WAY SHE TALKED...
I ACT ARROGANT ONLY WHEN MY POSITION ENGENDERS THE EXPECTATION OF SUPERIORITY.
WHAT SENSE IS THERE IN A WAITRESS ACTING MORE IMPORTANT THAN A CUSTOMER?
SHE... SHE'S RIGHT!
BUT WE HAVE A LITTLE MORE ENERGY TO SPARE, NOW!
I THINK WE CAN MAKE IT TO THE END!

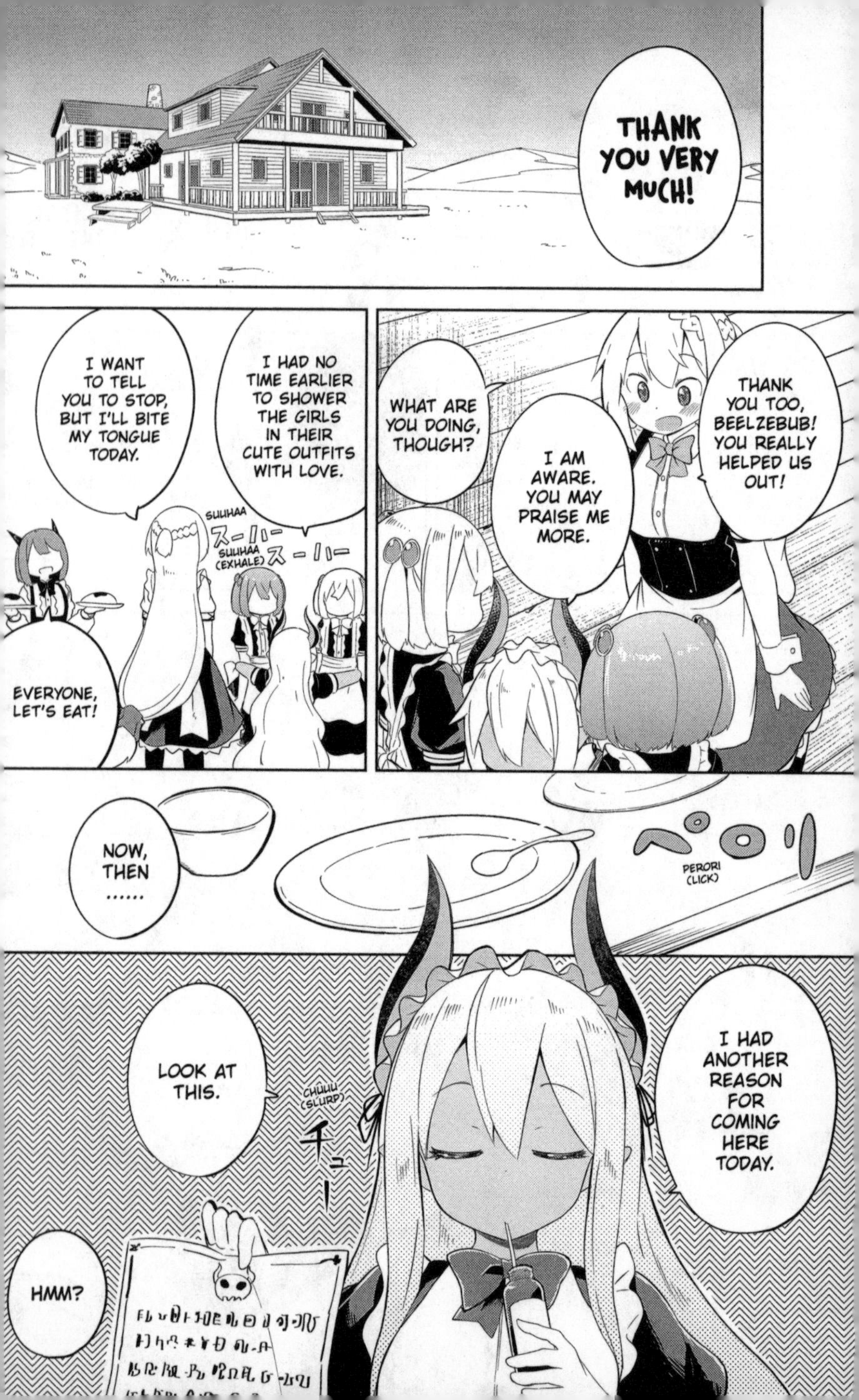
THANK YOU VERY MUCH!
THANK YOU TOO, BEELZEBUB! YOU REALLY HELPED US OUT!
I AM AWARE. YOU MAY PRAISE ME MORE.
WHAT ARE YOU DOING, THOUGH?
I HAD NO TIME EARLIER TO SHOWER THE GIRLS IN THEIR CUTE OUTFITS WITH LOVE.
I WANT TO TELL YOU TO STOP, BUT I'LL BITE MY TONGUE TODAY.
SUUHAA スーハー
SUUHAA (EXHALE) スーハー
EVERYONE, LET'S EAT!
ペロリ
PERORI (LICK)
NOW, THEN ......
I HAD ANOTHER REASON FOR COMING HERE TODAY.
CHUUU (SLURP)
チュー
LOOK AT THIS.
HMM?

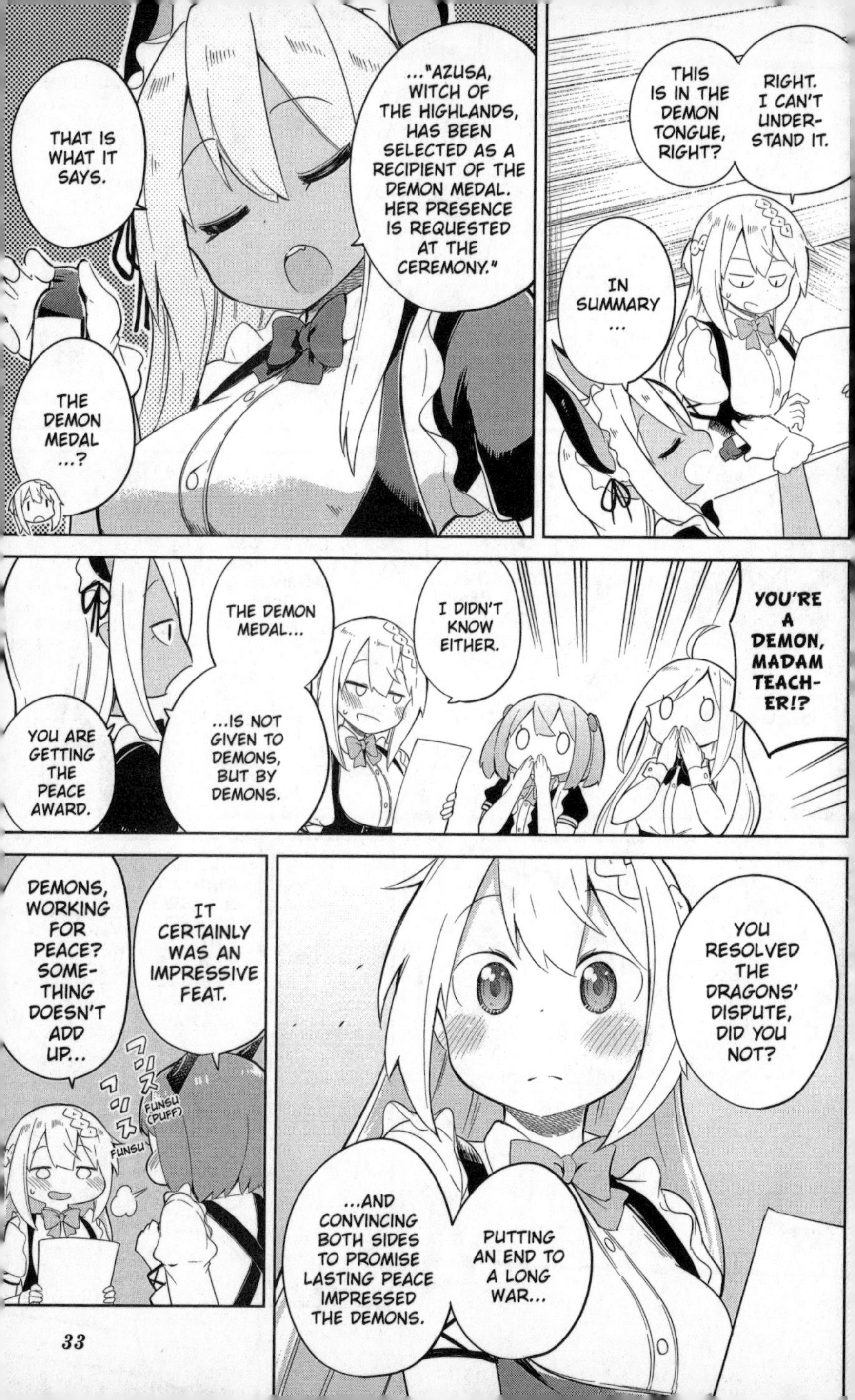
RIGHT. I CAN'T UNDER-STAND IT.
THIS IS IN THE DEMON TONGUE, RIGHT?
IN SUMMARY...
..."AZUSA, WITCH OF THE HIGHLANDS, HAS BEEN SELECTED AS A RECIPIENT OF THE DEMON MEDAL. HER PRESENCE IS REQUESTED AT THE CEREMONY."
THAT IS WHAT IT SAYS.
THE DEMON MEDAL...?
YOU'RE A DEMON, MADAM TEACHER!?
I DIDN'T KNOW EITHER.
THE DEMON MEDAL...
...IS NOT GIVEN TO DEMONS, BUT BY DEMONS.
YOU ARE GETTING THE PEACE AWARD.
YOU RESOLVED THE DRAGONS' DISPUTE, DID YOU NOT?
PUTTING AN END TO A LONG WAR...
...AND CONVINCING BOTH SIDES TO PROMISE LASTING PEACE IMPRESSED THE DEMONS.
IT CERTAINLY WAS AN IMPRESSIVE FEAT.
DEMONS, WORKING FOR PEACE? SOME-THING DOESN'T ADD UP...
FUNSU (PUFF)
FUNSU

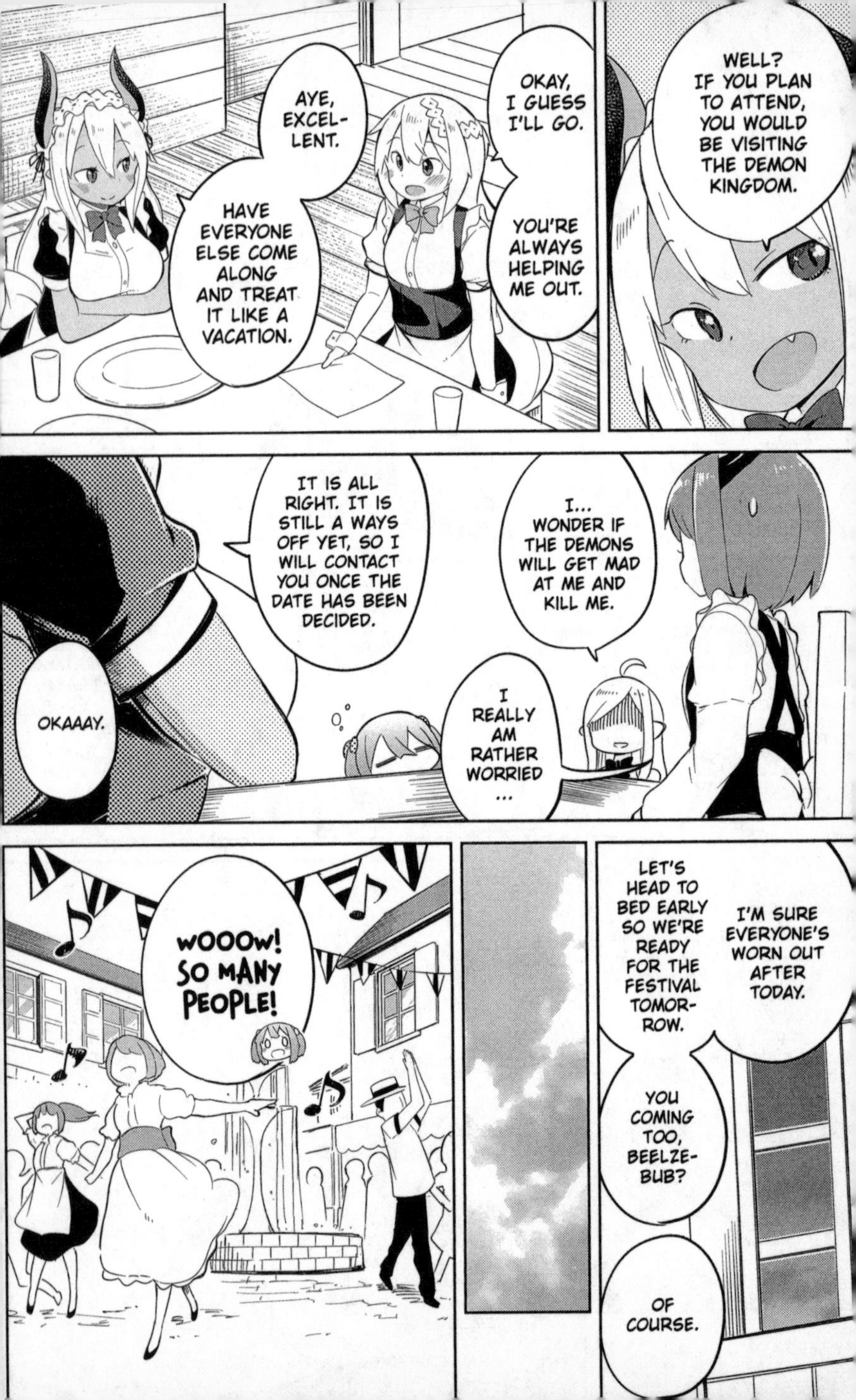
WELL? IF YOU PLAN TO ATTEND, YOU WOULD BE VISITING THE DEMON KINGDOM.
OKAY, I GUESS I'LL GO.
YOU'RE ALWAYS HELPING ME OUT.
AYE, EXCEL-LENT.
HAVE EVERYONE ELSE COME ALONG AND TREAT IT LIKE A VACATION.
I... WONDER IF THE DEMONS WILL GET MAD AT ME AND KILL ME.
IT IS ALL RIGHT. IT IS STILL A WAYS OFF YET, SO I WILL CONTACT YOU ONCE THE DATE HAS BEEN DECIDED.
I REALLY AM RATHER WORRIED ...
OKAAAY.
I'M SURE EVERYONE'S WORN OUT AFTER TODAY.
LET'S HEAD TO BED EARLY SO WE'RE READY FOR THE FESTIVAL TOMOR-ROW.
YOU COMING TOO, BEELZE-BUB?
OF COURSE.
WOOOW! SO MANY PEOPLE!

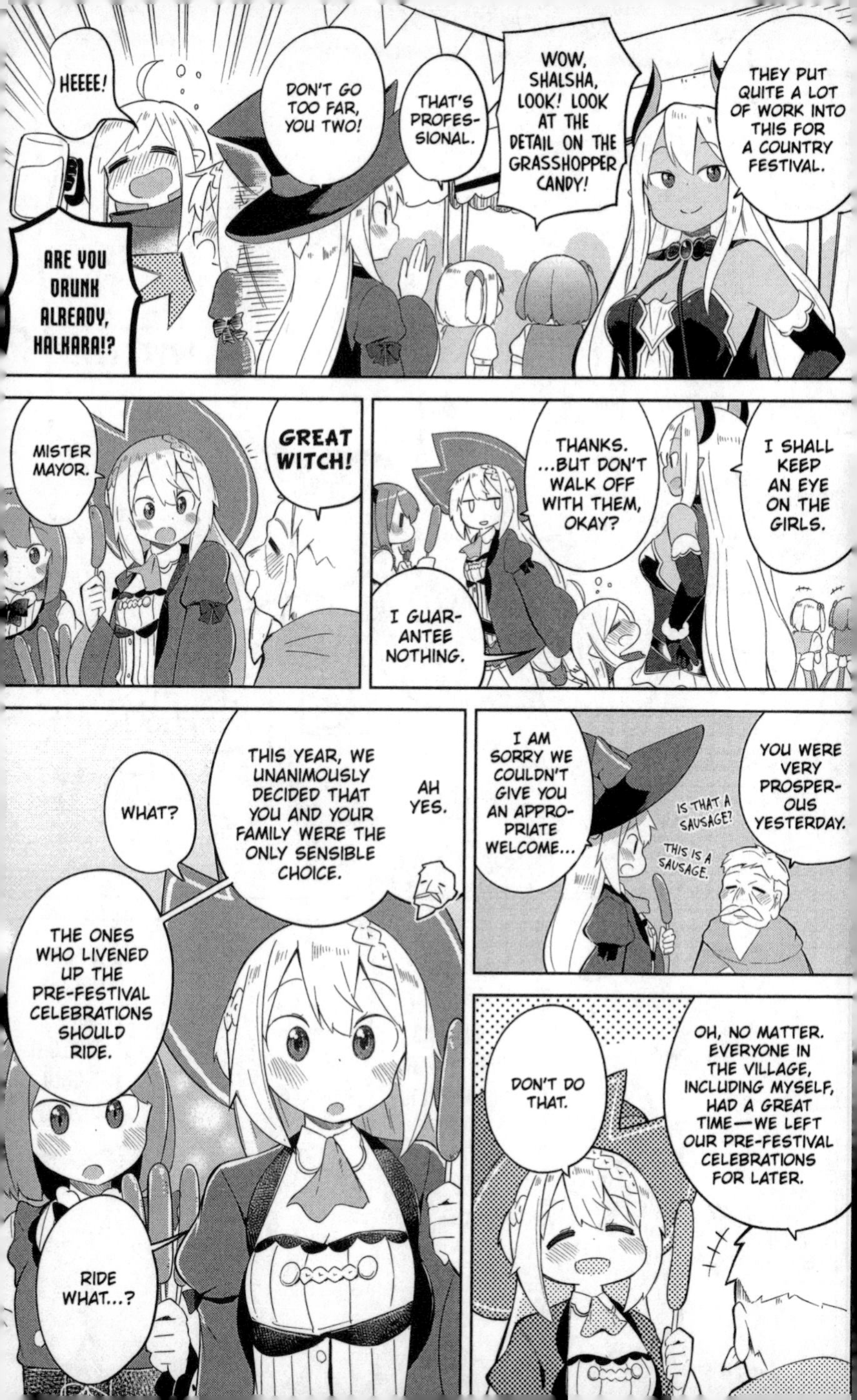
THEY PUT QUITE A LOT OF WORK INTO THIS FOR A COUNTRY FESTIVAL.
WOW, SHALSHA, LOOK! LOOK AT THE DETAIL ON THE GRASSHOPPER CANDY!
THAT'S PROFES-SIONAL.
DON'T GO TOO FAR, YOU TWO!
HEEEE!
ARE YOU DRUNK ALREADY, HALKARA!?
I SHALL KEEP AN EYE ON THE GIRLS.
THANKS. ...BUT DON'T WALK OFF WITH THEM, OKAY?
I GUAR-ANTEE NOTHING.
GREAT WITCH!
MISTER MAYOR.
YOU WERE VERY PROSPER-OUS YESTERDAY.
IS THAT A SAUSAGE?
THIS IS A SAUSAGE.
I AM SORRY WE COULDN'T GIVE YOU AN APPRO-PRIATE WELCOME...
OH, NO MATTER. EVERYONE IN THE VILLAGE, INCLUDING MYSELF, HAD A GREAT TIME—WE LEFT OUR PRE-FESTIVAL CELEBRATIONS FOR LATER.
DON'T DO THAT.
AH YES.
THIS YEAR, WE UNANIMOUSLY DECIDED THAT YOU AND YOUR FAMILY WERE THE ONLY SENSIBLE CHOICE.
WHAT?
THE ONES WHO LIVENED UP THE PRE-FESTIVAL CELEBRATIONS SHOULD RIDE.
RIDE WHAT...?

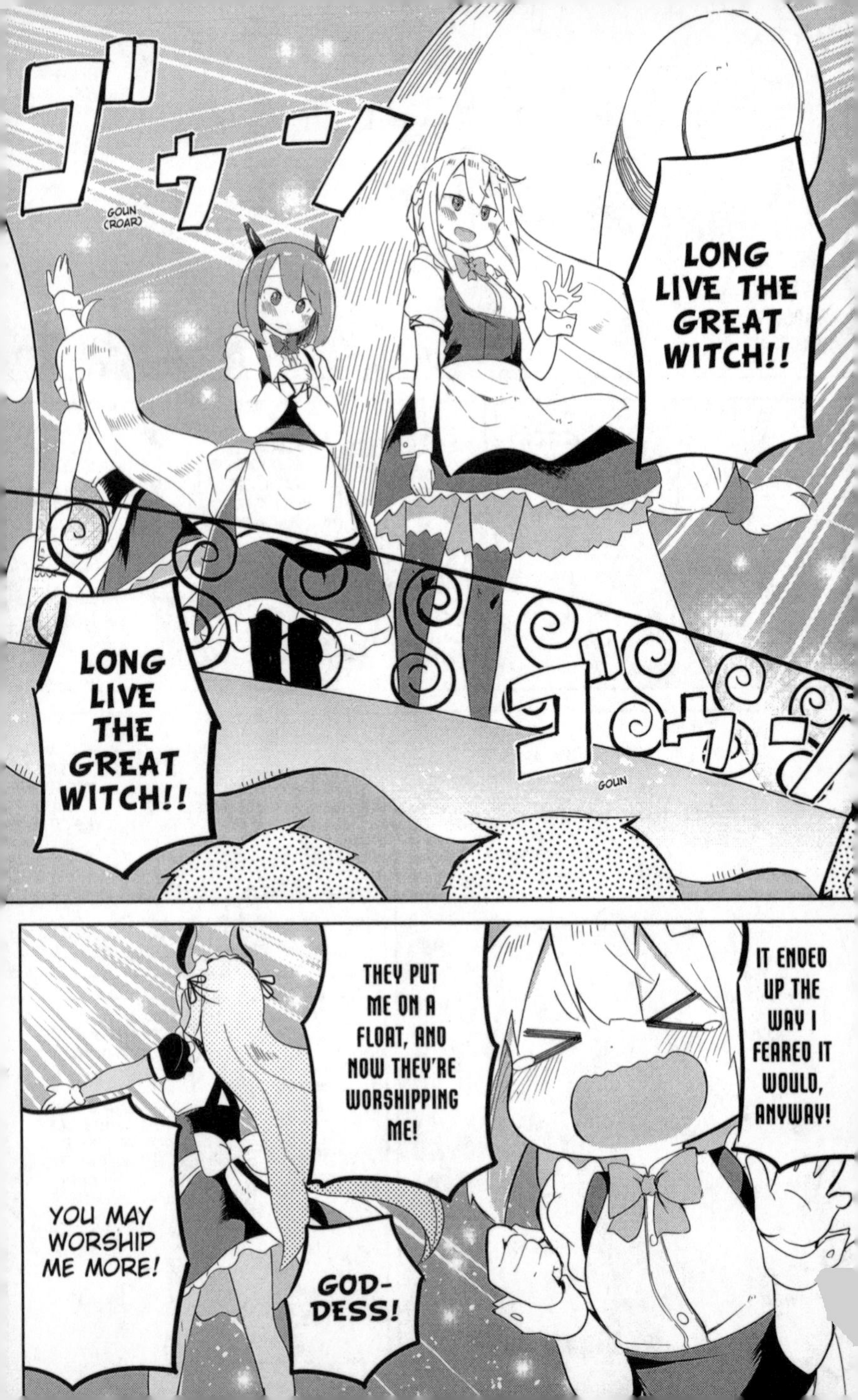
LONG LIVE THE GREAT WITCH!!
ゴゥーン
GOUN (ROAR)
LONG LIVE THE GREAT WITCH!!
ゴゥーン
GOUN
IT ENDED UP THE WAY I FEARED IT WOULD, ANYWAY!
THEY PUT ME ON A FLOAT, AND NOW THEY'RE WORSHIPPING ME!
GOD-DESS!
YOU MAY WORSHIP ME MORE!

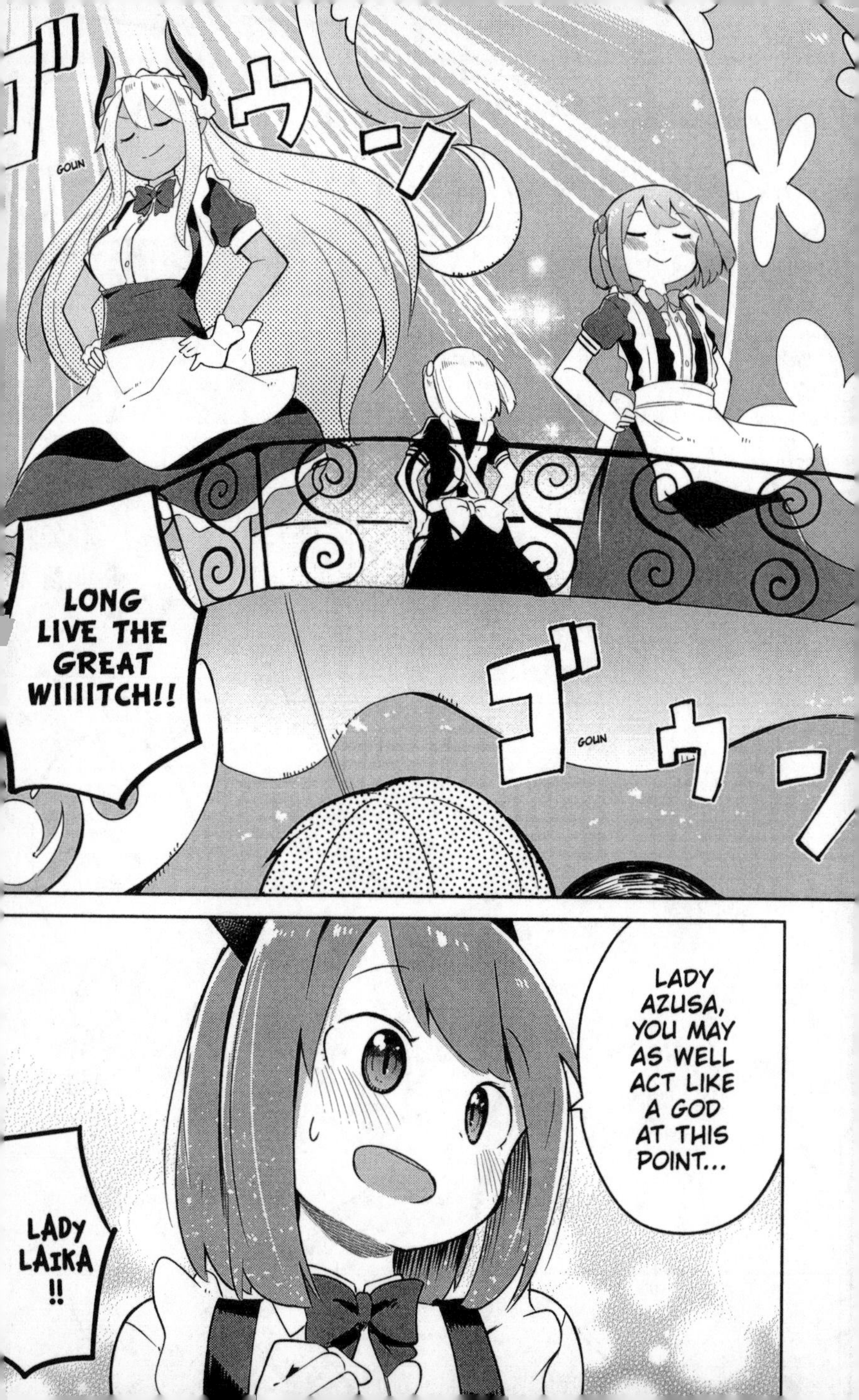

ゴウーン
GOUN
LONG LIVE THE GREAT WIIIITCH!!
ゴウーン
GOUN
LADY AZUSA, YOU MAY AS WELL ACT LIKE A GOD AT THIS POINT...
LADY LAIKA!!

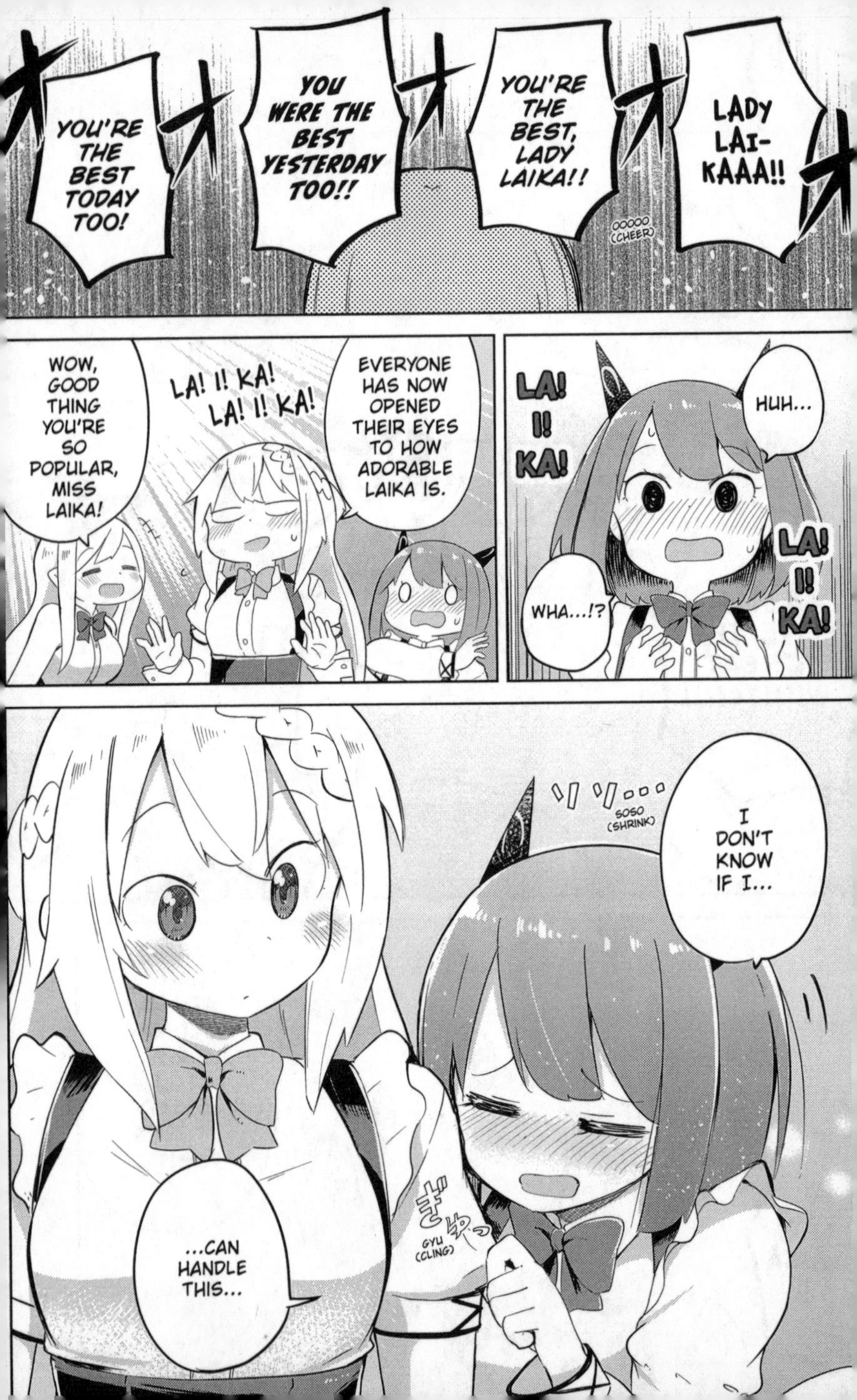
LADY LAI-KAAA!!
OOOOO (CHEER)
YOU'RE THE BEST, LADY LAIKA!!
YOU WERE THE BEST YESTERDAY TOO!!
YOU'RE THE BEST TODAY TOO!
HUH...
LA! I! KA!
LA! I! KA!
WHA...!?
EVERYONE HAS NOW OPENED THEIR EYES TO HOW ADORABLE LAIKA IS.
LA! I! KA! LA! I! KA!
WOW, GOOD THING YOU'RE SO POPULAR, MISS LAIKA!
I DON'T KNOW IF I...
SOSO (SHRINK)
GYU (CLING)
...CAN HANDLE THIS...

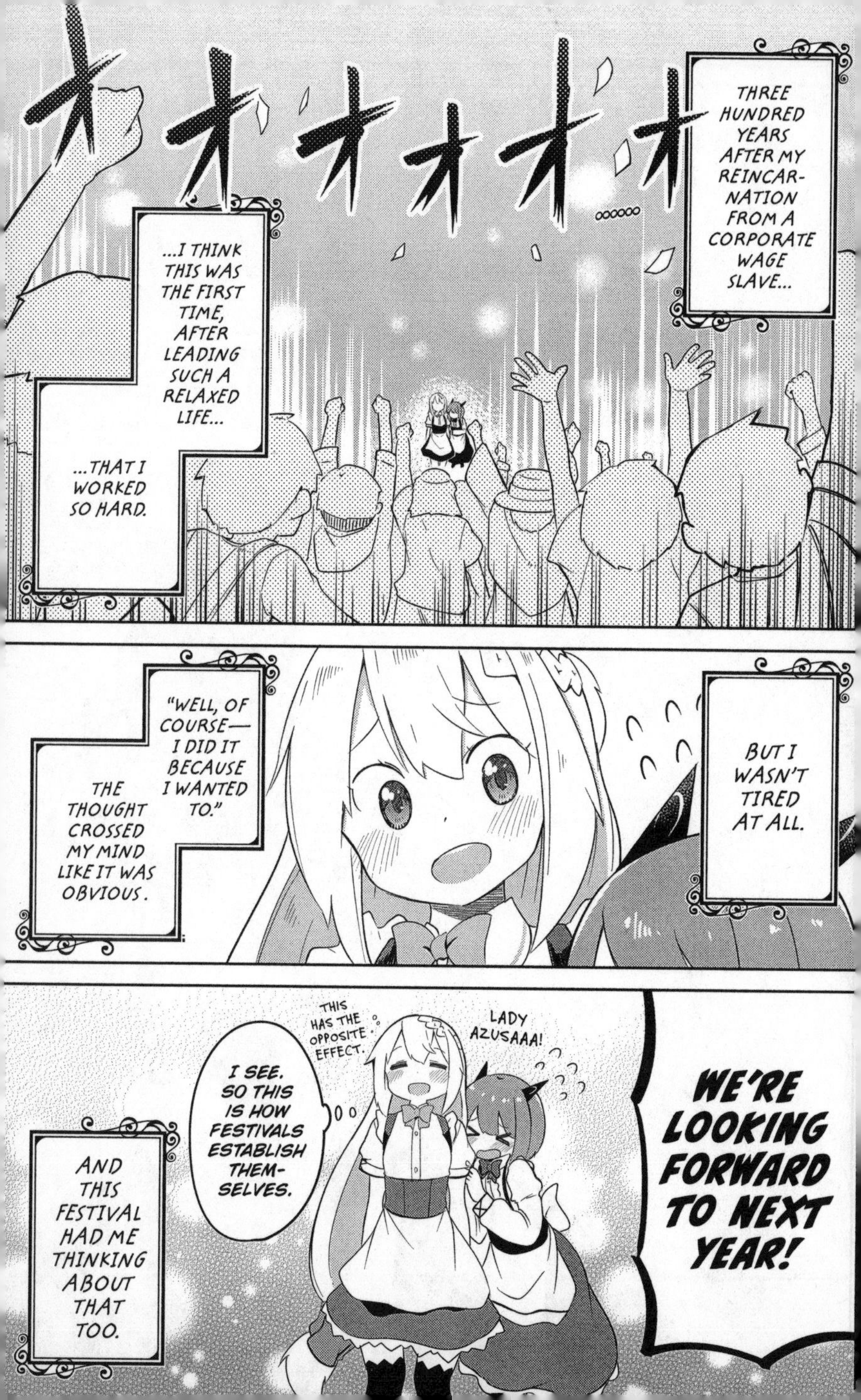
THREE HUNDRED YEARS AFTER MY REINCARNATION FROM A CORPORATE WAGE SLAVE...
オオオオオ
...I THINK THIS WAS THE FIRST TIME, AFTER LEADING SUCH A RELAXED LIFE...
...THAT I WORKED SO HARD.
BUT I WASN'T TIRED AT ALL.
“WELL, OF COURSE— I DID IT BECAUSE I WANTED TO.”
THE THOUGHT CROSSED MY MIND LIKE IT WAS OBVIOUS.
WE'RE LOOKING FORWARD TO NEXT YEAR!
LADY AZUSAAA!
THIS HAS THE OPPOSITE EFFECT.
I SEE. SO THIS IS HOW FESTIVALS ESTABLISH THEM-SELVES.
AND THIS FESTIVAL HAD ME THINKING ABOUT THAT TOO.

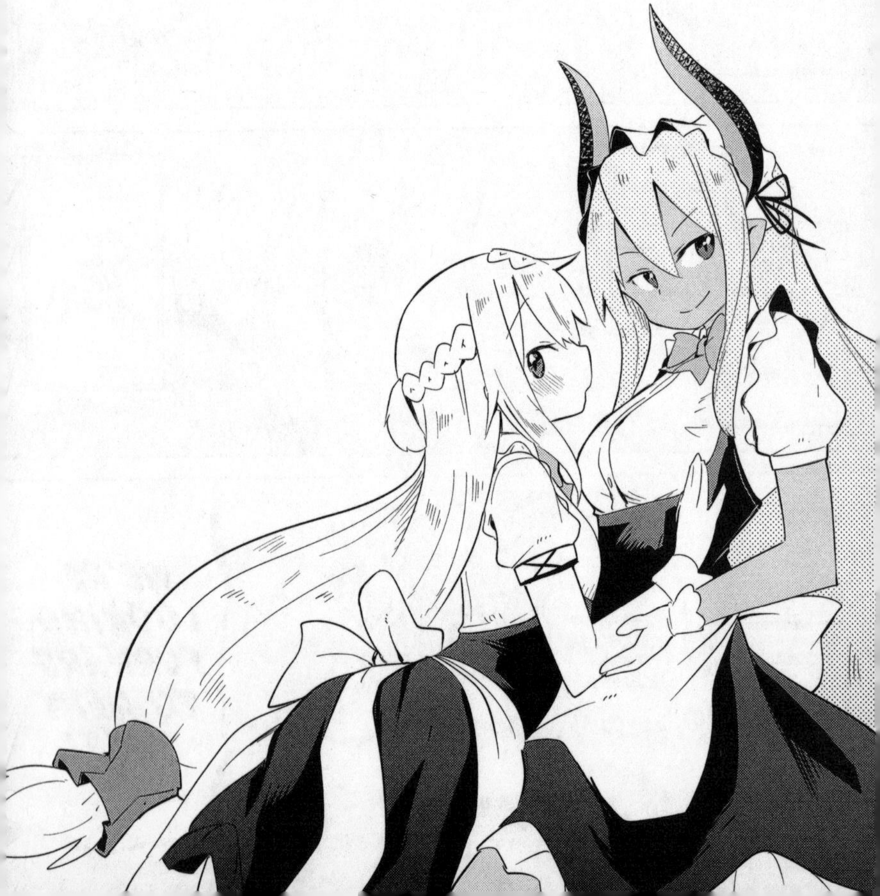

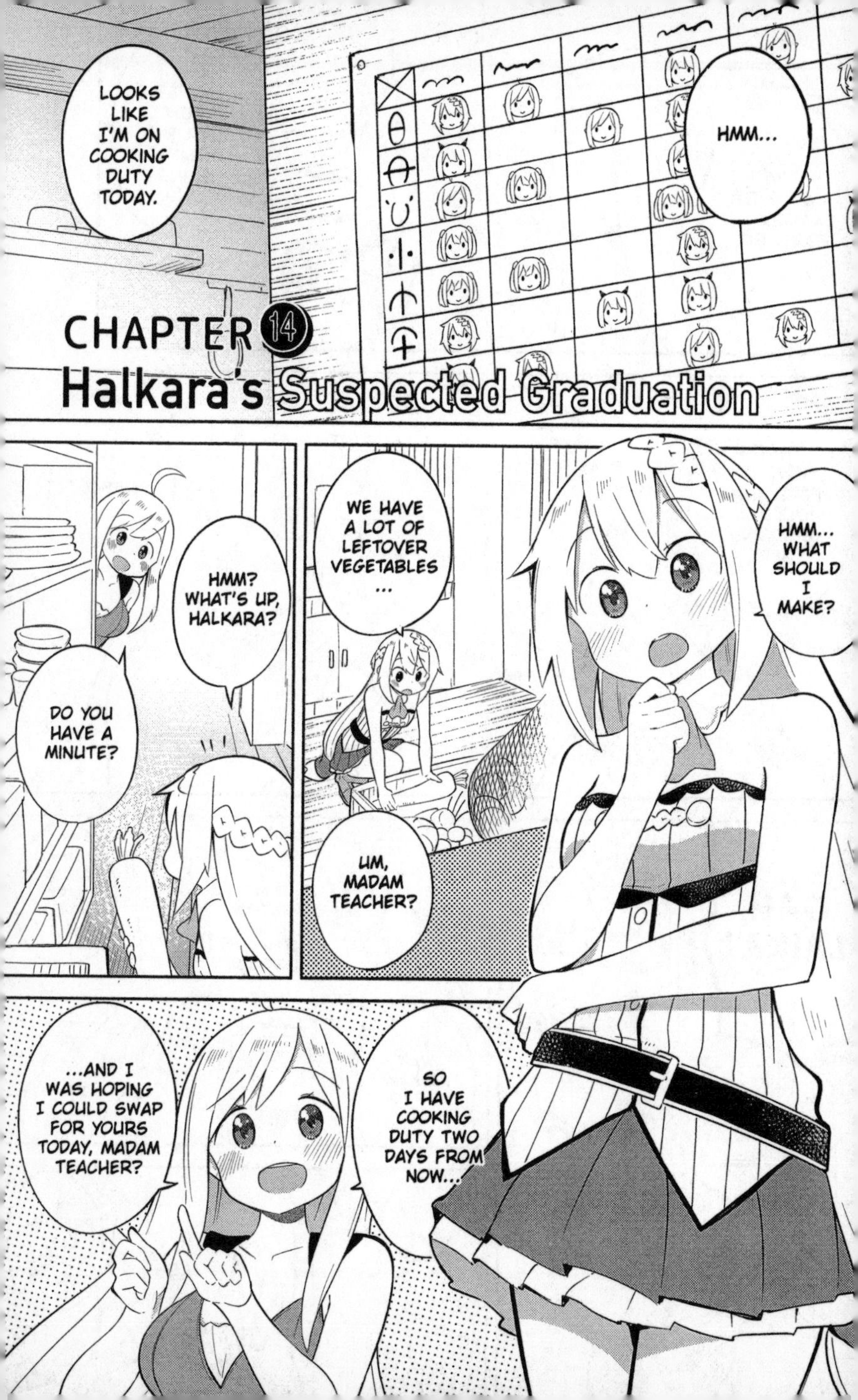
HMM...
LOOKS LIKE I'M ON COOKING DUTY TODAY.
CHAPTER 14
Halkara's Suspected Graduation
HMM... WHAT SHOULD I MAKE?
WE HAVE A LOT OF LEFTOVER VEGETABLES ...
UM, MADAM TEACHER?
HMM? WHAT'S UP, HALKARA?
DO YOU HAVE A MINUTE?
SO I HAVE COOKING DUTY TWO DAYS FROM NOW...
...AND I WAS HOPING I COULD SWAP FOR YOURS TODAY, MADAM TEACHER?

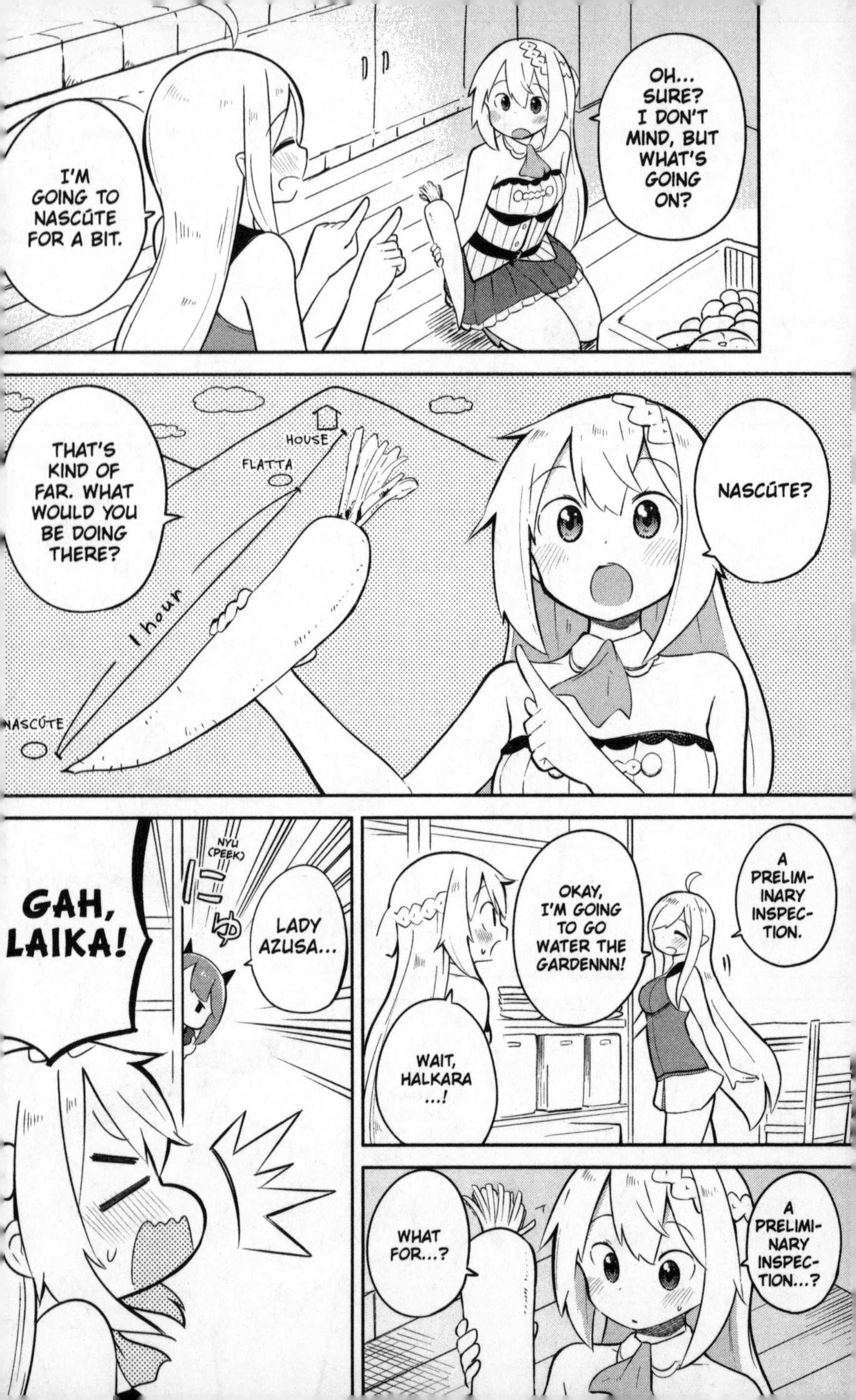
OH... SURE? I DON'T MIND, BUT WHAT'S GOING ON?
I'M GOING TO NASCÚTE FOR A BIT.
NASCÚTE?
THAT'S KIND OF FAR. WHAT WOULD YOU BE DOING THERE?
HOUSE
FLATTA
1 hour
NASCÚTE
A PRELIMINARY INSPECTION.
OKAY, I'M GOING TO GO WATER THE GARDENNN!
WAIT, HALKARA...!
A PRELIMINARY INSPECTION...?
WHAT FOR...?
NYU (PEEK)
LADY AZUSA...
GAH, LAIKA!

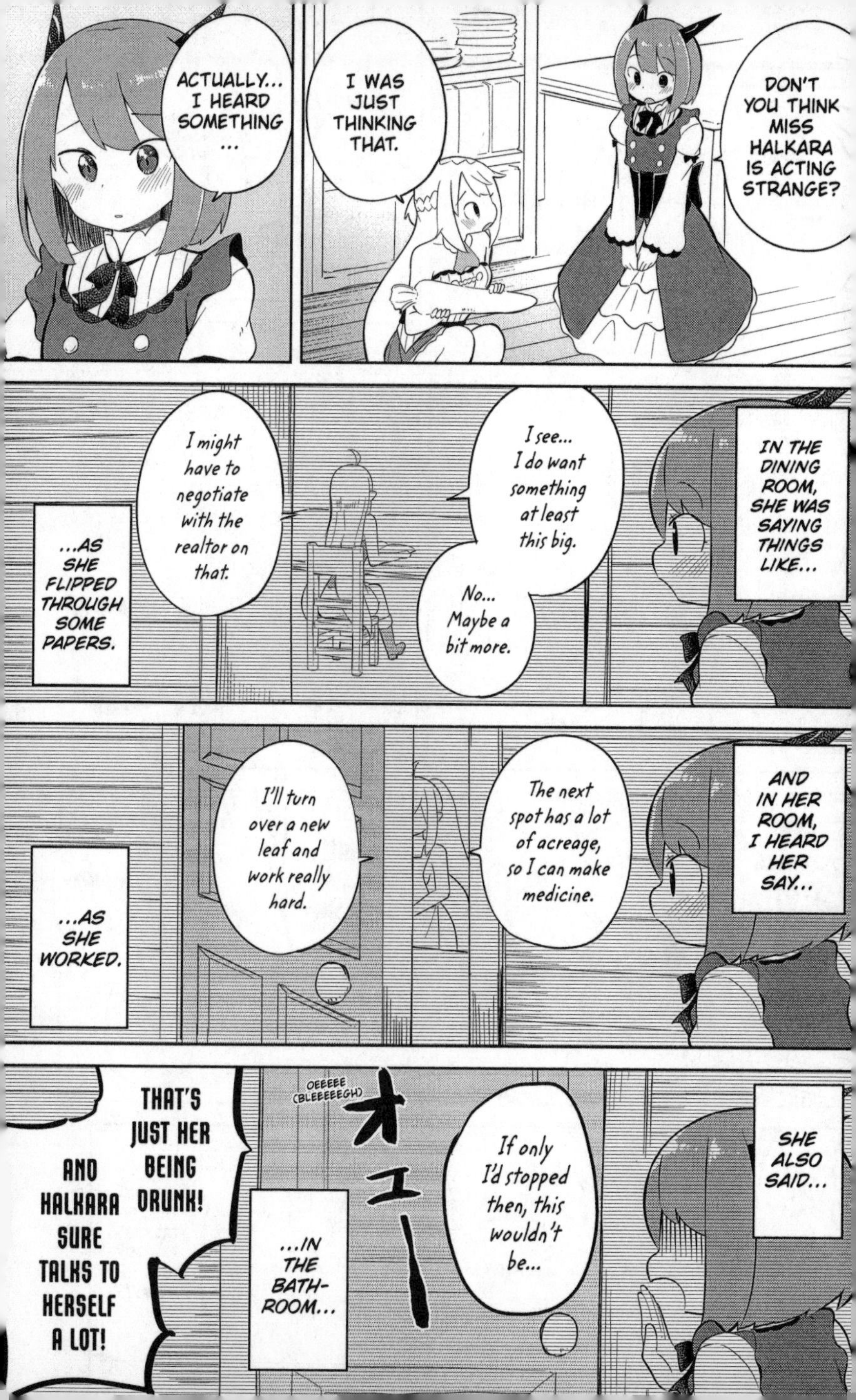
DON'T YOU THINK MISS HALKARA IS ACTING STRANGE?
I WAS JUST THINKING THAT.
ACTUALLY... I HEARD SOMETHING...
IN THE DINING ROOM, SHE WAS SAYING THINGS LIKE...
I see... I do want something at least this big.
No... Maybe a bit more.
I might have to negotiate with the realtor on that.
...AS SHE FLIPPED THROUGH SOME PAPERS.
AND IN HER ROOM, I HEARD HER SAY...
The next spot has a lot of acreage, so I can make medicine.
I'll turn over a new leaf and work really hard.
...AS SHE WORKED.
SHE ALSO SAID...
If only I'd stopped then, this wouldn't be...
OEEEEE (BLEEEEEGH)
...IN THE BATHROOM...
THAT'S JUST HER BEING DRUNK!
AND HALKARA SURE TALKS TO HERSELF A LOT!

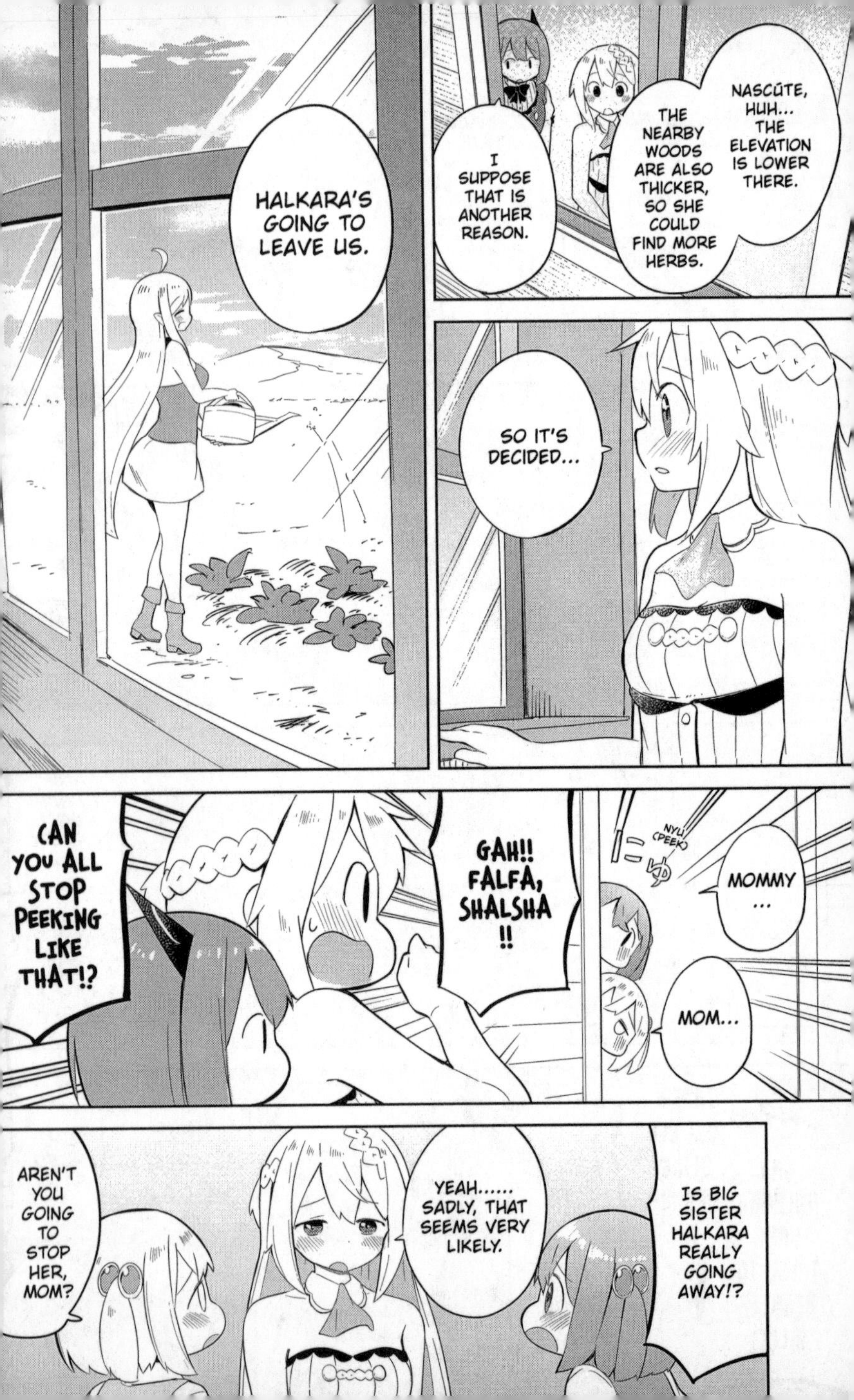
NASCÛTE, HUH... THE ELEVATION IS LOWER THERE.
THE NEARBY WOODS ARE ALSO THICKER, SO SHE COULD FIND MORE HERBS.
I SUPPOSE THAT IS ANOTHER REASON.
SO IT'S DECIDED...
HALKARA'S GOING TO LEAVE US.
NYU (PEEK)
MOMMY...
MOM...
GAH!! FALFA, SHALSHA!!
CAN YOU ALL STOP PEEKING LIKE THAT!?
IS BIG SISTER HALKARA REALLY GOING AWAY!?
YEAH...... SADLY, THAT SEEMS VERY LIKELY.
AREN'T YOU GOING TO STOP HER, MOM?

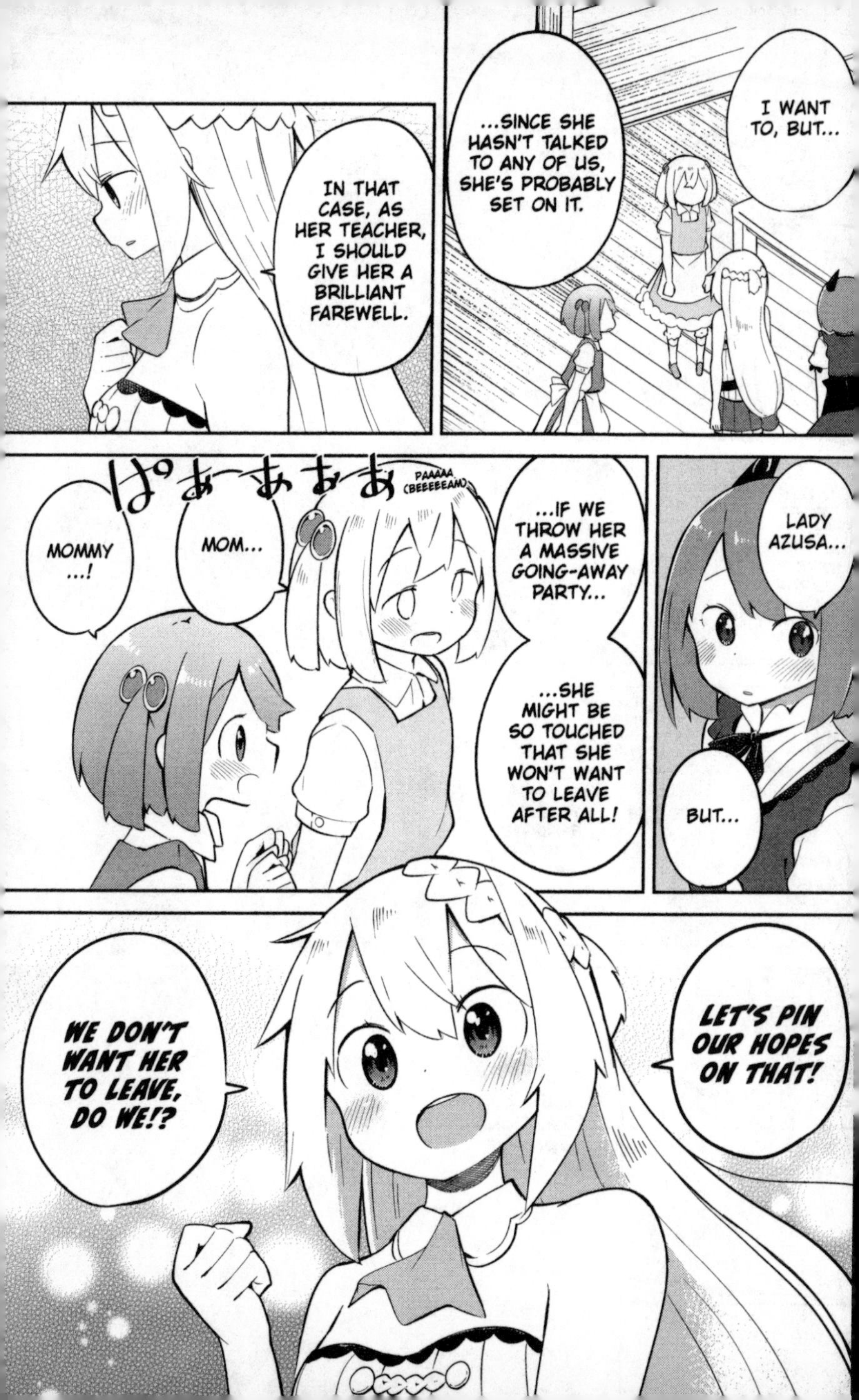
I WANT TO, BUT...
...SINCE SHE HASN'T TALKED TO ANY OF US, SHE'S PROBABLY SET ON IT.
IN THAT CASE, AS HER TEACHER, I SHOULD GIVE HER A BRILLIANT FAREWELL.
LADY AZUSA...
BUT...
...IF WE THROW HER A MASSIVE GOING-AWAY PARTY...
...SHE MIGHT BE SO TOUCHED THAT SHE WON'T WANT TO LEAVE AFTER ALL!
ぱぁあおあ
PAAAAA (BEEEEEAM)
MOM...
MOMMY...!
LET'S PIN OUR HOPES ON THAT!
WE DON'T WANT HER TO LEAVE, DO WE!?

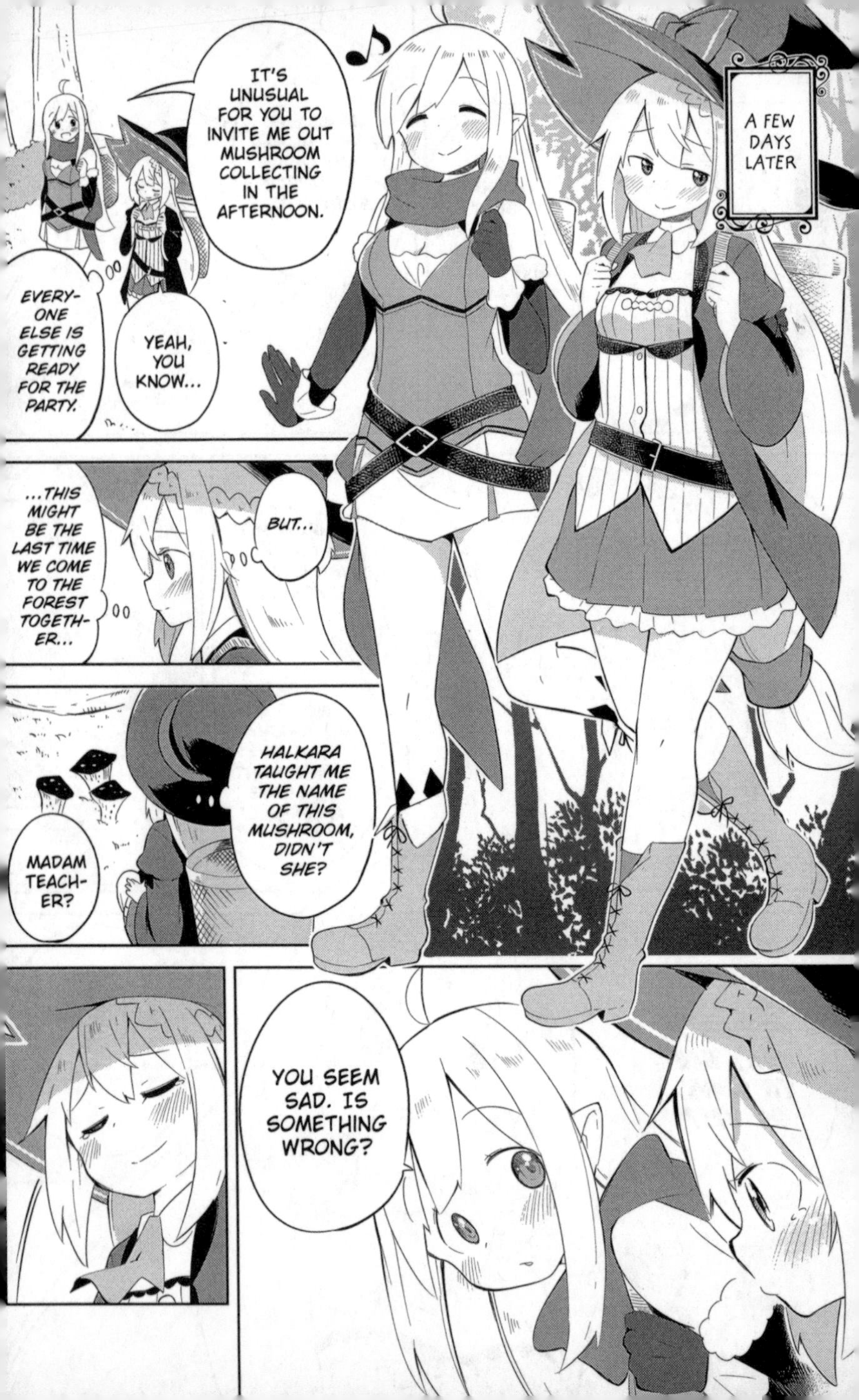
A FEW DAYS LATER
IT'S UNUSUAL FOR YOU TO INVITE ME OUT MUSHROOM COLLECTING IN THE AFTERNOON.
YEAH, YOU KNOW...
EVERYONE ELSE IS GETTING READY FOR THE PARTY.
BUT...
...THIS MIGHT BE THE LAST TIME WE COME TO THE FOREST TOGETHER...
HALKARA TAUGHT ME THE NAME OF THIS MUSHROOM, DIDN'T SHE?
MADAM TEACHER?
YOU SEEM SAD. IS SOMETHING WRONG?

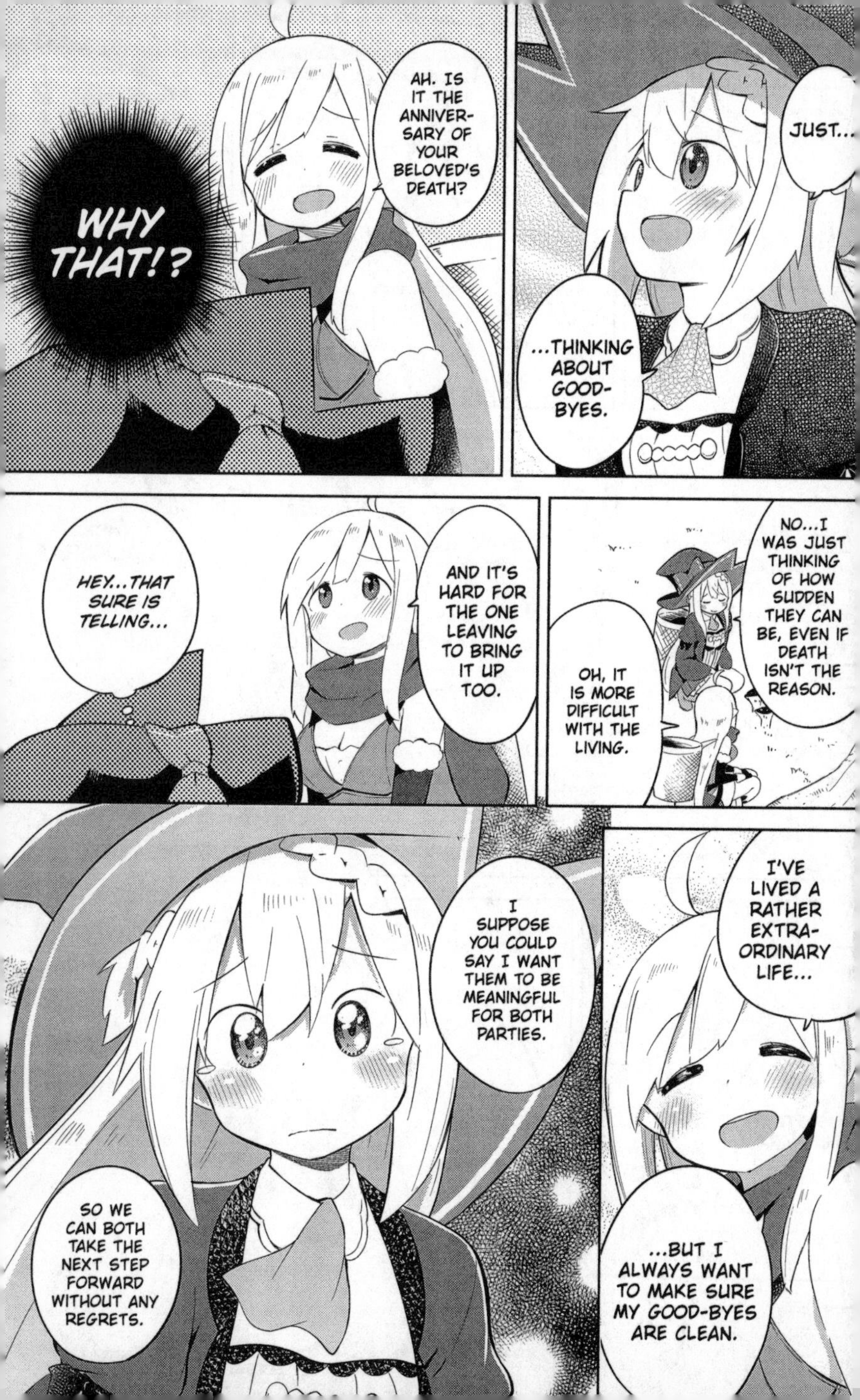
JUST...
...THINKING ABOUT GOOD-BYES.
AH. IS IT THE ANNIVER-SARY OF YOUR BELOVED'S DEATH?
WHY THAT!?
NO...I WAS JUST THINKING OF HOW SUDDEN THEY CAN BE, EVEN IF DEATH ISN'T THE REASON.
OH, IT IS MORE DIFFICULT WITH THE LIVING.
AND IT'S HARD FOR THE ONE LEAVING TO BRING IT UP TOO.
HEY...THAT SURE IS TELLING...
I'VE LIVED A RATHER EXTRA-ORDINARY LIFE...
...BUT I ALWAYS WANT TO MAKE SURE MY GOOD-BYES ARE CLEAN.
I SUPPOSE YOU COULD SAY I WANT THEM TO BE MEANINGFUL FOR BOTH PARTIES.
SO WE CAN BOTH TAKE THE NEXT STEP FORWARD WITHOUT ANY REGRETS.

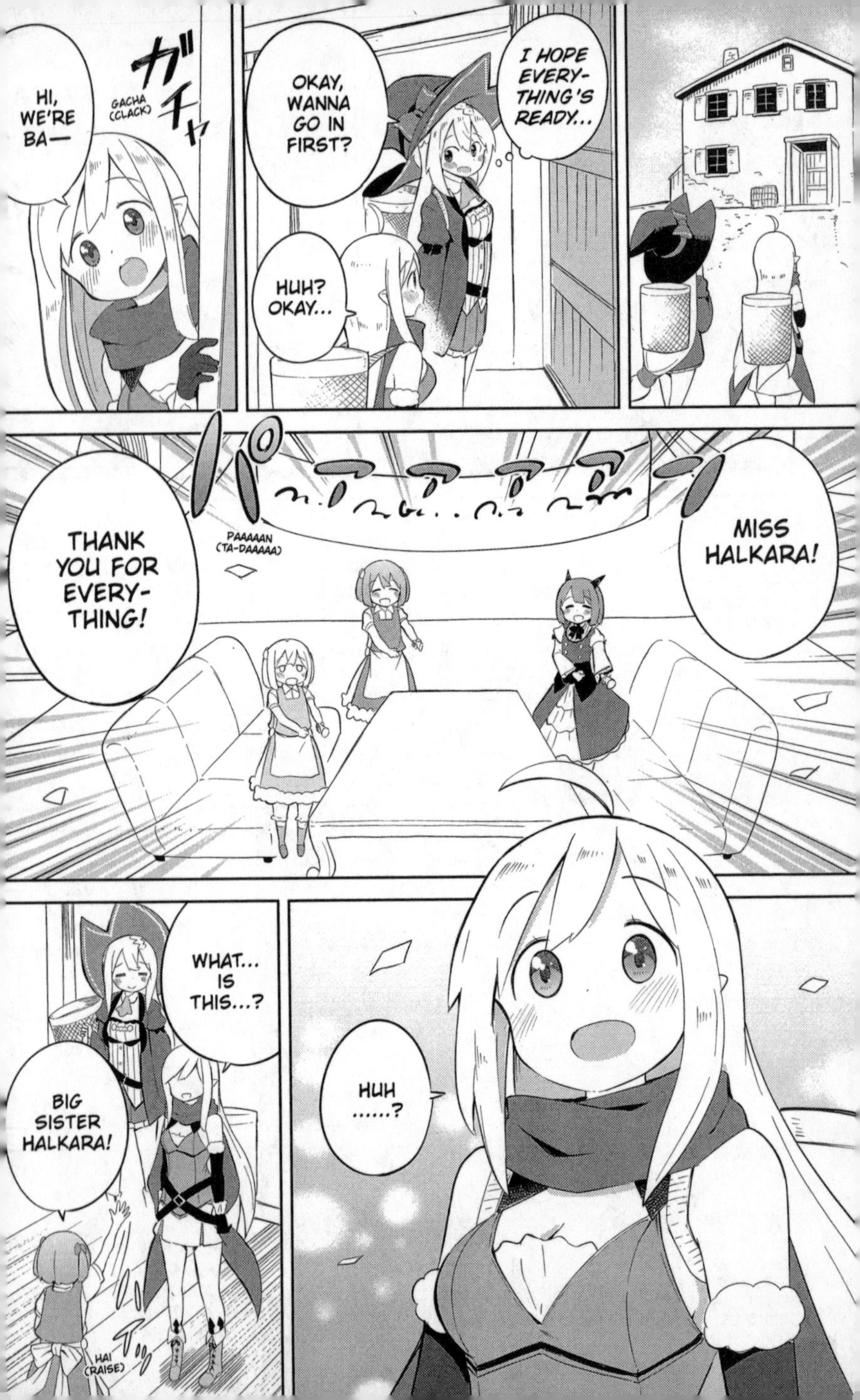
I HOPE EVERY-THING'S READY...
OKAY, WANNA GO IN FIRST?
HUH? OKAY...
GACHA (CLACK)
HI, WE'RE BA—
PAAAAAN (TA-DAAAAA)
MISS HALKARA!
THANK YOU FOR EVERY-THING!
HUH ......?
WHAT... IS THIS...?
BIG SISTER HALKARA!
HAI (RAISE)

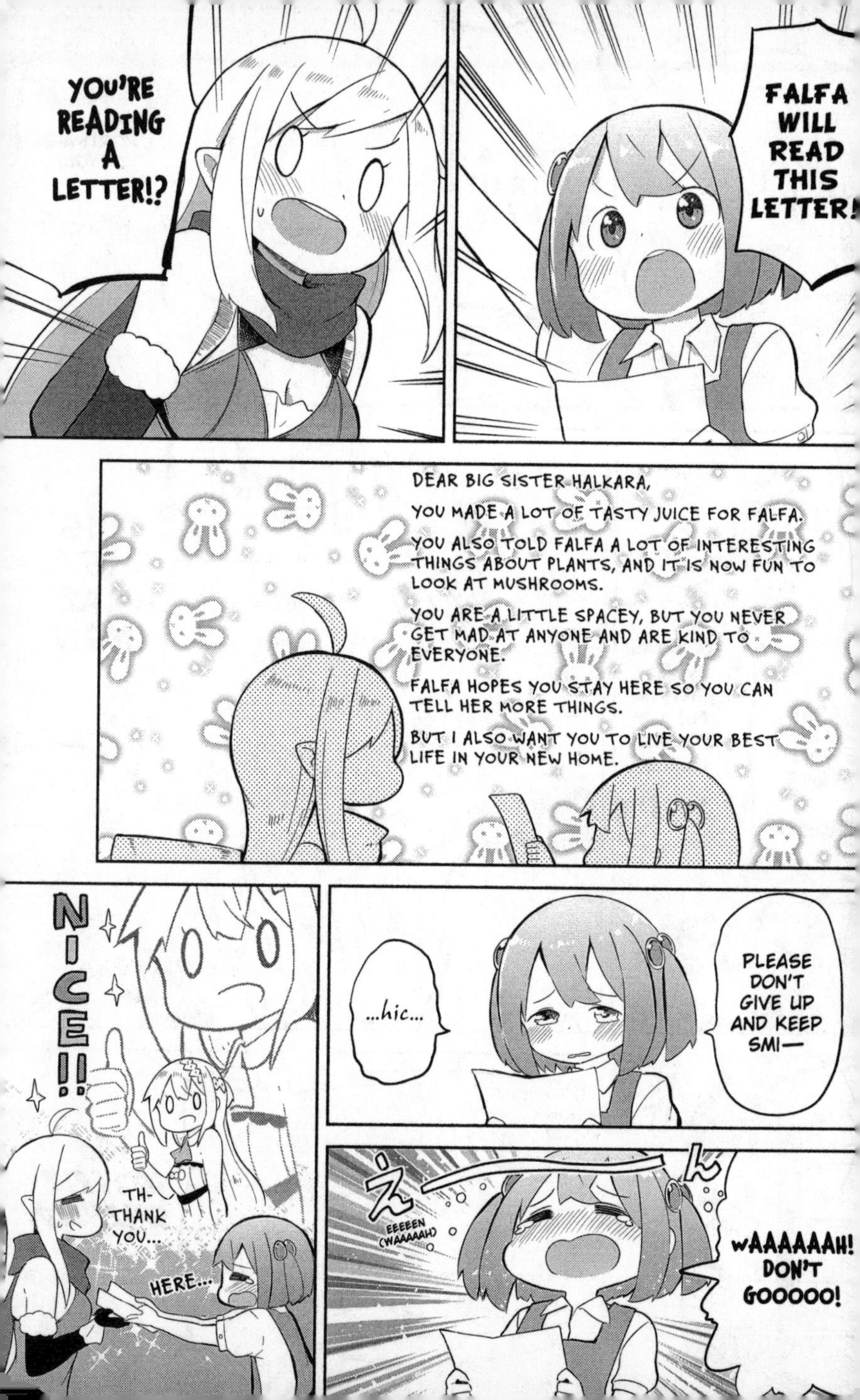
FALFA WILL READ THIS LETTER!
YOU'RE READING A LETTER!?
DEAR BIG SISTER HALKARA,
YOU MADE A LOT OF TASTY JUICE FOR FALFA.
YOU ALSO TOLD FALFA A LOT OF INTERESTING THINGS ABOUT PLANTS, AND IT IS NOW FUN TO LOOK AT MUSHROOMS.
YOU ARE A LITTLE SPACEY, BUT YOU NEVER GET MAD AT ANYONE AND ARE KIND TO EVERYONE.
FALFA HOPES YOU STAY HERE SO YOU CAN TELL HER MORE THINGS.
BUT I ALSO WANT YOU TO LIVE YOUR BEST LIFE IN YOUR NEW HOME.
PLEASE DON'T GIVE UP AND KEEP SMI—
...hic...
えーーーん
EEEEEN (WAAAAAH)
WAAAAAAH! DON'T GOOOOO!
NICE!!
TH-THANK YOU...
HERE...

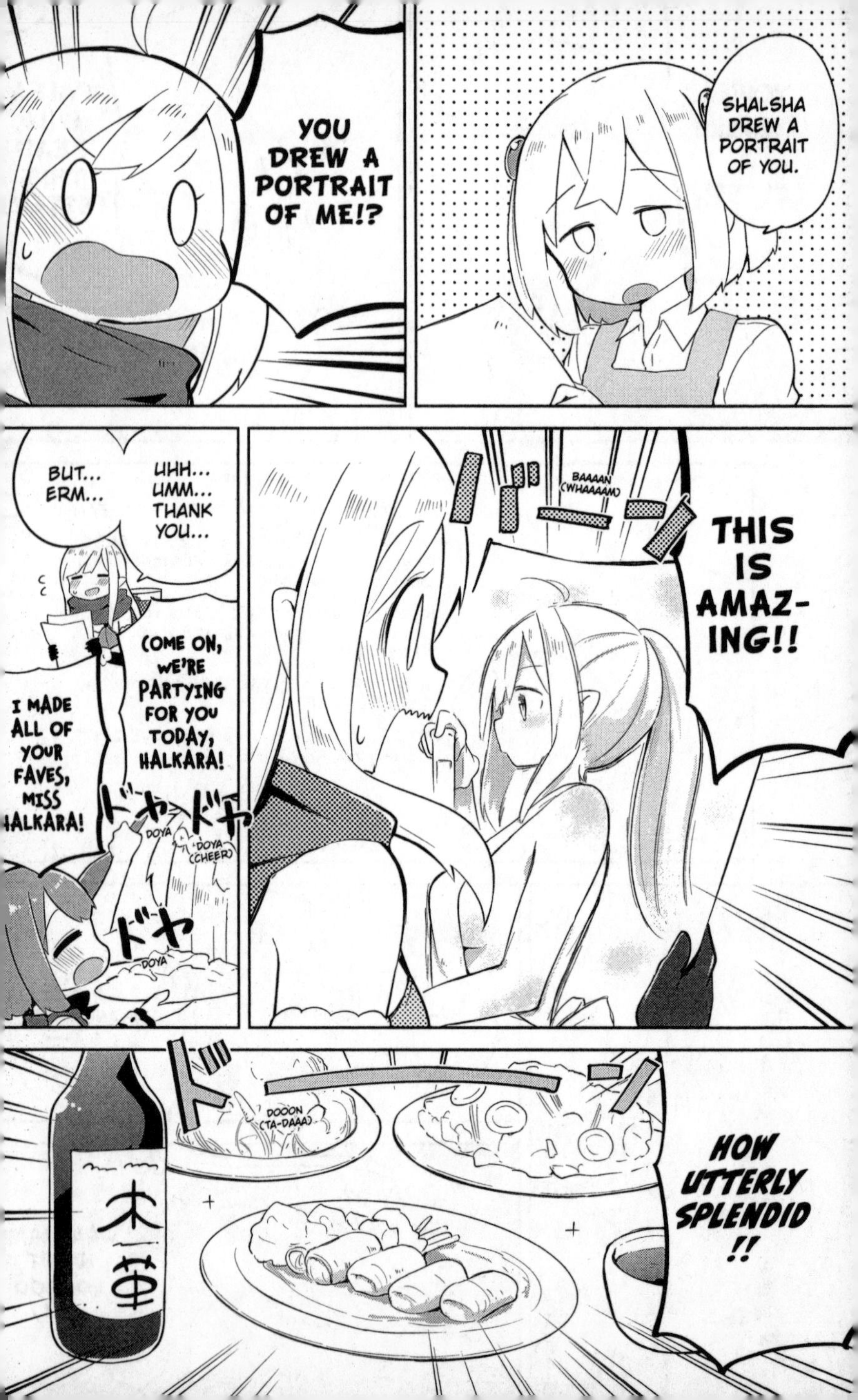
SHALSHA DREW A PORTRAIT OF YOU.
YOU DREW A PORTRAIT OF ME!?
バーン
BAAAAN (WHAAAAM)
THIS IS AMAZING!!
UHH... UMM... THANK YOU...
BUT... ERM...
COME ON, WE'RE PARTYING FOR YOU TODAY, HALKARA!
I MADE ALL OF YOUR FAVES, MISS HALKARA!
ドヤドヤ
DOYA DOYA (CHEER)
ドヤ
DOYA
ドーン
DOOON (TA-DAAA)
HOW UTTERLY SPLENDID!!

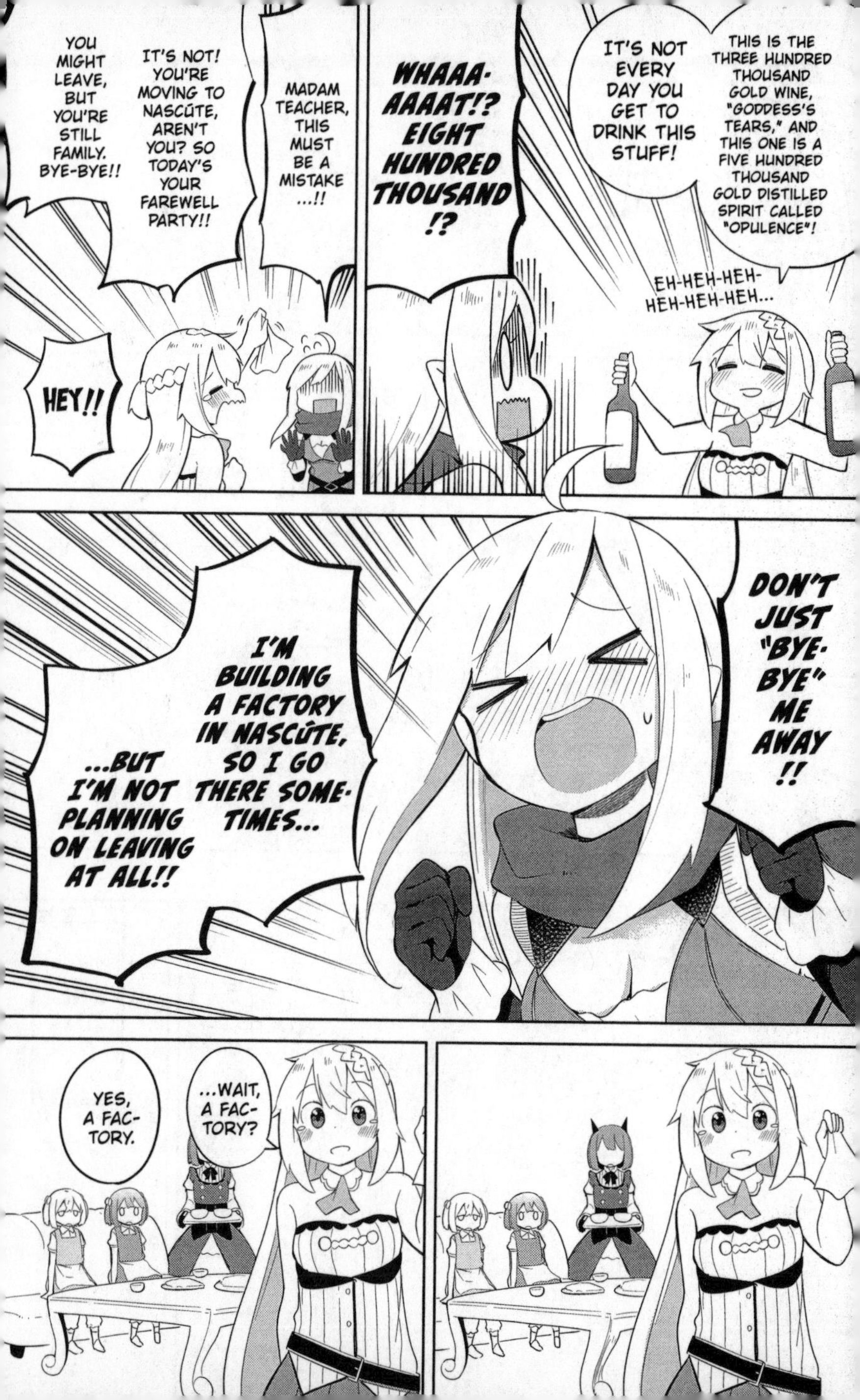
THIS IS THE THREE HUNDRED THOUSAND GOLD WINE, "GODDESS'S TEARS," AND THIS ONE IS A FIVE HUNDRED THOUSAND GOLD DISTILLED SPIRIT CALLED "OPULENCE"!
IT'S NOT EVERY DAY YOU GET TO DRINK THIS STUFF!
EH-HEH-HEH-HEH-HEH-HEH...
WHAAAA-AAAAT!? EIGHT HUNDRED THOUSAND!?
MADAM TEACHER, THIS MUST BE A MISTAKE...!!
IT'S NOT! YOU'RE MOVING TO NASCÛTE, AREN'T YOU? SO TODAY'S YOUR FAREWELL PARTY!!
YOU MIGHT LEAVE, BUT YOU'RE STILL FAMILY. BYE-BYE!!
HEY!!
DON'T JUST "BYE-BYE" ME AWAY!!
I'M BUILDING A FACTORY IN NASCÛTE, SO I GO THERE SOMETIMES...
...BUT I'M NOT PLANNING ON LEAVING AT ALL!!
...WAIT, A FACTORY?
YES, A FACTORY.

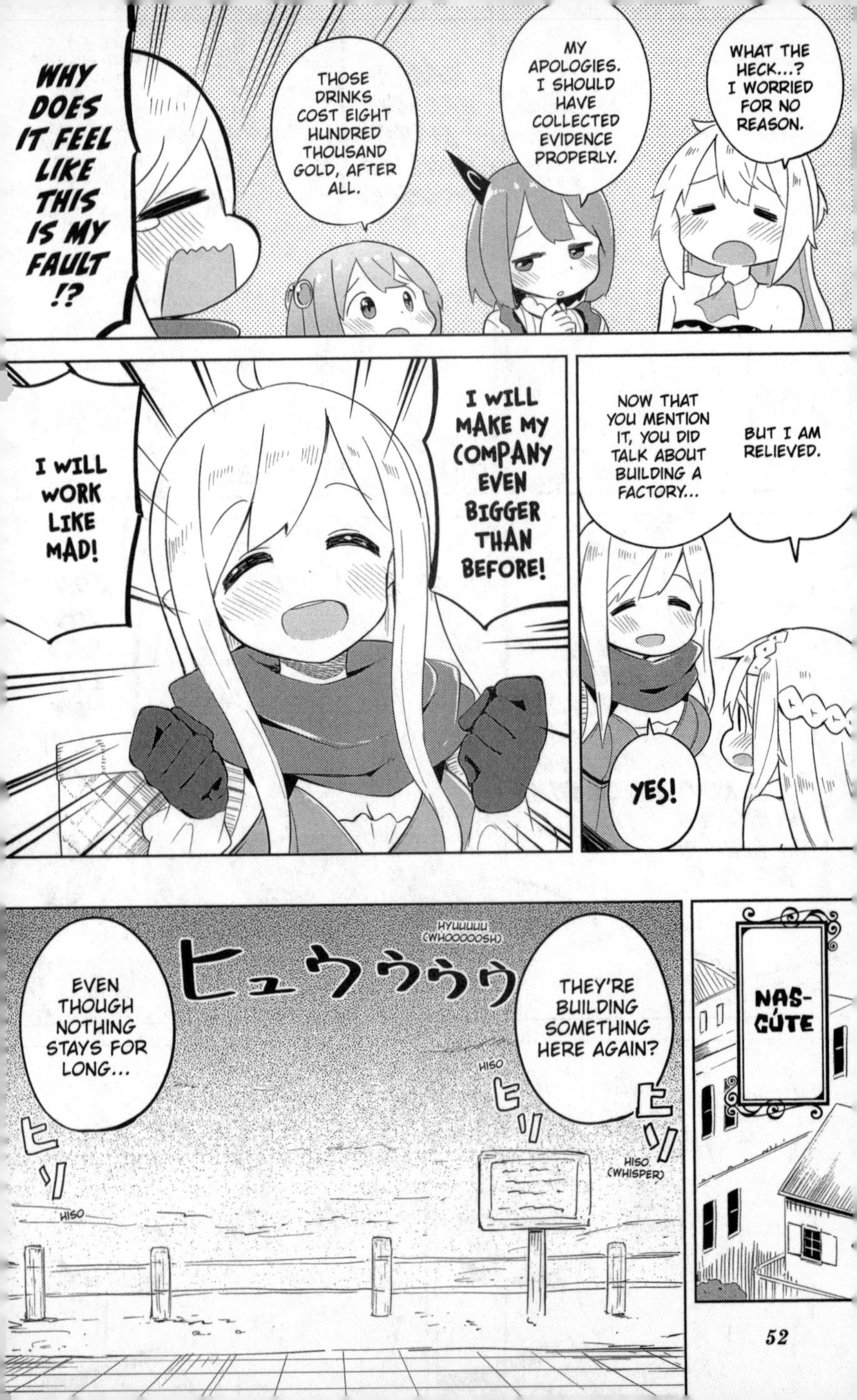
WHAT THE HECK...? I WORRIED FOR NO REASON.
MY APOLOGIES. I SHOULD HAVE COLLECTED EVIDENCE PROPERLY.
THOSE DRINKS COST EIGHT HUNDRED THOUSAND GOLD, AFTER ALL.
WHY DOES IT FEEL LIKE THIS IS MY FAULT!?
BUT I AM RELIEVED.
NOW THAT YOU MENTION IT, YOU DID TALK ABOUT BUILDING A FACTORY...
YES!
I WILL MAKE MY COMPANY EVEN BIGGER THAN BEFORE!
I WILL WORK LIKE MAD!
NAS-CÚTE
ヒュウウウウウ
HYUUUUU (WHOOOOOSH)
ヒソ
HISO. (WHISPER)
THEY'RE BUILDING SOMETHING HERE AGAIN?
ヒソ
HISO
EVEN THOUGH NOTHING STAYS FOR LONG...
ヒソ
HISO

I've Been Killing Slimes for 300 Years and Maxed Out My Level

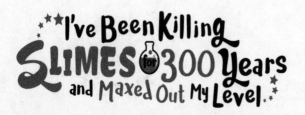

HAH!

THAT IS THE EXTREMELY RARE RAINBOW SLIME, SAID TO GIVE...

50K EXP

...WHEN DEFEATED!!

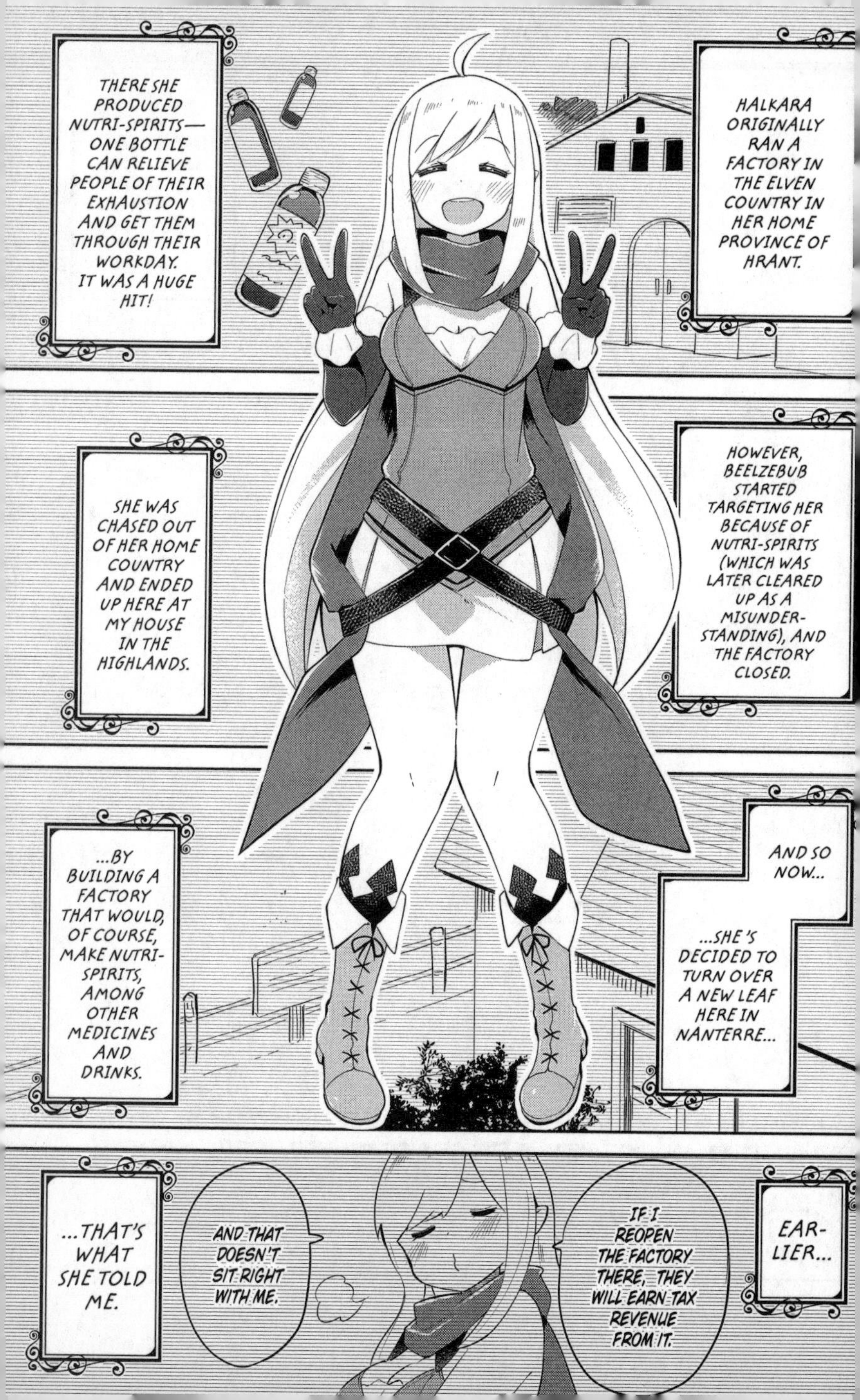
HALKARA ORIGINALLY RAN A FACTORY IN THE ELVEN COUNTRY IN HER HOME PROVINCE OF HRANT.
THERE SHE PRODUCED NUTRI-SPIRITS—ONE BOTTLE CAN RELIEVE PEOPLE OF THEIR EXHAUSTION AND GET THEM THROUGH THEIR WORKDAY. IT WAS A HUGE HIT!
HOWEVER, BEELZEBUB STARTED TARGETING HER BECAUSE OF NUTRI-SPIRITS (WHICH WAS LATER CLEARED UP AS A MISUNDER-STANDING), AND THE FACTORY CLOSED.
SHE WAS CHASED OUT OF HER HOME COUNTRY AND ENDED UP HERE AT MY HOUSE IN THE HIGHLANDS.
AND SO NOW...
...SHE'S DECIDED TO TURN OVER A NEW LEAF HERE IN NANTERRE...
...BY BUILDING A FACTORY THAT WOULD, OF COURSE, MAKE NUTRI-SPIRITS, AMONG OTHER MEDICINES AND DRINKS.
EAR-LIER...
IF I REOPEN THE FACTORY THERE, THEY WILL EARN TAX REVENUE FROM IT.
AND THAT DOESN'T SIT RIGHT WITH ME.
...THAT'S WHAT SHE TOLD ME.

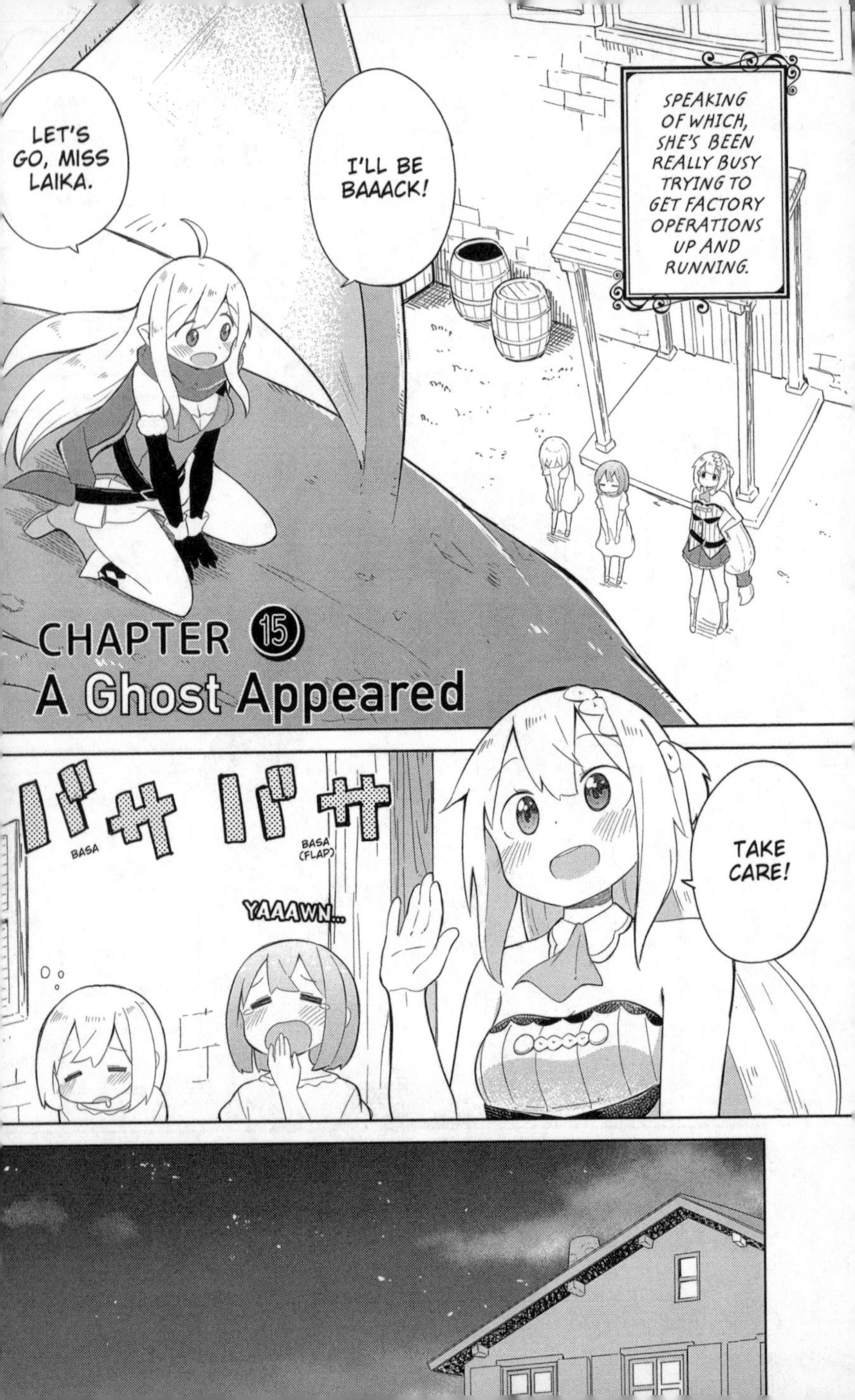
SPEAKING OF WHICH, SHE'S BEEN REALLY BUSY TRYING TO GET FACTORY OPERATIONS UP AND RUNNING.
I'LL BE BAAACK!
LET'S GO, MISS LAIKA.
CHAPTER 15
A Ghost Appeared
TAKE CARE!
バサ
BASA (FLAP)
YAAAWN...
バサ
BASA

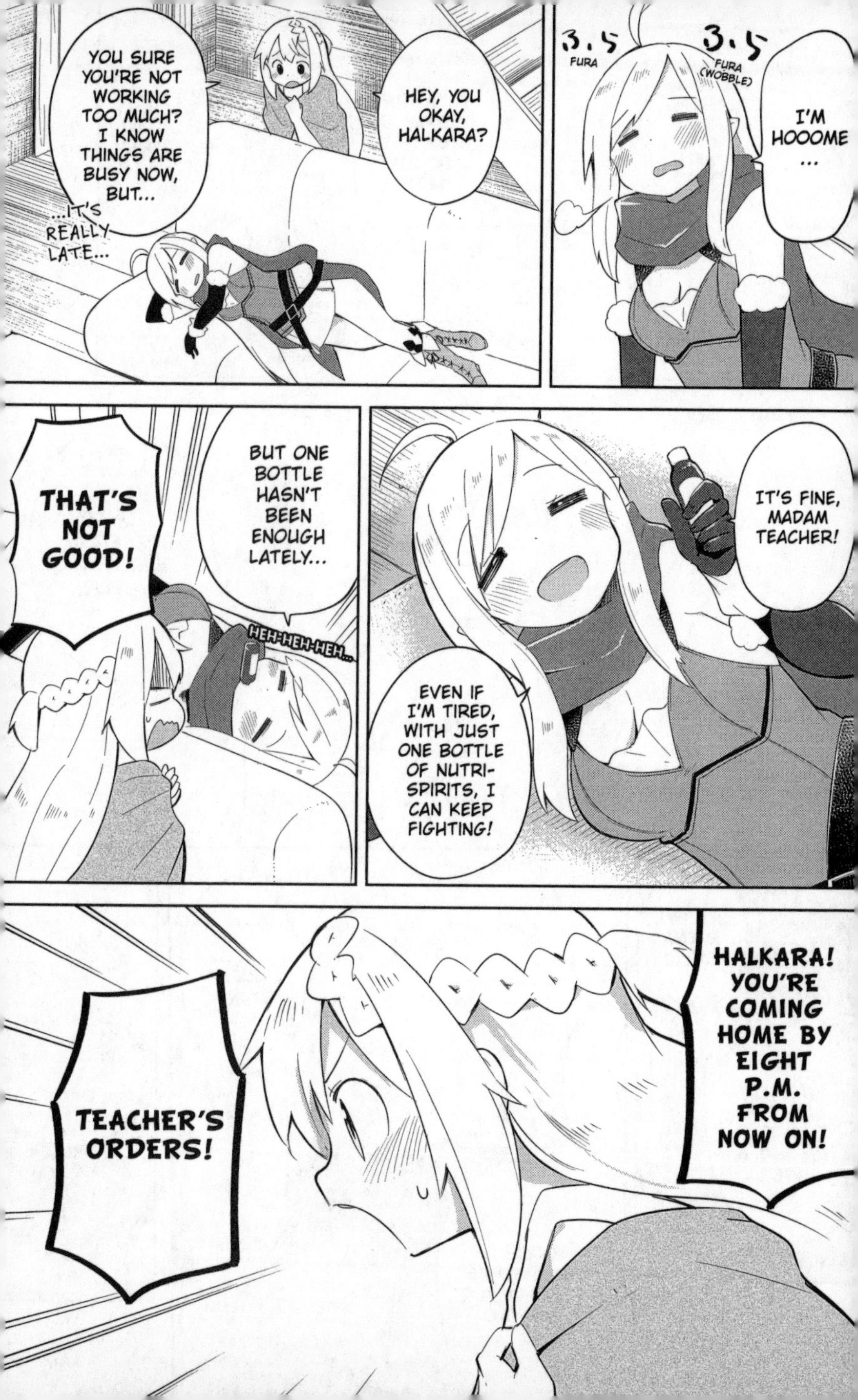
ふら
FURA
ふら
FURA (WOBBLE)
I'M HOOOME...
HEY, YOU OKAY, HALKARA?
YOU SURE YOU'RE NOT WORKING TOO MUCH? I KNOW THINGS ARE BUSY NOW, BUT...
...IT'S REALLY LATE...
IT'S FINE, MADAM TEACHER!
EVEN IF I'M TIRED, WITH JUST ONE BOTTLE OF NUTRI-SPIRITS, I CAN KEEP FIGHTING!
HEH-HEH-HEH...
BUT ONE BOTTLE HASN'T BEEN ENOUGH LATELY...
THAT'S NOT GOOD!
HALKARA! YOU'RE COMING HOME BY EIGHT P.M. FROM NOW ON!
TEACHER'S ORDERS!

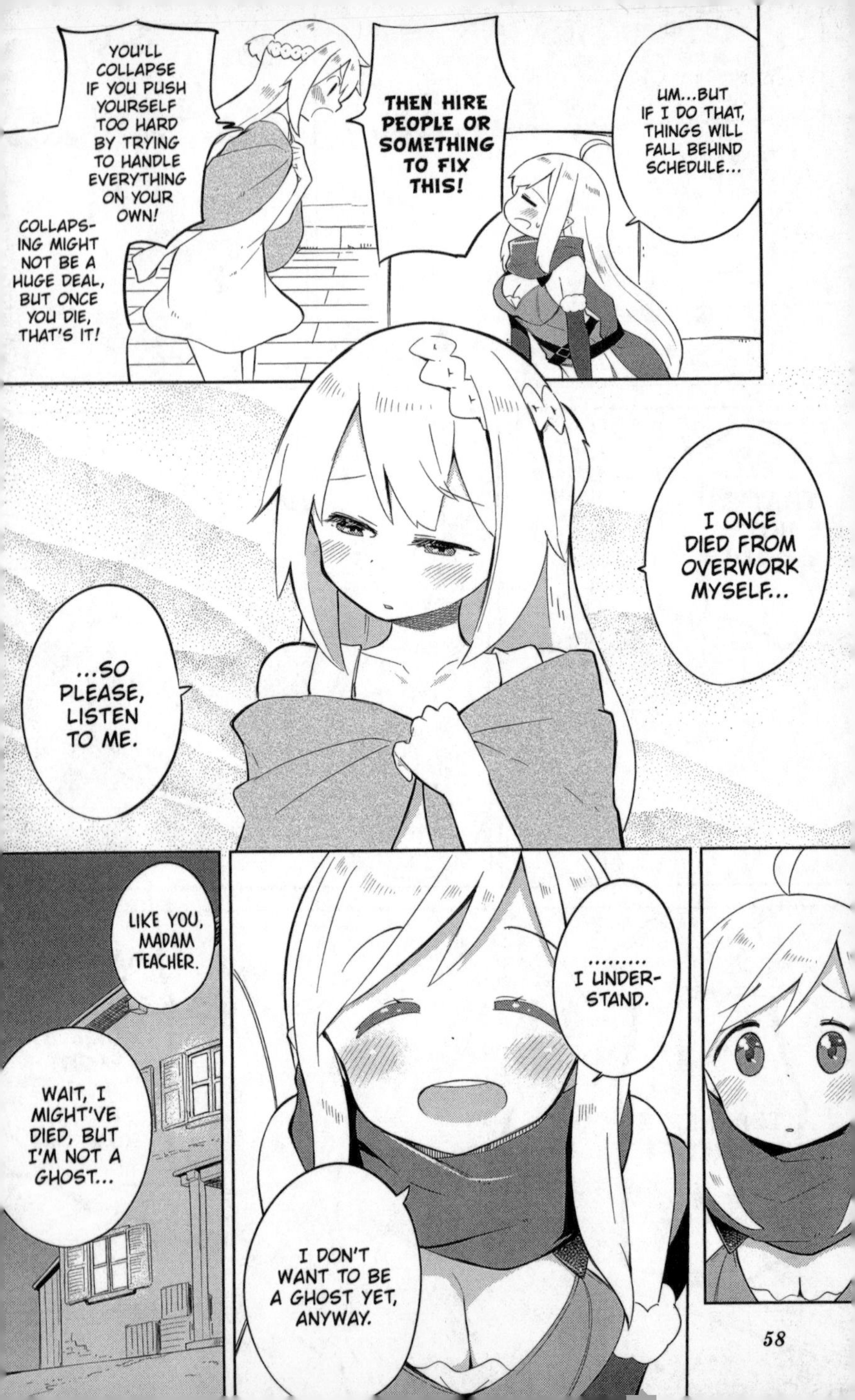
UM...BUT IF I DO THAT, THINGS WILL FALL BEHIND SCHEDULE...
THEN HIRE PEOPLE OR SOMETHING TO FIX THIS!
YOU'LL COLLAPSE IF YOU PUSH YOURSELF TOO HARD BY TRYING TO HANDLE EVERYTHING ON YOUR OWN!
COLLAPS-ING MIGHT NOT BE A HUGE DEAL, BUT ONCE YOU DIE, THAT'S IT!
I ONCE DIED FROM OVERWORK MYSELF...
...SO PLEASE, LISTEN TO ME.
.... I UNDER-STAND.
I DON'T WANT TO BE A GHOST YET, ANYWAY.
LIKE YOU, MADAM TEACHER.
WAIT, I MIGHT'VE DIED, BUT I'M NOT A GHOST...

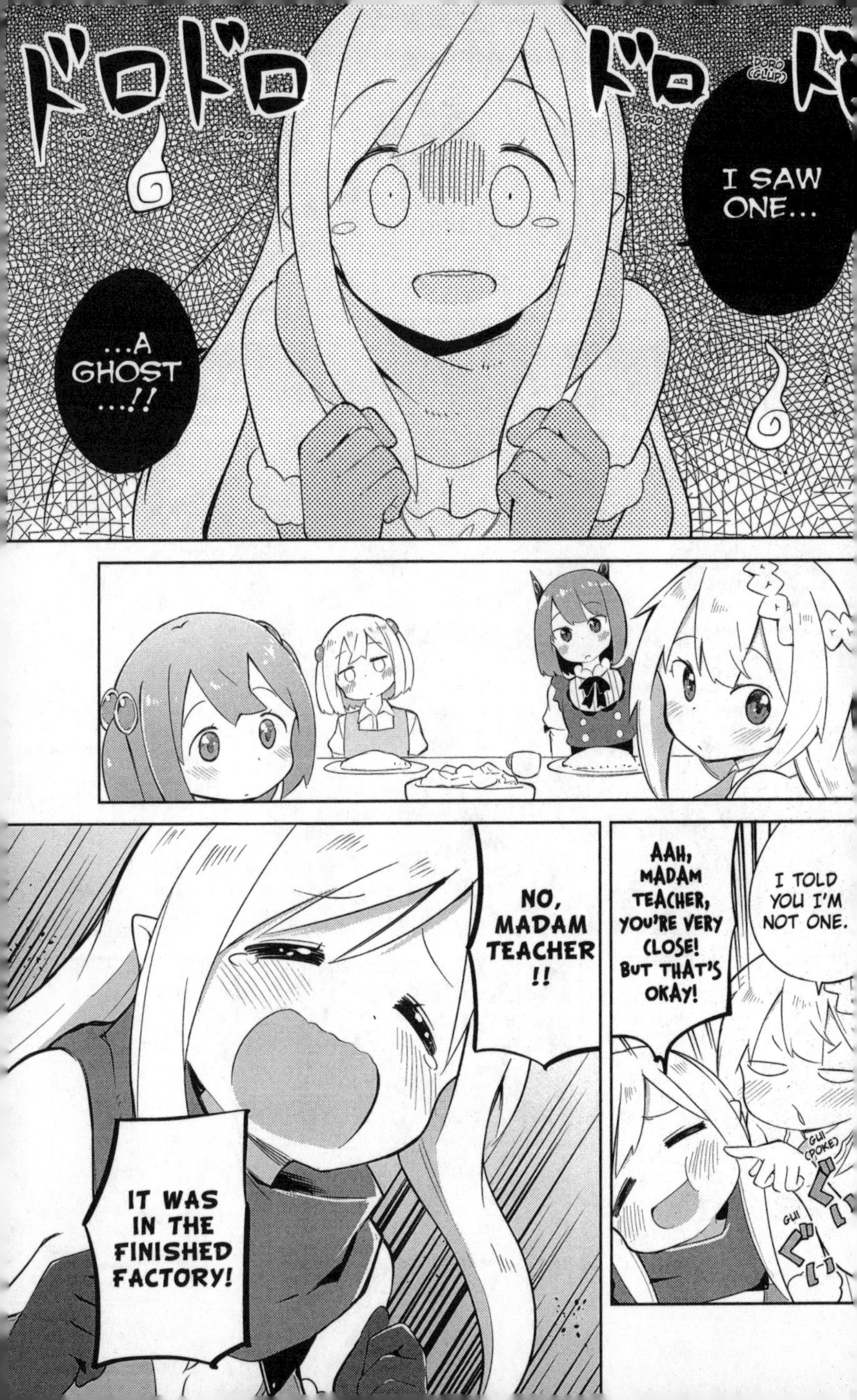
DORO (GLUP)
DORO
I SAW ONE...
ドロドロ
DORO
DORO
...A GHOST ...!!
I TOLD YOU I'M NOT ONE.
AAH, MADAM TEACHER, YOU'RE VERY CLOSE! BUT THAT'S OKAY!
GUI (POKE)
GUI
NO, MADAM TEACHER!!
IT WAS IN THE FINISHED FACTORY!

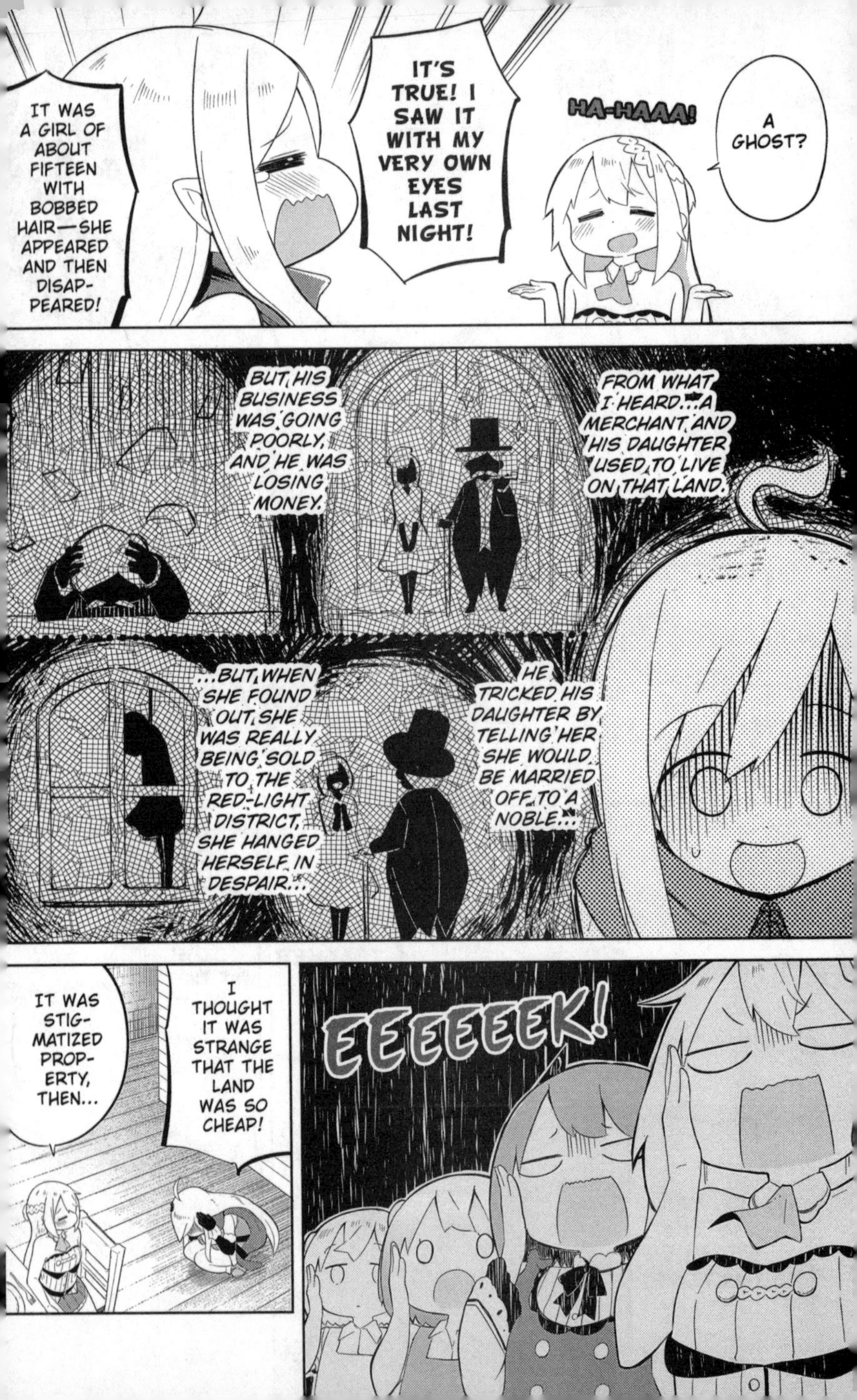
A GHOST?
HA-HAAA!
IT'S TRUE! I SAW IT WITH MY VERY OWN EYES LAST NIGHT!
IT WAS A GIRL OF ABOUT FIFTEEN WITH BOBBED HAIR—SHE APPEARED AND THEN DISAP-PEARED!
FROM WHAT I HEARD... A MERCHANT AND HIS DAUGHTER USED TO LIVE ON THAT LAND.
BUT HIS BUSINESS WAS GOING POORLY, AND HE WAS LOSING MONEY.
HE TRICKED HIS DAUGHTER BY TELLING HER SHE WOULD BE MARRIED OFF TO A NOBLE...
...BUT WHEN SHE FOUND OUT SHE WAS REALLY BEING SOLD TO THE RED-LIGHT DISTRICT, SHE HANGED HERSELF IN DESPAIR...
EEEEEEK!
I THOUGHT IT WAS STRANGE THAT THE LAND WAS SO CHEAP!
IT WAS STIG-MATIZED PROP-ERTY, THEN...

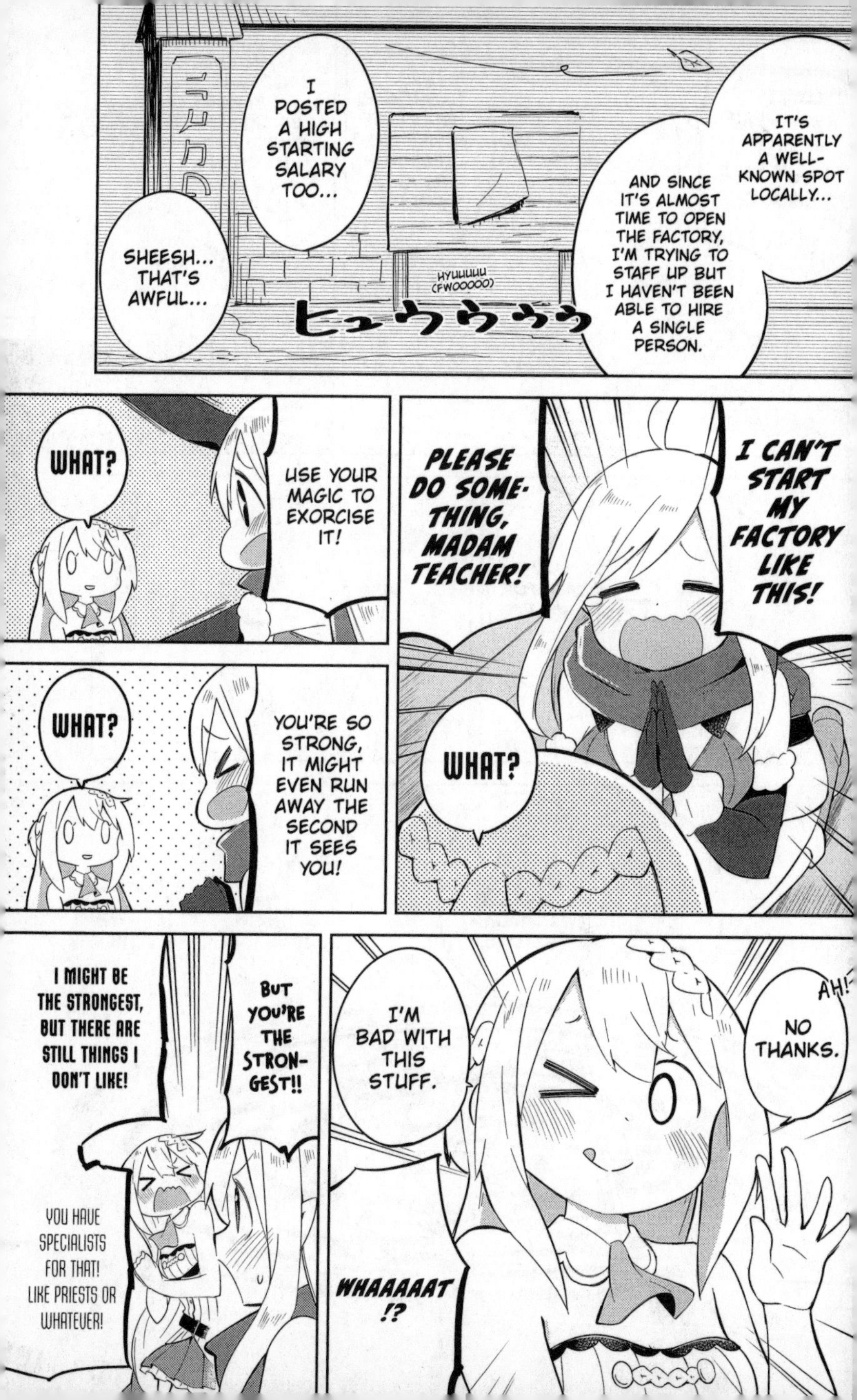
IT'S APPARENTLY A WELL-KNOWN SPOT LOCALLY...
AND SINCE IT'S ALMOST TIME TO OPEN THE FACTORY, I'M TRYING TO STAFF UP BUT I HAVEN'T BEEN ABLE TO HIRE A SINGLE PERSON.
HYUUUUU (FWOOOOO)
I POSTED A HIGH STARTING SALARY TOO...
SHEESH... THAT'S AWFUL...
I CAN'T START MY FACTORY LIKE THIS!
PLEASE DO SOME-THING, MADAM TEACHER!
WHAT?
USE YOUR MAGIC TO EXORCISE IT!
WHAT?
YOU'RE SO STRONG, IT MIGHT EVEN RUN AWAY THE SECOND IT SEES YOU!
WHAT?
AH!
NO THANKS.
I'M BAD WITH THIS STUFF.
WHAAAAAT!?
BUT YOU'RE THE STRON-GEST!!
I MIGHT BE THE STRONGEST, BUT THERE ARE STILL THINGS I DON'T LIKE!
YOU HAVE SPECIALISTS FOR THAT! LIKE PRIESTS OR WHATEVER!

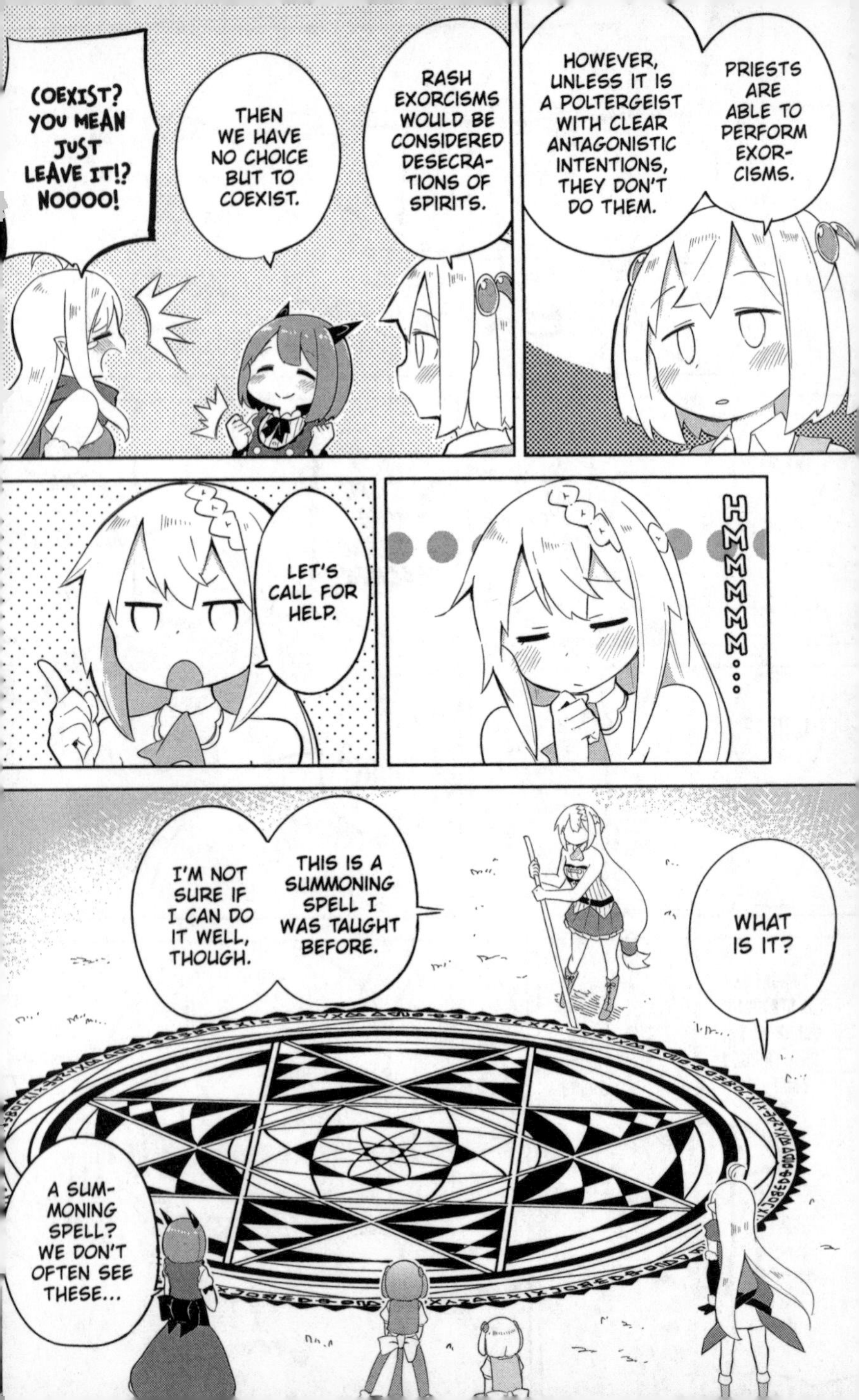
PRIESTS ARE ABLE TO PERFORM EXOR-CISMS.
HOWEVER, UNLESS IT IS A POLTERGEIST WITH CLEAR ANTAGONISTIC INTENTIONS, THEY DON'T DO THEM.
RASH EXORCISMS WOULD BE CONSIDERED DESECRA-TIONS OF SPIRITS.
THEN WE HAVE NO CHOICE BUT TO COEXIST.
COEXIST? YOU MEAN JUST LEAVE IT!? NOOOO!
HMMMMM...
LET'S CALL FOR HELP.
WHAT IS IT?
THIS IS A SUMMONING SPELL I WAS TAUGHT BEFORE.
I'M NOT SURE IF I CAN DO IT WELL, THOUGH.
A SUM-MONING SPELL? WE DON'T OFTEN SEE THESE...

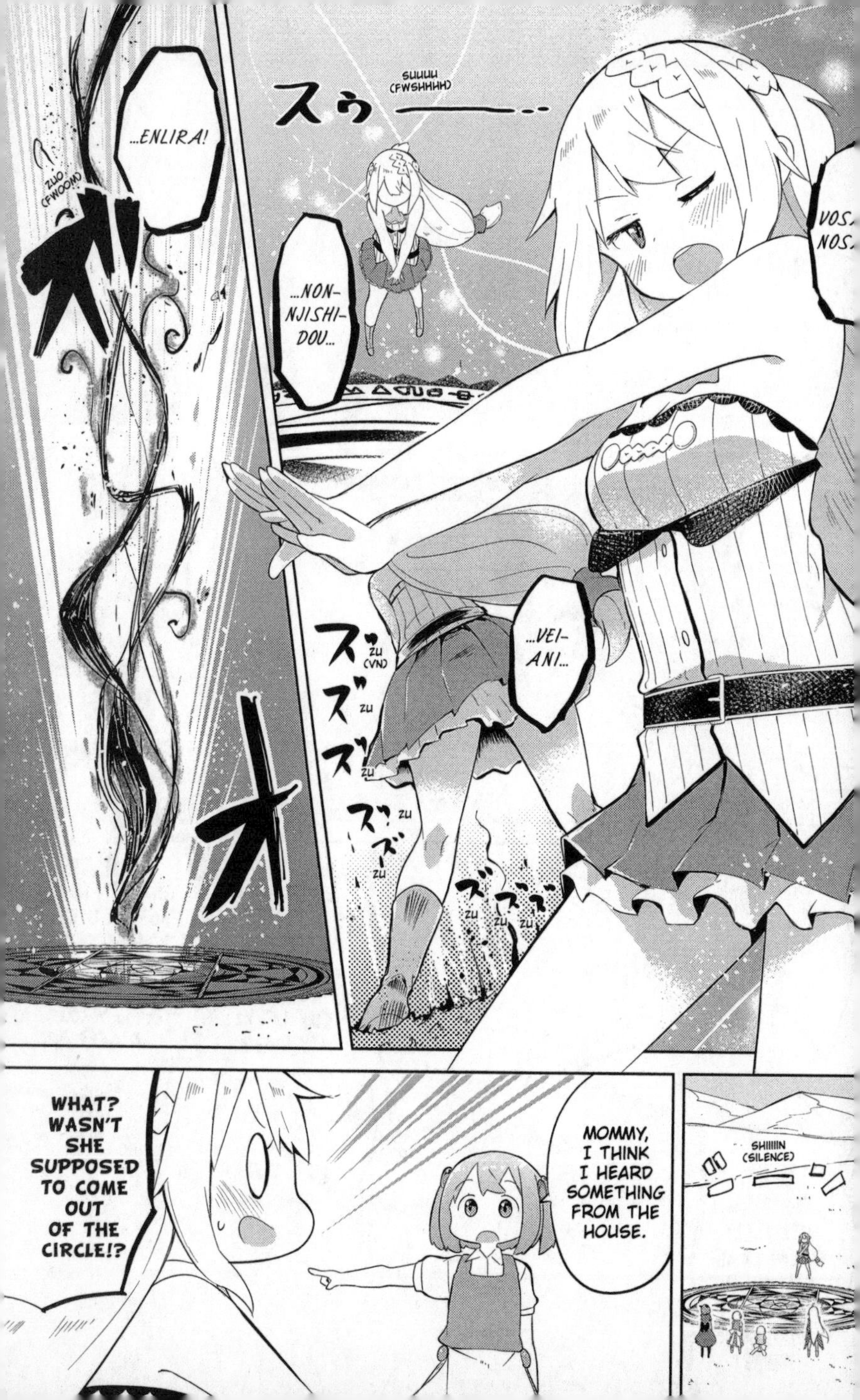
VOS NOS
...VEI-ANI...
ズ ZU (VN)
ズ ZU
ズ ZU
ズ ZU
ズ ZU
ズ ZU ズ ZU ズ ZU
スゥーー
SUUUU (FWSHHH)
...NON-NJISHI-DOU...
...ENLIRA!
ZUO (FWOOM)
SHIIIIN (SILENCE)
MOMMY, I THINK I HEARD SOMETHING FROM THE HOUSE.
WHAT? WASN'T SHE SUPPOSED TO COME OUT OF THE CIRCLE!?

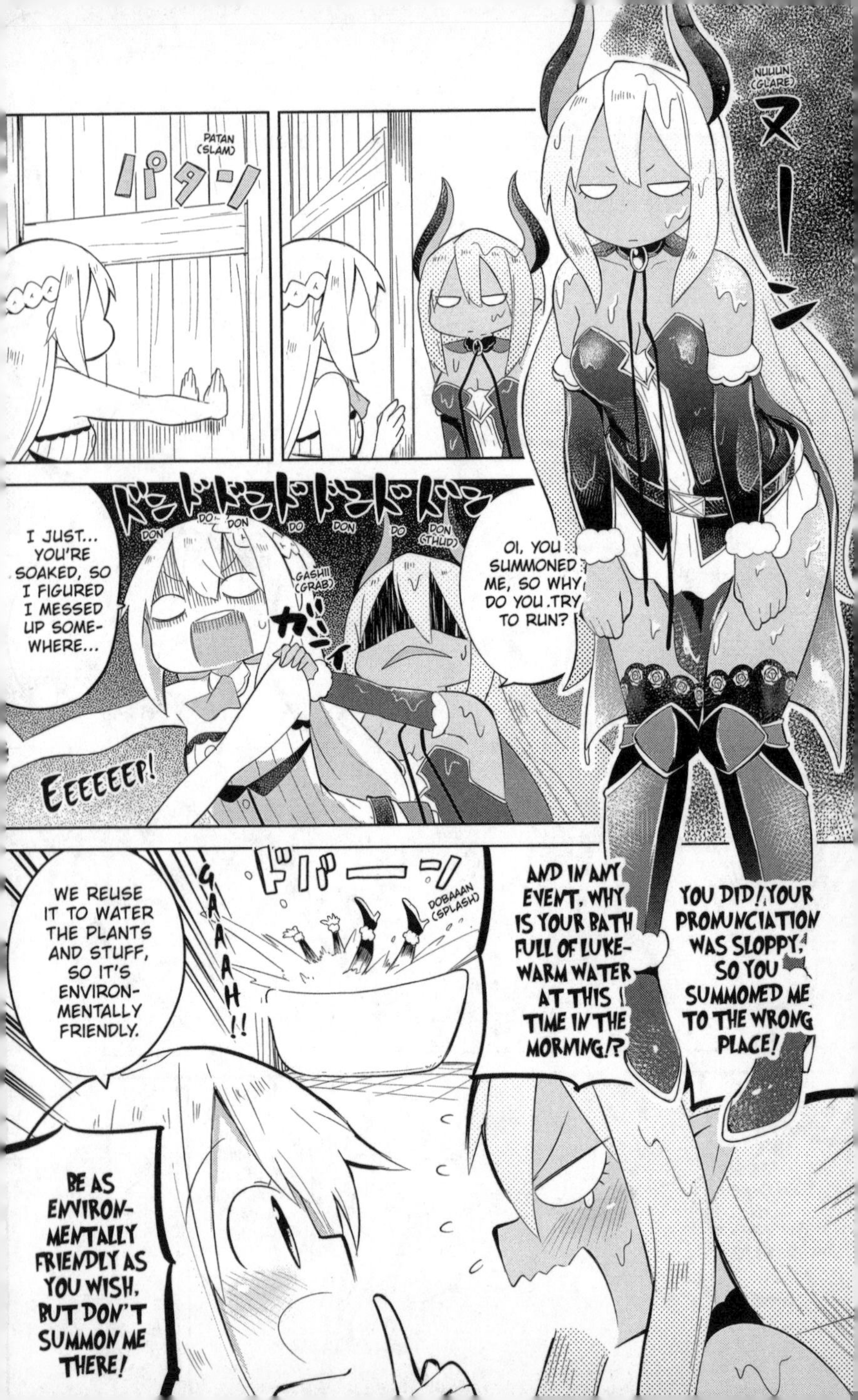
NUUUN (GLARE)
ヌー
PATAN (SLAM)
パターン
ドンドドンドドンドドン
DON DON DON DO DON DO DON (THUD)
OI, YOU SUMMONED ME, SO WHY DO YOU TRY TO RUN?
GASHI! (GRAB)
ガシ
I JUST... YOU'RE SOAKED, SO I FIGURED I MESSED UP SOME-WHERE...
EEEEEEP!
YOU DID! YOUR PRONUNCIATION WAS SLOPPY, SO YOU SUMMONED ME TO THE WRONG PLACE!
AND IN ANY EVENT, WHY IS YOUR BATH FULL OF LUKE-WARM WATER AT THIS TIME IN THE MORNING!?
ドバーン
DOBAAAN (SPLASH)
GYAAAAH!!
WE REUSE IT TO WATER THE PLANTS AND STUFF, SO IT'S ENVIRON-MENTALLY FRIENDLY.
BE AS ENVIRON-MENTALLY FRIENDLY AS YOU WISH, BUT DON'T SUMMON ME THERE!

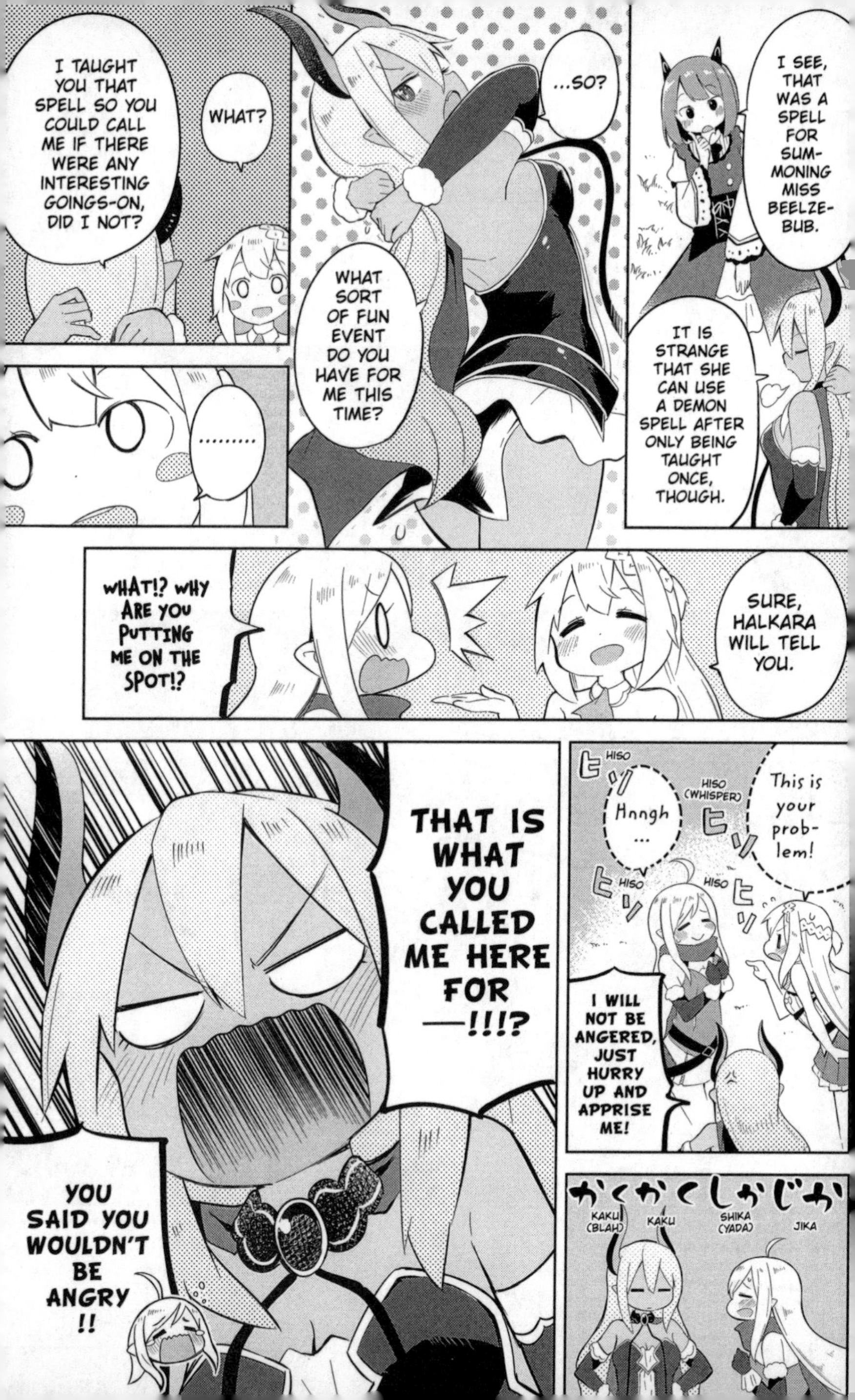
I SEE, THAT WAS A SPELL FOR SUMMONING MISS BEELZEBUB.
IT IS STRANGE THAT SHE CAN USE A DEMON SPELL AFTER ONLY BEING TAUGHT ONCE, THOUGH.
...SO?
WHAT SORT OF FUN EVENT DO YOU HAVE FOR ME THIS TIME?
WHAT?
I TAUGHT YOU THAT SPELL SO YOU COULD CALL ME IF THERE WERE ANY INTERESTING GOINGS-ON, DID I NOT?
....
SURE, HALKARA WILL TELL YOU.
WHAT!? WHY ARE YOU PUTTING ME ON THE SPOT!?
HISO (WHISPER)
This is your problem!
HISO
Hnngh ...
HISO
HISO
I WILL NOT BE ANGERED, JUST HURRY UP AND APPRISE ME!
かくかくしかじか
KAKU (BLAH)
KAKU
SHIKA (YADA)
JIKA
THAT IS WHAT YOU CALLED ME HERE FOR—!!!?
YOU SAID YOU WOULDN'T BE ANGRY!!

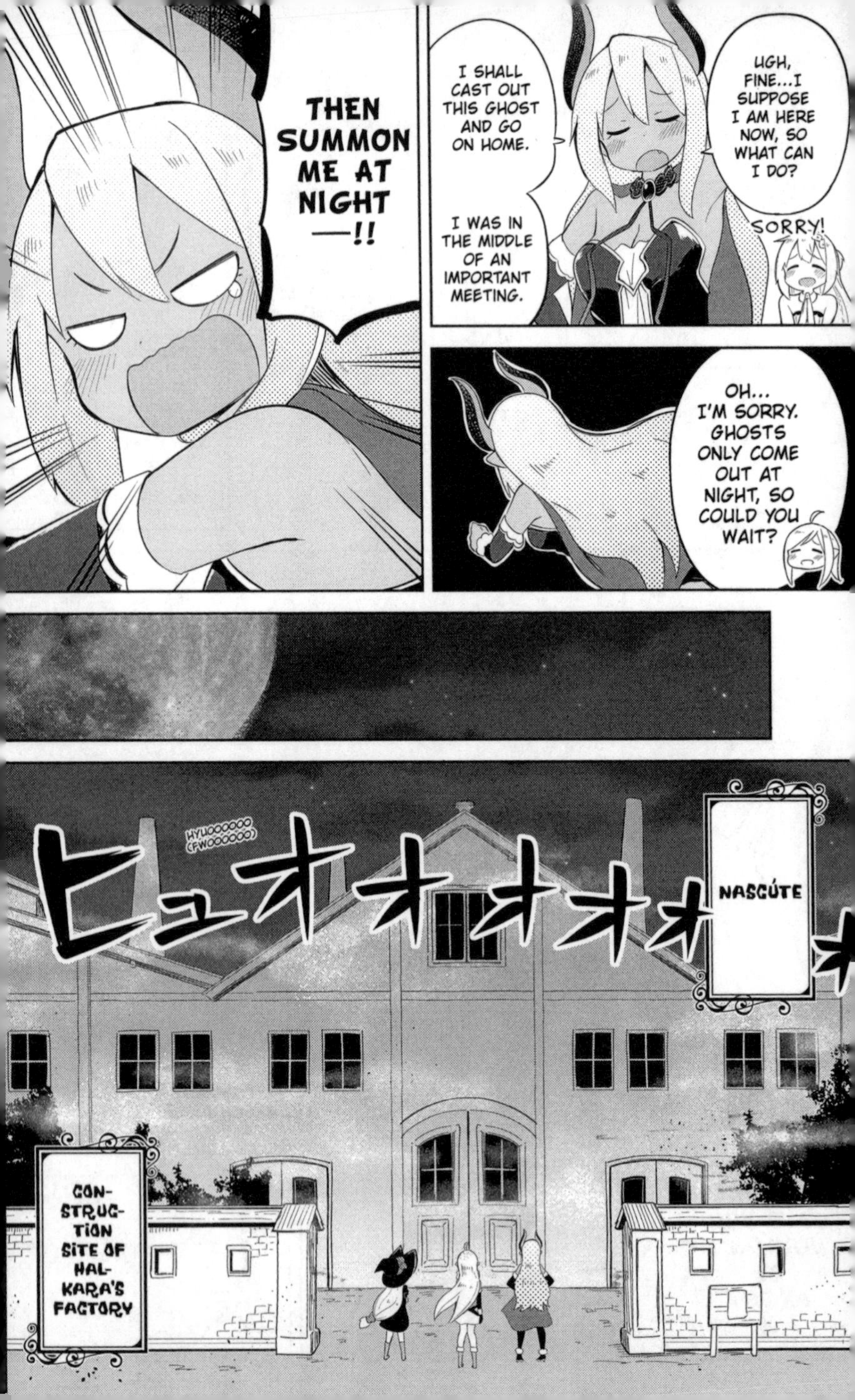
UGH, FINE...I SUPPOSE I AM HERE NOW, SO WHAT CAN I DO?
I SHALL CAST OUT THIS GHOST AND GO ON HOME.
I WAS IN THE MIDDLE OF AN IMPORTANT MEETING.
SORRY!
OH... I'M SORRY. GHOSTS ONLY COME OUT AT NIGHT, SO COULD YOU WAIT?
THEN SUMMON ME AT NIGHT—!!
NASCÚTE
ヒュオオオオオ
HYUOOOOOO (FWOOOOOO)
CON-STRUC-TION SITE OF HAL-KARA'S FACTORY

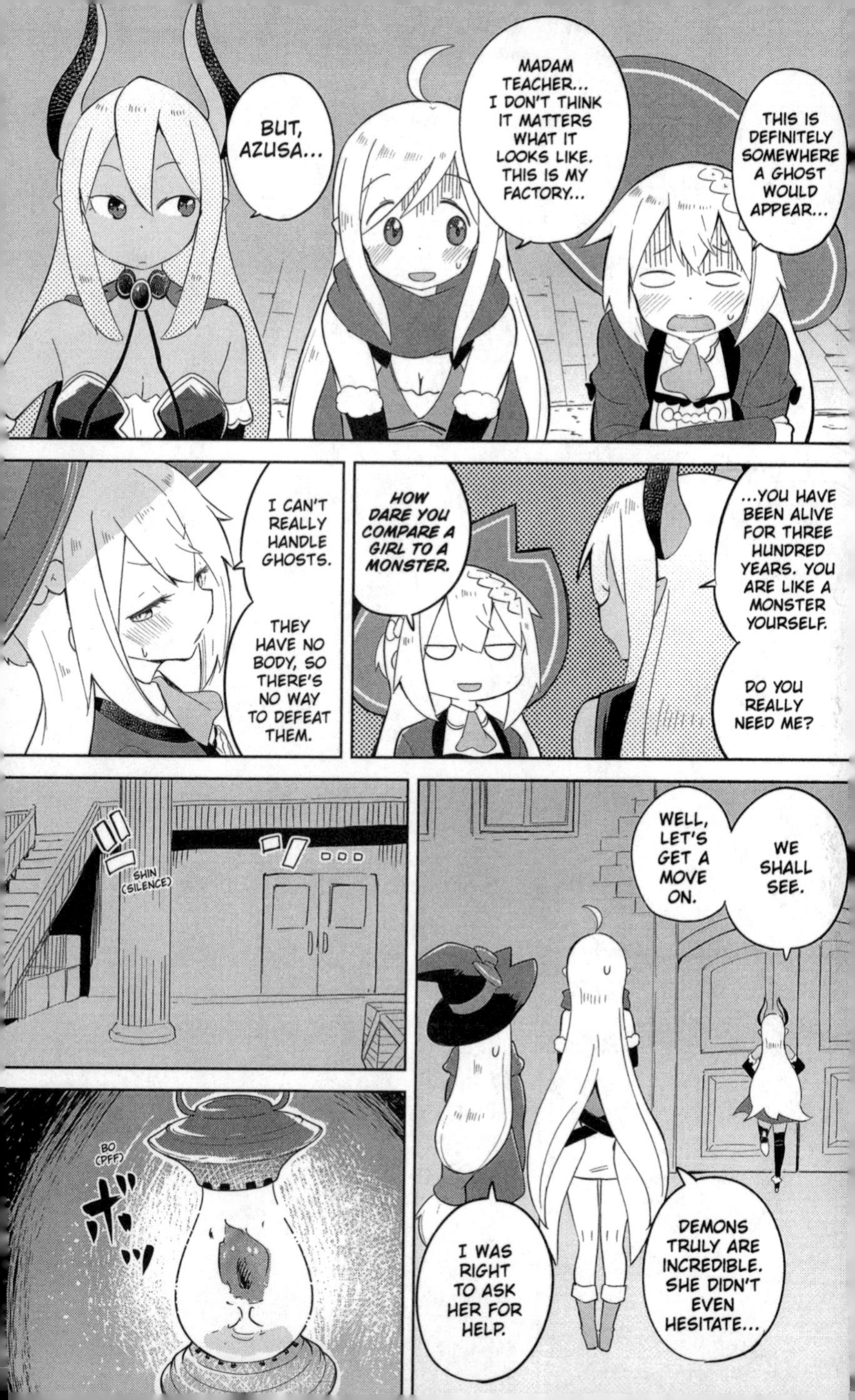
THIS IS DEFINITELY SOMEWHERE A GHOST WOULD APPEAR...
MADAM TEACHER... I DON'T THINK IT MATTERS WHAT IT LOOKS LIKE. THIS IS MY FACTORY...
BUT, AZUSA...
...YOU HAVE BEEN ALIVE FOR THREE HUNDRED YEARS. YOU ARE LIKE A MONSTER YOURSELF.
DO YOU REALLY NEED ME?
HOW DARE YOU COMPARE A GIRL TO A MONSTER.
I CAN'T REALLY HANDLE GHOSTS.
THEY HAVE NO BODY, SO THERE'S NO WAY TO DEFEAT THEM.
WE SHALL SEE.
WELL, LET'S GET A MOVE ON.
DEMONS TRULY ARE INCREDIBLE. SHE DIDN'T EVEN HESITATE...
I WAS RIGHT TO ASK HER FOR HELP.
SHIN (SILENCE)
BO (PFF)

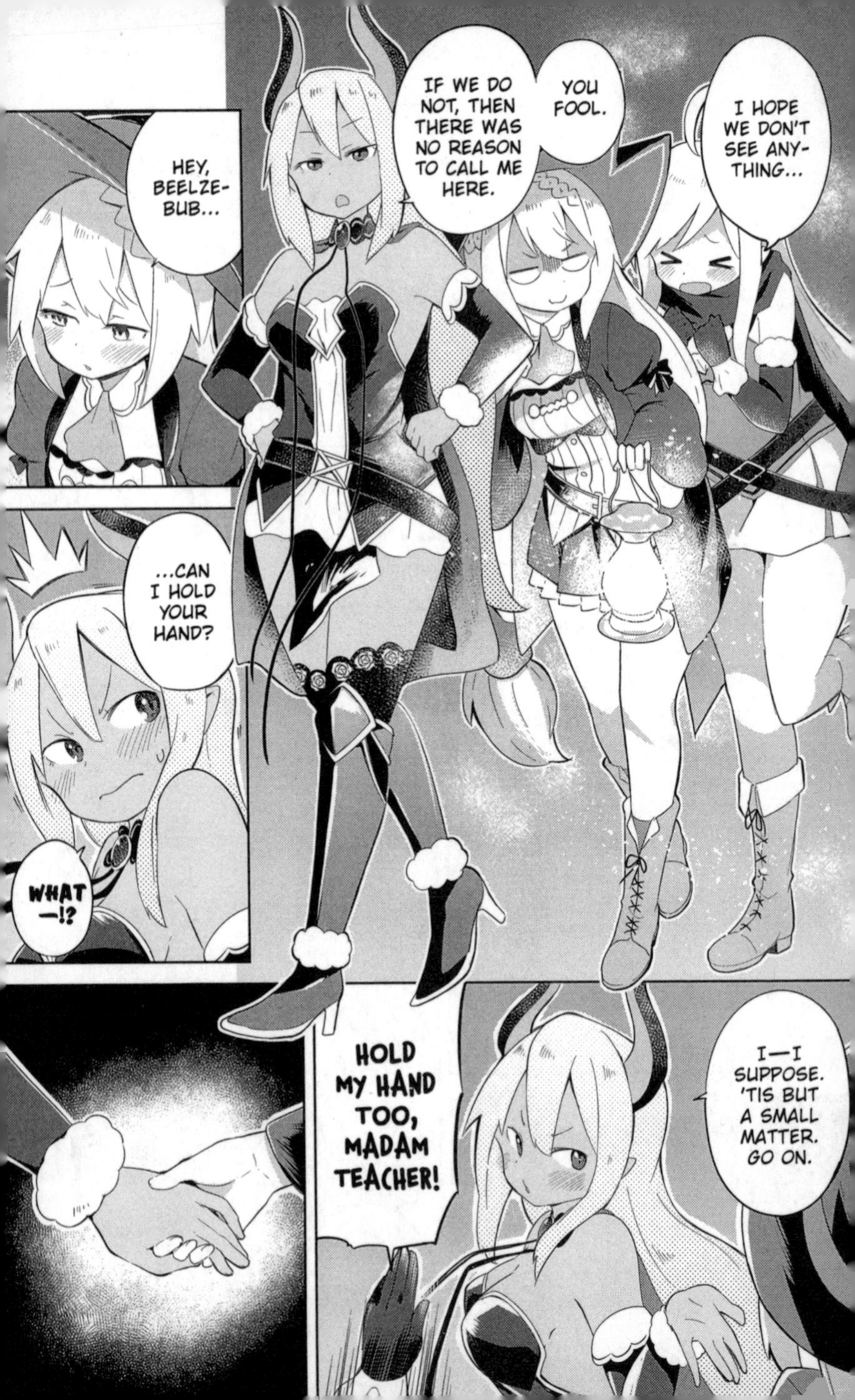
I HOPE WE DON'T SEE ANYTHING...
YOU FOOL.
IF WE DO NOT, THEN THERE WAS NO REASON TO CALL ME HERE.
HEY, BEELZEBUB...
...CAN I HOLD YOUR HAND?
WHAT—!?
I—I SUPPOSE. 'TIS BUT A SMALL MATTER. GO ON.
HOLD MY HAND TOO, MADAM TEACHER!

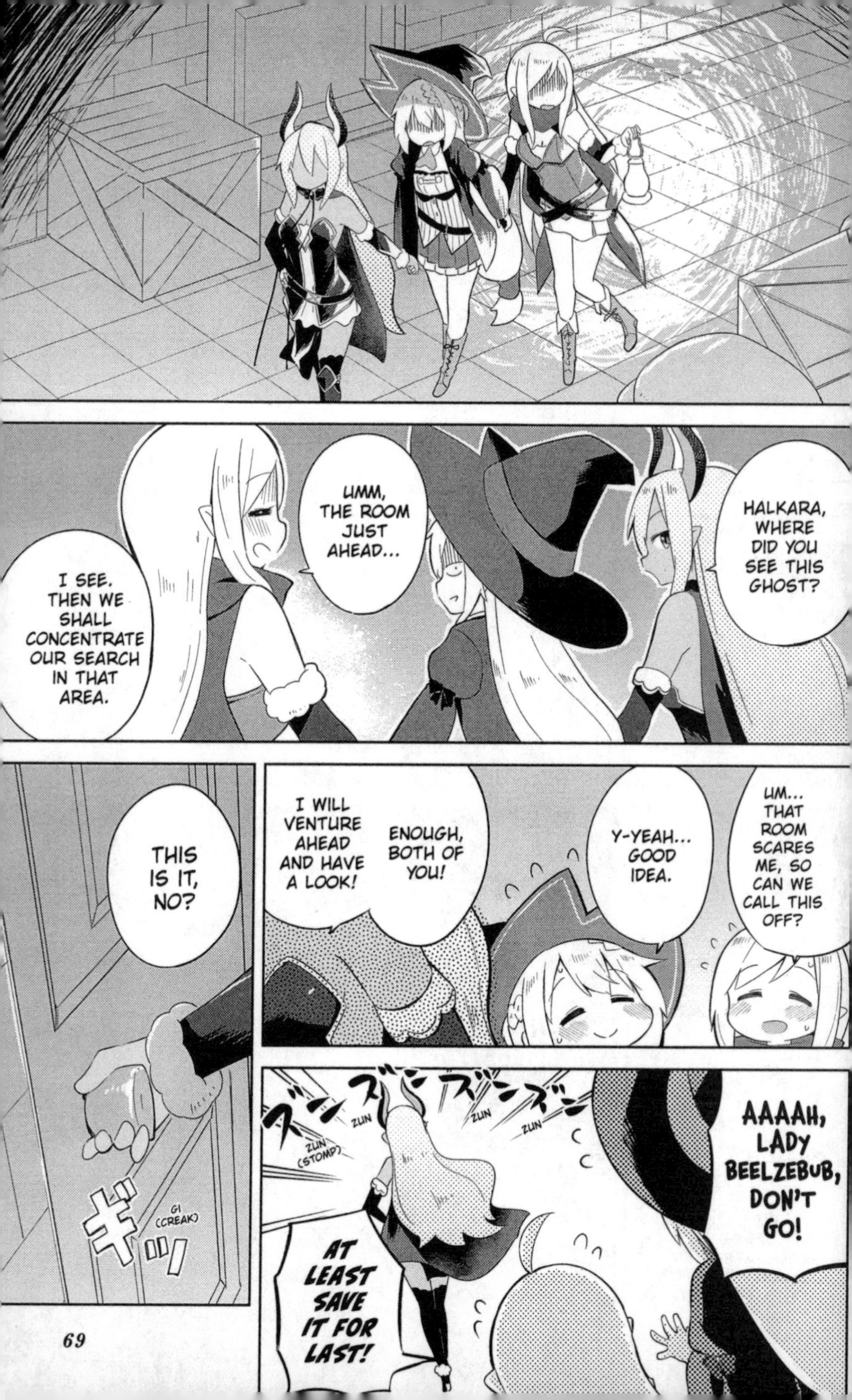
HALKARA, WHERE DID YOU SEE THIS GHOST?
UMM, THE ROOM JUST AHEAD...
I SEE. THEN WE SHALL CONCENTRATE OUR SEARCH IN THAT AREA.
UM... THAT ROOM SCARES ME, SO CAN WE CALL THIS OFF?
Y-YEAH... GOOD IDEA.
ENOUGH, BOTH OF YOU!
I WILL VENTURE AHEAD AND HAVE A LOOK!
AAAAH, LADY BEELZEBUB, DON'T GO!
ZUN
ZUN
ZUN
ZUN (STOMP)
AT LEAST SAVE IT FOR LAST!
THIS IS IT, NO?
GI (CREAK)

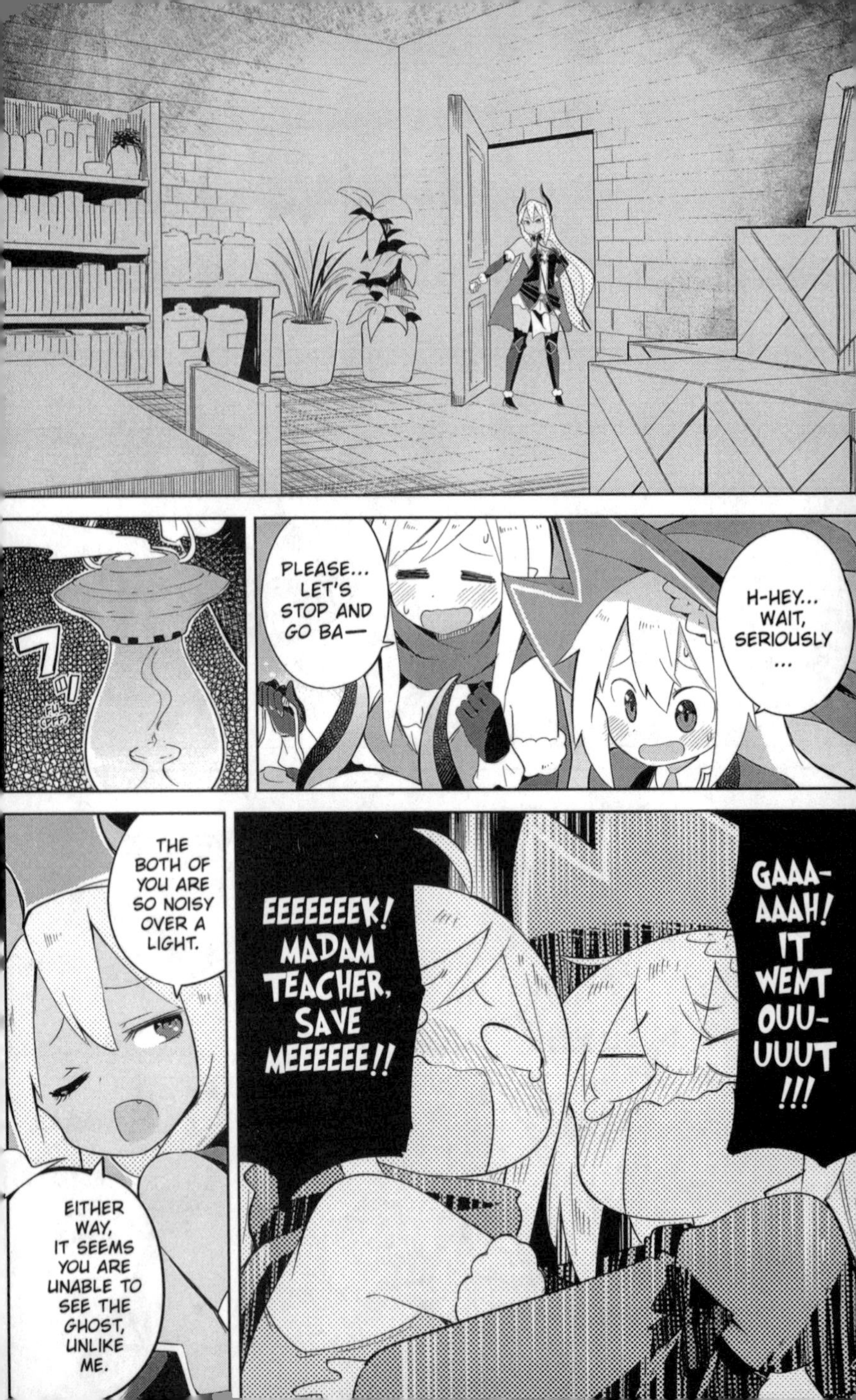

H-HEY... WAIT, SERIOUSLY...
PLEASE... LET'S STOP AND GO BA—
フッ
FU (PFF)
GAAA-AAAH! IT WENT OUU-UUUT!!!
EEEEEEEK! MADAM TEACHER, SAVE MEEEEEE!!
THE BOTH OF YOU ARE SO NOISY OVER A LIGHT.
EITHER WAY, IT SEEMS YOU ARE UNABLE TO SEE THE GHOST, UNLIKE ME.

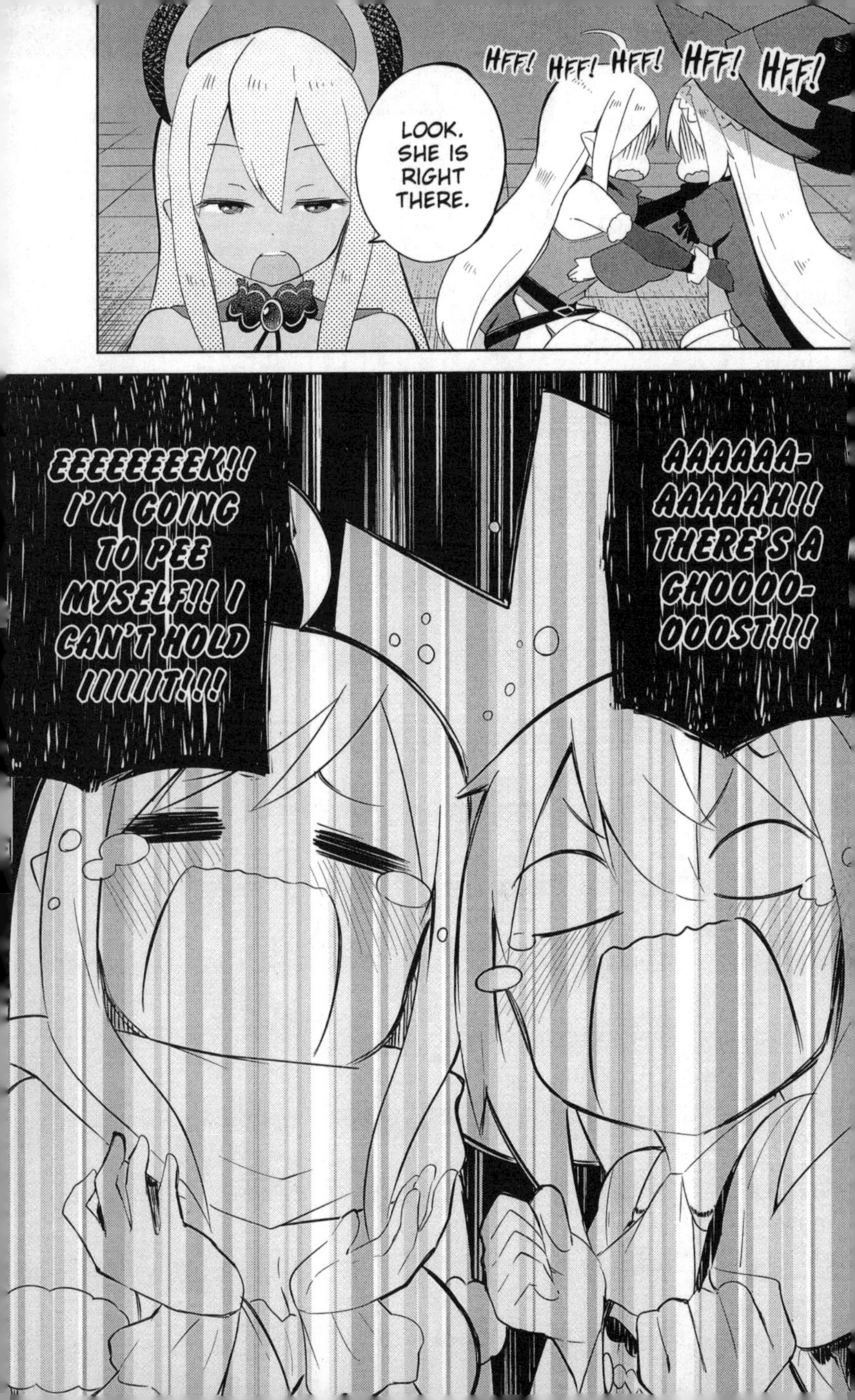
HFF! HFF! HFF! HFF! HFF!
LOOK. SHE IS RIGHT THERE.
AAAAAA-AAAAAH!! THERE'S A GHOOOO-OOOST!!!
EEEEEEEEK!!! I'M GOING TO PEE MYSELF!!! I CAN'T HOLD IIIIIIT!!!

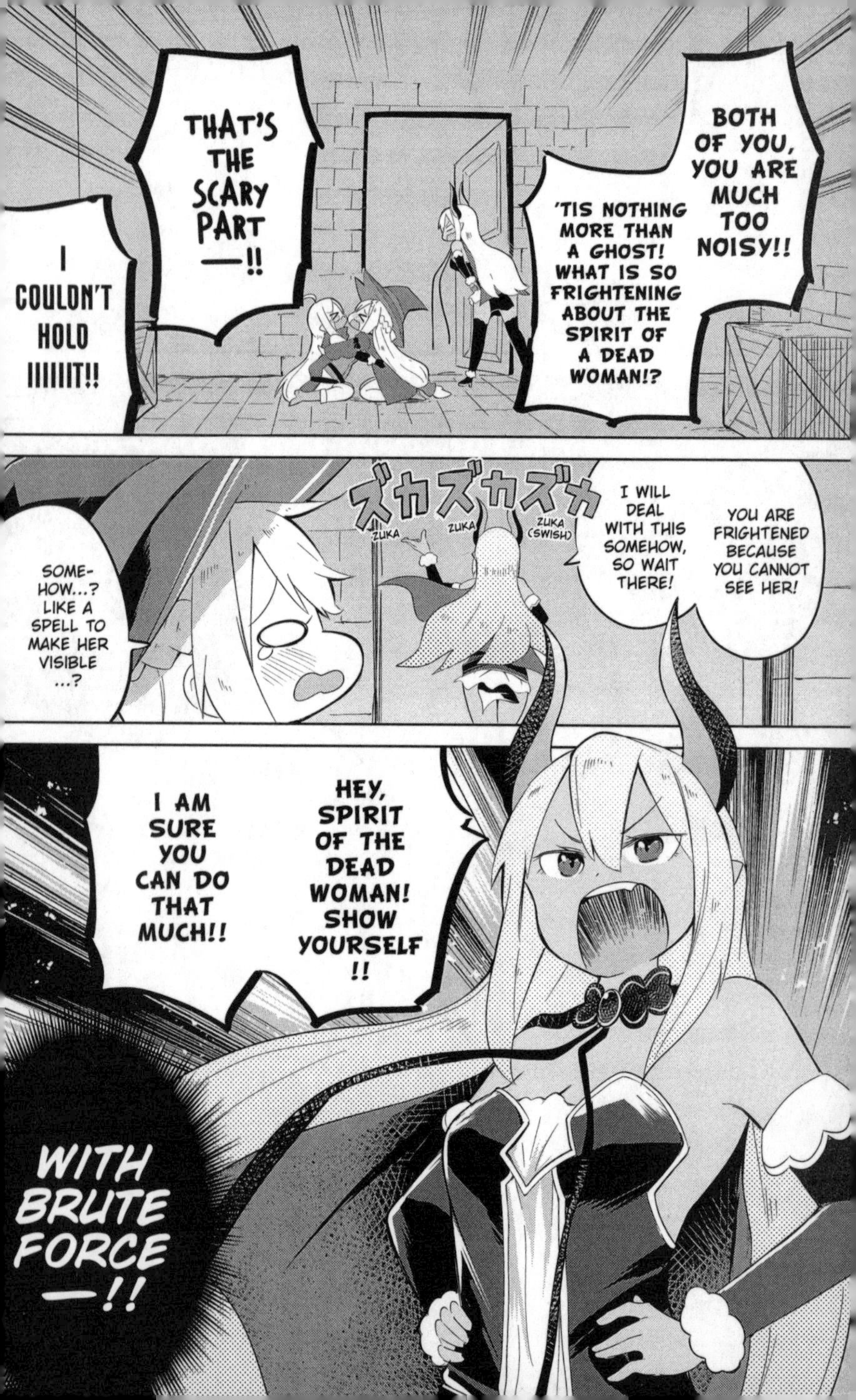
BOTH OF YOU, YOU ARE MUCH TOO NOISY!!
'TIS NOTHING MORE THAN A GHOST! WHAT IS SO FRIGHTENING ABOUT THE SPIRIT OF A DEAD WOMAN!?
THAT'S THE SCARY PART—!!
I COULDN'T HOLD IIIIIIIT!!
YOU ARE FRIGHTENED BECAUSE YOU CANNOT SEE HER!
I WILL DEAL WITH THIS SOMEHOW, SO WAIT THERE!
ズカズカズカ
ZUKA ZUKA ZUKA (SWISH)
SOME-HOW...? LIKE A SPELL TO MAKE HER VISIBLE ...?
HEY, SPIRIT OF THE DEAD WOMAN! SHOW YOURSELF!!
I AM SURE YOU CAN DO THAT MUCH!!
WITH BRUTE FORCE—!!

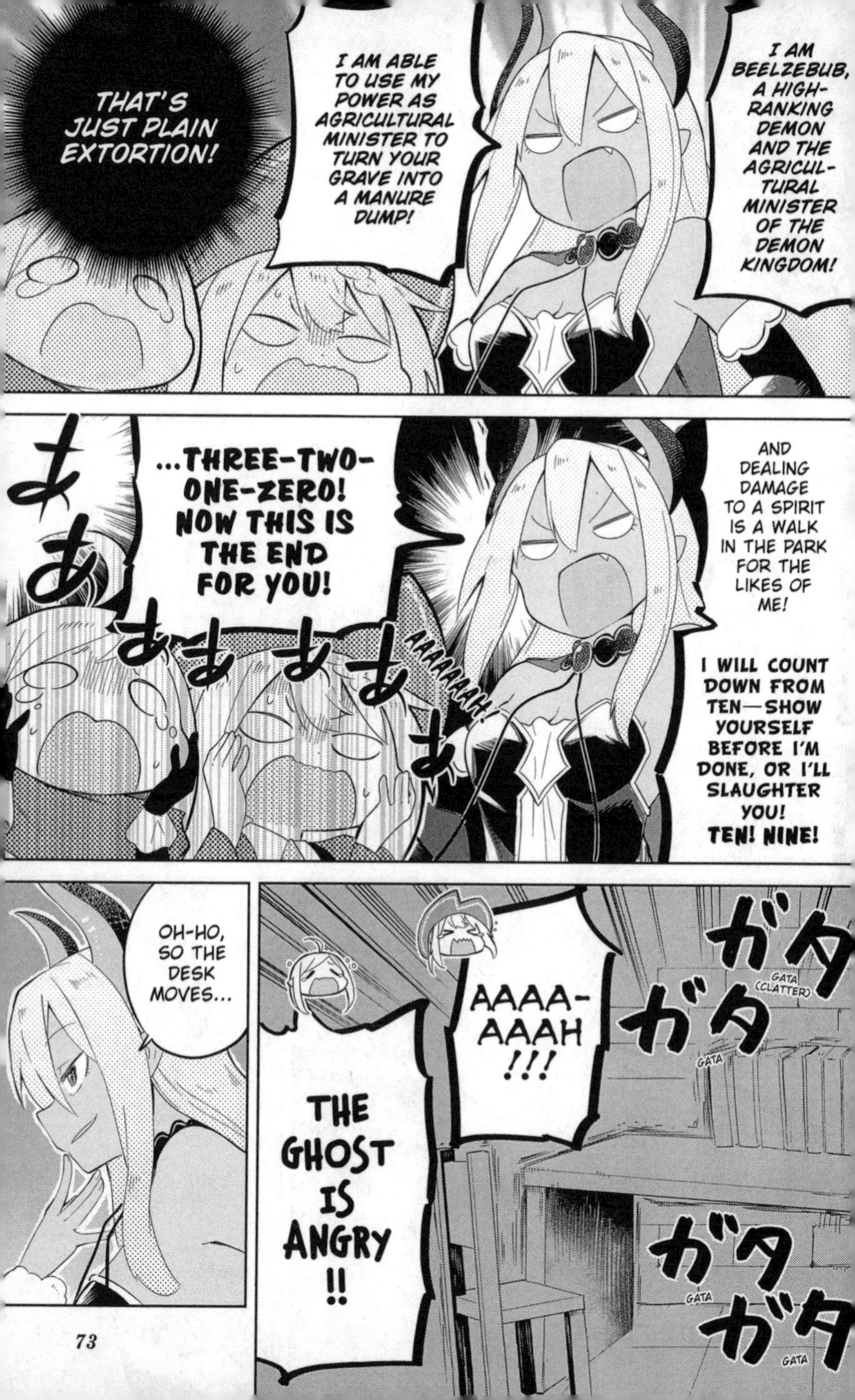
I AM BEELZEBUB, A HIGH-RANKING DEMON AND THE AGRICULTURAL MINISTER OF THE DEMON KINGDOM!
I AM ABLE TO USE MY POWER AS AGRICULTURAL MINISTER TO TURN YOUR GRAVE INTO A MANURE DUMP!
THAT'S JUST PLAIN EXTORTION!
AND DEALING DAMAGE TO A SPIRIT IS A WALK IN THE PARK FOR THE LIKES OF ME!
I WILL COUNT DOWN FROM TEN—SHOW YOURSELF BEFORE I'M DONE, OR I'LL SLAUGHTER YOU! TEN! NINE!
...THREE-TWO-ONE-ZERO! NOW THIS IS THE END FOR YOU!
ああああああああ
AAAAAAAAH!
ガタ
GATA (CLATTER)
ガタ
GATA
AAAA-AAAH!!!
THE GHOST IS ANGRY!!
ガタ
GATA
ガタ
GATA
OH-HO, SO THE DESK MOVES...

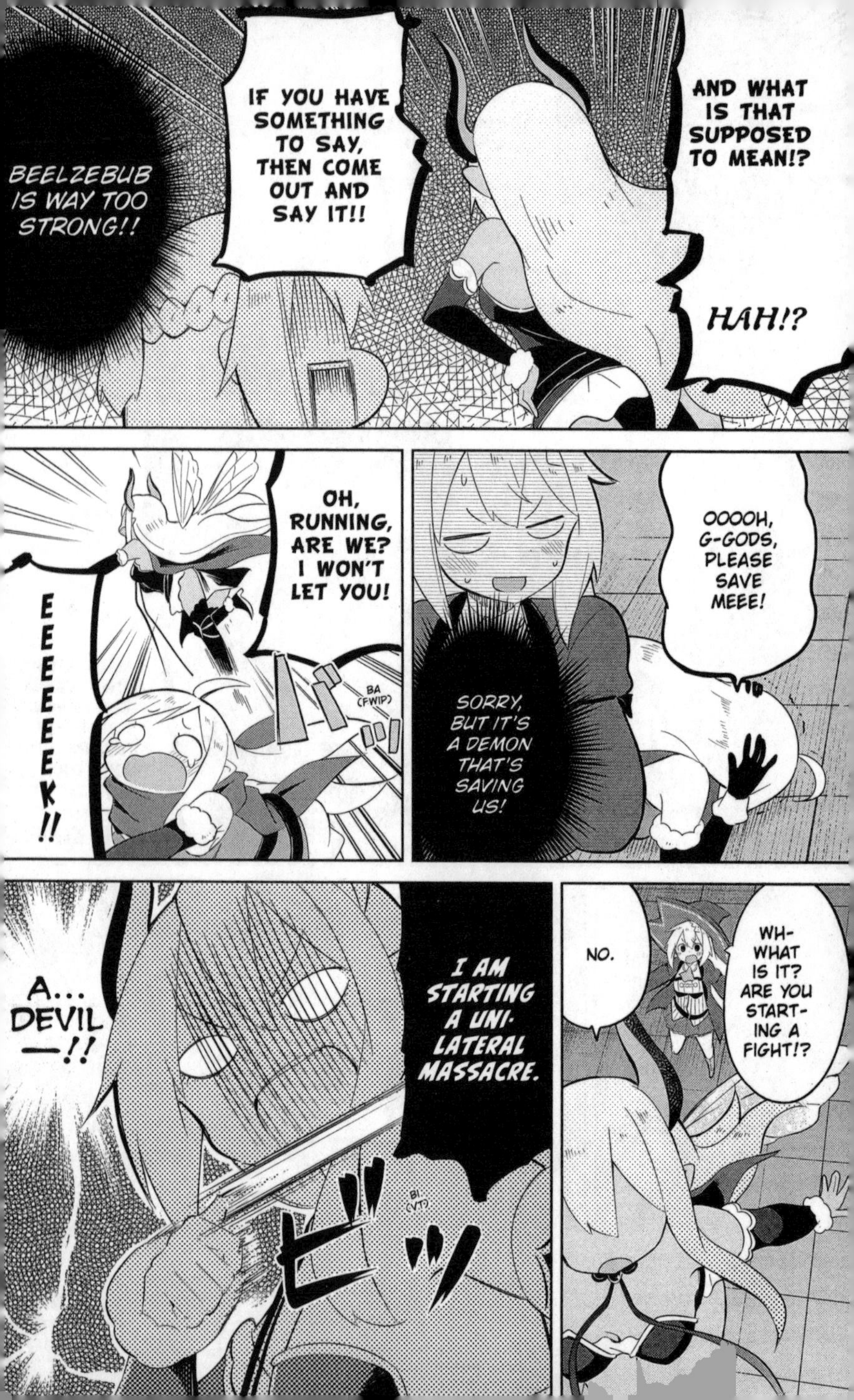
AND WHAT IS THAT SUPPOSED TO MEAN!?
HAH!?
IF YOU HAVE SOMETHING TO SAY, THEN COME OUT AND SAY IT!!
BEELZEBUB IS WAY TOO STRONG!!
OOOOH, G-GODS, PLEASE SAVE MEEE!
SORRY, BUT IT'S A DEMON THAT'S SAVING US!
OH, RUNNING, ARE WE? I WON'T LET YOU!
BA (FWIP)
EEEEEEEEK!!
WH-WHAT IS IT? ARE YOU START-ING A FIGHT!?
NO.
I AM STARTING A UNI-LATERAL MASSACRE.
BI (VT)
A... DEVIL—!!

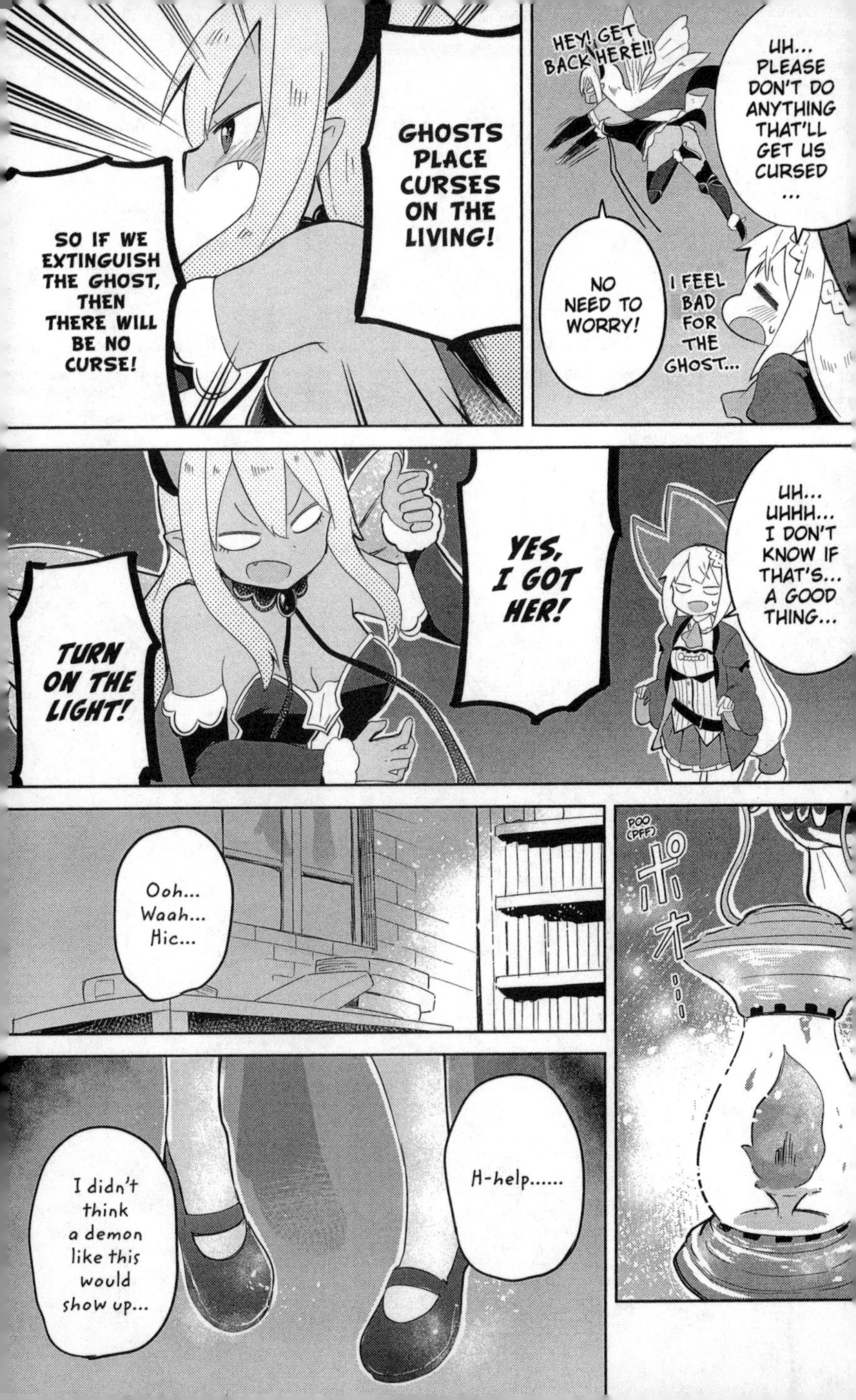
UH... PLEASE DON'T DO ANYTHING THAT'LL GET US CURSED ...
HEY! GET BACK HERE!!
I FEEL BAD FOR THE GHOST...
NO NEED TO WORRY!
GHOSTS PLACE CURSES ON THE LIVING!
SO IF WE EXTINGUISH THE GHOST, THEN THERE WILL BE NO CURSE!
UH... UHHH... I DON'T KNOW IF THAT'S... A GOOD THING...
YES, I GOT HER!
TURN ON THE LIGHT!
POO (PFF)
ポオ…
Ooh... Waah... Hic...
H-help......
I didn't think a demon like this would show up...

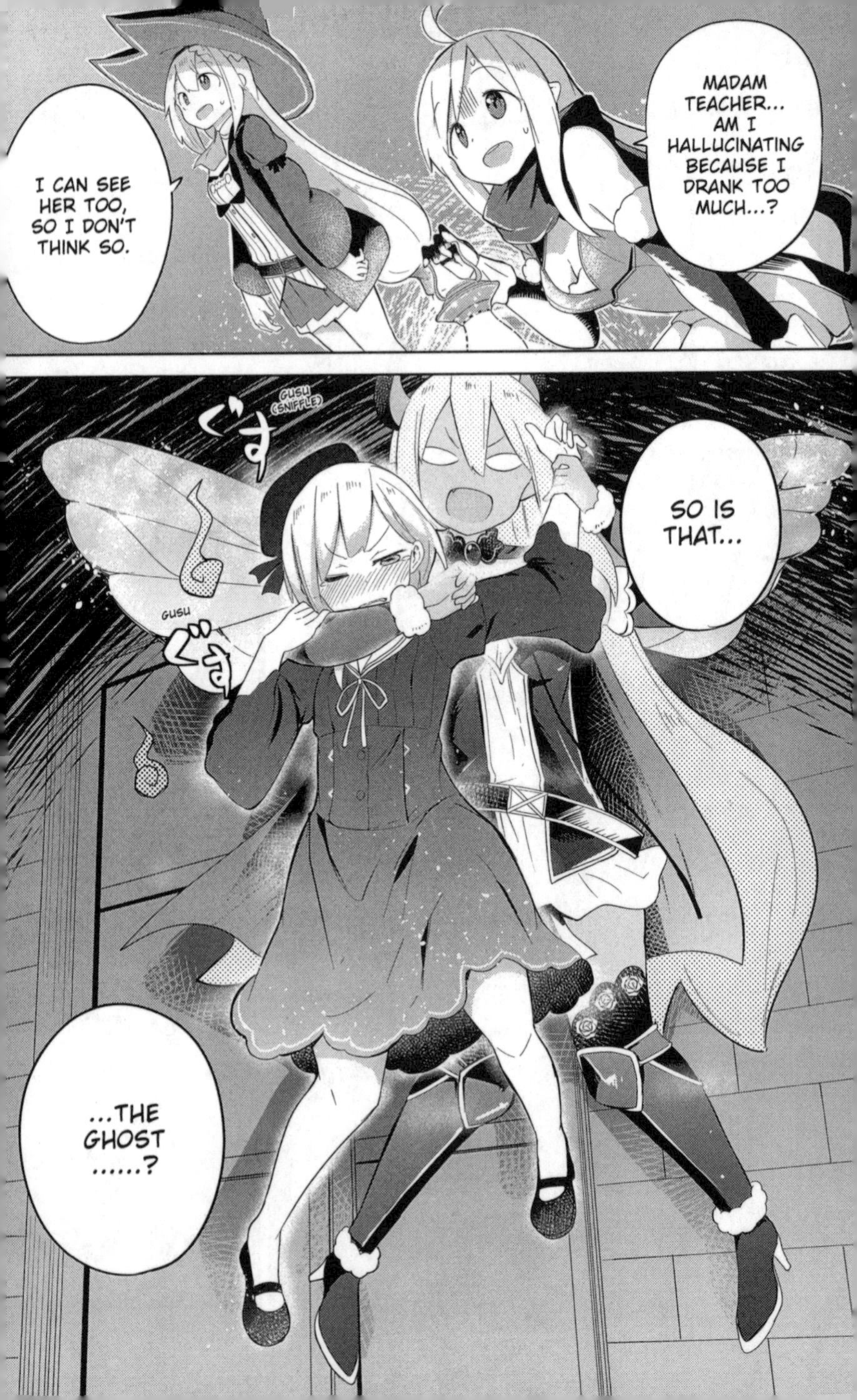
MADAM TEACHER... AM I HALLUCINATING BECAUSE I DRANK TOO MUCH...?
I CAN SEE HER TOO, SO I DON'T THINK SO.
ぐす
GUSU (SNIFFLE)
SO IS THAT...
ぐす
GUSU
...THE GHOST ......?

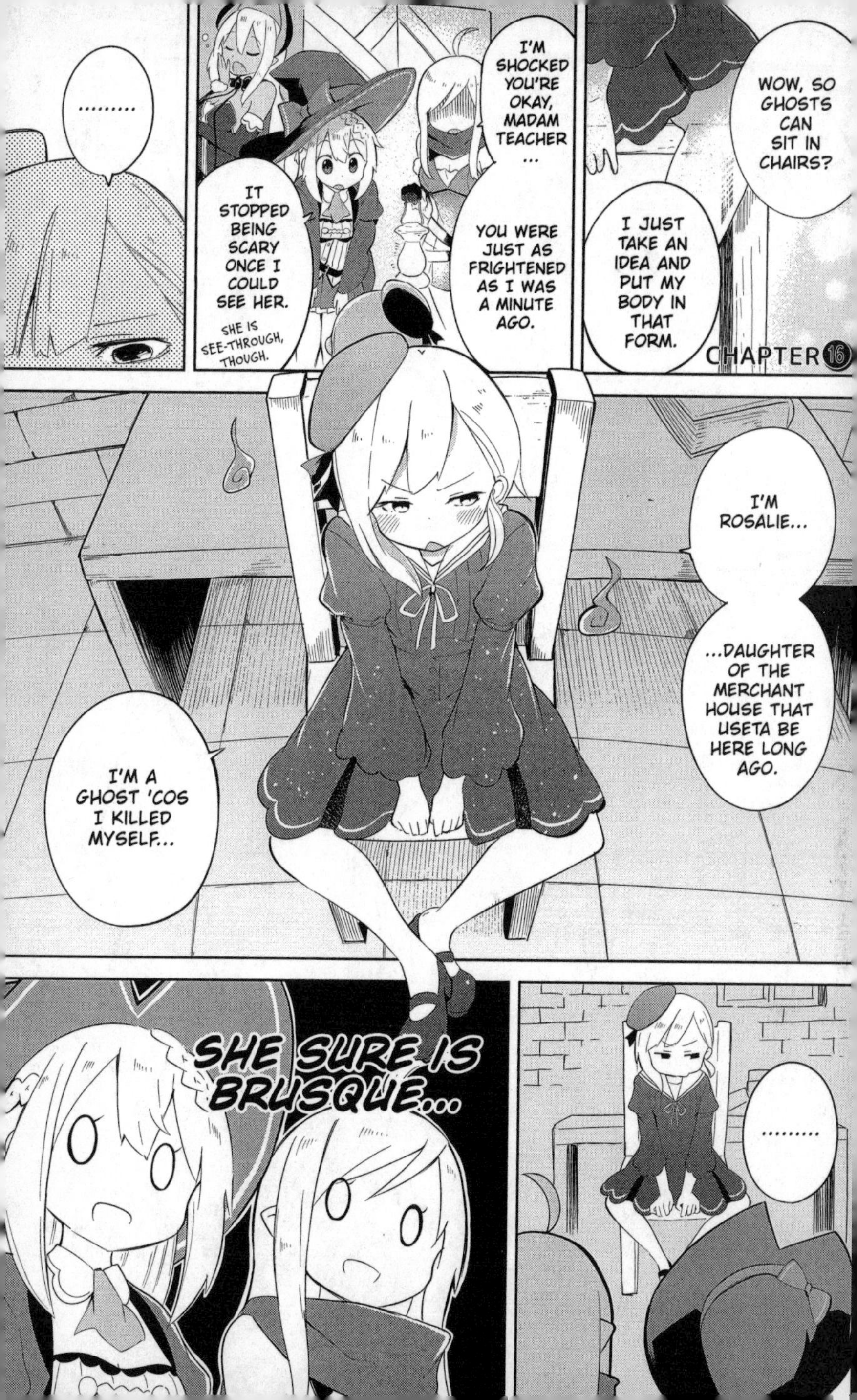
WOW, SO GHOSTS CAN SIT IN CHAIRS?
I JUST TAKE AN IDEA AND PUT MY BODY IN THAT FORM.
CHAPTER 16
I'M SHOCKED YOU'RE OKAY, MADAM TEACHER...
YOU WERE JUST AS FRIGHTENED AS I WAS A MINUTE AGO.
IT STOPPED BEING SCARY ONCE I COULD SEE HER.
SHE IS SEE-THROUGH, THOUGH.
....
I'M ROSALIE...
...DAUGHTER OF THE MERCHANT HOUSE THAT USETA BE HERE LONG AGO.
I'M A GHOST 'COS I KILLED MYSELF...
....
SHE SURE IS BRUSQUE...

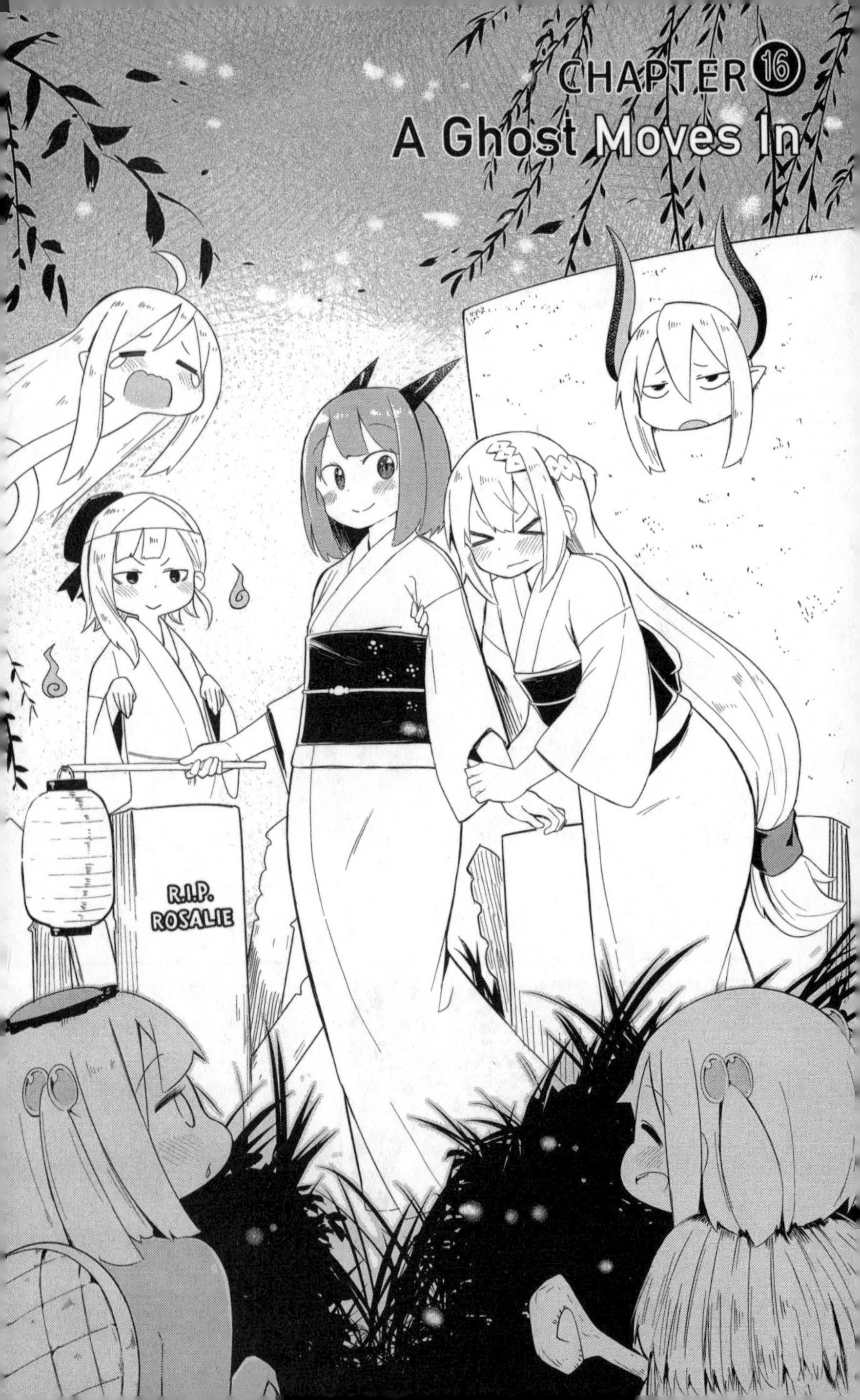
CHAPTER 16
A Ghost Moves In
R.I.P.
ROSALIE

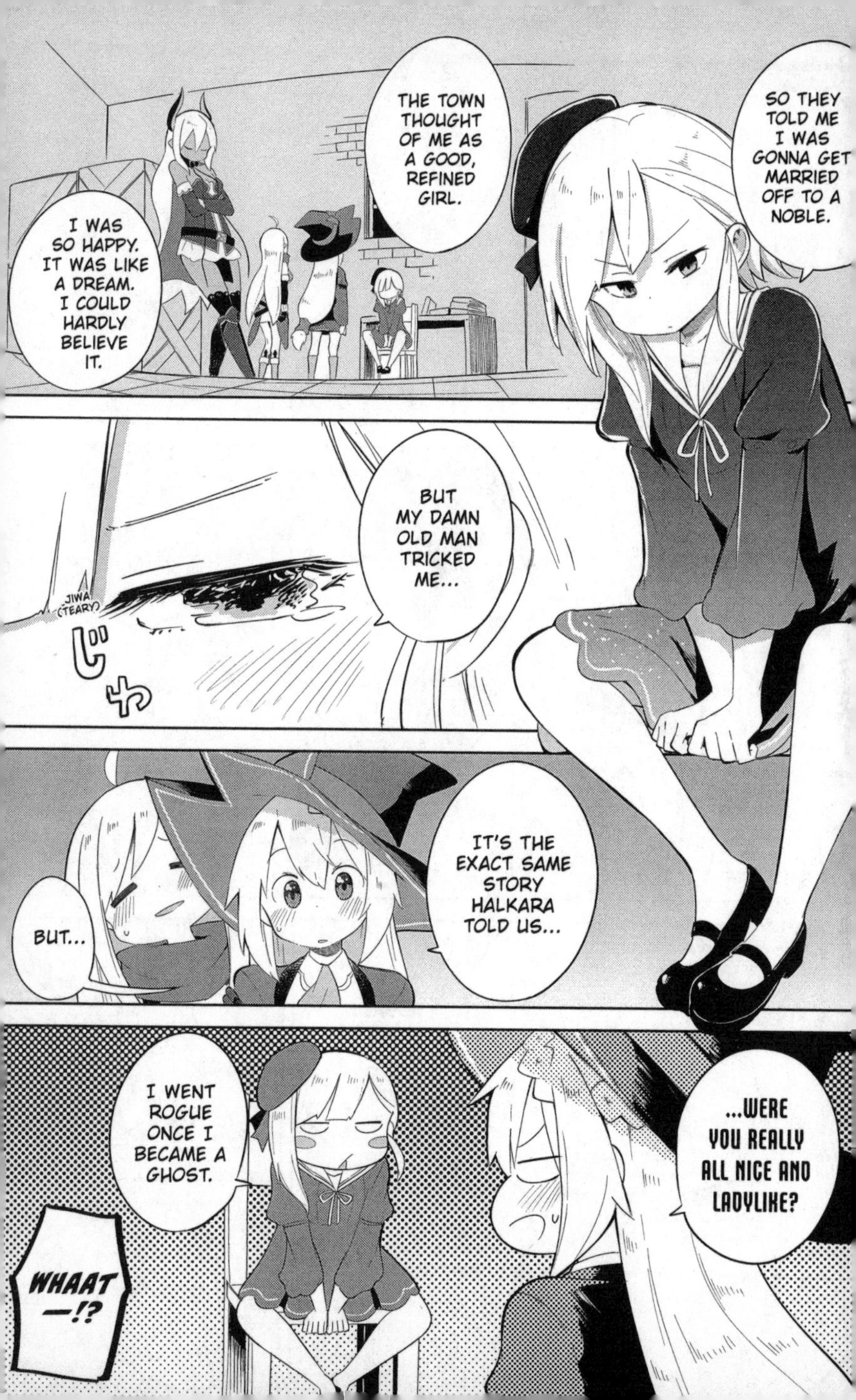
SO THEY TOLD ME I WAS GONNA GET MARRIED OFF TO A NOBLE.
THE TOWN THOUGHT OF ME AS A GOOD, REFINED GIRL.
I WAS SO HAPPY. IT WAS LIKE A DREAM. I COULD HARDLY BELIEVE IT.
BUT MY DAMN OLD MAN TRICKED ME...
JIWA (TEARY)
じわ
IT'S THE EXACT SAME STORY HALKARA TOLD US...
BUT...
...WERE YOU REALLY ALL NICE AND LADYLIKE?
I WENT ROGUE ONCE I BECAME A GHOST.
WHAAT—!?

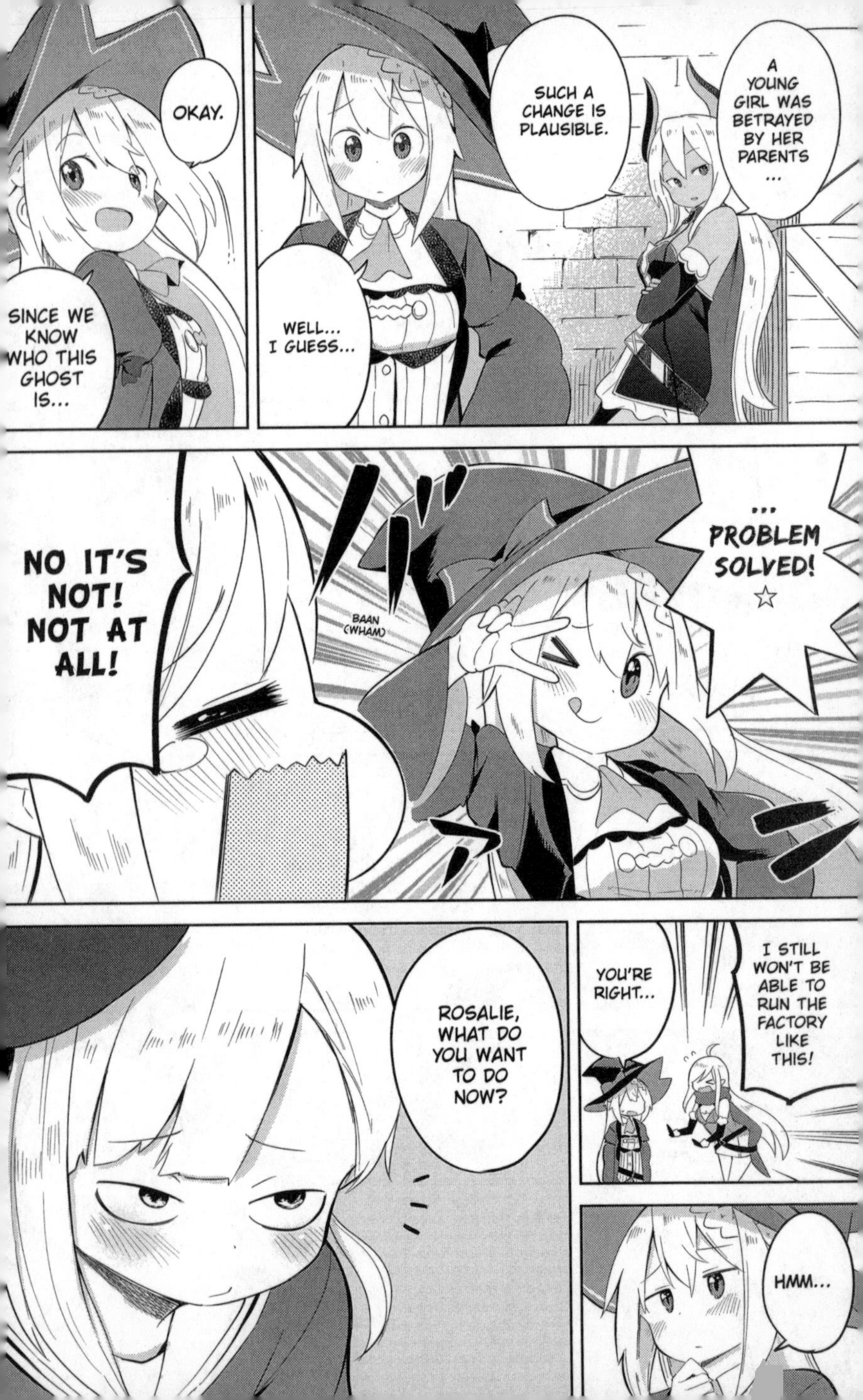
A YOUNG GIRL WAS BETRAYED BY HER PARENTS...
SUCH A CHANGE IS PLAUSIBLE.
WELL... I GUESS...
OKAY.
SINCE WE KNOW WHO THIS GHOST IS...
...PROBLEM SOLVED! ☆
BAAN (WHAM)
NO IT'S NOT! NOT AT ALL!
I STILL WON'T BE ABLE TO RUN THE FACTORY LIKE THIS!
YOU'RE RIGHT...
HMM...
ROSALIE, WHAT DO YOU WANT TO DO NOW?

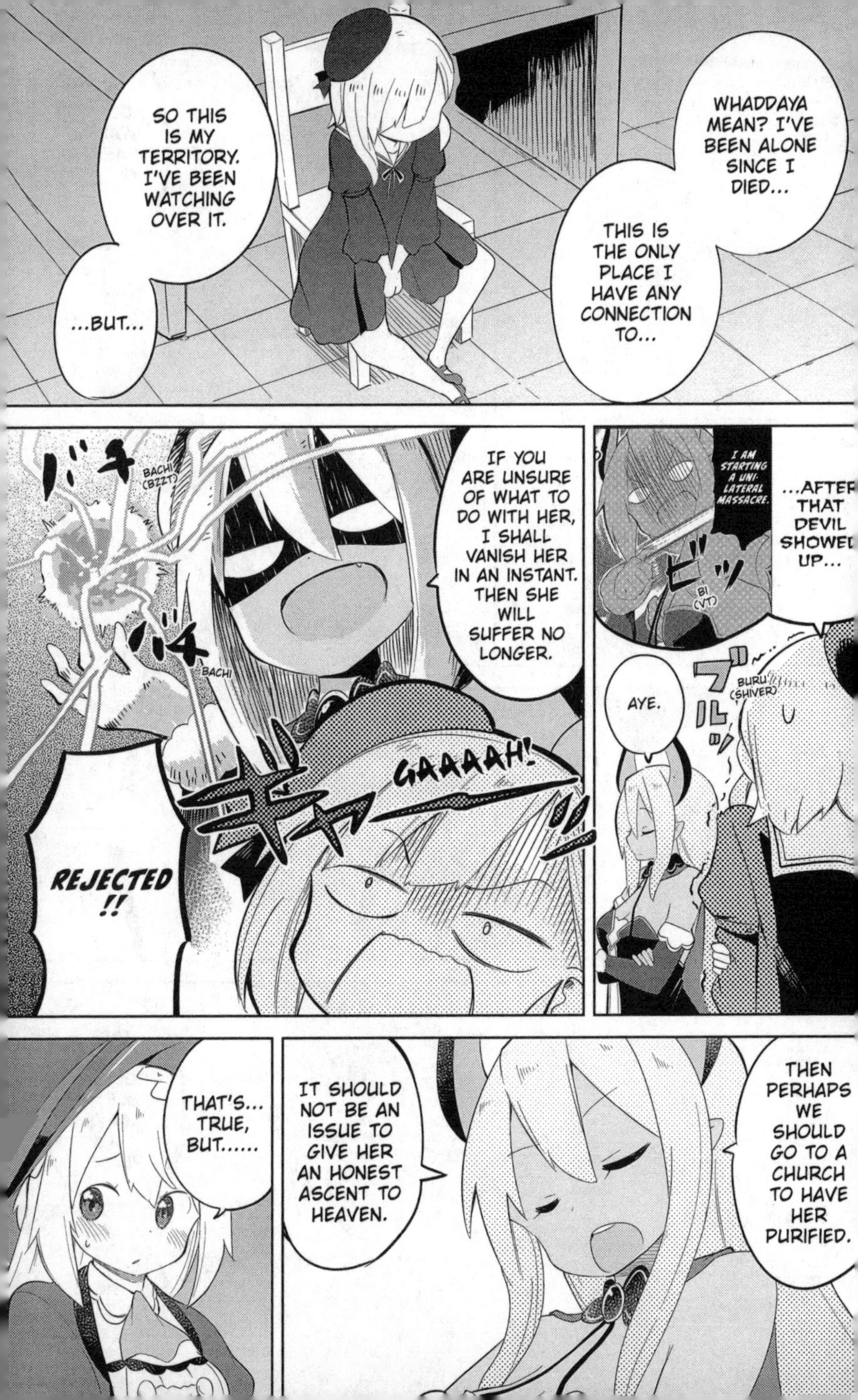
WHADDAYA MEAN? I'VE BEEN ALONE SINCE I DIED...
THIS IS THE ONLY PLACE I HAVE ANY CONNECTION TO...
SO THIS IS MY TERRITORY. I'VE BEEN WATCHING OVER IT.
...BUT...
...AFTER THAT DEVIL SHOWED UP...
I AM STARTING A UNI-LATERAL MASSACRE.
BI (VT)
BURU (SHIVER)
AYE.
IF YOU ARE UNSURE OF WHAT TO DO WITH HER, I SHALL VANISH HER IN AN INSTANT. THEN SHE WILL SUFFER NO LONGER.
BACHI (BZZT)
BACHI
GAAAAH!
REJECTED!!
THEN PERHAPS WE SHOULD GO TO A CHURCH TO HAVE HER PURIFIED.
IT SHOULD NOT BE AN ISSUE TO GIVE HER AN HONEST ASCENT TO HEAVEN.
THAT'S... TRUE, BUT......

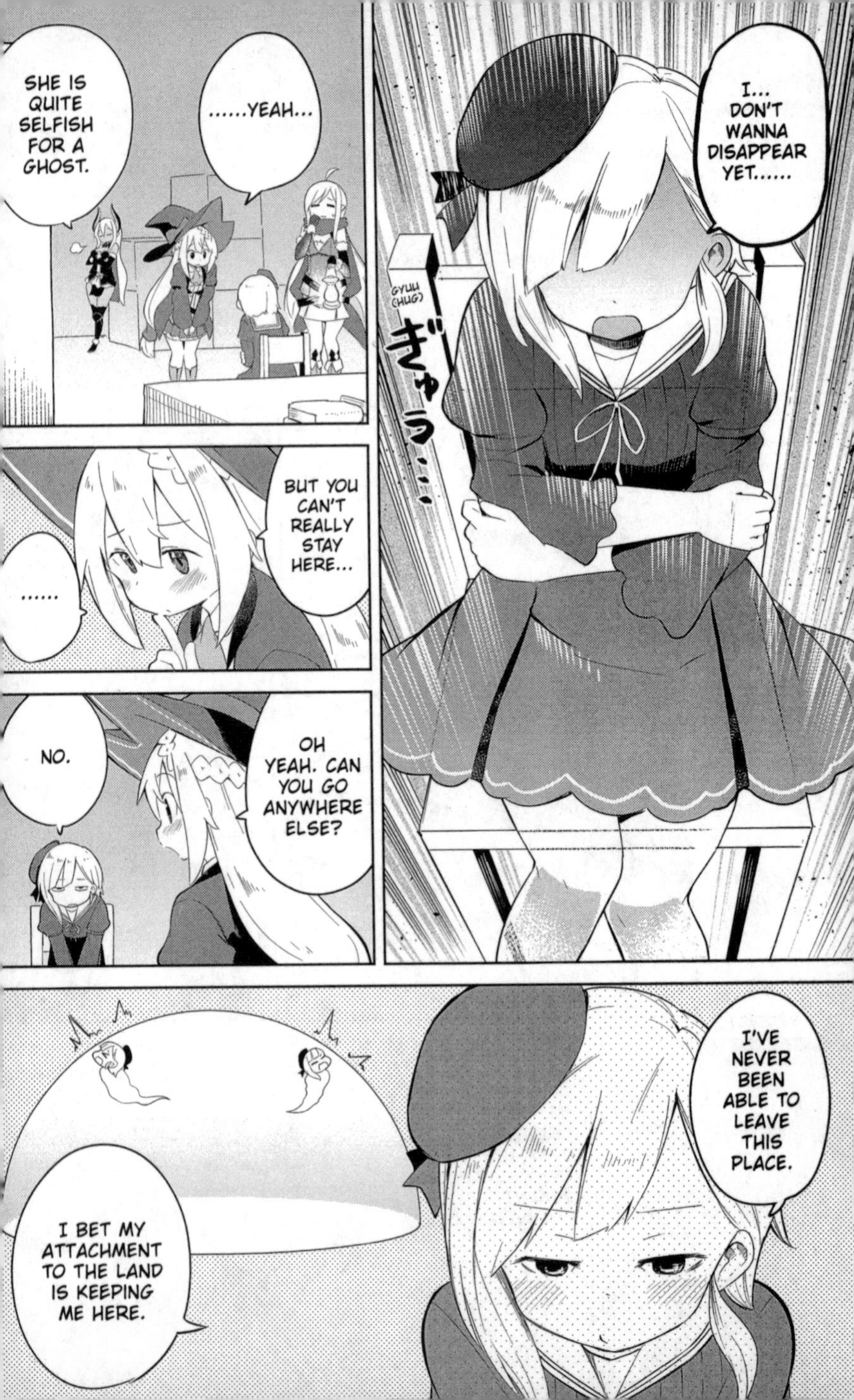
I... DON'T WANNA DISAPPEAR YET......
GYUU (HUG)
ぎゅう…
......YEAH...
SHE IS QUITE SELFISH FOR A GHOST.
BUT YOU CAN'T REALLY STAY HERE...
......
OH YEAH. CAN YOU GO ANYWHERE ELSE?
NO.
I'VE NEVER BEEN ABLE TO LEAVE THIS PLACE.
I BET MY ATTACHMENT TO THE LAND IS KEEPING ME HERE.

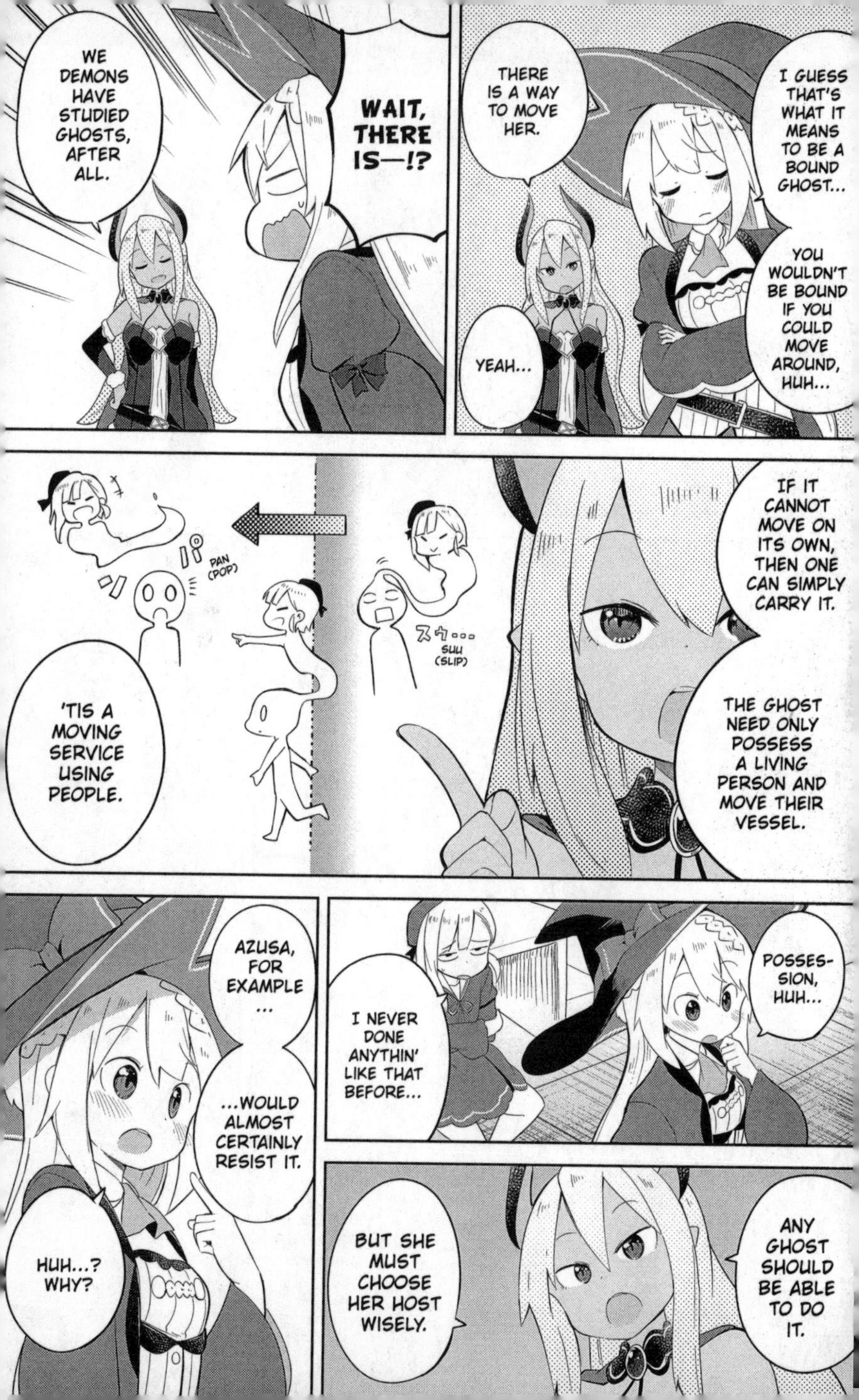
I GUESS THAT'S WHAT IT MEANS TO BE A BOUND GHOST...
YOU WOULDN'T BE BOUND IF YOU COULD MOVE AROUND, HUH...
YEAH...
THERE IS A WAY TO MOVE HER.
WAIT, THERE IS—!?
WE DEMONS HAVE STUDIED GHOSTS, AFTER ALL.
IF IT CANNOT MOVE ON ITS OWN, THEN ONE CAN SIMPLY CARRY IT.
THE GHOST NEED ONLY POSSESS A LIVING PERSON AND MOVE THEIR VESSEL.
スゥ...
SUU (SLIP)
PAN (POP)
'TIS A MOVING SERVICE USING PEOPLE.
POSSES-SION, HUH...
I NEVER DONE ANYTHIN' LIKE THAT BEFORE...
ANY GHOST SHOULD BE ABLE TO DO IT.
BUT SHE MUST CHOOSE HER HOST WISELY.
AZUSA, FOR EXAMPLE...
...WOULD ALMOST CERTAINLY RESIST IT.
HUH...? WHY?

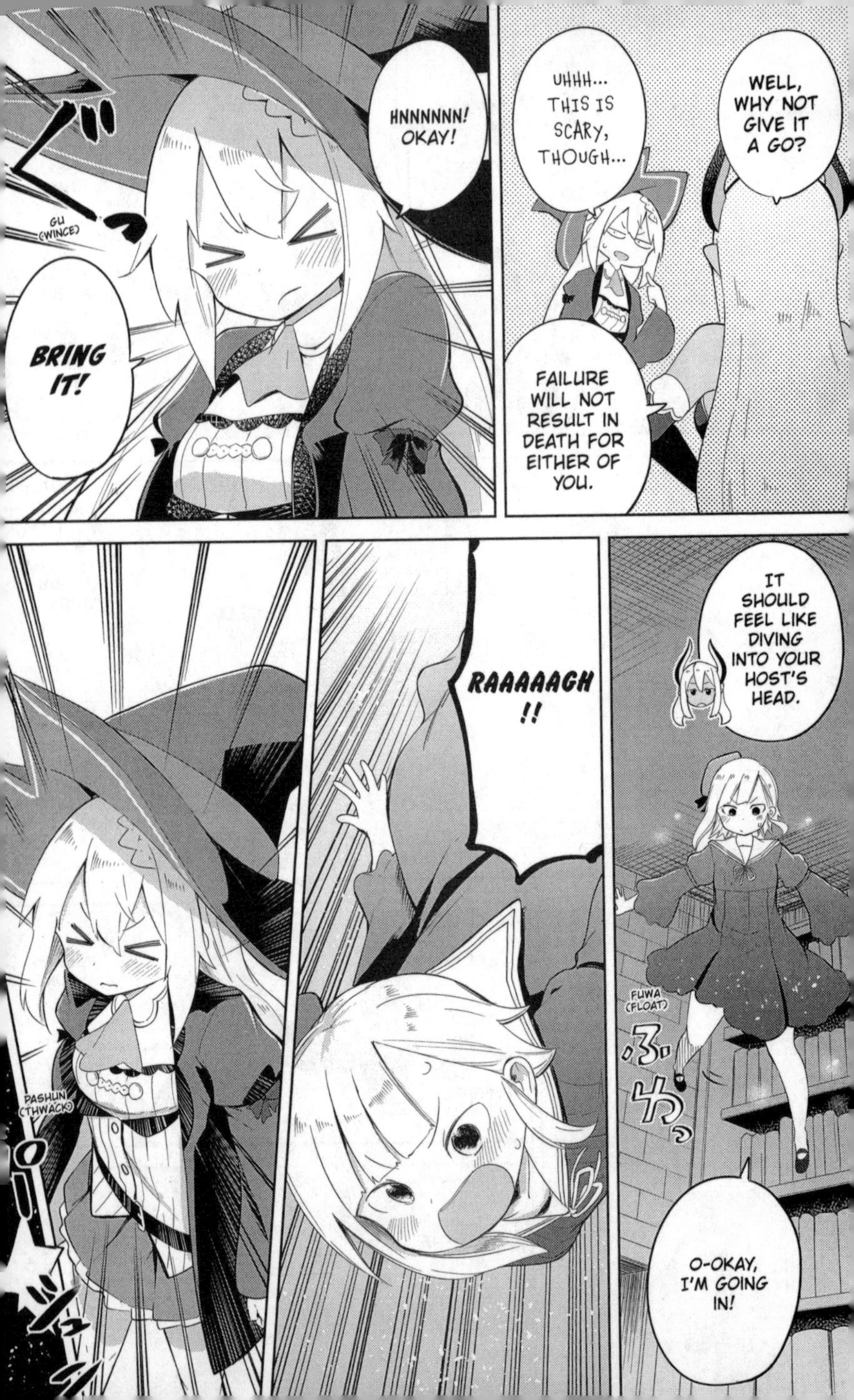
WELL, WHY NOT GIVE IT A GO?
UHHH... THIS IS SCARY, THOUGH...
FAILURE WILL NOT RESULT IN DEATH FOR EITHER OF YOU.
HNNNNNN! OKAY!
GU (WINCE)
BRING IT!
IT SHOULD FEEL LIKE DIVING INTO YOUR HOST'S HEAD.
FUWA (FLOAT)
O-OKAY, I'M GOING IN!
RAAAAAGH!!
PASHUN (THWACK)

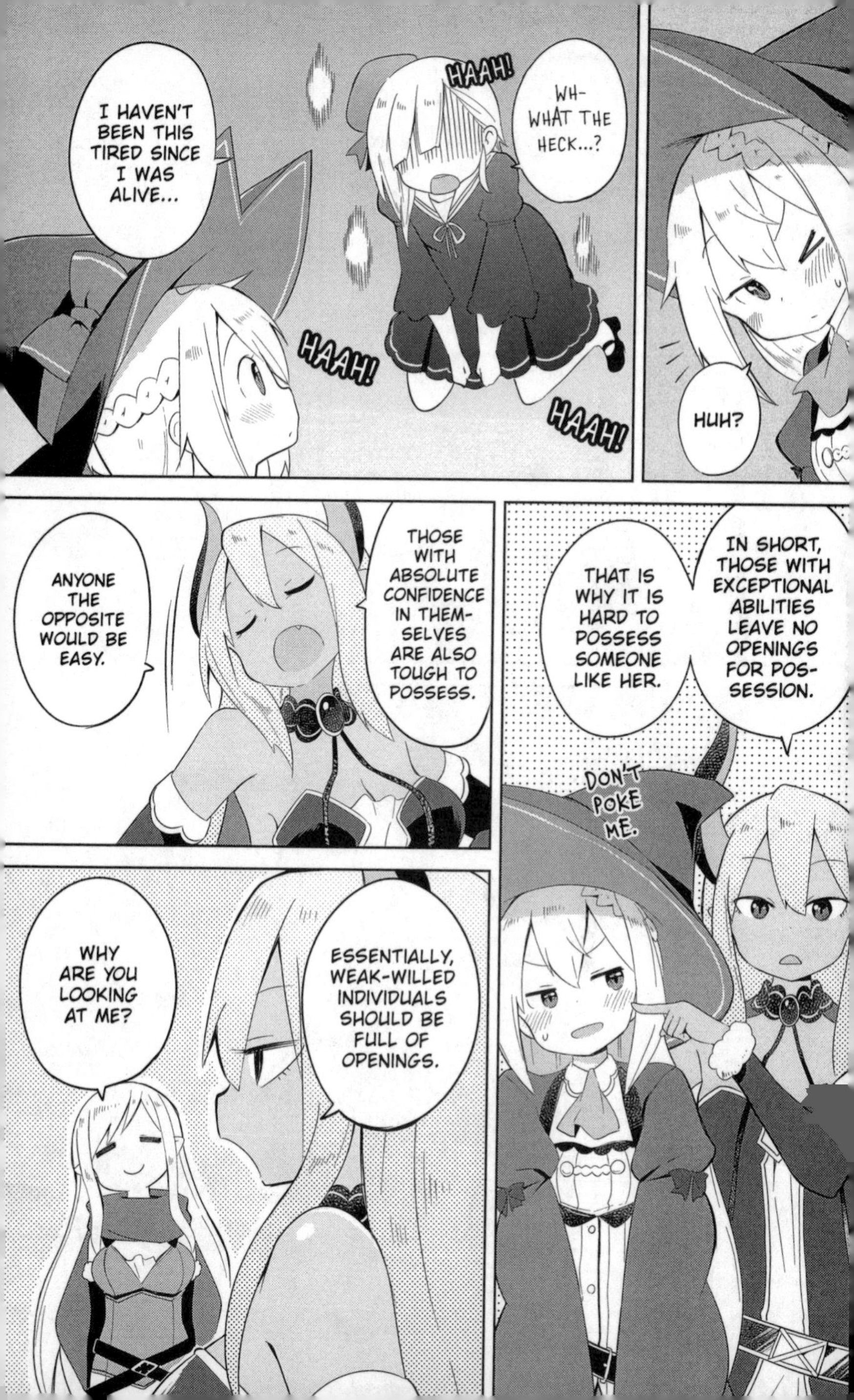
HUH?
HAAAH!
WH- WHAT THE HECK...?
I HAVEN'T BEEN THIS TIRED SINCE I WAS ALIVE...
HAAAH!
HAAAH!
IN SHORT, THOSE WITH EXCEPTIONAL ABILITIES LEAVE NO OPENINGS FOR POS- SESSION.
THAT IS WHY IT IS HARD TO POSSESS SOMEONE LIKE HER.
DON'T POKE ME.
THOSE WITH ABSOLUTE CONFIDENCE IN THEM- SELVES ARE ALSO TOUGH TO POSSESS.
ANYONE THE OPPOSITE WOULD BE EASY.
ESSENTIALLY, WEAK-WILLED INDIVIDUALS SHOULD BE FULL OF OPENINGS.
WHY ARE YOU LOOKING AT ME?

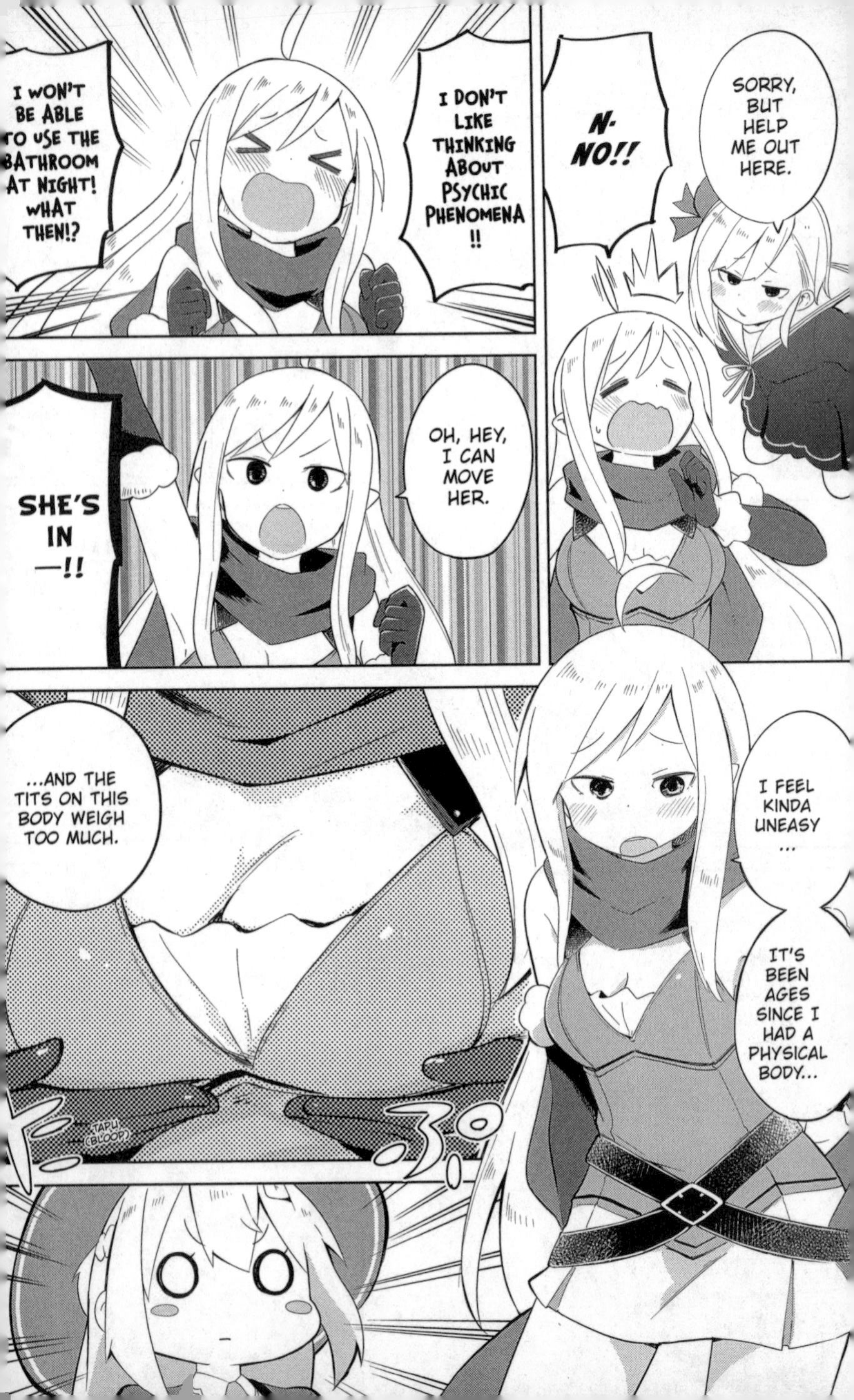
SORRY, BUT HELP ME OUT HERE.
N-NO!!
I DON'T LIKE THINKING ABOUT PSYCHIC PHENOMENA!!
I WON'T BE ABLE TO USE THE BATHROOM AT NIGHT! WHAT THEN!?
OH, HEY, I CAN MOVE HER.
SHE'S IN—!!
I FEEL KINDA UNEASY...
IT'S BEEN AGES SINCE I HAD A PHYSICAL BODY...
...AND THE TITS ON THIS BODY WEIGH TOO MUCH.
TAPU (BLOOP)

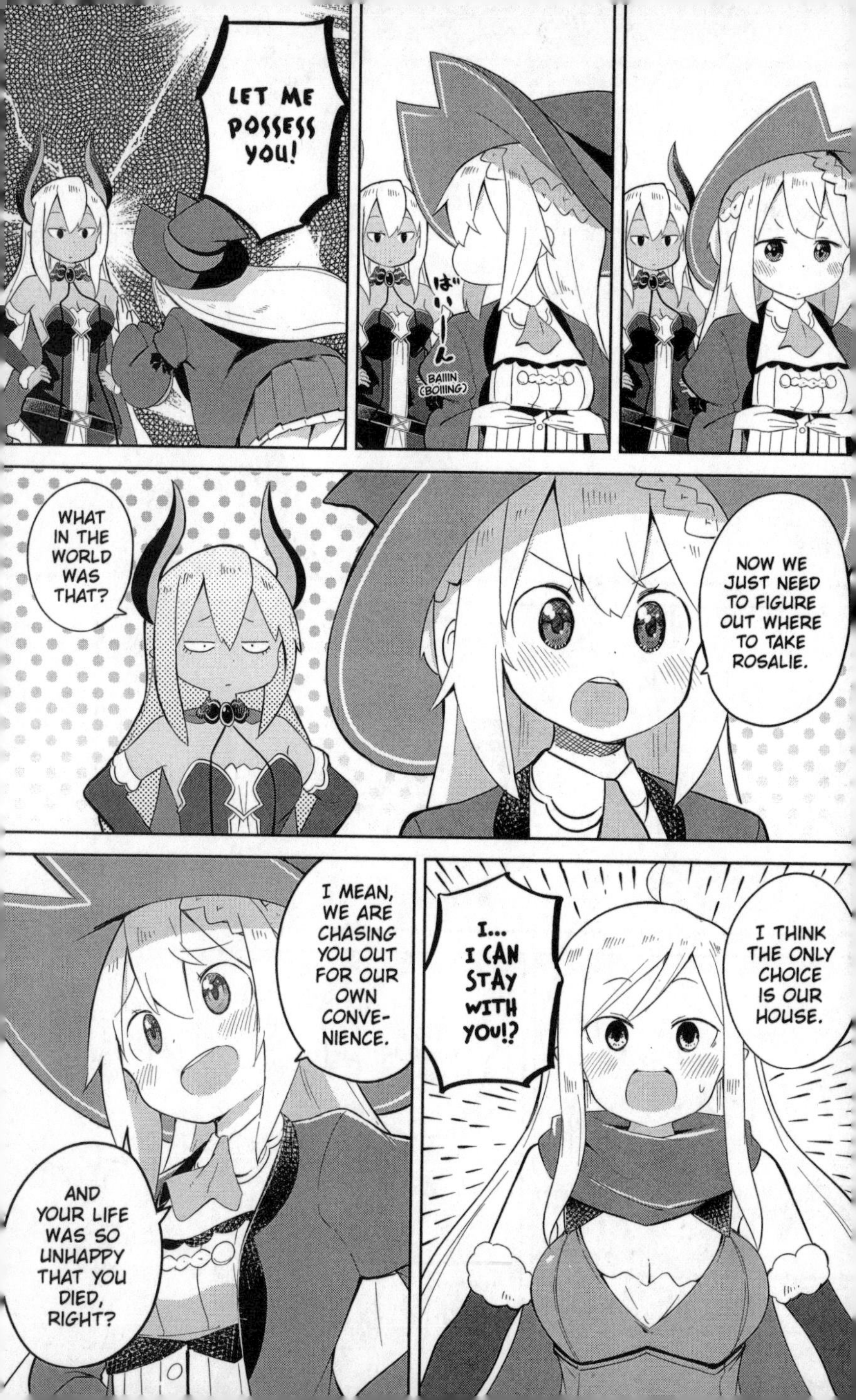
ばいーん
BAIIIN (BOIIING)
LET ME POSSESS YOU!
NOW WE JUST NEED TO FIGURE OUT WHERE TO TAKE ROSALIE.
WHAT IN THE WORLD WAS THAT?
I THINK THE ONLY CHOICE IS OUR HOUSE.
I... I CAN STAY WITH YOU!?
I MEAN, WE ARE CHASING YOU OUT FOR OUR OWN CONVENIENCE.
AND YOUR LIFE WAS SO UNHAPPY THAT YOU DIED, RIGHT?

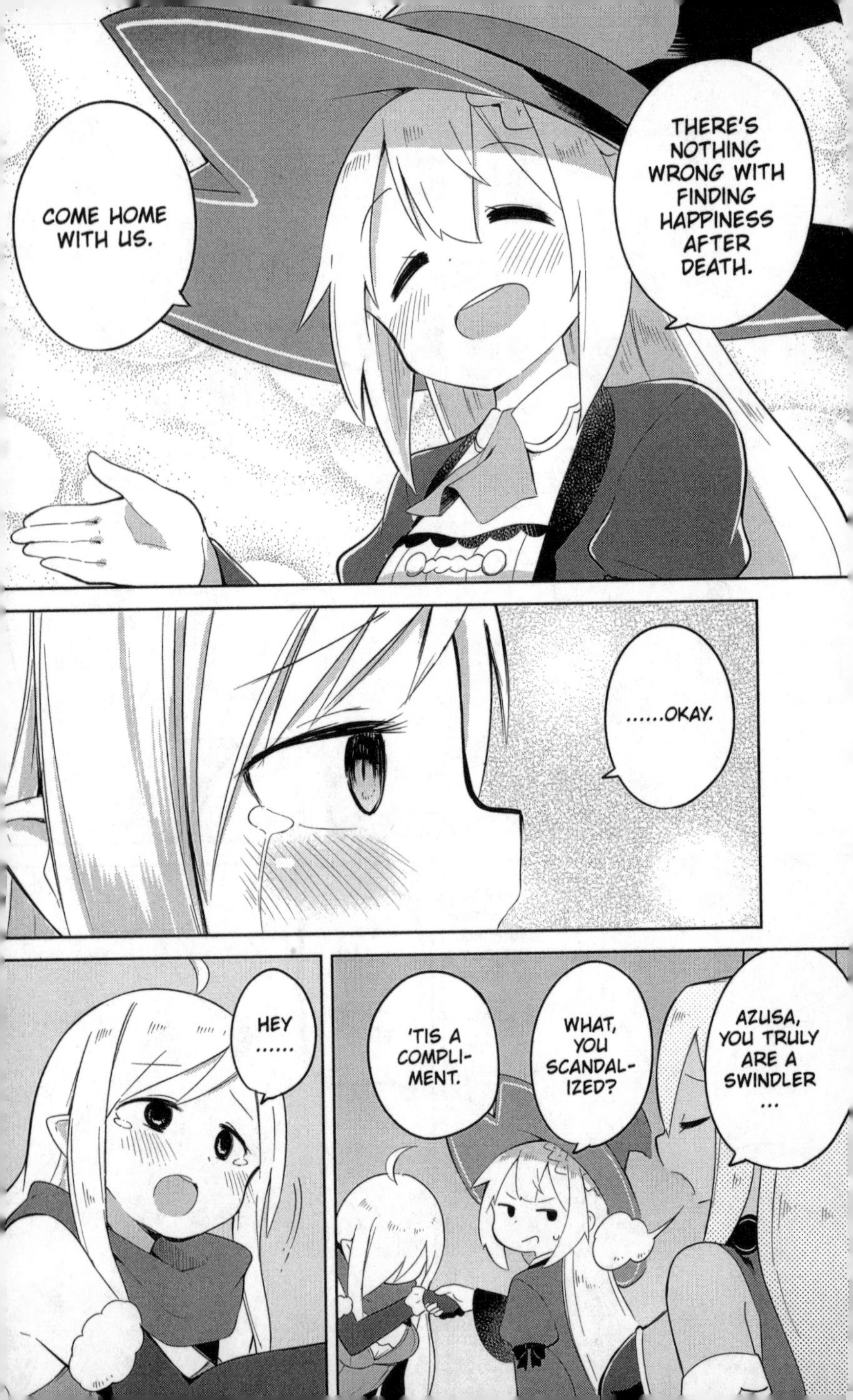
THERE'S NOTHING WRONG WITH FINDING HAPPINESS AFTER DEATH.
COME HOME WITH US.
......OKAY.
AZUSA, YOU TRULY ARE A SWINDLER ...
WHAT, YOU SCANDALIZED?
'TIS A COMPLIMENT.
HEY ......

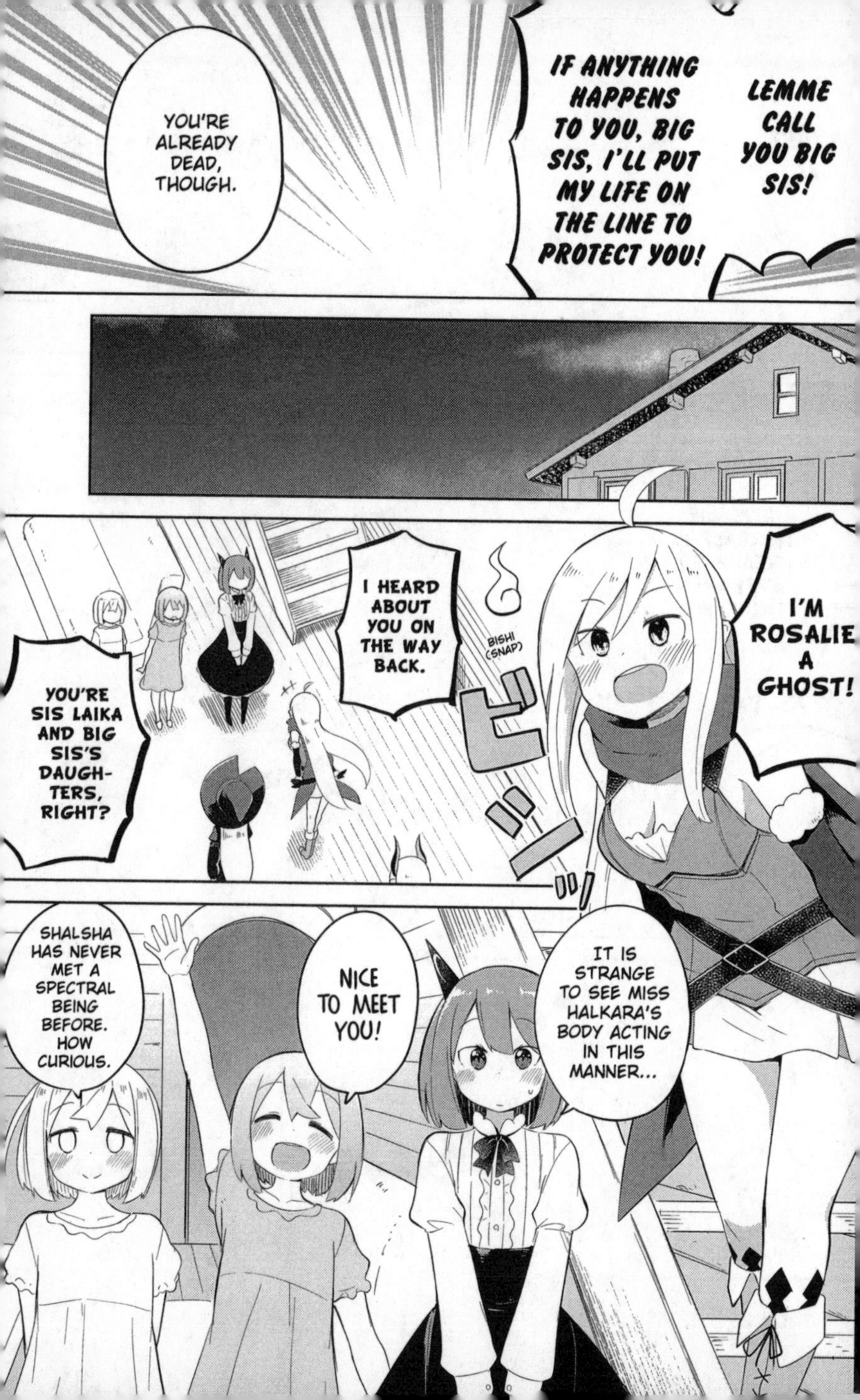
LEMME CALL YOU BIG SIS!
IF ANYTHING HAPPENS TO YOU, BIG SIS, I'LL PUT MY LIFE ON THE LINE TO PROTECT YOU!
YOU'RE ALREADY DEAD, THOUGH.
I'M ROSALIE A GHOST!
BISHI (SNAP)
I HEARD ABOUT YOU ON THE WAY BACK.
YOU'RE SIS LAIKA AND BIG SIS'S DAUGHTERS, RIGHT?
IT IS STRANGE TO SEE MISS HALKARA'S BODY ACTING IN THIS MANNER...
NICE TO MEET YOU!
SHALSHA HAS NEVER MET A SPECTRAL BEING BEFORE. HOW CURIOUS.

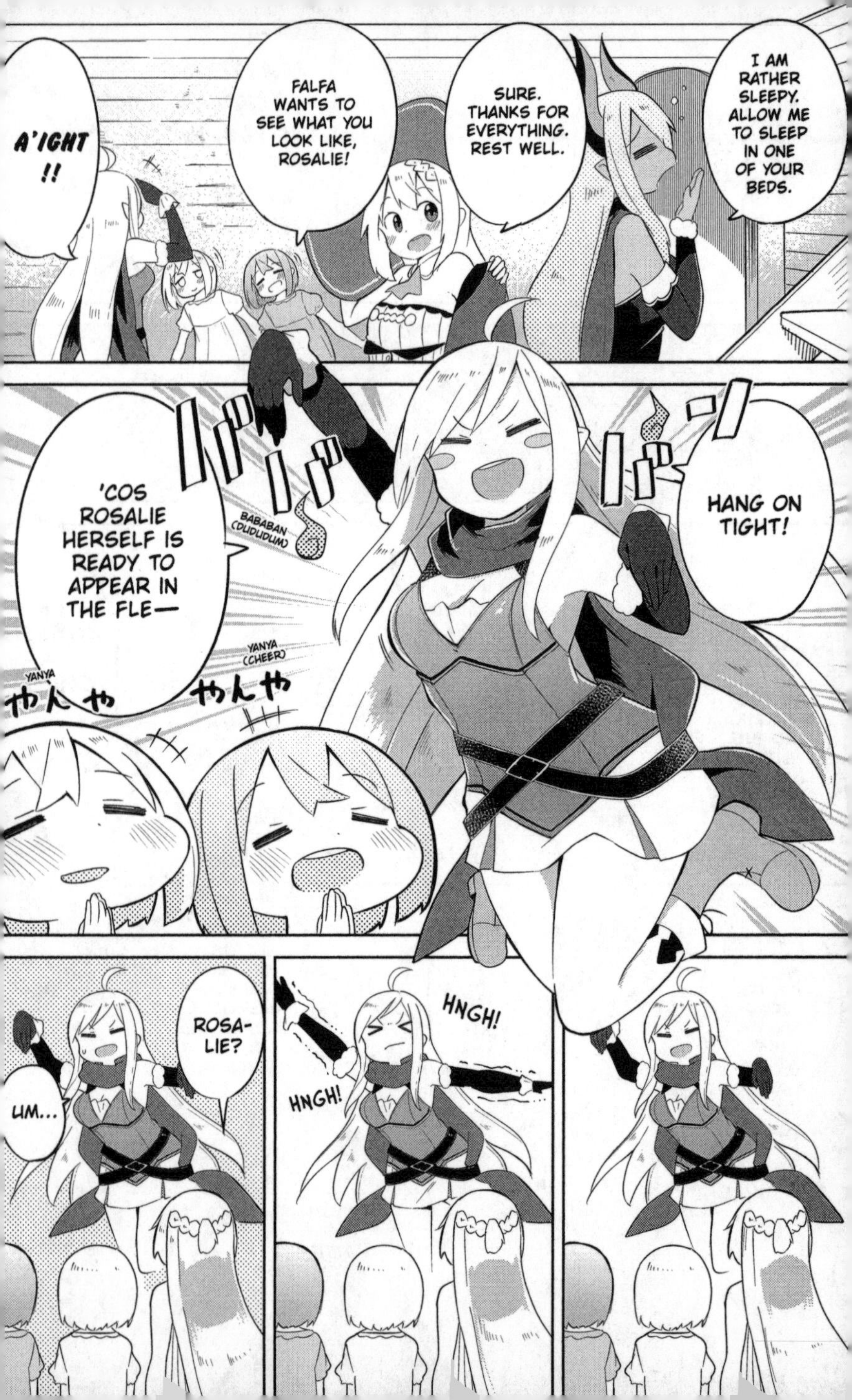
I AM RATHER SLEEPY. ALLOW ME TO SLEEP IN ONE OF YOUR BEDS.
SURE. THANKS FOR EVERYTHING. REST WELL.
FALFA WANTS TO SEE WHAT YOU LOOK LIKE, ROSALIE!
A'IGHT !!
HANG ON TIGHT!
BABABAN (DUDUDUM)
'COS ROSALIE HERSELF IS READY TO APPEAR IN THE FLE—
YANYA (CHEER)
やんや
YANYA
やんや
HNGH!
HNGH!
ROSA-LIE?
UM...

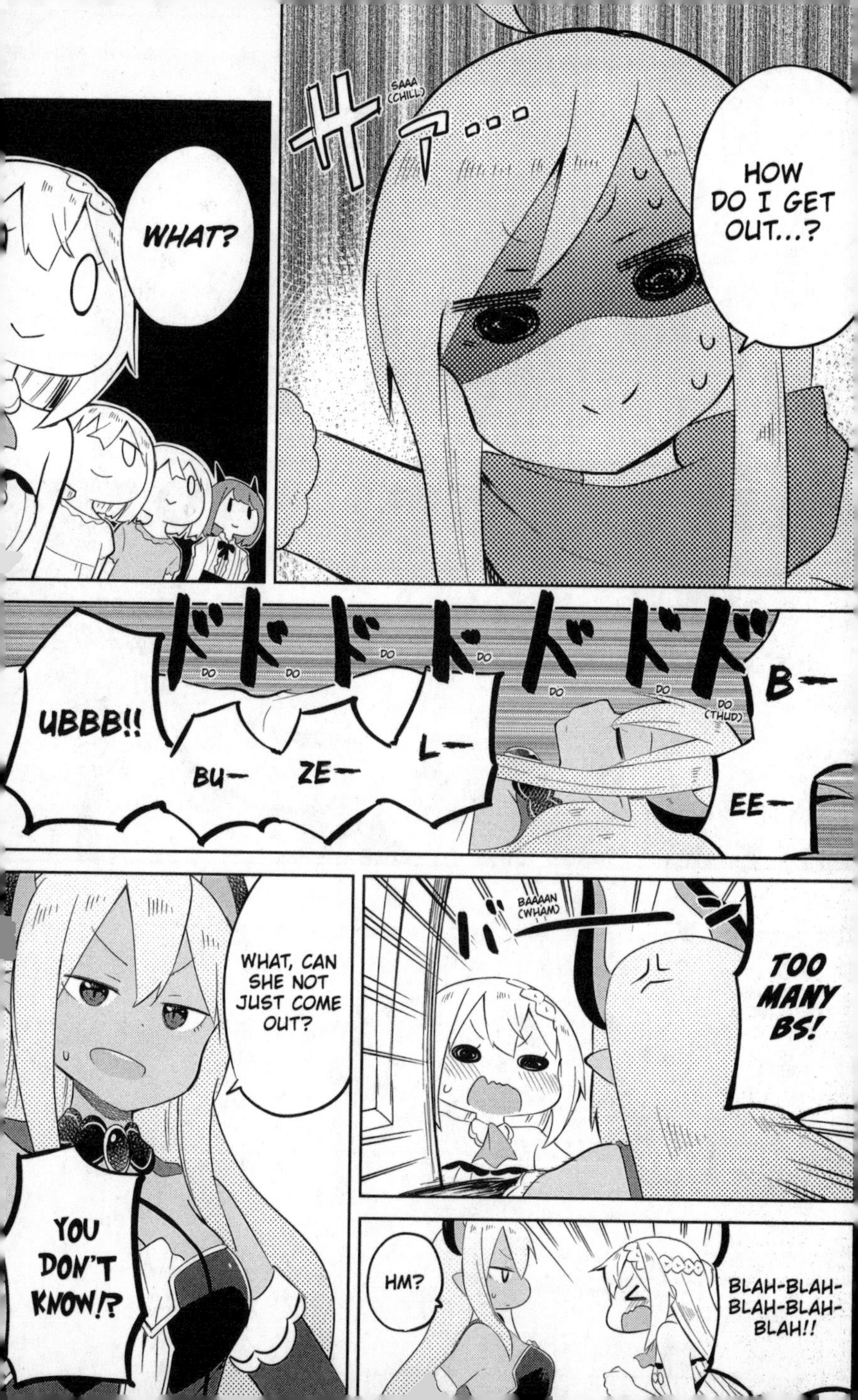
SAAA (CHILL)
HOW DO I GET OUT...?
WHAT?
B—
DO (THUD)
DO
DO
DO
DO
DO
EE—
L—
ZE—
BU—
UBBB!!
BAAAAN (WHAM)
TOO MANY BS!
BLAH-BLAH-BLAH-BLAH-BLAH!!
HM?
WHAT, CAN SHE NOT JUST COME OUT?
YOU DON'T KNOW!?

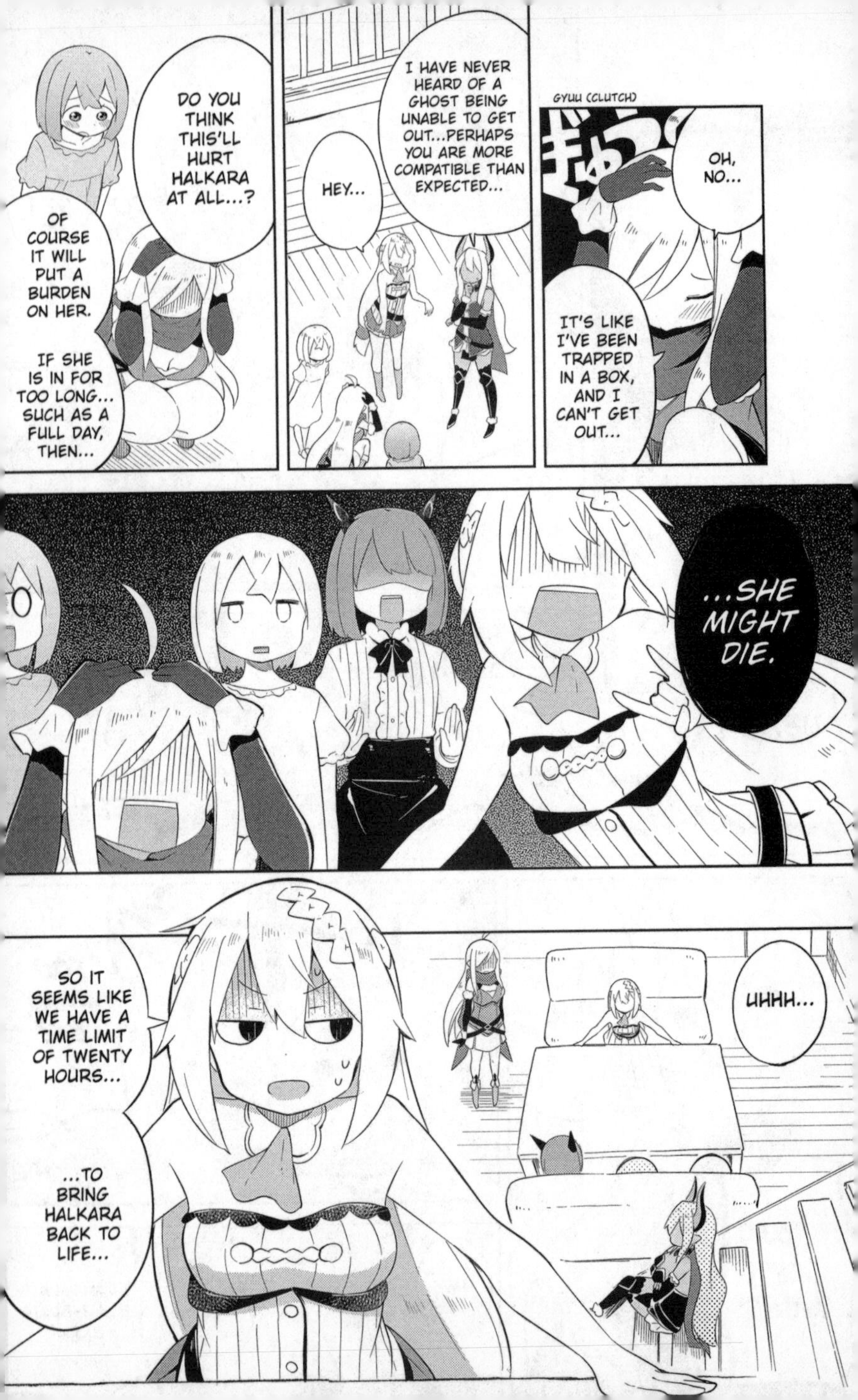
GYUU (CLUTCH)
OH, NO...
IT'S LIKE I'VE BEEN TRAPPED IN A BOX, AND I CAN'T GET OUT...
I HAVE NEVER HEARD OF A GHOST BEING UNABLE TO GET OUT...PERHAPS YOU ARE MORE COMPATIBLE THAN EXPECTED...
HEY...
DO YOU THINK THIS'LL HURT HALKARA AT ALL...?
OF COURSE IT WILL PUT A BURDEN ON HER.
IF SHE IS IN FOR TOO LONG... SUCH AS A FULL DAY, THEN...
...SHE MIGHT DIE.
UHHH...
...
...
SO IT SEEMS LIKE WE HAVE A TIME LIMIT OF TWENTY HOURS...
...TO BRING HALKARA BACK TO LIFE...

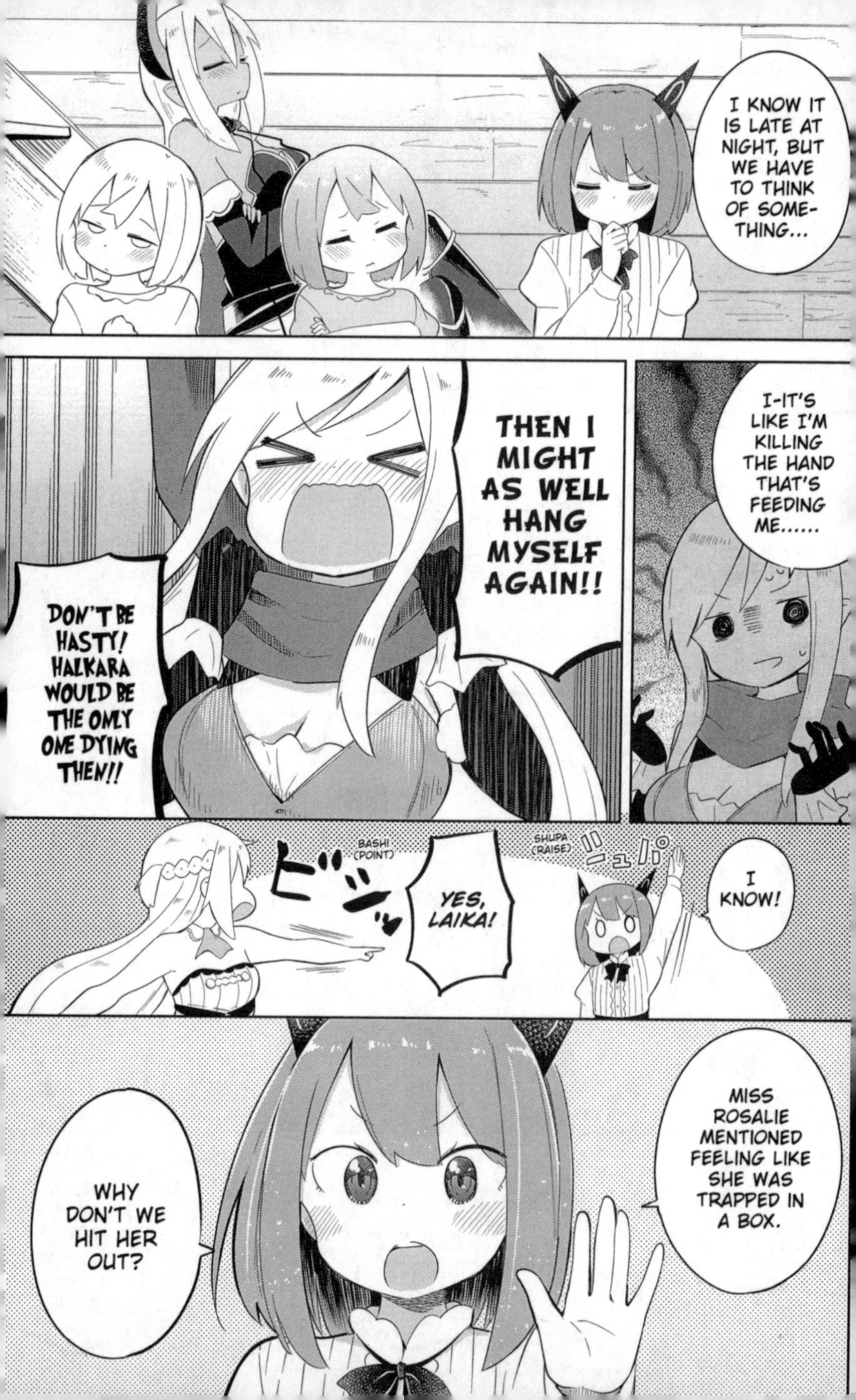
I KNOW IT IS LATE AT NIGHT, BUT WE HAVE TO THINK OF SOMETHING...
I-IT'S LIKE I'M KILLING THE HAND THAT'S FEEDING ME......
THEN I MIGHT AS WELL HANG MYSELF AGAIN!!
DON'T BE HASTY! HALKARA WOULD BE THE ONLY ONE DYING THEN!!
I KNOW!
SHUPA (RAISE)
YES, LAIKA!
BASHI (POINT)
MISS ROSALIE MENTIONED FEELING LIKE SHE WAS TRAPPED IN A BOX.
WHY DON'T WE HIT HER OUT?

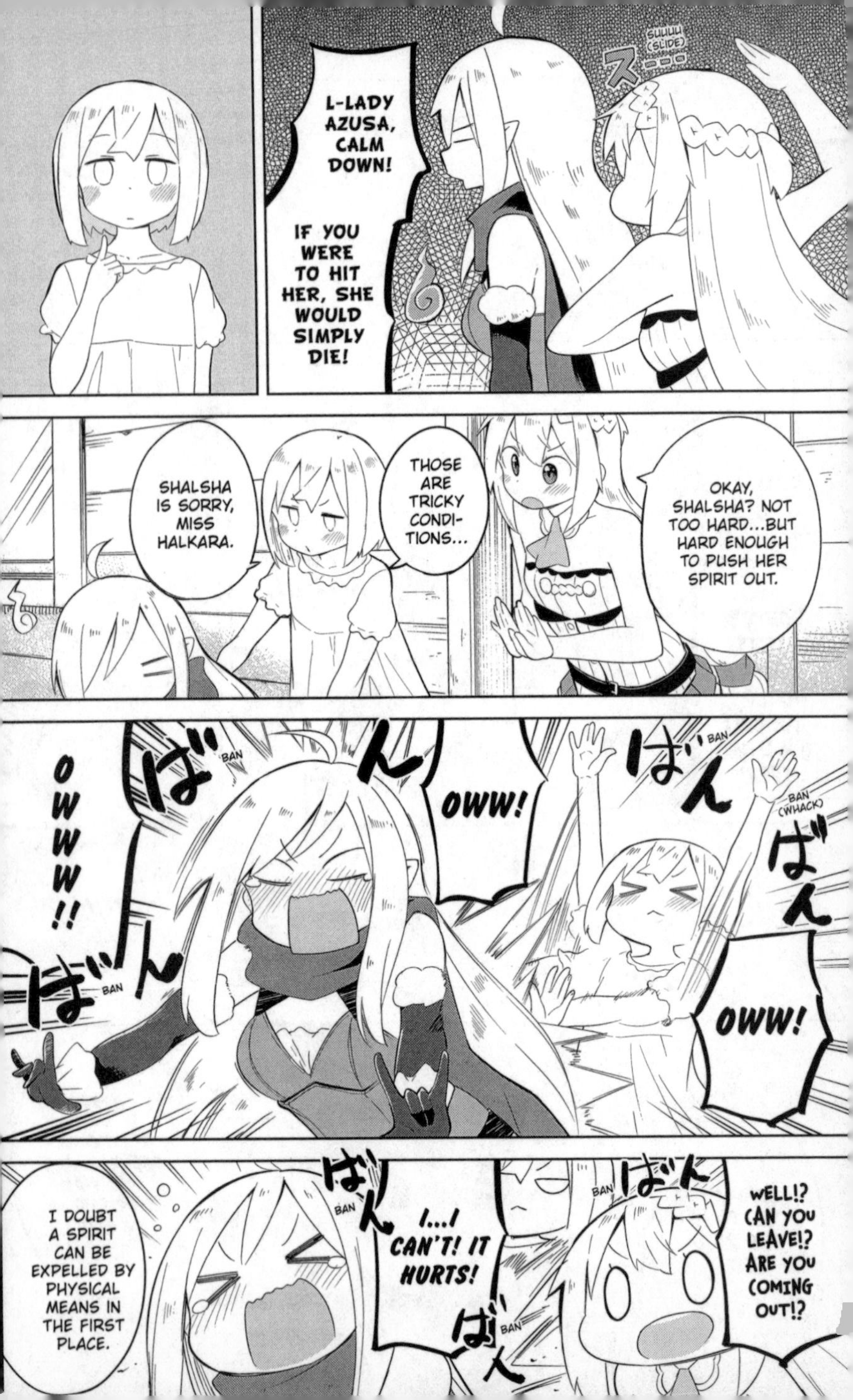

SUUUU (SLIDE)
L-LADY AZUSA, CALM DOWN!
IF YOU WERE TO HIT HER, SHE WOULD SIMPLY DIE!
OKAY, SHALSHA? NOT TOO HARD...BUT HARD ENOUGH TO PUSH HER SPIRIT OUT.
THOSE ARE TRICKY CONDI-TIONS...
SHALSHA IS SORRY, MISS HALKARA.
BAN
BAN (WHACK)
OWW!
OWW!
BAN
OWWWW!!
BAN
WELL!? CAN YOU LEAVE!? ARE YOU COMING OUT!?
BAN
BAN
I...I CAN'T! IT HURTS!
BAN
BAN
I DOUBT A SPIRIT CAN BE EXPELLED BY PHYSICAL MEANS IN THE FIRST PLACE.

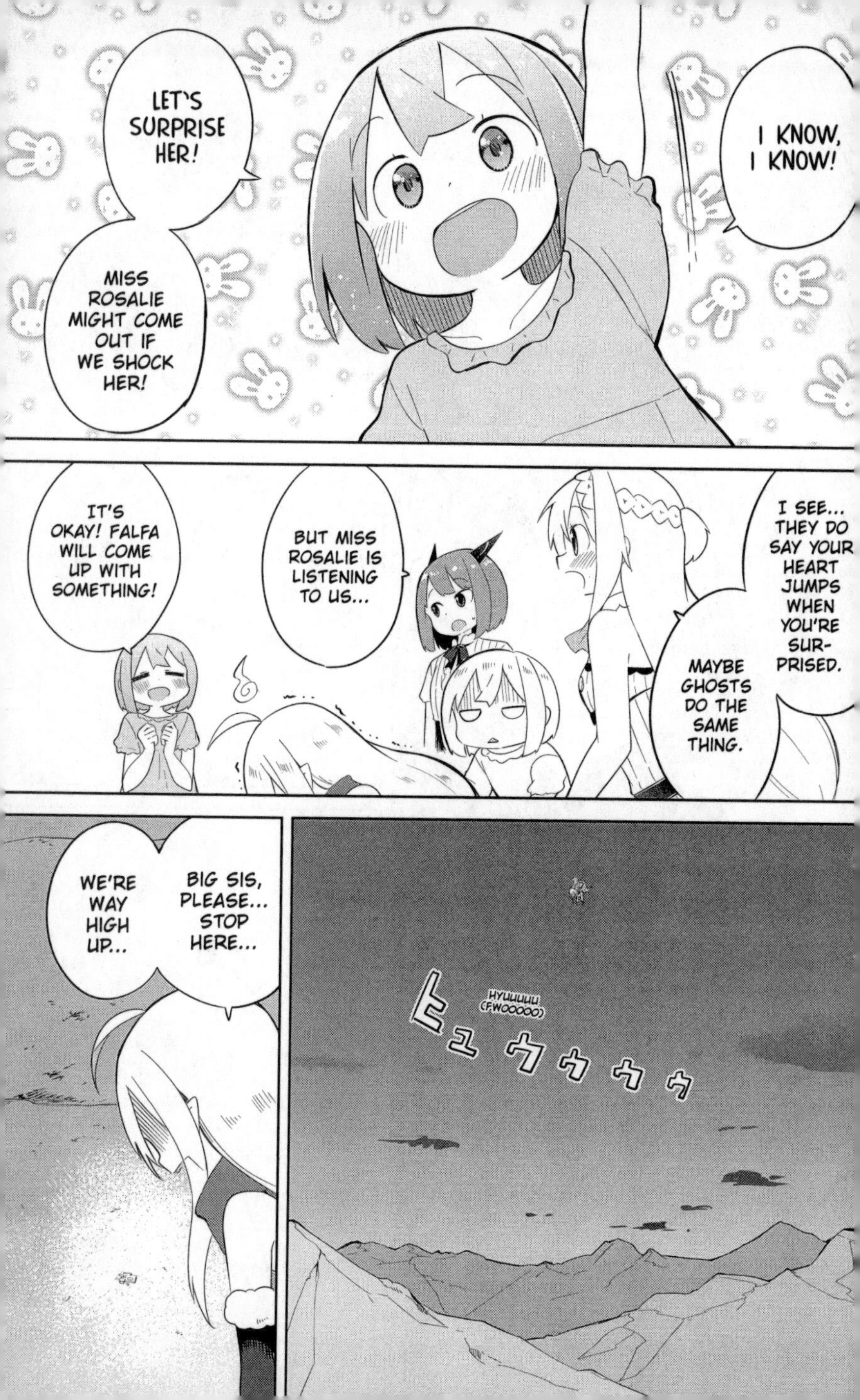
I KNOW, I KNOW!
LET'S SURPRISE HER!
MISS ROSALIE MIGHT COME OUT IF WE SHOCK HER!
I SEE... THEY DO SAY YOUR HEART JUMPS WHEN YOU'RE SUR-PRISED.
MAYBE GHOSTS DO THE SAME THING.
BUT MISS ROSALIE IS LISTENING TO US...
IT'S OKAY! FALFA WILL COME UP WITH SOMETHING!
ヒュウウウウ
HYUUUUU (FWOOOOO)
BIG SIS, PLEASE... STOP HERE...
WE'RE WAY HIGH UP...

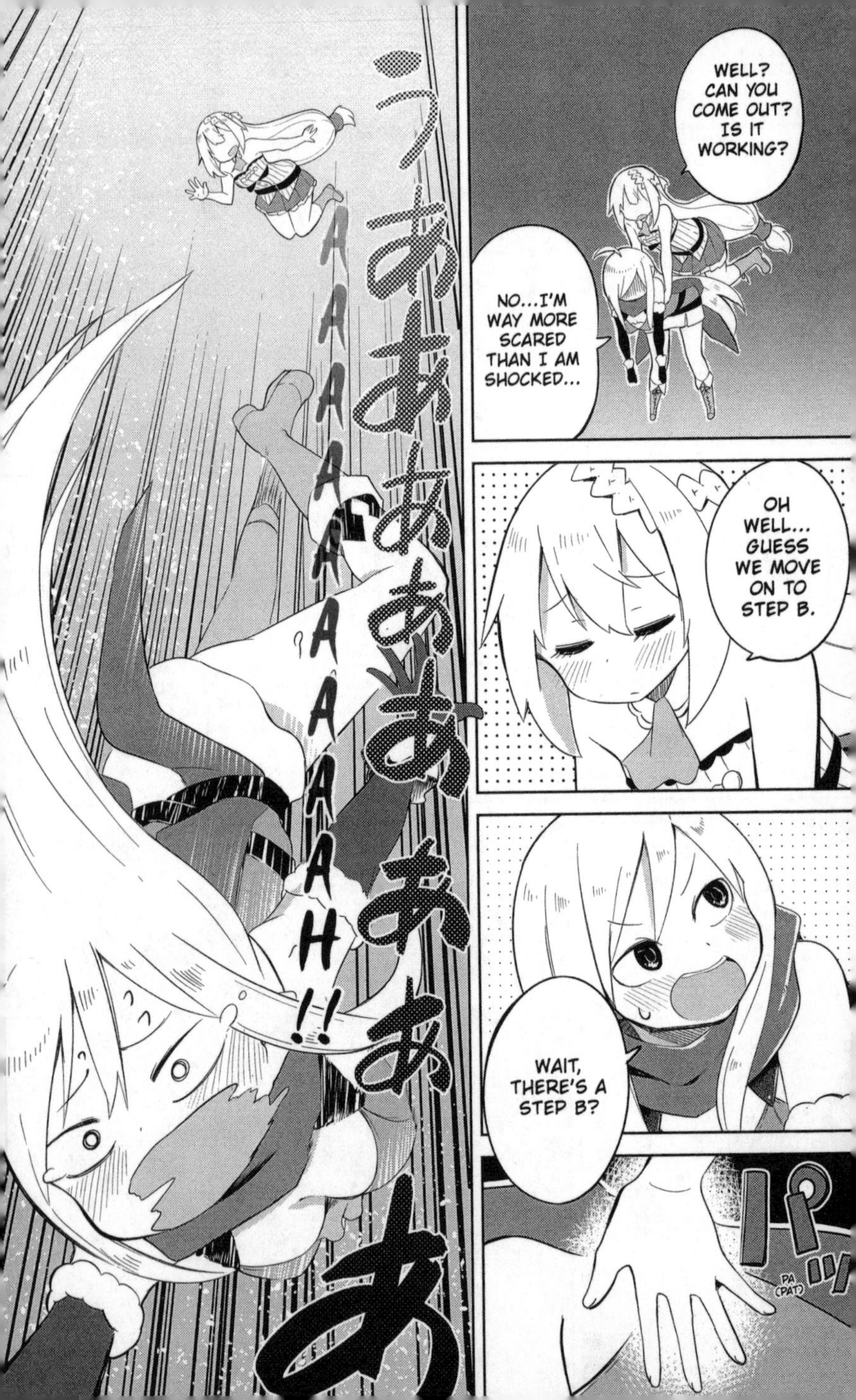

WELL? CAN YOU COME OUT? IS IT WORKING?
NO...I'M WAY MORE SCARED THAN I AM SHOCKED...
OH WELL... GUESS WE MOVE ON TO STEP B.
WAIT, THERE'S A STEP B?
パッ
PA (PAT)
うあああああああ
AAAAAAAAAH!!

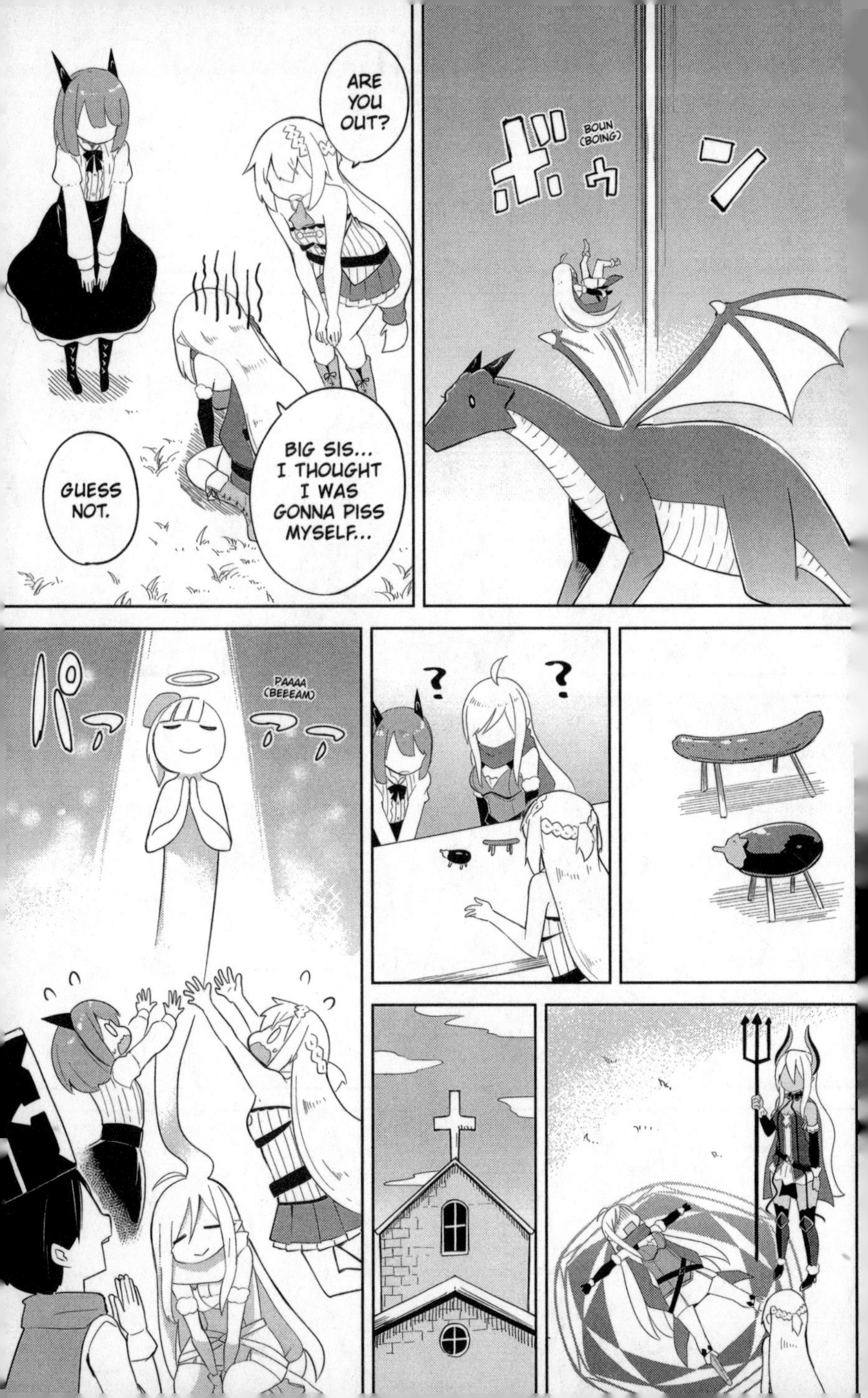
BOUN
(BOING)
ARE YOU OUT?
BIG SIS... I THOUGHT I WAS GONNA PISS MYSELF...
GUESS NOT.
?
?
PAAAA
(BEEEAM)

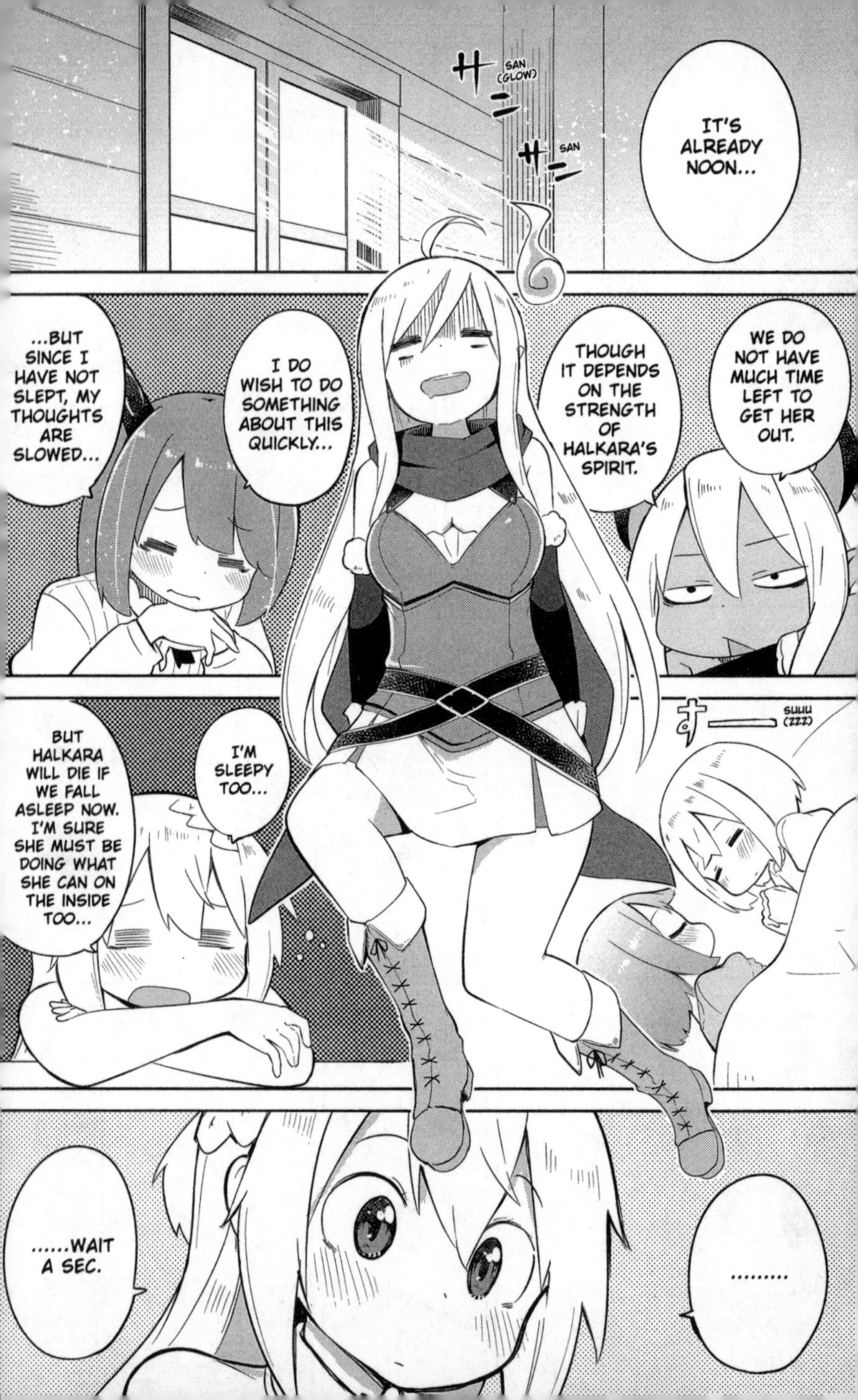
IT'S ALREADY NOON...
SAN (GLOW)
SAN
WE DO NOT HAVE MUCH TIME LEFT TO GET HER OUT.
THOUGH IT DEPENDS ON THE STRENGTH OF HALKARA'S SPIRIT.
I DO WISH TO DO SOMETHING ABOUT THIS QUICKLY...
...BUT SINCE I HAVE NOT SLEPT, MY THOUGHTS ARE SLOWED...
SUUU (ZZZ)
I'M SLEEPY TOO...
BUT HALKARA WILL DIE IF WE FALL ASLEEP NOW. I'M SURE SHE MUST BE DOING WHAT SHE CAN ON THE INSIDE TOO...
....
......WAIT A SEC.

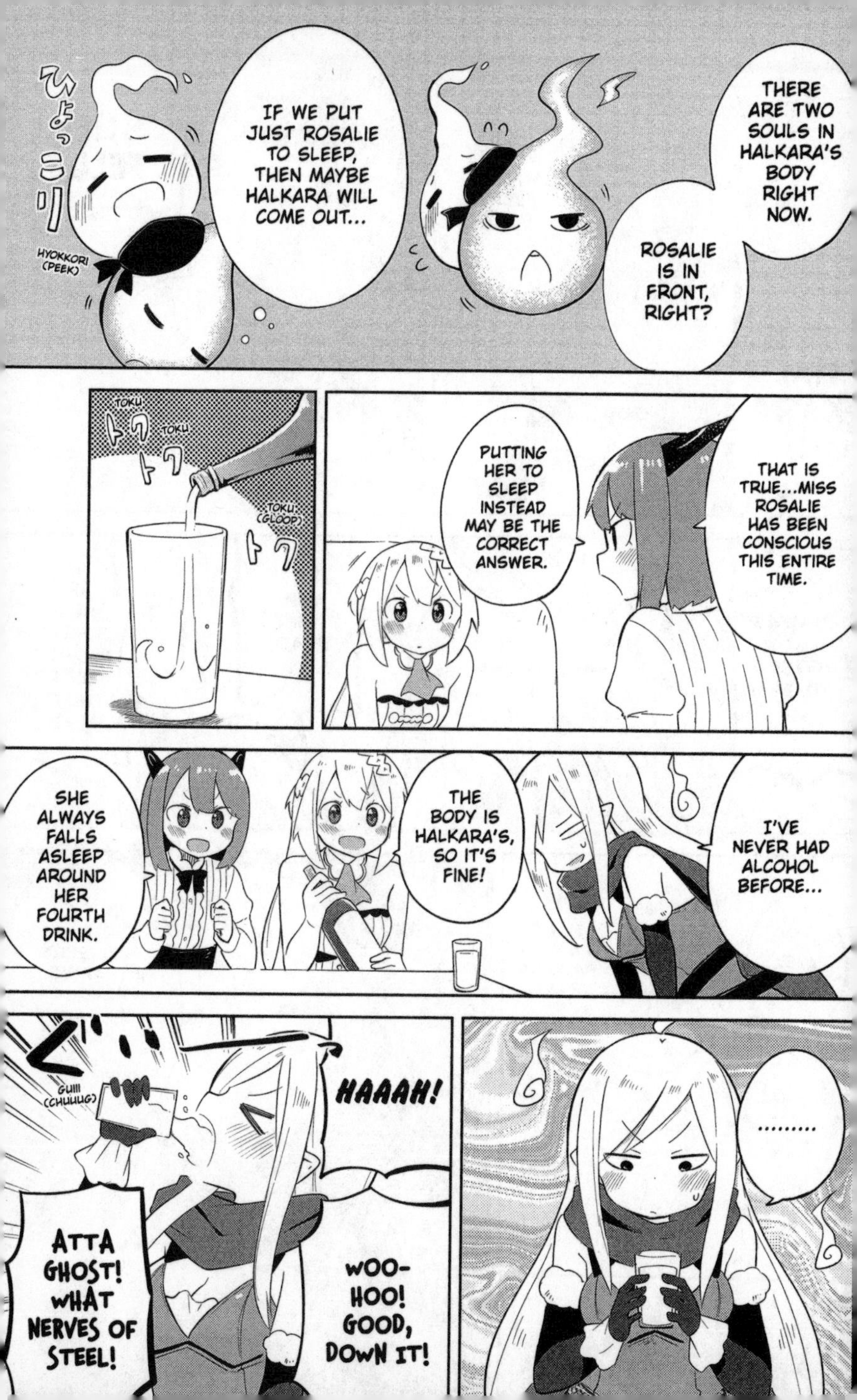
THERE ARE TWO SOULS IN HALKARA'S BODY RIGHT NOW.
ROSALIE IS IN FRONT, RIGHT?
IF WE PUT JUST ROSALIE TO SLEEP, THEN MAYBE HALKARA WILL COME OUT...
ひょっこり
HYOKKORI (PEEK)
THAT IS TRUE...MISS ROSALIE HAS BEEN CONSCIOUS THIS ENTIRE TIME.
PUTTING HER TO SLEEP INSTEAD MAY BE THE CORRECT ANSWER.
トク TOKU
トク TOKU
トク TOKU (GLOOP)
I'VE NEVER HAD ALCOHOL BEFORE...
THE BODY IS HALKARA'S, SO IT'S FINE!
SHE ALWAYS FALLS ASLEEP AROUND HER FOURTH DRINK.
....
HAAAH!
GUIII (CHUUUG)
WOO-HOO! GOOD, DOWN IT!
ATTA GHOST! WHAT NERVES OF STEEL!

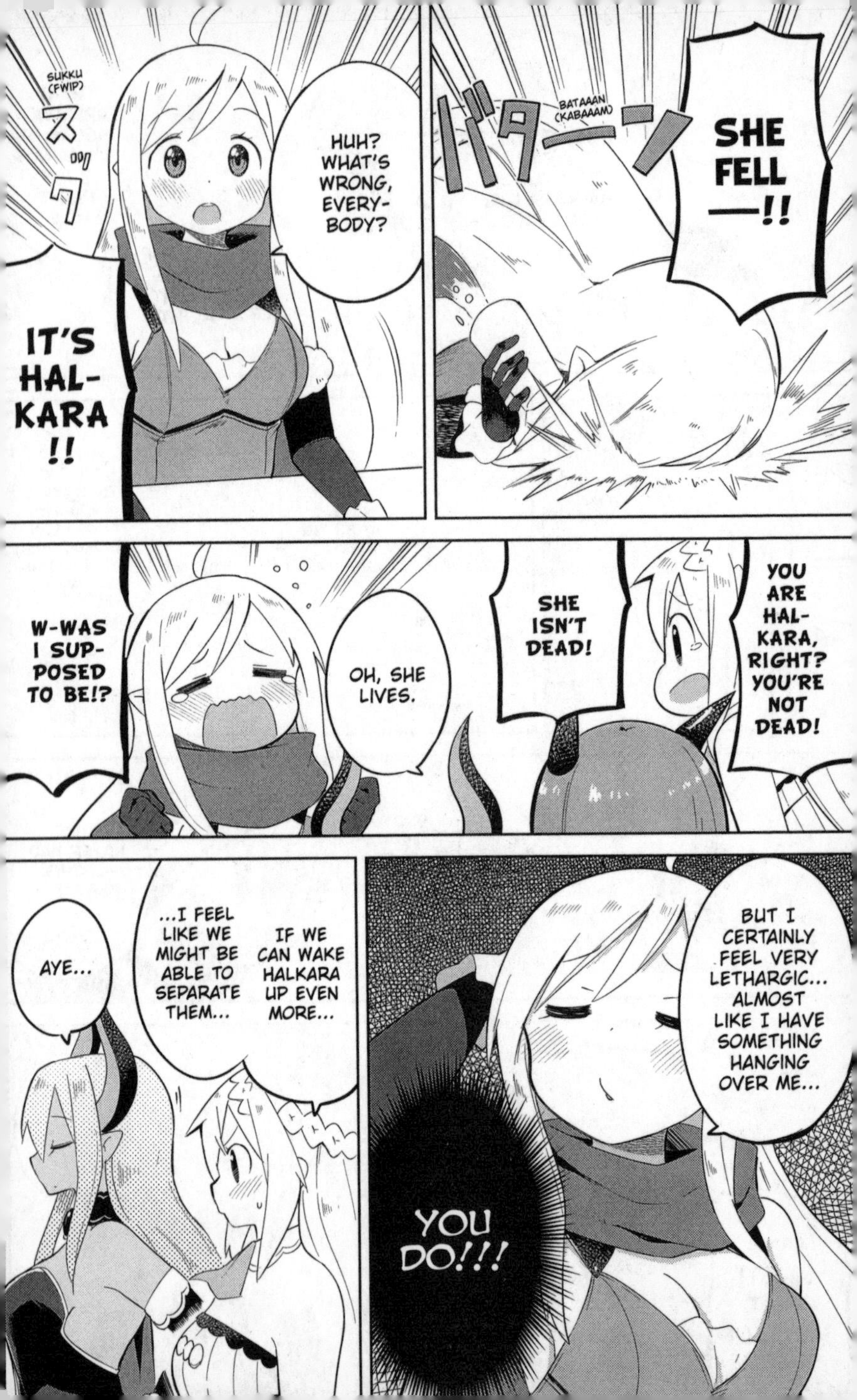
SHE FELL—!!
BATAAAN (KABAAAM)
バターーン
HUH? WHAT'S WRONG, EVERYBODY?
SUKKU (FWIP)
スック
IT'S HALKARA!!
YOU ARE HALKARA, RIGHT? YOU'RE NOT DEAD!
SHE ISN'T DEAD!
OH, SHE LIVES.
W-WAS I SUPPOSED TO BE!?
BUT I CERTAINLY FEEL VERY LETHARGIC... ALMOST LIKE I HAVE SOMETHING HANGING OVER ME...
YOU DO!!!
IF WE CAN WAKE HALKARA UP EVEN MORE...
...I FEEL LIKE WE MIGHT BE ABLE TO SEPARATE THEM...
AYE...

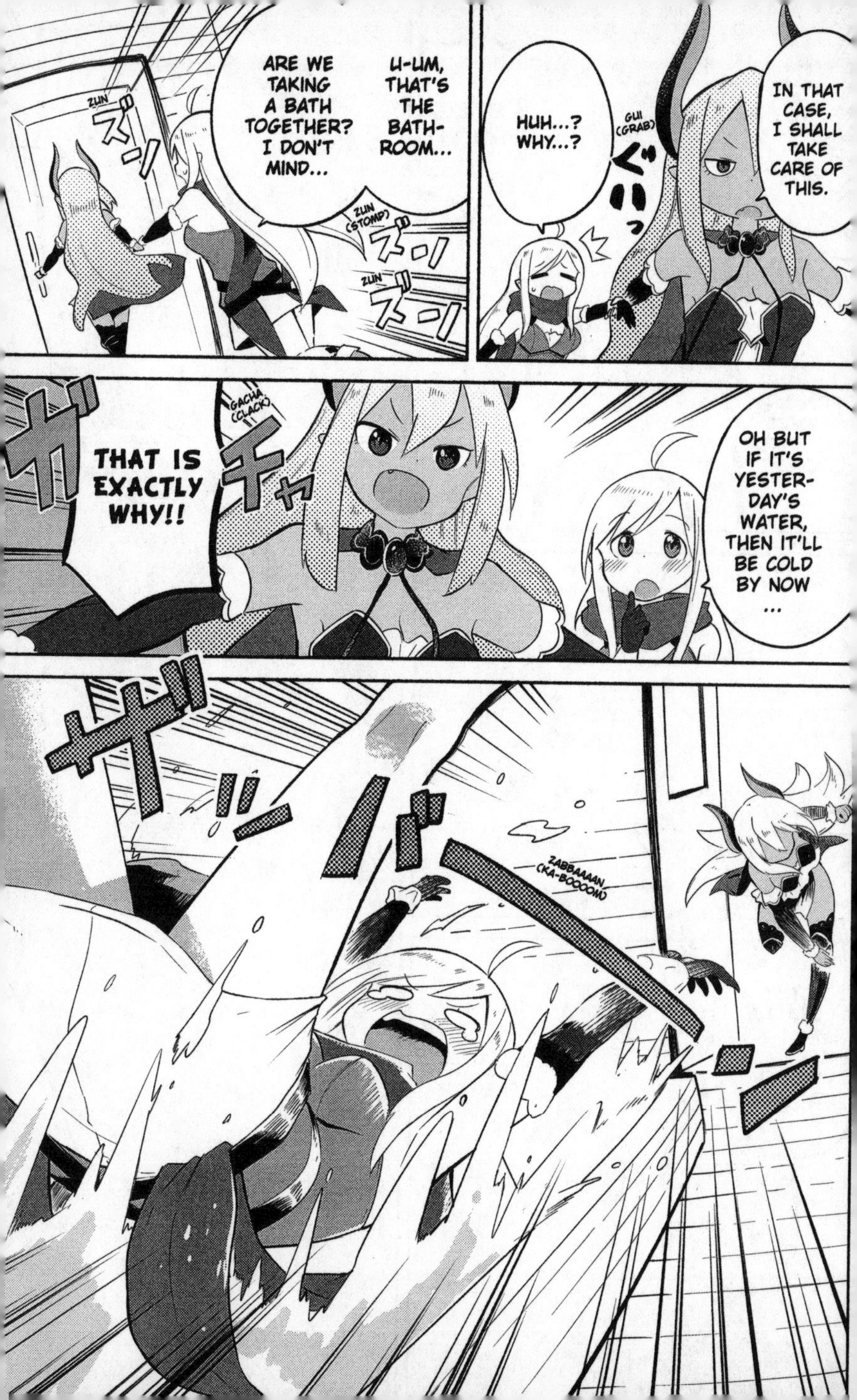
IN THAT CASE, I SHALL TAKE CARE OF THIS.
GUI (GRAB)
HUH...? WHY...?
ZUN (STOMP)
ZUN
U-UM, THAT'S THE BATH-ROOM...
ARE WE TAKING A BATH TOGETHER? I DON'T MIND...
ZUN
OH BUT IF IT'S YESTER-DAY'S WATER, THEN IT'LL BE COLD BY NOW ...
GACHA (CLACK)
THAT IS EXACTLY WHY!!
ZABBAAAAN (KA-BOOOOM)

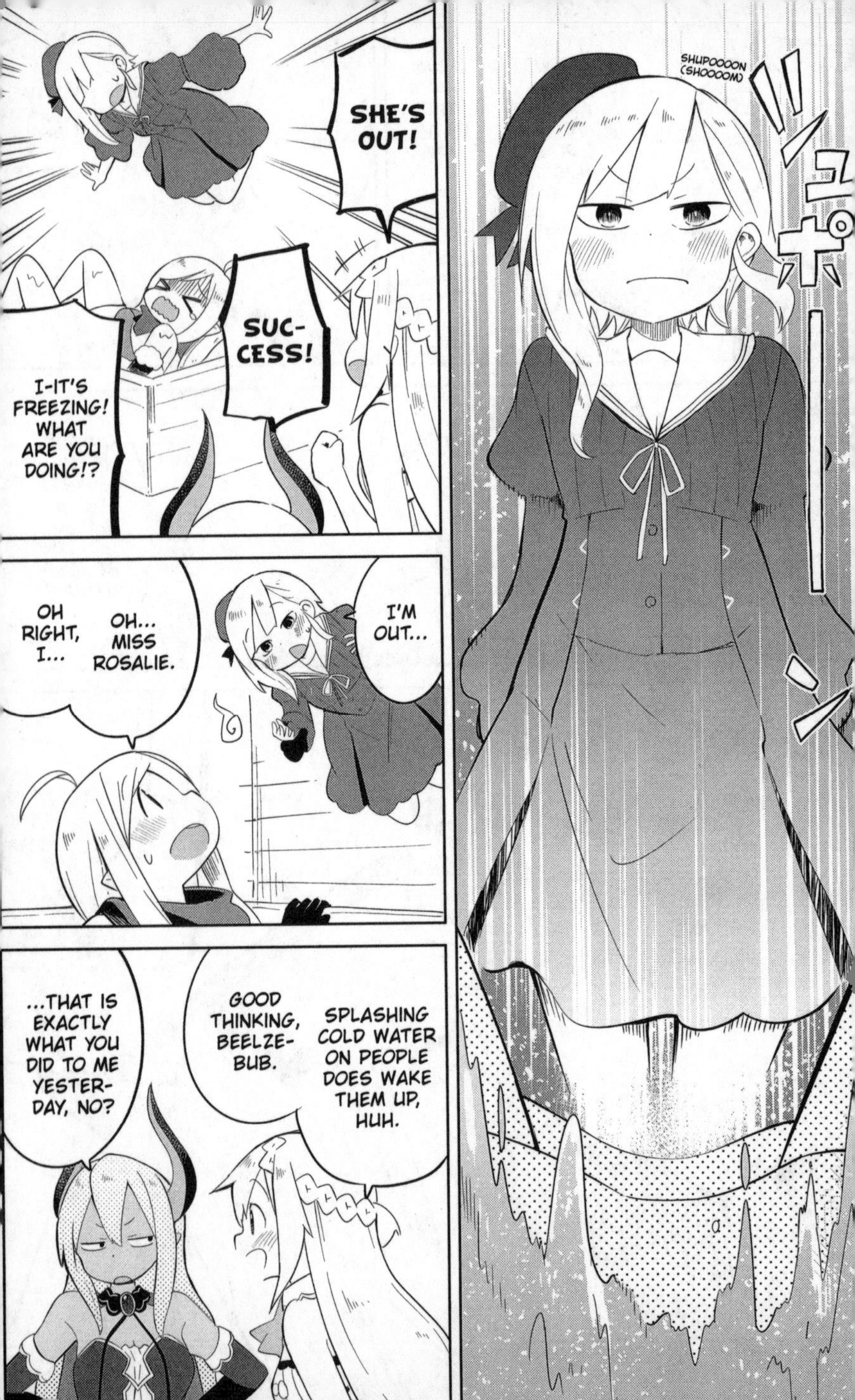
SHUPOOOON (SHOOOOM)
SHE'S OUT!
SUC-CESS!
I-IT'S FREEZING! WHAT ARE YOU DOING!?
I'M OUT...
OH... MISS ROSALIE.
OH RIGHT, I...
SPLASHING COLD WATER ON PEOPLE DOES WAKE THEM UP, HUH.
GOOD THINKING, BEELZE-BUB.
...THAT IS EXACTLY WHAT YOU DID TO ME YESTER-DAY, NO?

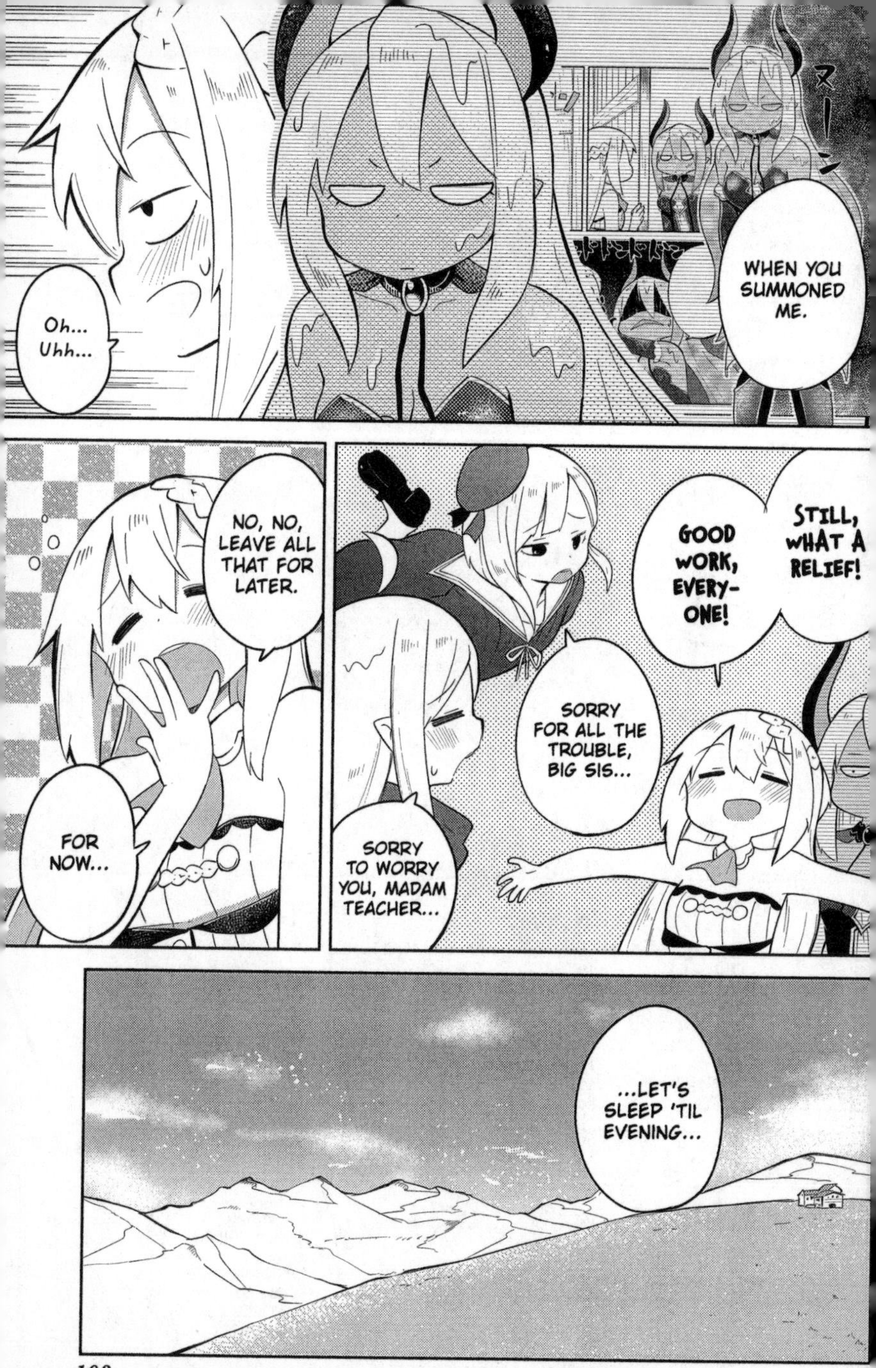
WHEN YOU SUMMONED ME.
Oh... Uhh...
STILL, WHAT A RELIEF!
GOOD WORK, EVERY-ONE!
SORRY FOR ALL THE TROUBLE, BIG SIS...
SORRY TO WORRY YOU, MADAM TEACHER...
NO, NO, LEAVE ALL THAT FOR LATER.
FOR NOW...
...LET'S SLEEP 'TIL EVENING...

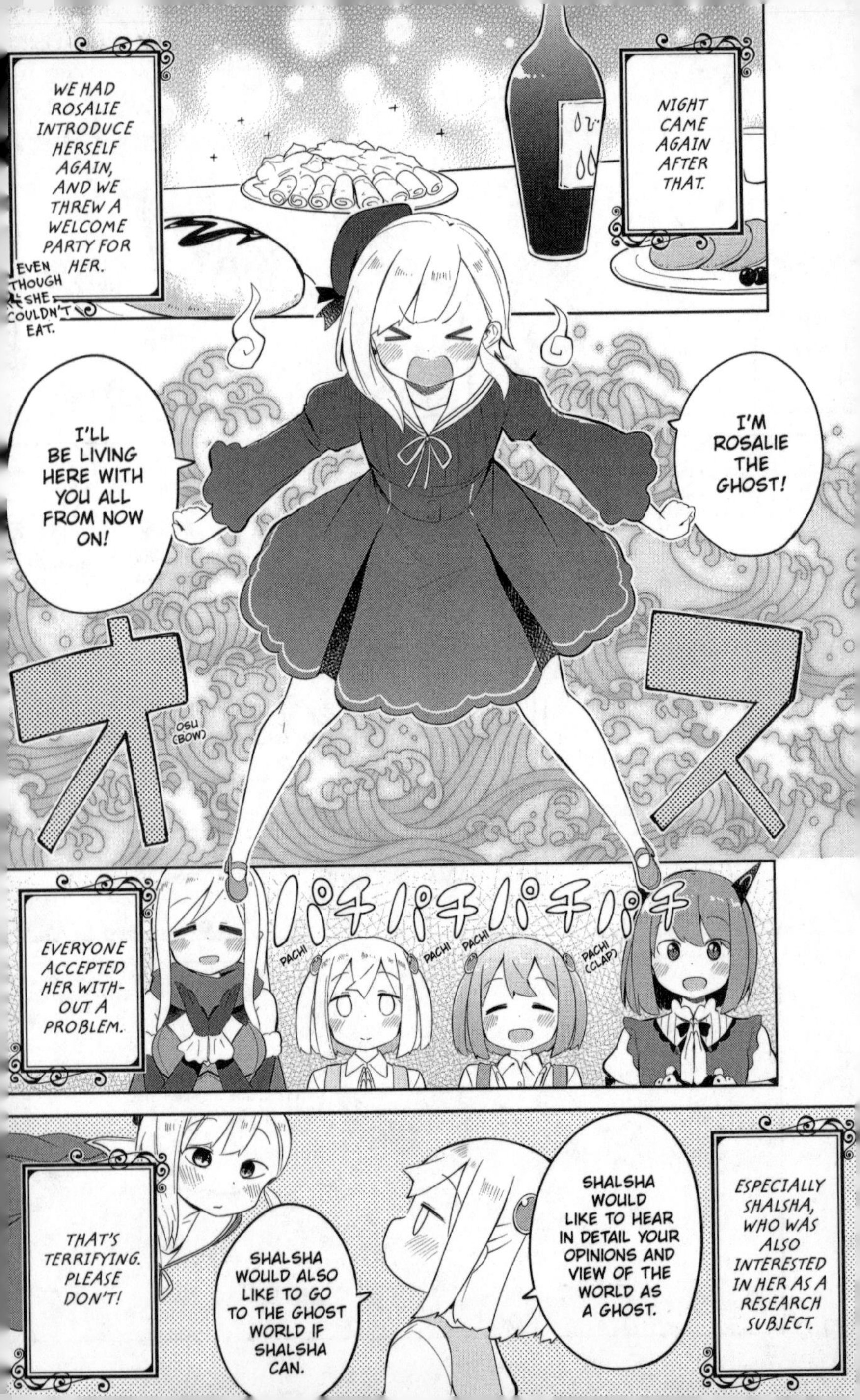
NIGHT CAME AGAIN AFTER THAT.
WE HAD ROSALIE INTRODUCE HERSELF AGAIN, AND WE THREW A WELCOME PARTY FOR HER.
EVEN THOUGH SHE COULDN'T EAT.
I'M ROSALIE THE GHOST!
I'LL BE LIVING HERE WITH YOU ALL FROM NOW ON!
OSU (BOW)
PACHI PACHI PACHI PACHI (CLAP)
EVERYONE ACCEPTED HER WITH-OUT A PROBLEM.
ESPECIALLY SHALSHA, WHO WAS ALSO INTERESTED IN HER AS A RESEARCH SUBJECT.
SHALSHA WOULD LIKE TO HEAR IN DETAIL YOUR OPINIONS AND VIEW OF THE WORLD AS A GHOST.
SHALSHA WOULD ALSO LIKE TO GO TO THE GHOST WORLD IF SHALSHA CAN.
THAT'S TERRIFYING. PLEASE DON'T!

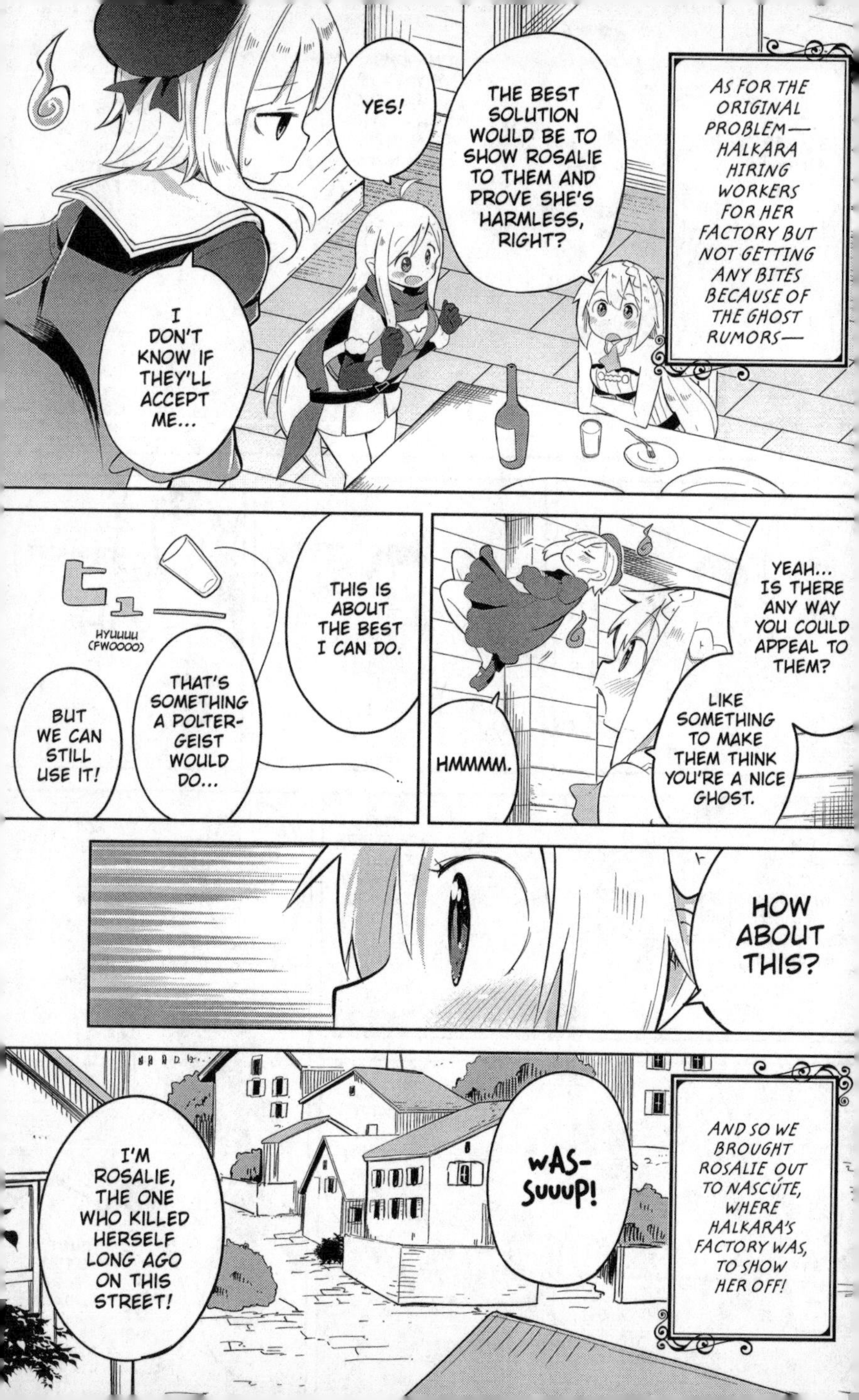

AS FOR THE ORIGINAL PROBLEM—HALKARA HIRING WORKERS FOR HER FACTORY BUT NOT GETTING ANY BITES BECAUSE OF THE GHOST RUMORS—
THE BEST SOLUTION WOULD BE TO SHOW ROSALIE TO THEM AND PROVE SHE'S HARMLESS, RIGHT?
YES!
I DON'T KNOW IF THEY'LL ACCEPT ME...
YEAH... IS THERE ANY WAY YOU COULD APPEAL TO THEM?
LIKE SOMETHING TO MAKE THEM THINK YOU'RE A NICE GHOST.
HMMMM.
THIS IS ABOUT THE BEST I CAN DO.
HYUUUU (FWOOOO)
THAT'S SOMETHING A POLTER-GEIST WOULD DO...
BUT WE CAN STILL USE IT!
HOW ABOUT THIS?
AND SO WE BROUGHT ROSALIE OUT TO NASCÚTE, WHERE HALKARA'S FACTORY WAS, TO SHOW HER OFF!
WAS-SUUUP!
I'M ROSALIE, THE ONE WHO KILLED HERSELF LONG AGO ON THIS STREET!

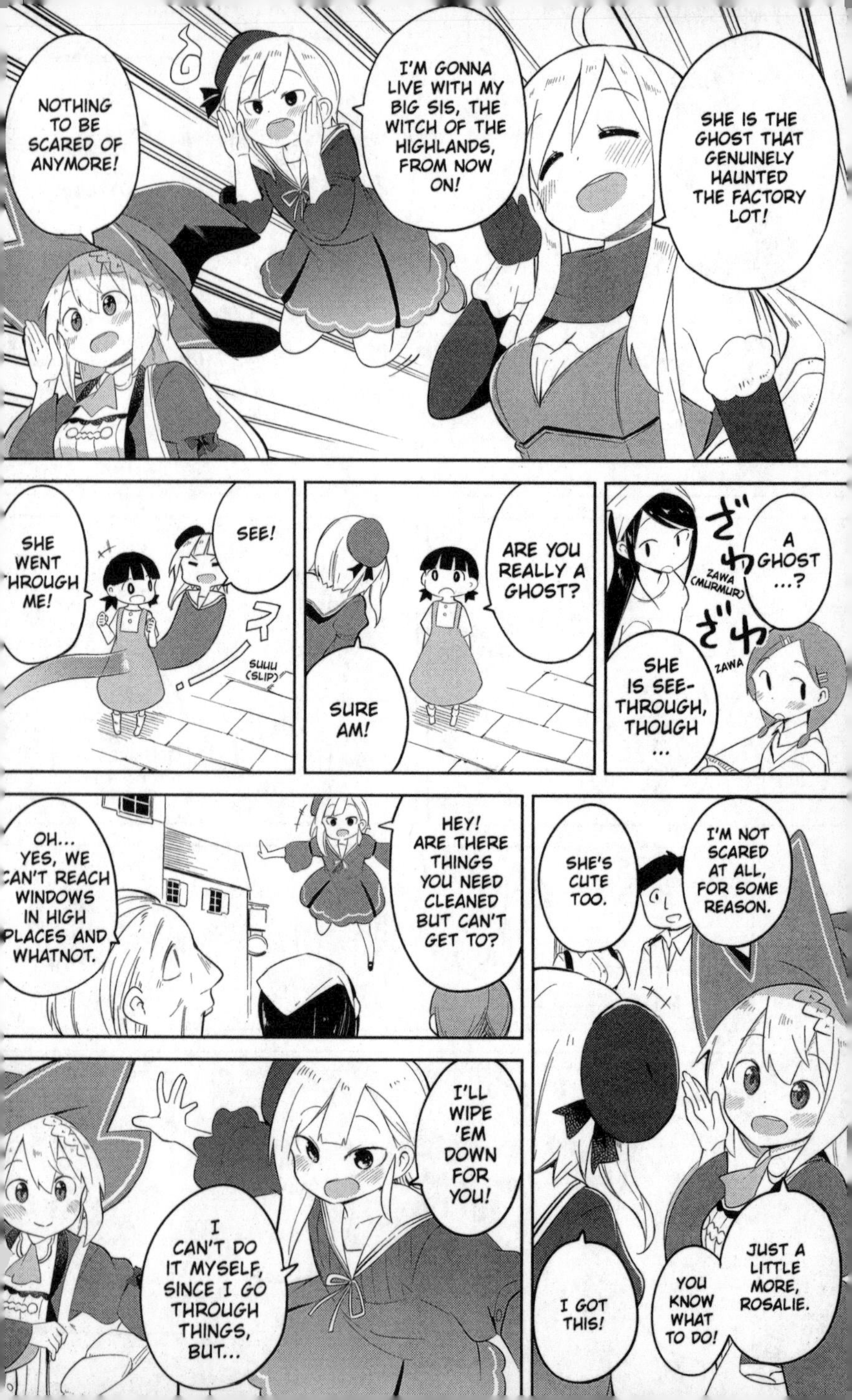

SHE IS THE GHOST THAT GENUINELY HAUNTED THE FACTORY LOT!
I'M GONNA LIVE WITH MY BIG SIS, THE WITCH OF THE HIGHLANDS, FROM NOW ON!
NOTHING TO BE SCARED OF ANYMORE!
A GHOST...?
ざわ
ZAWA (MURMUR)
ざわ
ZAWA
SHE IS SEE-THROUGH, THOUGH...
ARE YOU REALLY A GHOST?
SURE AM!
SEE!
SHE WENT THROUGH ME!
ス
SUUU (SLIP)
I'M NOT SCARED AT ALL, FOR SOME REASON.
SHE'S CUTE TOO.
JUST A LITTLE MORE, ROSALIE.
YOU KNOW WHAT TO DO!
I GOT THIS!
HEY! ARE THERE THINGS YOU NEED CLEANED BUT CAN'T GET TO?
OH... YES, WE CAN'T REACH WINDOWS IN HIGH PLACES AND WHATNOT.
I'LL WIPE 'EM DOWN FOR YOU!
I CAN'T DO IT MYSELF, SINCE I GO THROUGH THINGS, BUT...

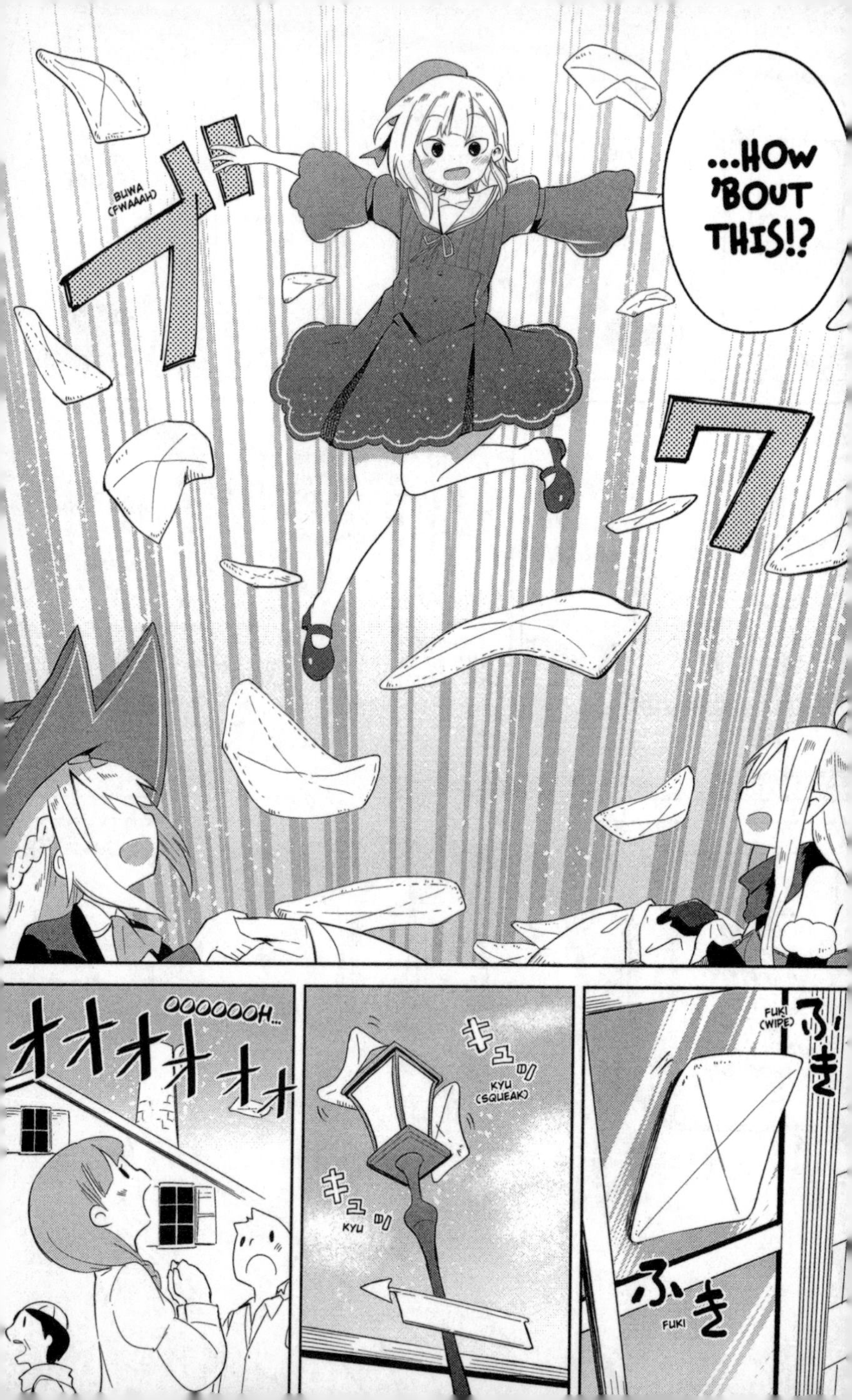
...HOW 'BOUT THIS!?
BUWA (FWAAAH)
ふき
FUKI (WIPE)
ふき
FUKI
キュッ
KYU (SQUEAK)
キュッ
KYU
OOOOOOOH...

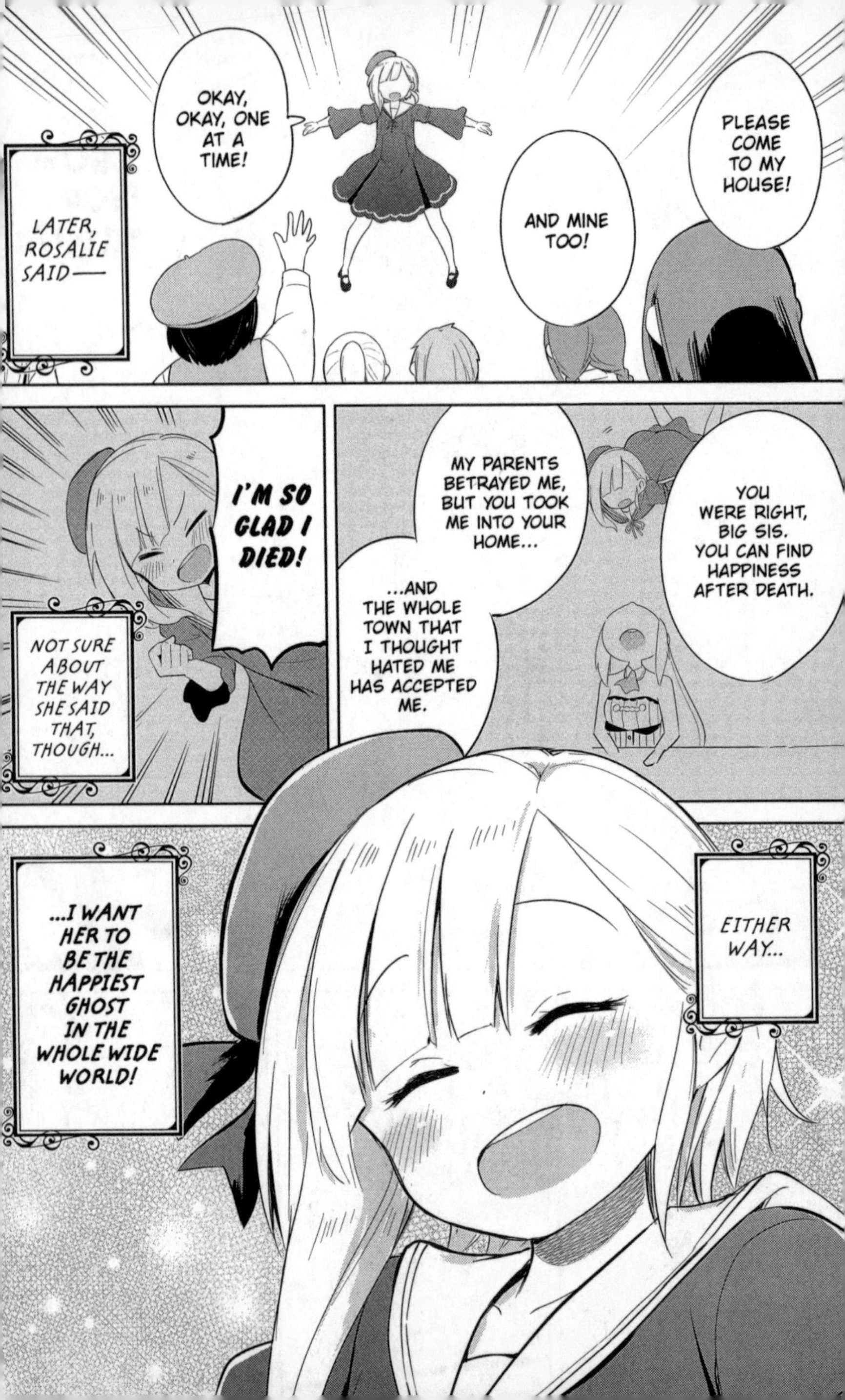
PLEASE COME TO MY HOUSE!
AND MINE TOO!
OKAY, OKAY, ONE AT A TIME!
LATER, ROSALIE SAID—
YOU WERE RIGHT, BIG SIS. YOU CAN FIND HAPPINESS AFTER DEATH.
MY PARENTS BETRAYED ME, BUT YOU TOOK ME INTO YOUR HOME...
...AND THE WHOLE TOWN THAT I THOUGHT HATED ME HAS ACCEPTED ME.
I'M SO GLAD I DIED!
NOT SURE ABOUT THE WAY SHE SAID THAT, THOUGH...
EITHER WAY...
...I WANT HER TO BE THE HAPPIEST GHOST IN THE WHOLE WIDE WORLD!

I've Been Killing SLIMES for 300 Years and Maxed Out My Level

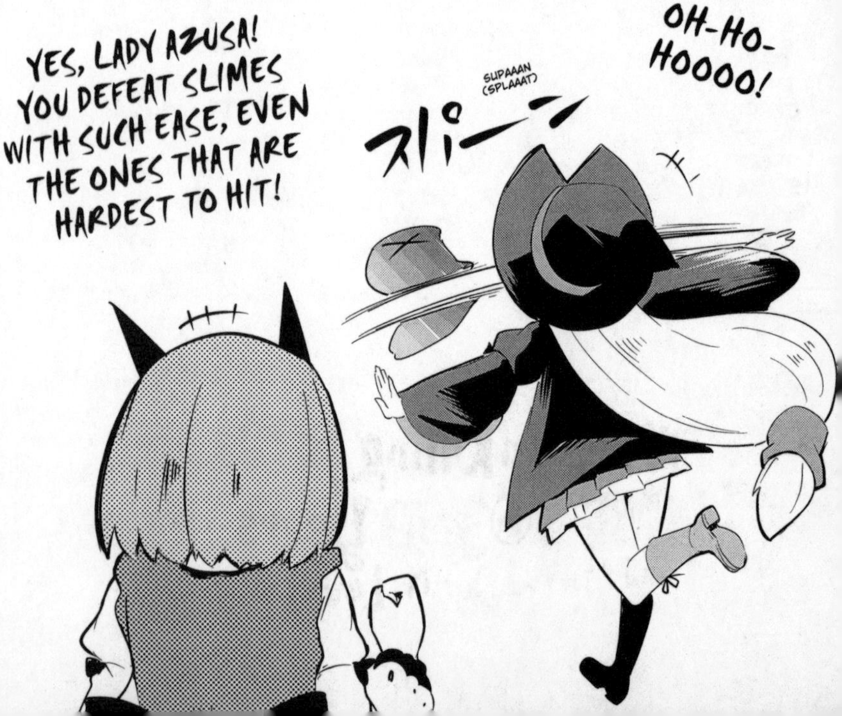
OH-HO-HOOOOO!
SUPAAAN (SPLAAAT)
スパーン
YES, LADY AZUSA! YOU DEFEAT SLIMES WITH SUCH EASE, EVEN THE ONES THAT ARE HARDEST TO HIT!

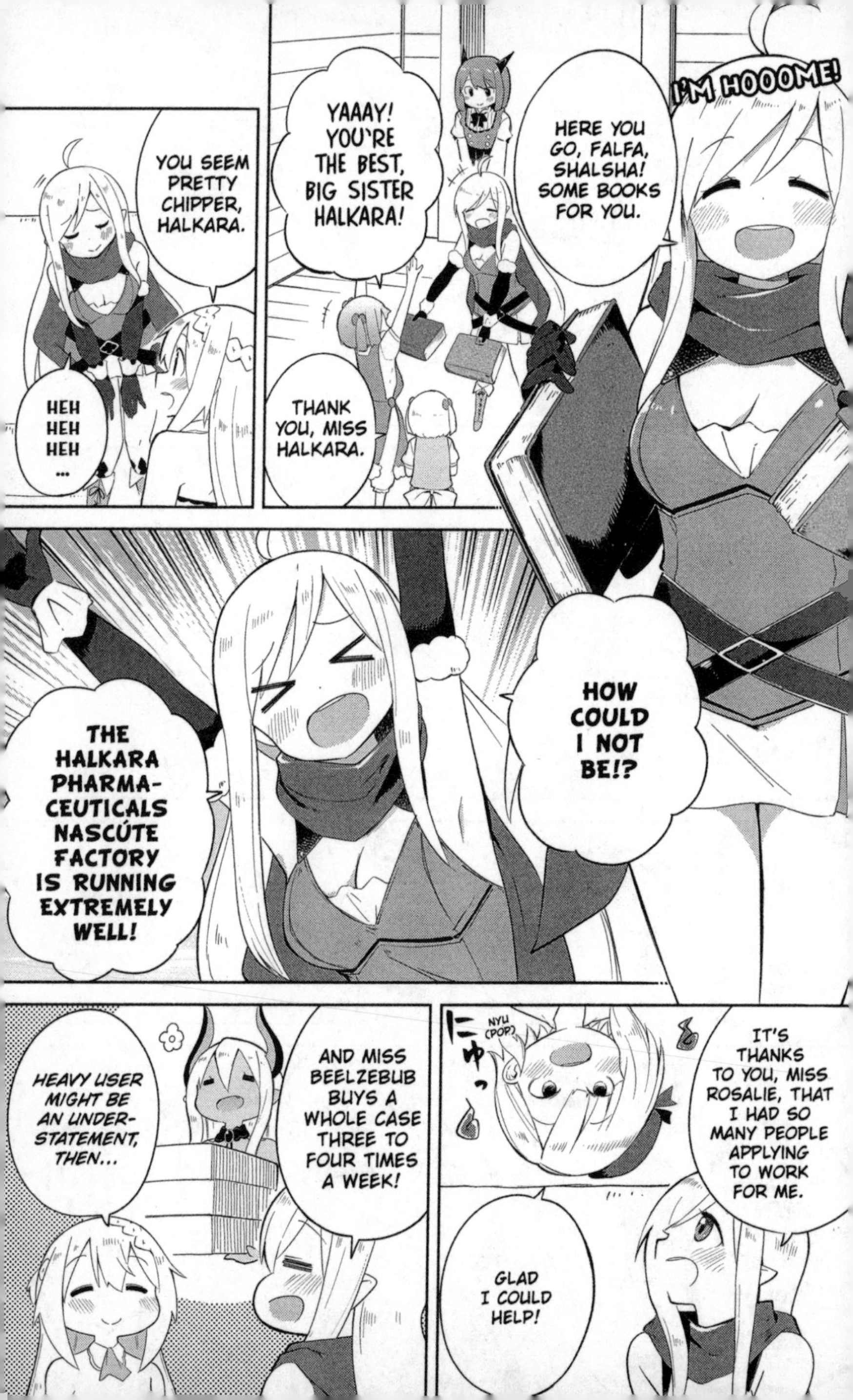
I'M HOOOME!
HERE YOU GO, FALFA, SHALSHA! SOME BOOKS FOR YOU.
YAAAY! YOU'RE THE BEST, BIG SISTER HALKARA!
THANK YOU, MISS HALKARA.
YOU SEEM PRETTY CHIPPER, HALKARA.
HEH HEH HEH ...
HOW COULD I NOT BE!?
THE HALKARA PHARMA-CEUTICALS NASCÚTE FACTORY IS RUNNING EXTREMELY WELL!
NYU (POP)
IT'S THANKS TO YOU, MISS ROSALIE, THAT I HAD SO MANY PEOPLE APPLYING TO WORK FOR ME.
GLAD I COULD HELP!
AND MISS BEELZEBUB BUYS A WHOLE CASE THREE TO FOUR TIMES A WEEK!
HEAVY USER MIGHT BE AN UNDER-STATEMENT, THEN...

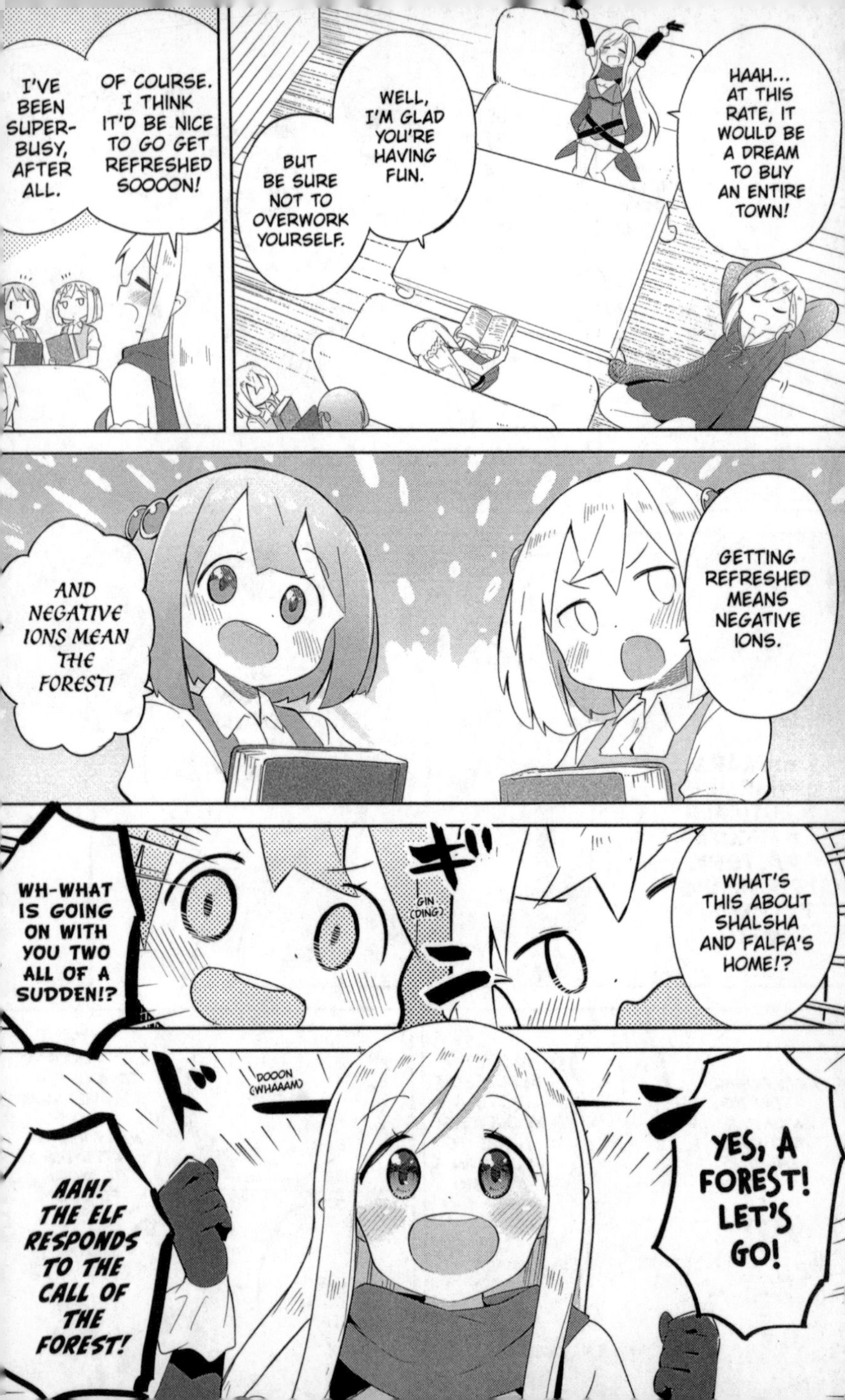
HAAH... AT THIS RATE, IT WOULD BE A DREAM TO BUY AN ENTIRE TOWN!
WELL, I'M GLAD YOU'RE HAVING FUN.
BUT BE SURE NOT TO OVERWORK YOURSELF.
OF COURSE. I THINK IT'D BE NICE TO GO GET REFRESHED SOOOON!
I'VE BEEN SUPER-BUSY, AFTER ALL.
GETTING REFRESHED MEANS NEGATIVE IONS.
AND NEGATIVE IONS MEAN THE FOREST!
WHAT'S THIS ABOUT SHALSHA AND FALFA'S HOME!?
GIN (DING)
WH-WHAT IS GOING ON WITH YOU TWO ALL OF A SUDDEN!?
YES, A FOREST! LET'S GO!
DOOON (WHAAAM)
AAH! THE ELF RESPONDS TO THE CALL OF THE FOREST!

CHAPTER 17
The Girls Go Home for a Visit

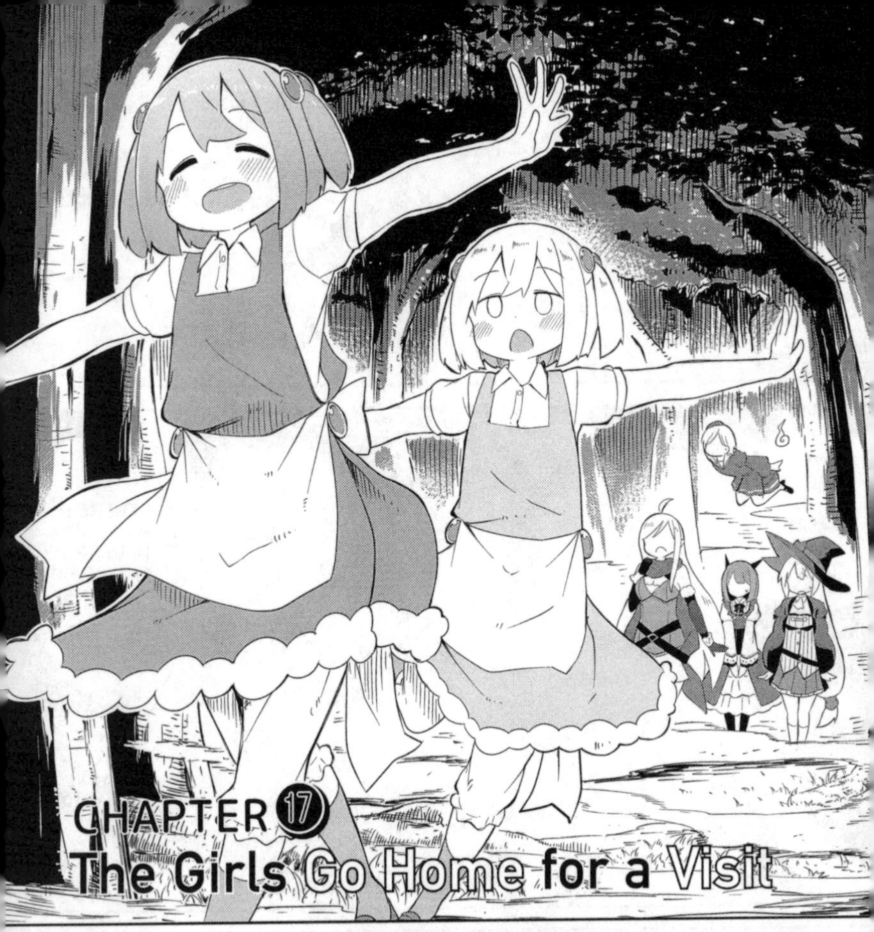

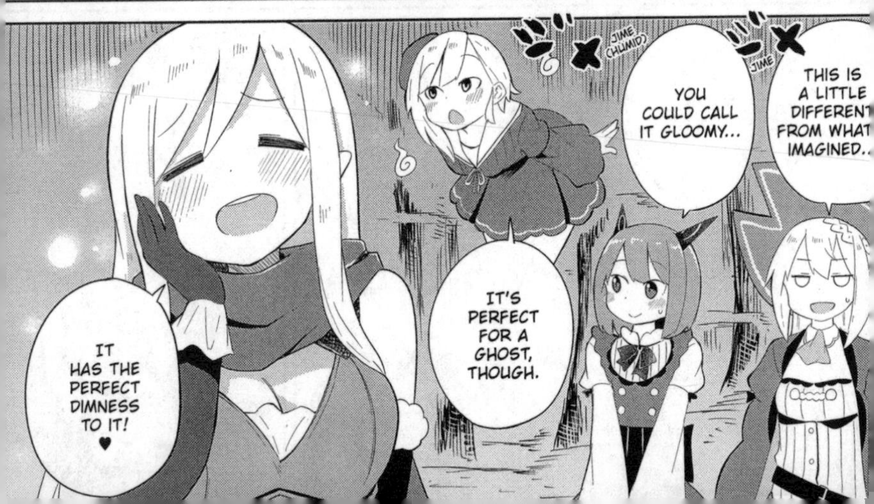
JIME
THIS IS A LITTLE DIFFERENT FROM WHAT IMAGINED...
JIME (HUMID)
YOU COULD CALL IT GLOOMY...
IT'S PERFECT FOR A GHOST, THOUGH.
IT HAS THE PERFECT DIMNESS TO IT! ♥

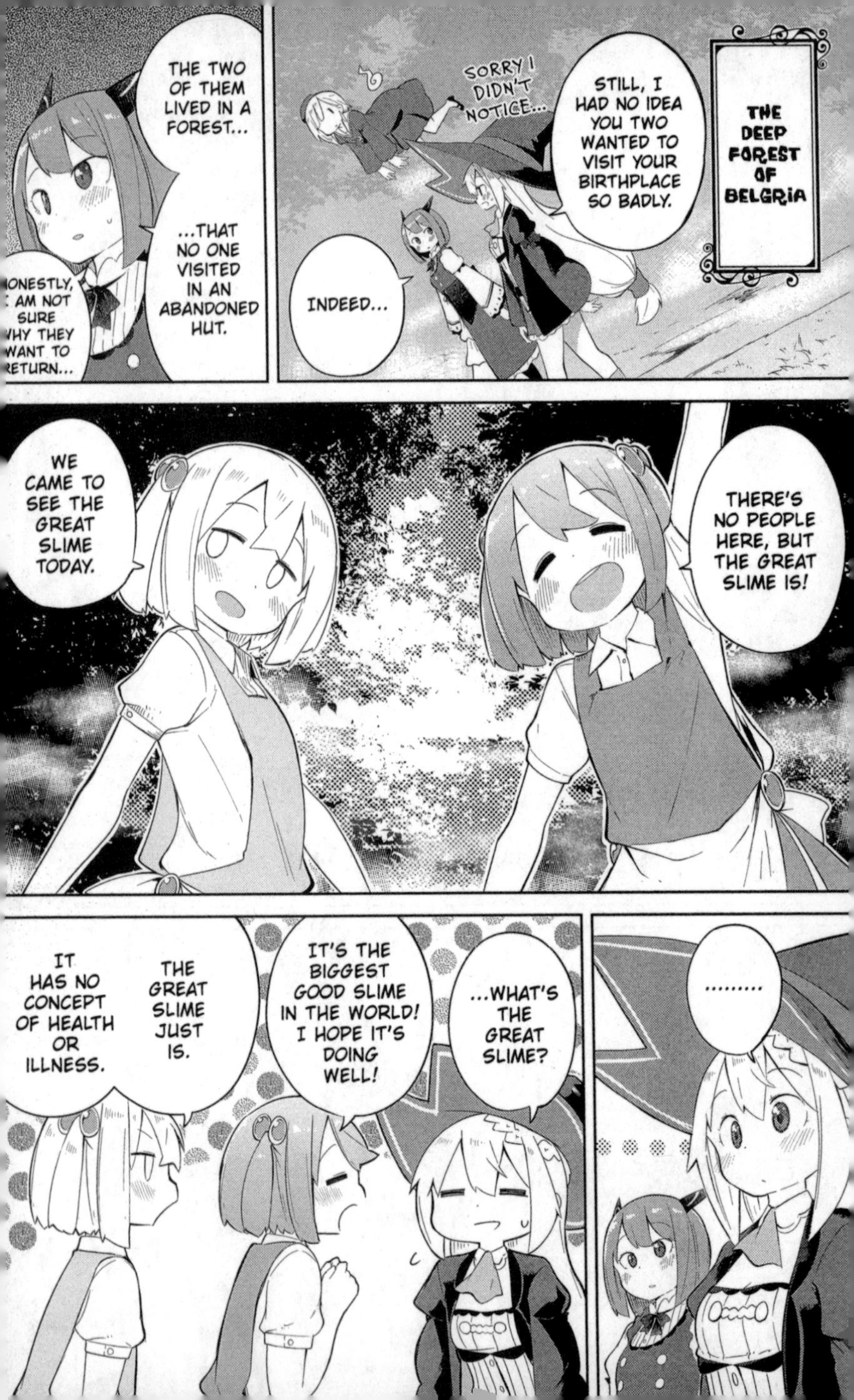
THE DEEP FOREST OF BELGRIA
STILL, I HAD NO IDEA YOU TWO WANTED TO VISIT YOUR BIRTHPLACE SO BADLY.
SORRY I DIDN'T NOTICE...
INDEED...
THE TWO OF THEM LIVED IN A FOREST...
...THAT NO ONE VISITED IN AN ABANDONED HUT.
HONESTLY, I AM NOT SURE WHY THEY WANT TO RETURN...
THERE'S NO PEOPLE HERE, BUT THE GREAT SLIME IS!
WE CAME TO SEE THE GREAT SLIME TODAY.
....
...WHAT'S THE GREAT SLIME?
IT'S THE BIGGEST GOOD SLIME IN THE WORLD! I HOPE IT'S DOING WELL!
THE GREAT SLIME JUST IS.
IT HAS NO CONCEPT OF HEALTH OR ILLNESS.

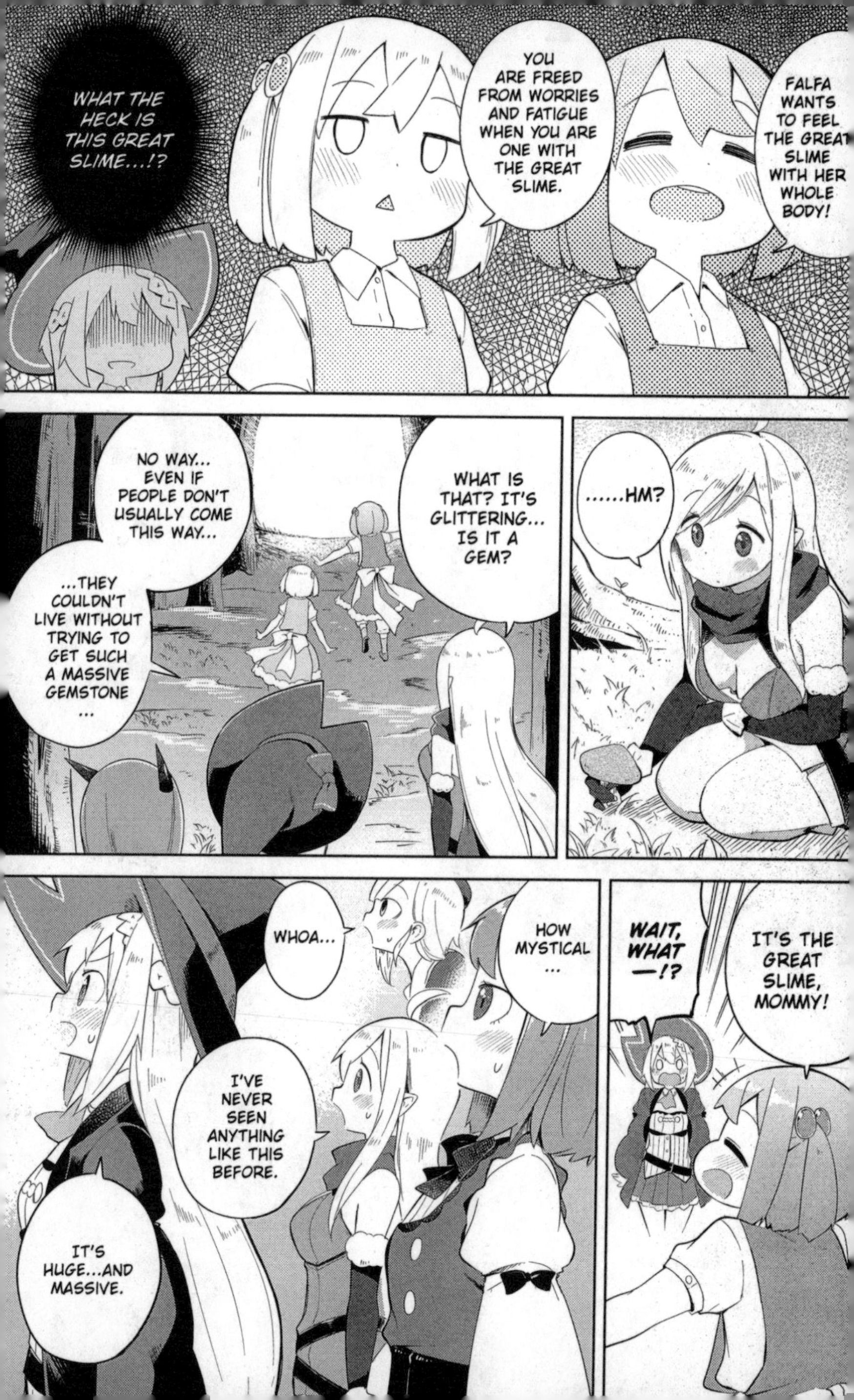
FALFA WANTS TO FEEL THE GREAT SLIME WITH HER WHOLE BODY!
YOU ARE FREED FROM WORRIES AND FATIGUE WHEN YOU ARE ONE WITH THE GREAT SLIME.
WHAT THE HECK IS THIS GREAT SLIME...!?
......HM?
WHAT IS THAT? IT'S GLITTERING... IS IT A GEM?
NO WAY... EVEN IF PEOPLE DON'T USUALLY COME THIS WAY...
...THEY COULDN'T LIVE WITHOUT TRYING TO GET SUCH A MASSIVE GEMSTONE ...
IT'S THE GREAT SLIME, MOMMY!
WAIT, WHAT—!?
HOW MYSTICAL ...
WHOA...
I'VE NEVER SEEN ANYTHING LIKE THIS BEFORE.
IT'S HUGE...AND MASSIVE.

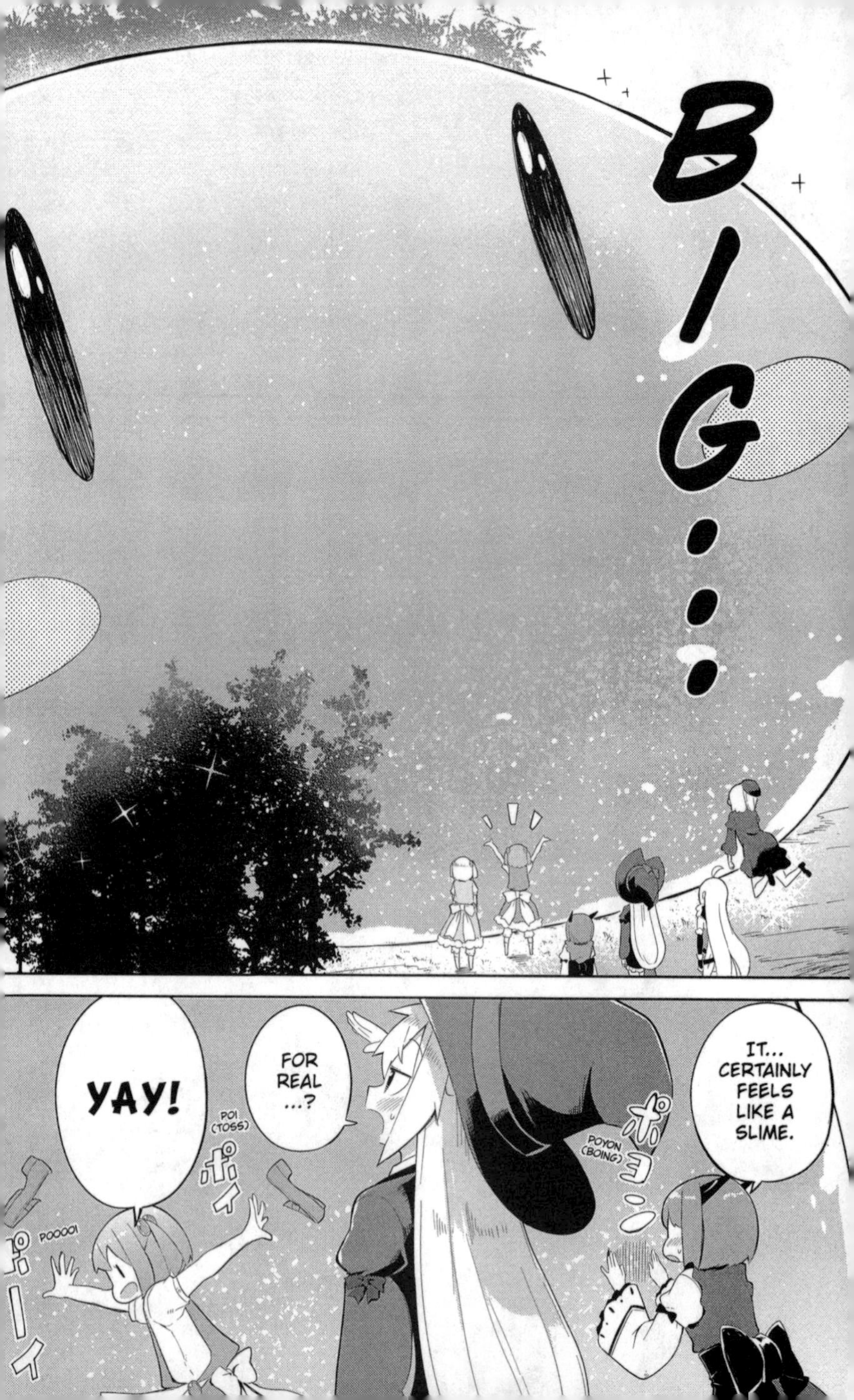
BIG...
IT... CERTAINLY FEELS LIKE A SLIME.
POYON (BOING)
ポヨン
FOR REAL ...?
POI (TOSS)
ポイ
YAY!
POOOOI
ポーーイ

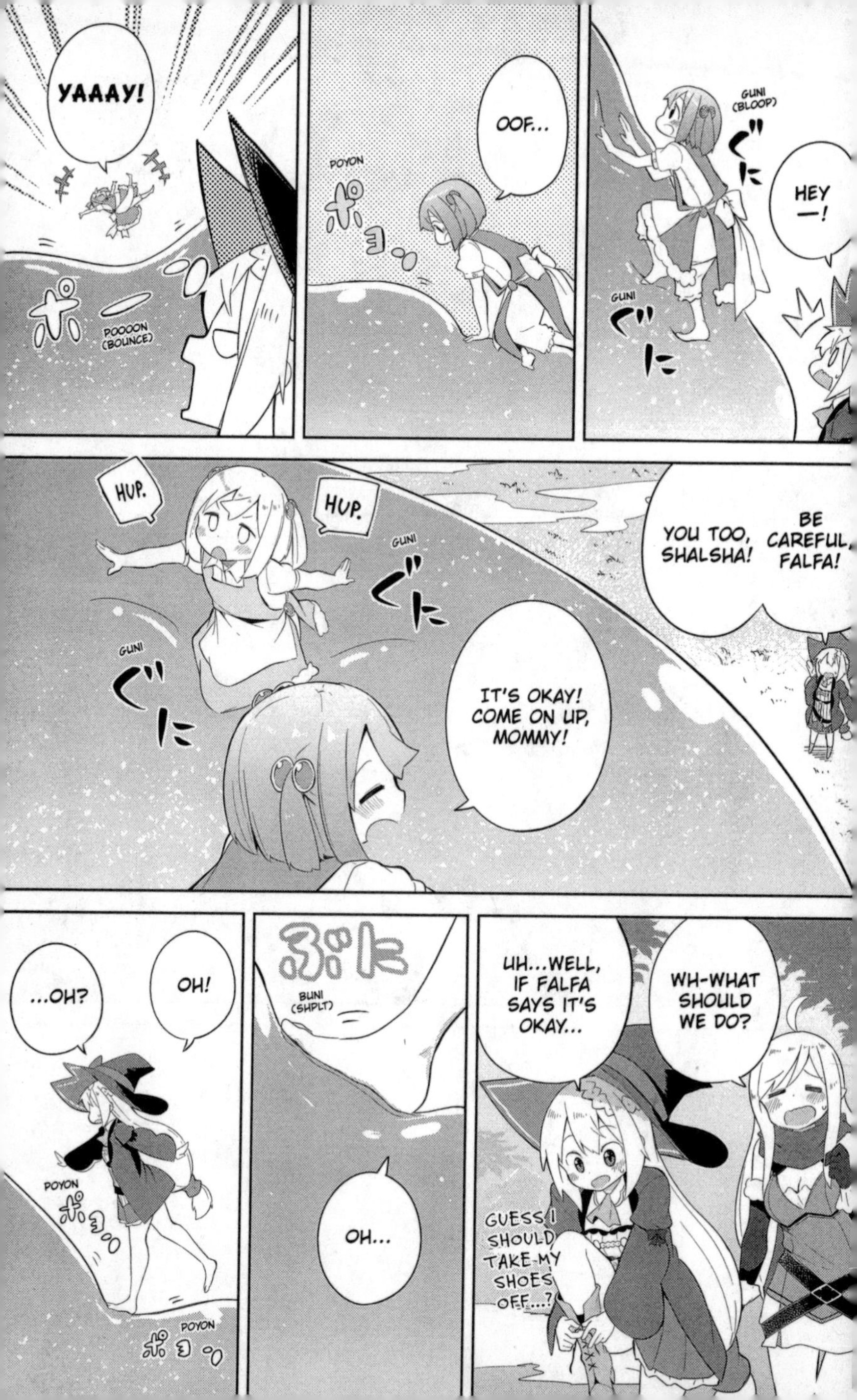
GUNI (BLOOP)
HEY—!
GUNI
OOF...
POYON
YAAAY!
POOOON (BOUNCE)
BE CAREFUL, FALFA!
YOU TOO, SHALSHA!
HUP.
HUP.
GUNI
GUNI
IT'S OKAY! COME ON UP, MOMMY!
WH-WHAT SHOULD WE DO?
UH...WELL, IF FALFA SAYS IT'S OKAY...
GUESS I SHOULD TAKE MY SHOES OFF...?
BUNI (SHPLT)
OH...
OH!
...OH?
POYON
POYON

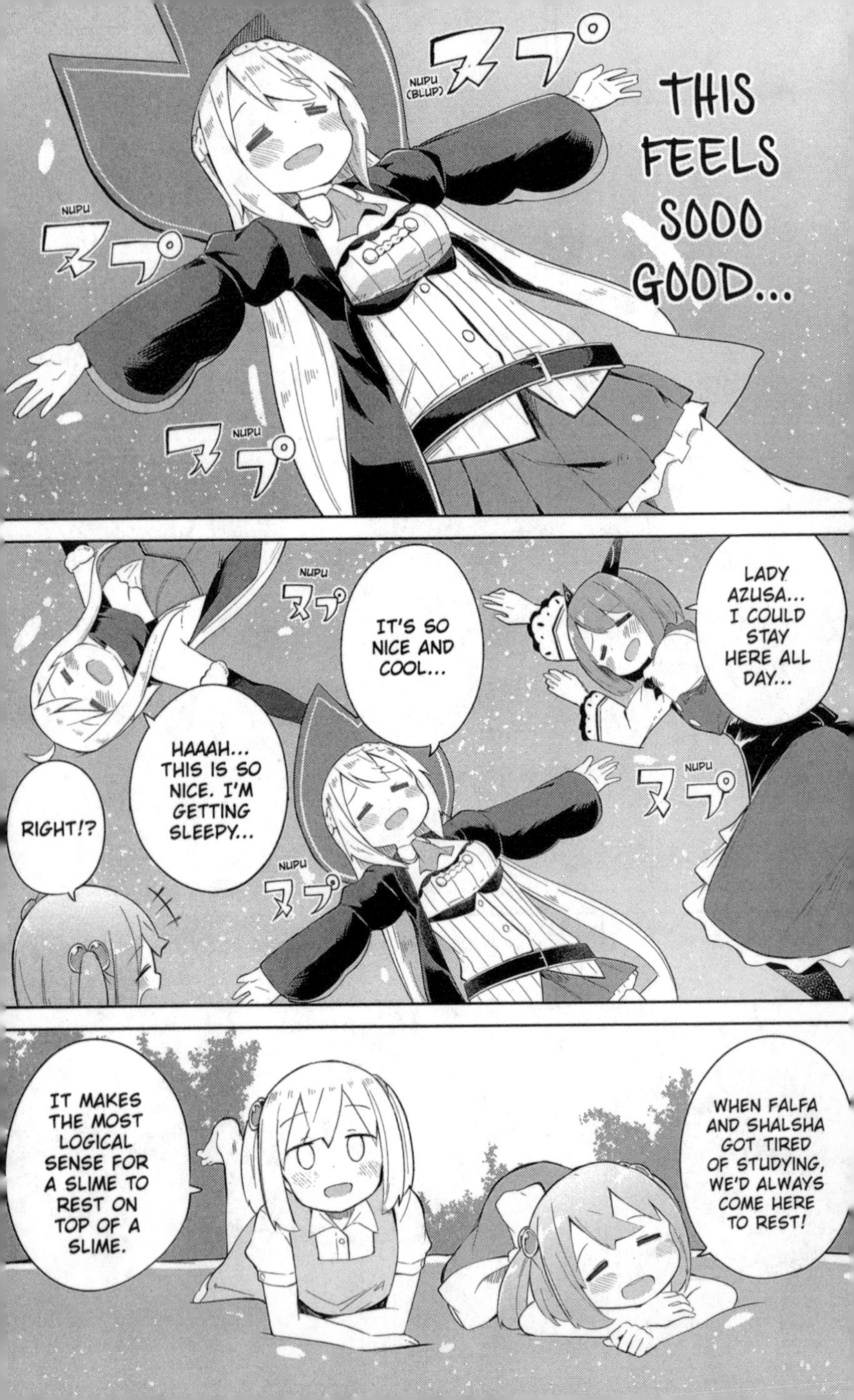
THIS FEELS SOOO GOOD...
NUPU (BLUP)
NUPU
NUPU
LADY AZUSA... I COULD STAY HERE ALL DAY...
NUPU
IT'S SO NICE AND COOL...
NUPU
HAAAH... THIS IS SO NICE. I'M GETTING SLEEPY...
NUPU
RIGHT!?
WHEN FALFA AND SHALSHA GOT TIRED OF STUDYING, WE'D ALWAYS COME HERE TO REST!
IT MAKES THE MOST LOGICAL SENSE FOR A SLIME TO REST ON TOP OF A SLIME.

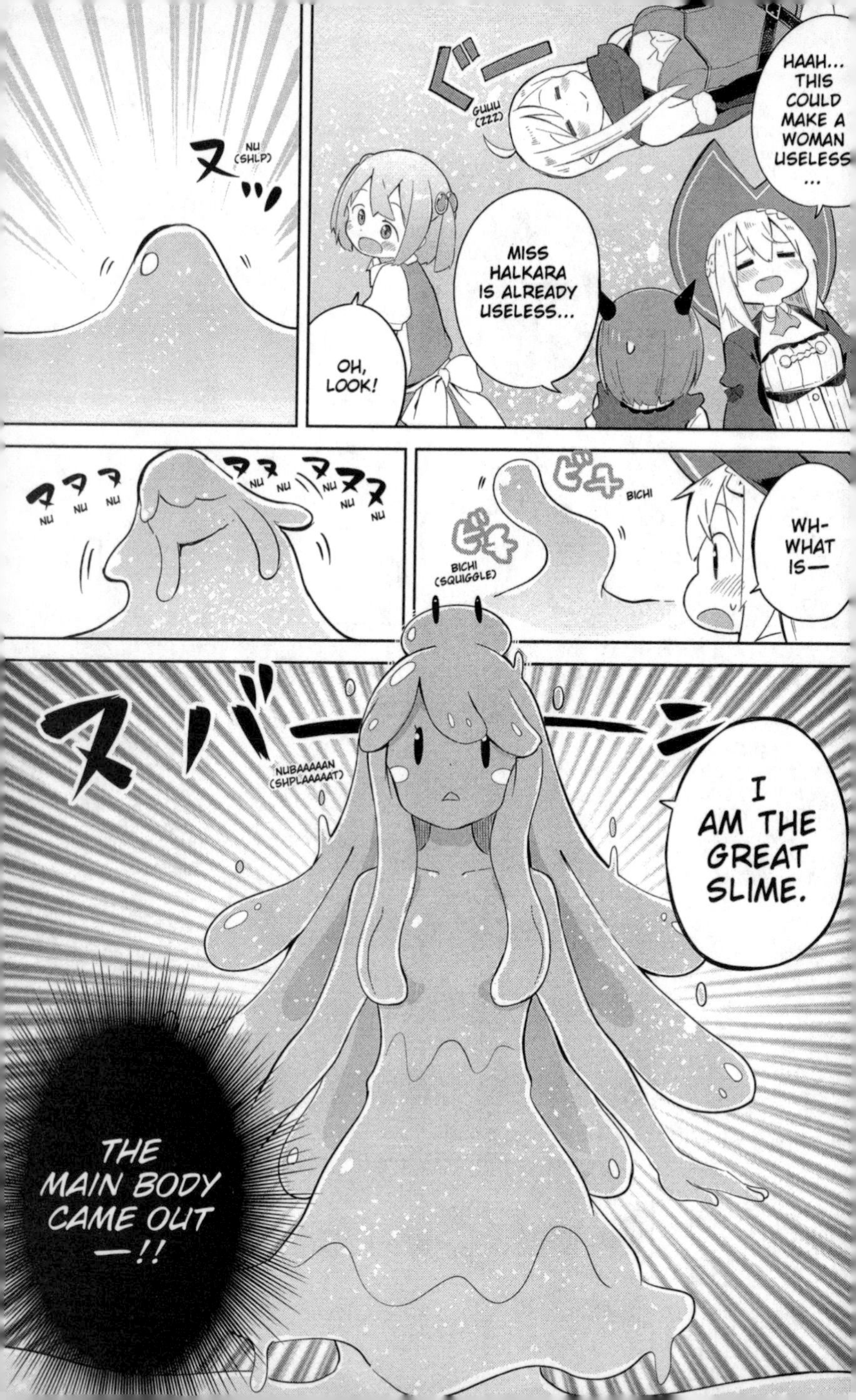
HAAH... THIS COULD MAKE A WOMAN USELESS...
GUUU (ZZZ)
MISS HALKARA IS ALREADY USELESS...
OH, LOOK!
NU (SHLP)
WH-WHAT IS—
BICHI
BICHI (SQUIGGLE)
NU NU NU NU NU NU NU NU NU
NUBAAAAAN (SHPLAAAAAT)
I AM THE GREAT SLIME.
THE MAIN BODY CAME OUT—!!

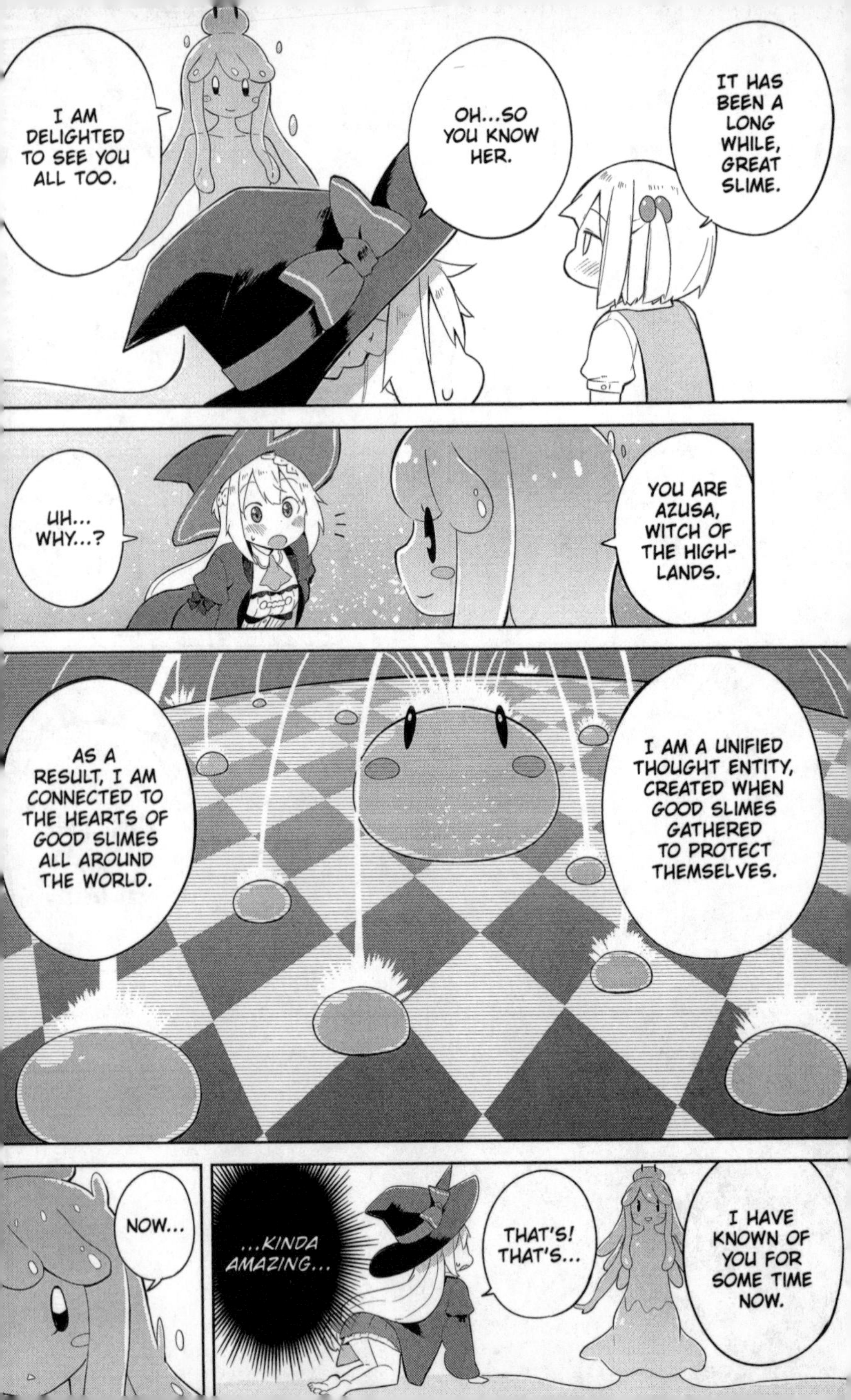
IT HAS BEEN A LONG WHILE, GREAT SLIME.
OH...SO YOU KNOW HER.
I AM DELIGHTED TO SEE YOU ALL TOO.
YOU ARE AZUSA, WITCH OF THE HIGH-LANDS.
UH... WHY...?
I AM A UNIFIED THOUGHT ENTITY, CREATED WHEN GOOD SLIMES GATHERED TO PROTECT THEMSELVES.
AS A RESULT, I AM CONNECTED TO THE HEARTS OF GOOD SLIMES ALL AROUND THE WORLD.
I HAVE KNOWN OF YOU FOR SOME TIME NOW.
THAT'S! THAT'S...
...KINDA AMAZING...
NOW...

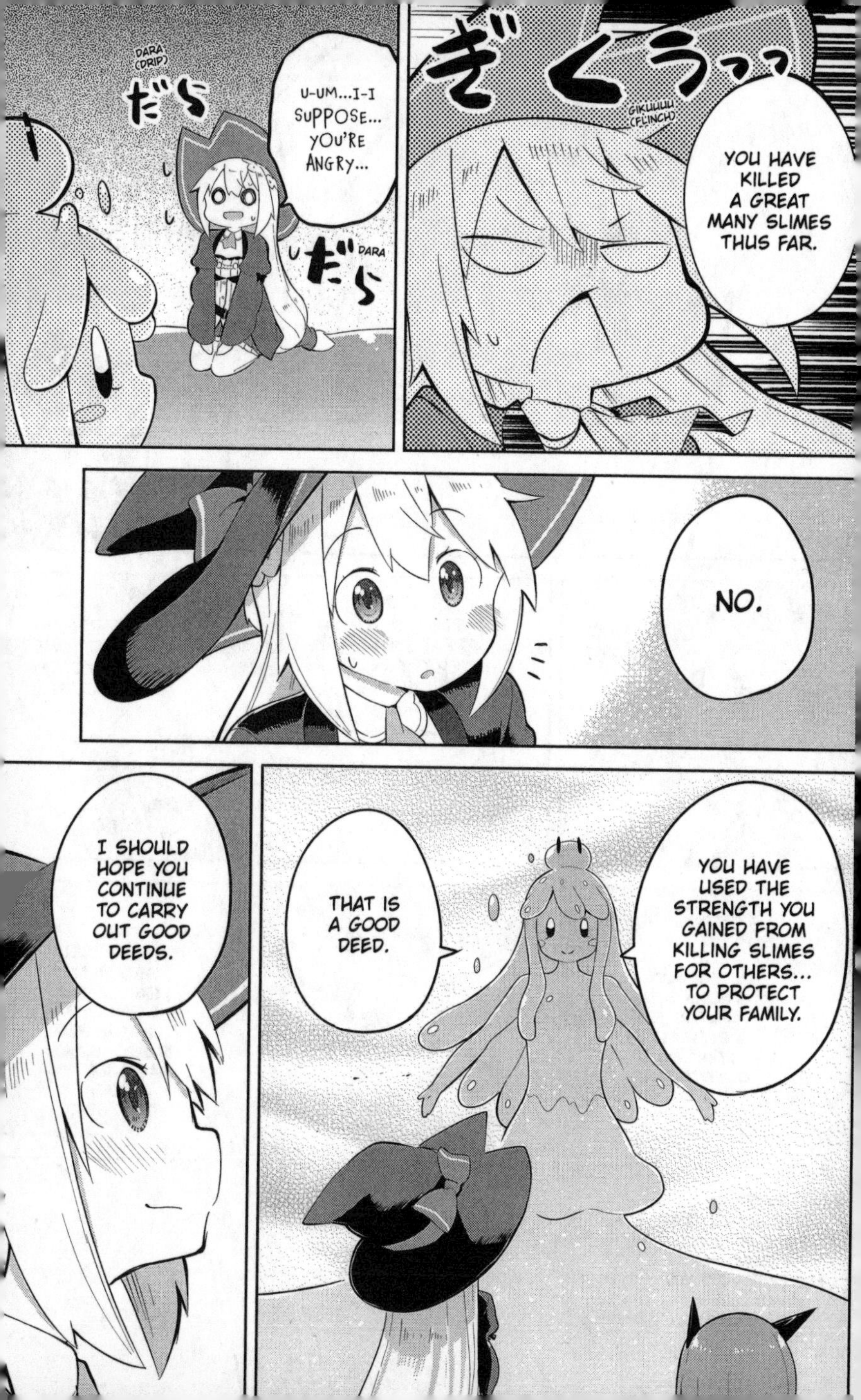
ぎくぅっっ
GIKUUUU (FLINCH)
YOU HAVE KILLED A GREAT MANY SLIMES THUS FAR.
DARA (DRIP)
だら
U-UM...I-I SUPPOSE... YOU'RE ANGRY...
だら
DARA
NO.
YOU HAVE USED THE STRENGTH YOU GAINED FROM KILLING SLIMES FOR OTHERS... TO PROTECT YOUR FAMILY.
THAT IS A GOOD DEED.
I SHOULD HOPE YOU CONTINUE TO CARRY OUT GOOD DEEDS.

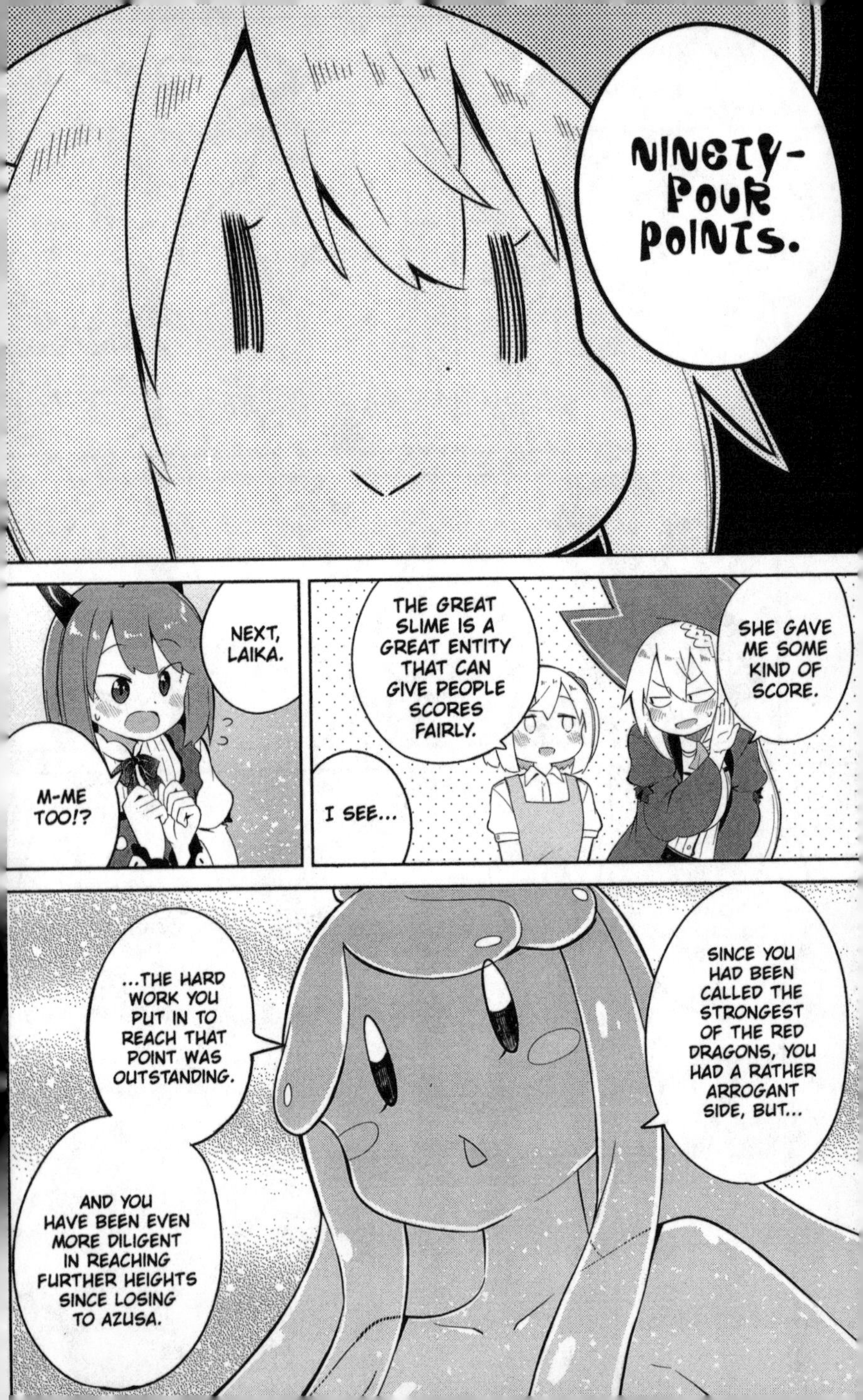
NINETY-FOUR POINTS.
SHE GAVE ME SOME KIND OF SCORE.
THE GREAT SLIME IS A GREAT ENTITY THAT CAN GIVE PEOPLE SCORES FAIRLY.
I SEE...
NEXT, LAIKA.
M-ME TOO!?
SINCE YOU HAD BEEN CALLED THE STRONGEST OF THE RED DRAGONS, YOU HAD A RATHER ARROGANT SIDE, BUT...
...THE HARD WORK YOU PUT IN TO REACH THAT POINT WAS OUTSTANDING.
AND YOU HAVE BEEN EVEN MORE DILIGENT IN REACHING FURTHER HEIGHTS SINCE LOSING TO AZUSA.

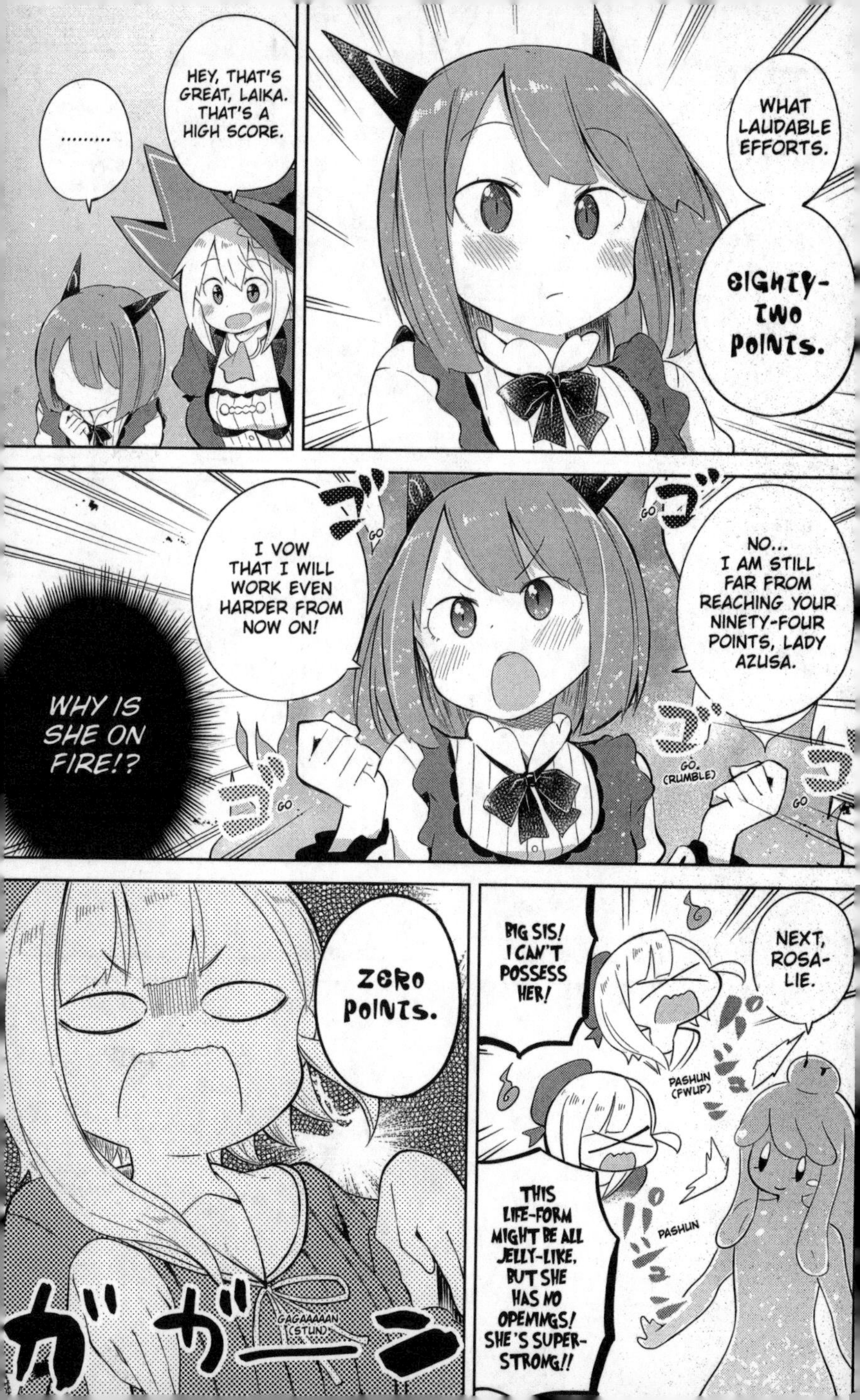
WHAT LAUDABLE EFFORTS.
EIGHTY-TWO POINTS.
HEY, THAT'S GREAT, LAIKA. THAT'S A HIGH SCORE.
....
GO
NO... I AM STILL FAR FROM REACHING YOUR NINETY-FOUR POINTS, LADY AZUSA.
GO
I VOW THAT I WILL WORK EVEN HARDER FROM NOW ON!
GO (RUMBLE)
GO
GO
WHY IS SHE ON FIRE!?
NEXT, ROSA-LIE.
BIG SIS! I CAN'T POSSESS HER!
PASHUN (FWUP)
PASHUN
THIS LIFE-FORM MIGHT BE ALL JELLY-LIKE, BUT SHE HAS NO OPEMINGS! SHE'S SUPER-STRONG!!
ZERO POINTS.
GAGAAAAAN (STUN)

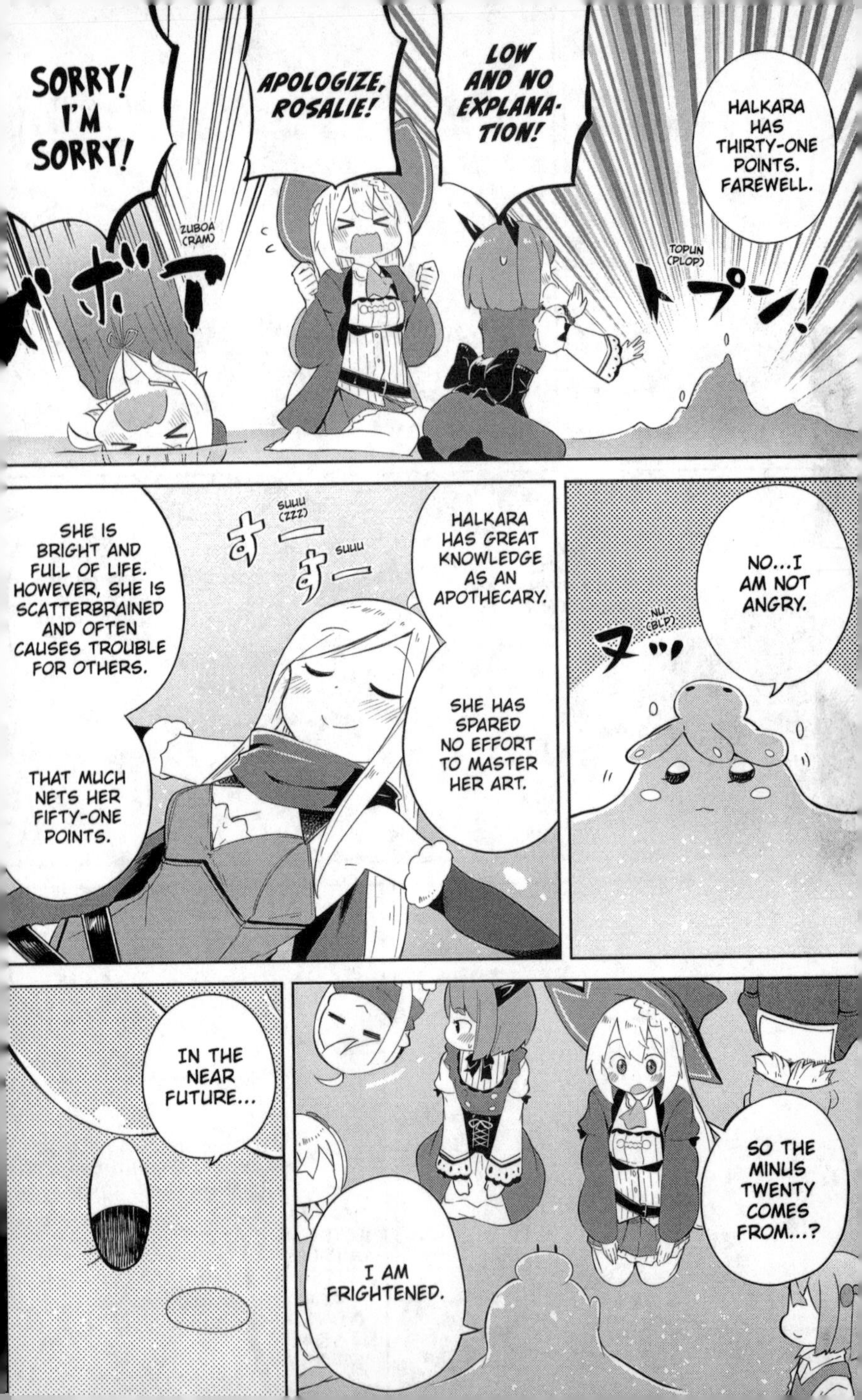
HALKARA HAS THIRTY-ONE POINTS. FAREWELL.
TOPUN (PLOP)
トプン!
LOW AND NO EXPLANATION!
APOLOGIZE, ROSALIE!
SORRY! I'M SORRY!
ZUBOA (RAM)
ズボァ
NO...I AM NOT ANGRY.
NU (BLP)
ヌッ
HALKARA HAS GREAT KNOWLEDGE AS AN APOTHECARY.
SUUU (ZZZ)
すー
SUUU
すー
SHE HAS SPARED NO EFFORT TO MASTER HER ART.
SHE IS BRIGHT AND FULL OF LIFE. HOWEVER, SHE IS SCATTERBRAINED AND OFTEN CAUSES TROUBLE FOR OTHERS.
THAT MUCH NETS HER FIFTY-ONE POINTS.
SO THE MINUS TWENTY COMES FROM...?
I AM FRIGHTENED.
IN THE NEAR FUTURE...

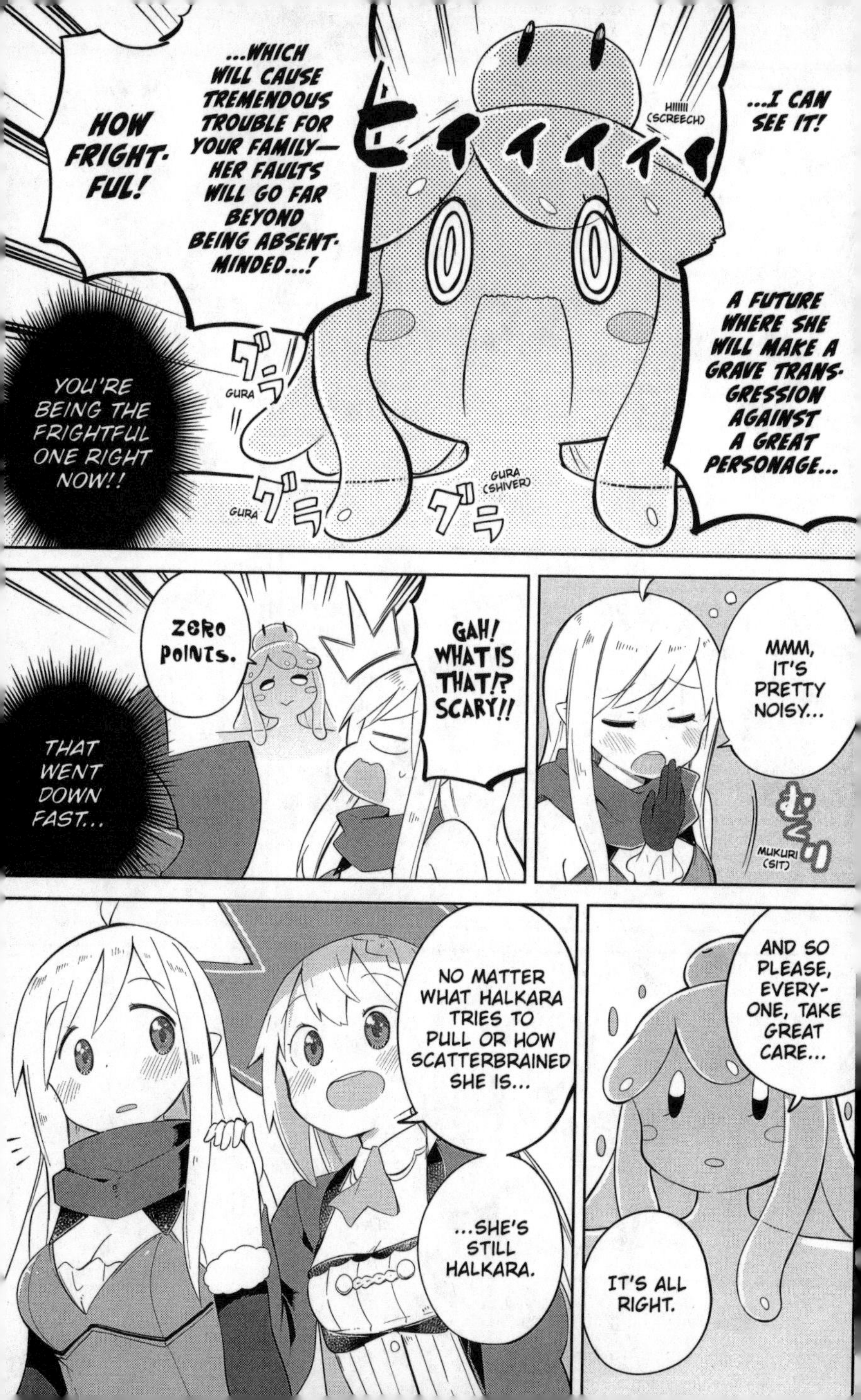
...I CAN SEE IT!
A FUTURE WHERE SHE WILL MAKE A GRAVE TRANSGRESSION AGAINST A GREAT PERSONAGE...
HIIIIII (SCREECH)
...WHICH WILL CAUSE TREMENDOUS TROUBLE FOR YOUR FAMILY—HER FAULTS WILL GO FAR BEYOND BEING ABSENT-MINDED...!
HOW FRIGHTFUL!
GURA (SHIVER)
GURA
GURA
YOU'RE BEING THE FRIGHTFUL ONE RIGHT NOW!!
MMM, IT'S PRETTY NOISY...
MUKURI (SIT)
GAH! WHAT IS THAT!? SCARY!!
ZERO POINTS.
THAT WENT DOWN FAST...
AND SO PLEASE, EVERYONE, TAKE GREAT CARE...
IT'S ALL RIGHT.
NO MATTER WHAT HALKARA TRIES TO PULL OR HOW SCATTERBRAINED SHE IS...
...SHE'S STILL HALKARA.

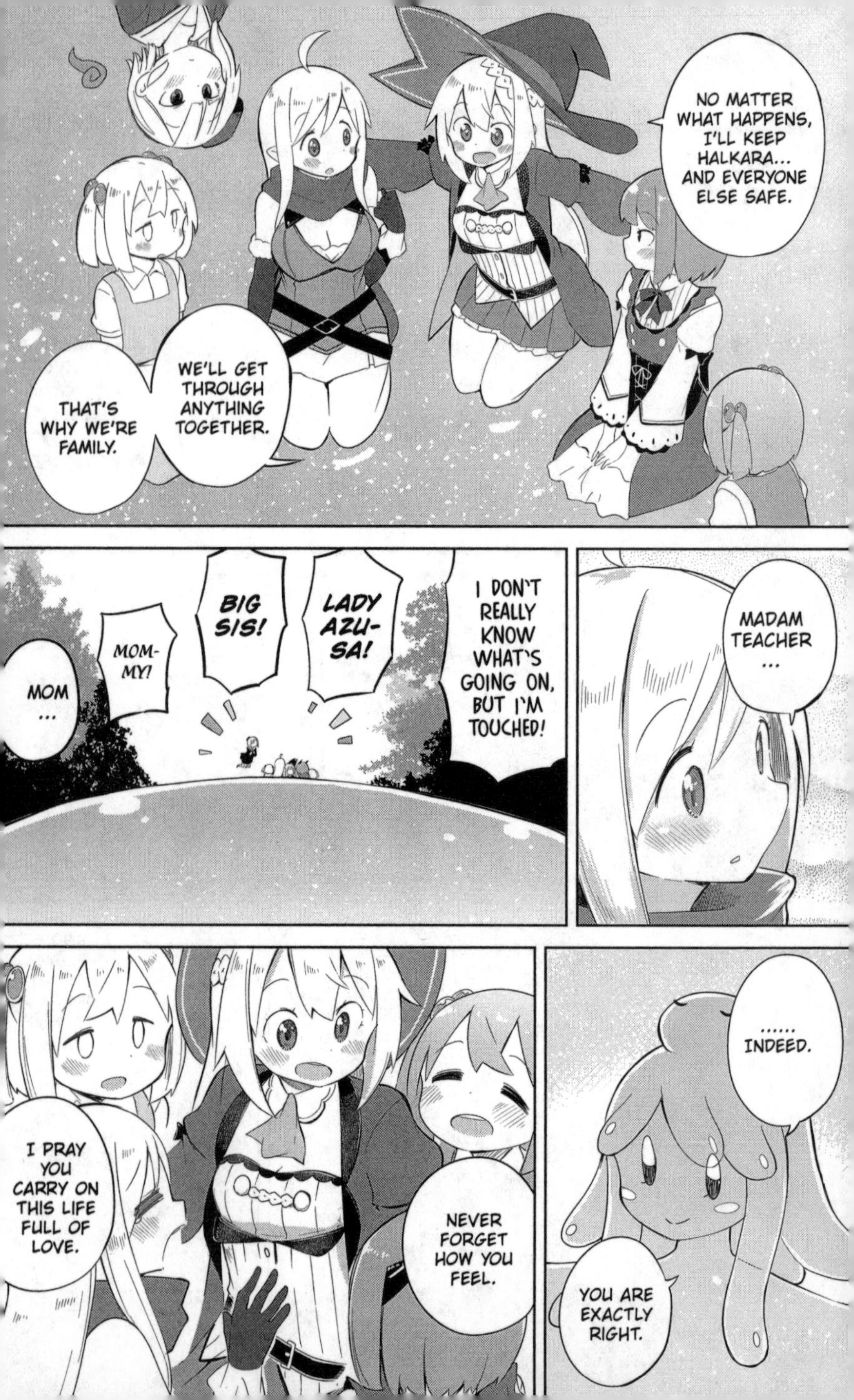
NO MATTER WHAT HAPPENS, I'LL KEEP HALKARA... AND EVERYONE ELSE SAFE.
WE'LL GET THROUGH ANYTHING TOGETHER.
THAT'S WHY WE'RE FAMILY.
MADAM TEACHER ...
I DON'T REALLY KNOW WHAT'S GOING ON, BUT I'M TOUCHED!
LADY AZU-SA!
BIG SIS!
MOM-MY!
MOM ...
...... INDEED.
YOU ARE EXACTLY RIGHT.
NEVER FORGET HOW YOU FEEL.
I PRAY YOU CARRY ON THIS LIFE FULL OF LOVE.

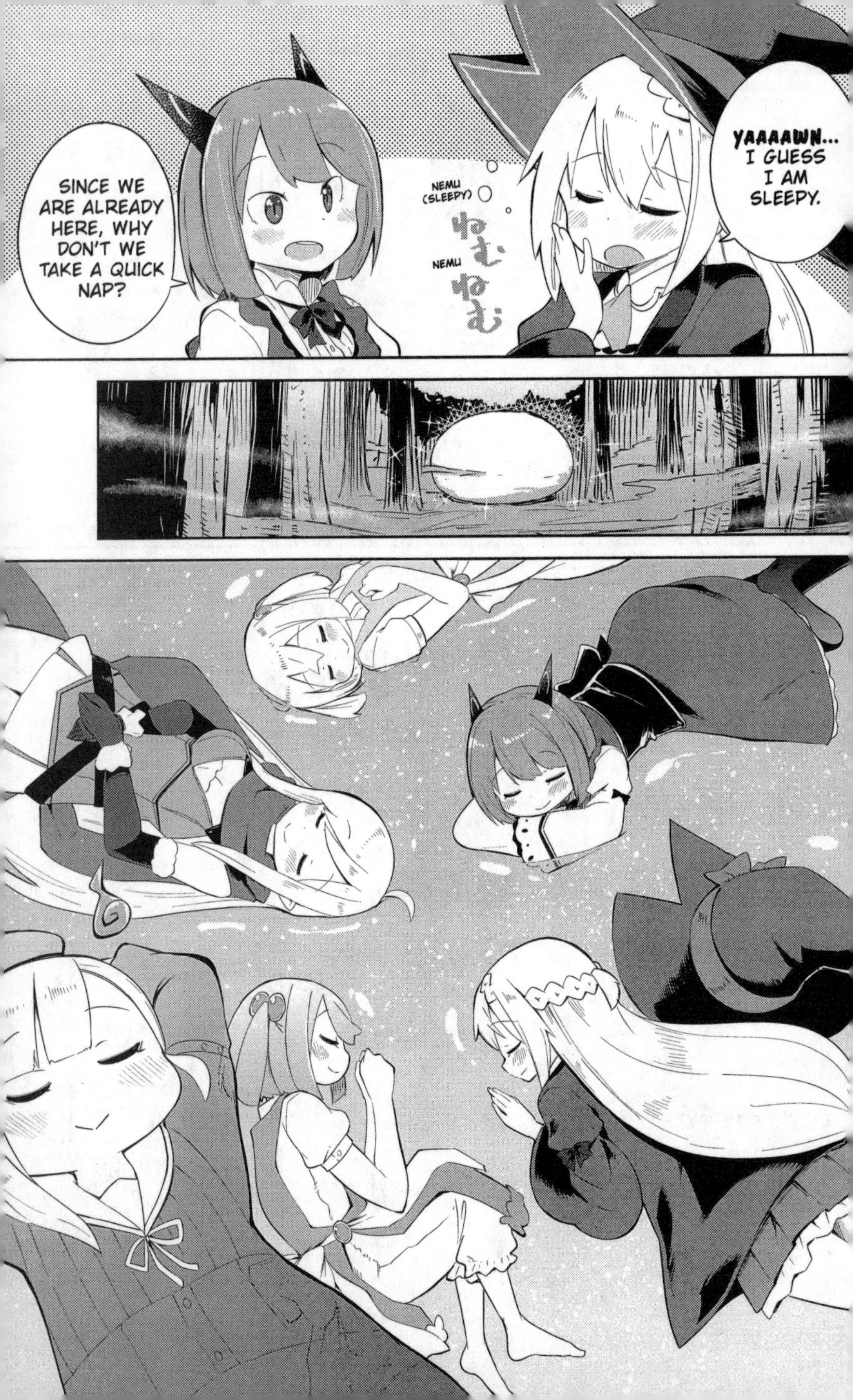

YAAAAWN... I GUESS I AM SLEEPY.
NEMU (SLEEPY)
ねむ
NEMU
ねむ
SINCE WE ARE ALREADY HERE, WHY DON'T WE TAKE A QUICK NAP?

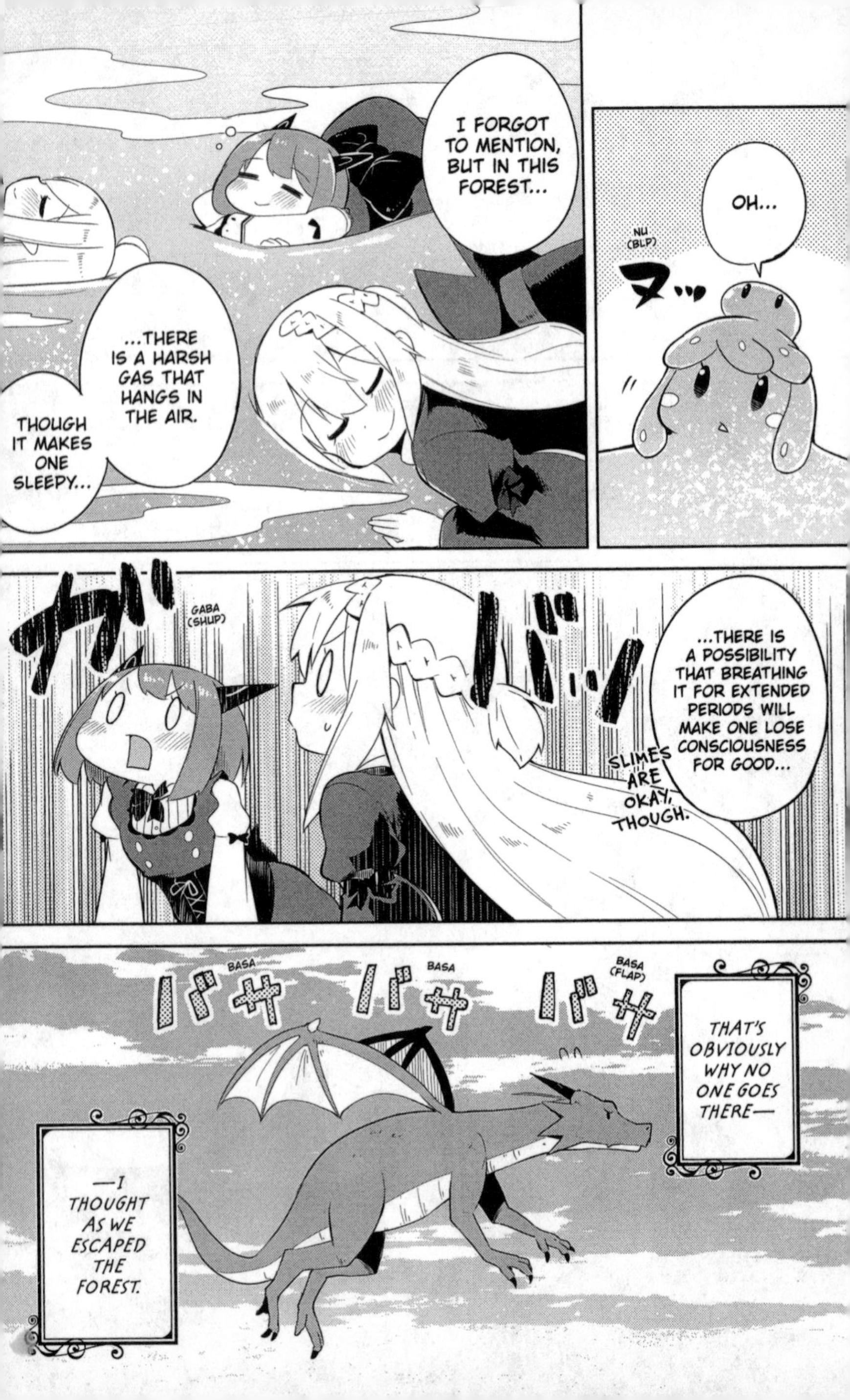
NU (BLP)
OH...
I FORGOT TO MENTION, BUT IN THIS FOREST...
...THERE IS A HARSH GAS THAT HANGS IN THE AIR.
THOUGH IT MAKES ONE SLEEPY...
...THERE IS A POSSIBILITY THAT BREATHING IT FOR EXTENDED PERIODS WILL MAKE ONE LOSE CONSCIOUSNESS FOR GOOD...
SLIMES ARE OKAY, THOUGH.
GABA (SHUP)
BASA (FLAP)
BASA
BASA
THAT'S OBVIOUSLY WHY NO ONE GOES THERE—
—I THOUGHT AS WE ESCAPED THE FOREST.

I've Been Killing SLIMES for 300 Years and Maxed Out My Level

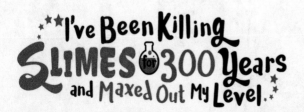

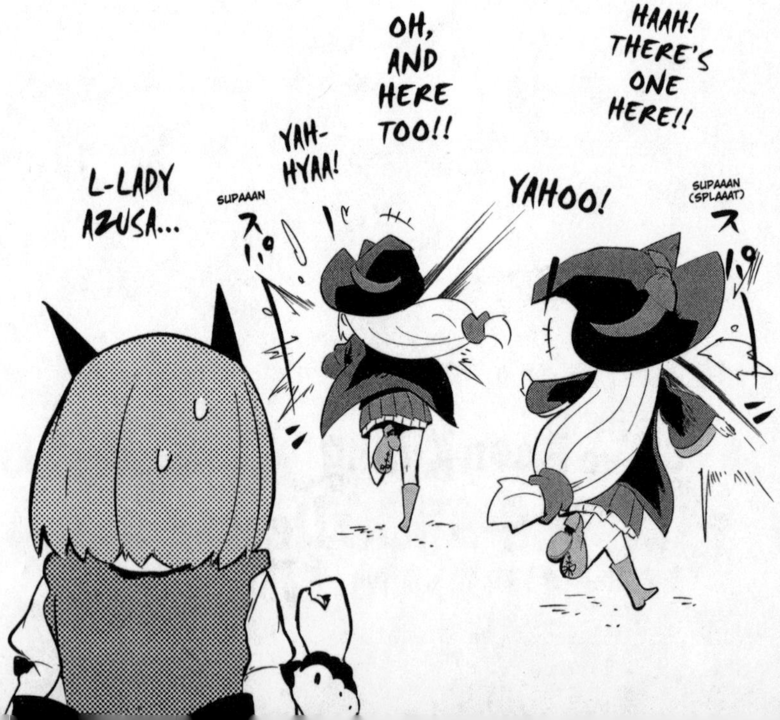
HAAH! THERE'S ONE HERE!!
SUPAAAN (SPLAAAT)
YAHOO!
OH, AND HERE TOO!!
YAH-HYAA!
SUPAAAN
L-LADY AZUSA...

CHAPTER 18 I Made a Dress for a Ghost

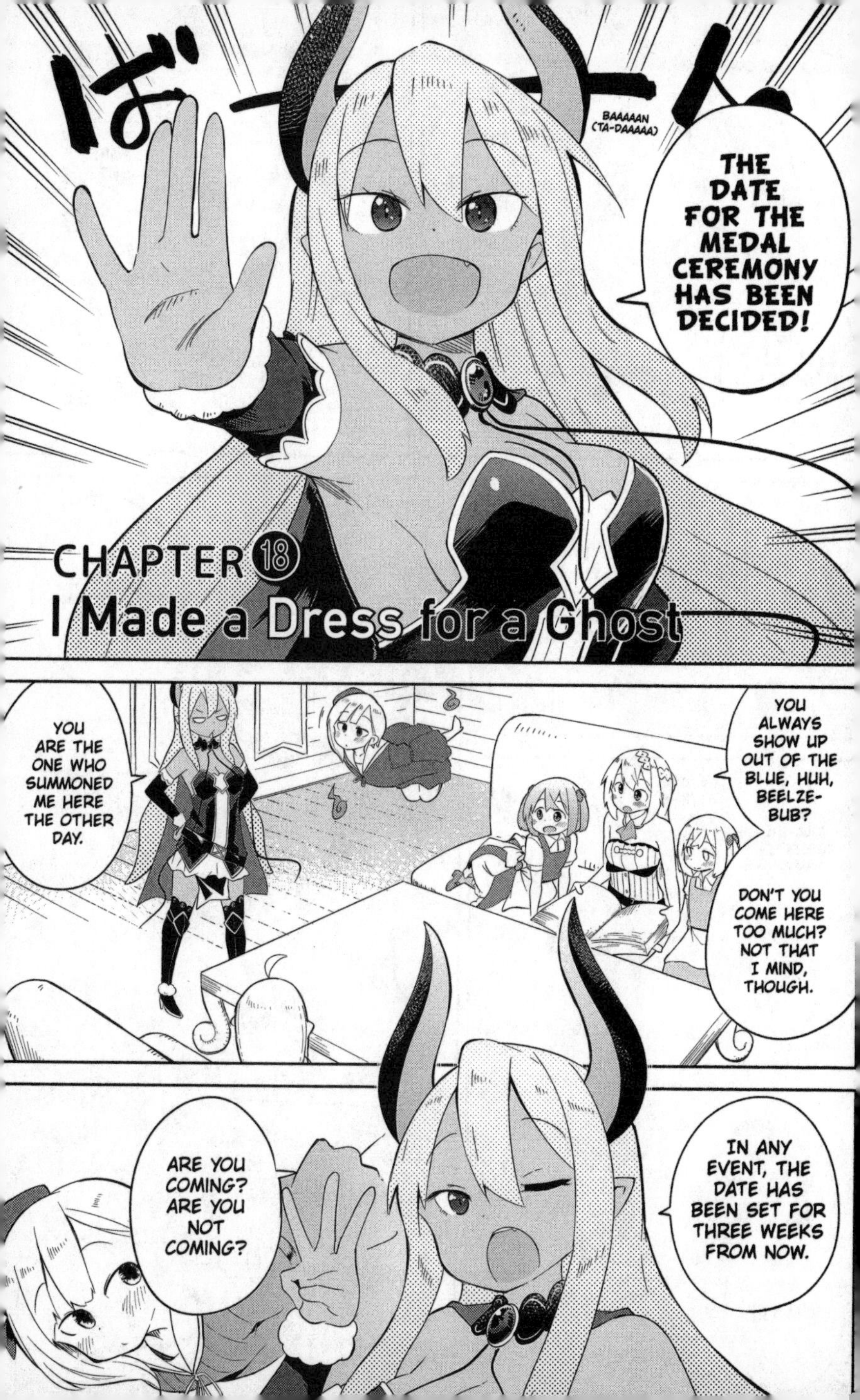
ばーん
BAAAAAN (TA-DAAAAA)
THE DATE FOR THE MEDAL CEREMONY HAS BEEN DECIDED!
YOU ALWAYS SHOW UP OUT OF THE BLUE, HUH, BEELZE-BUB?
DON'T YOU COME HERE TOO MUCH? NOT THAT I MIND, THOUGH.
YOU ARE THE ONE WHO SUMMONED ME HERE THE OTHER DAY.
IN ANY EVENT, THE DATE HAS BEEN SET FOR THREE WEEKS FROM NOW.
ARE YOU COMING? ARE YOU NOT COMING?

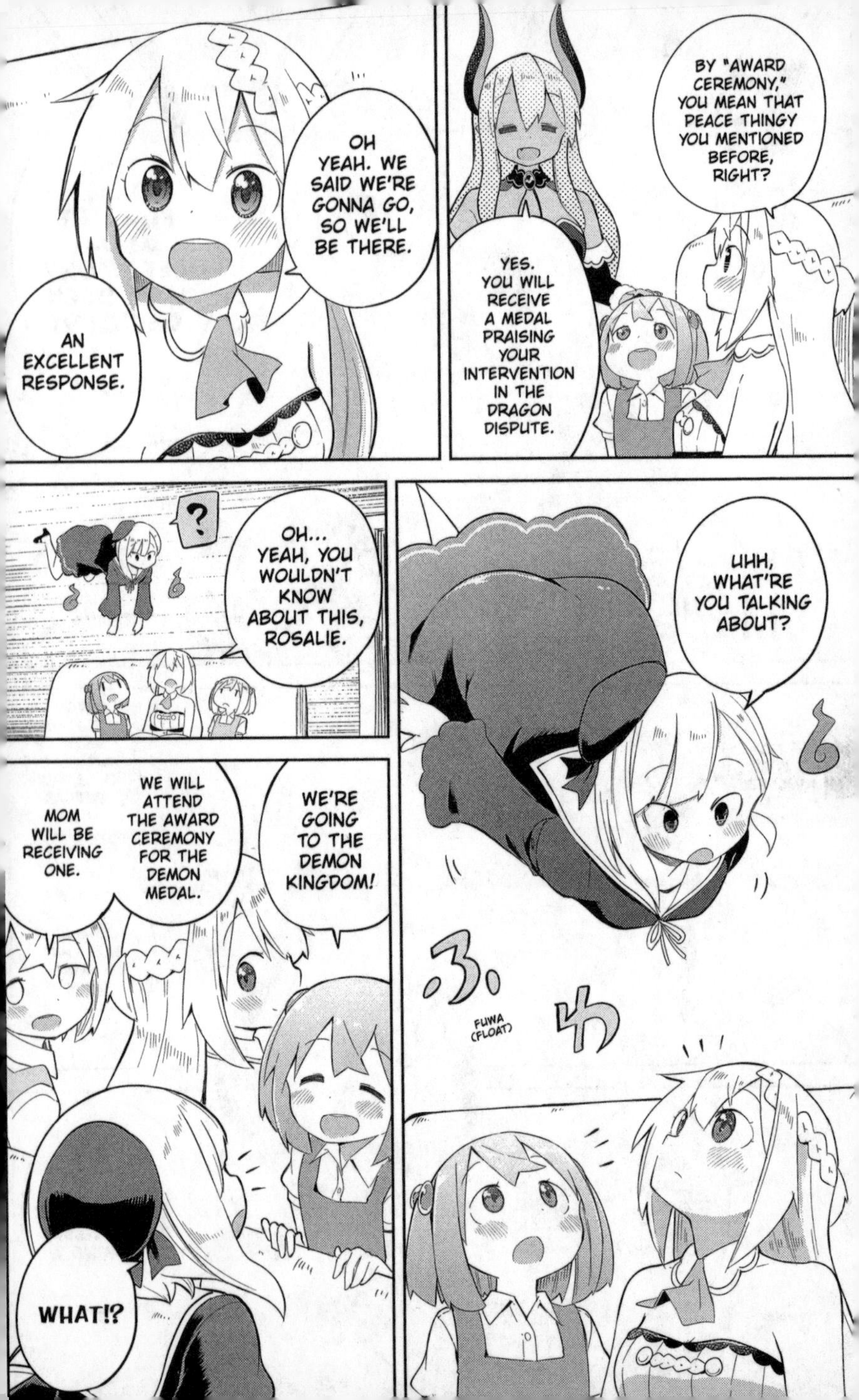
BY "AWARD CEREMONY," YOU MEAN THAT PEACE THINGY YOU MENTIONED BEFORE, RIGHT?
YES. YOU WILL RECEIVE A MEDAL PRAISING YOUR INTERVENTION IN THE DRAGON DISPUTE.
OH YEAH. WE SAID WE'RE GONNA GO, SO WE'LL BE THERE.
AN EXCELLENT RESPONSE.
UHH, WHAT'RE YOU TALKING ABOUT?
FUWA (FLOAT)
?
OH... YEAH, YOU WOULDN'T KNOW ABOUT THIS, ROSALIE.
WE'RE GOING TO THE DEMON KINGDOM!
WE WILL ATTEND THE AWARD CEREMONY FOR THE DEMON MEDAL.
MOM WILL BE RECEIVING ONE.
WHAT!?

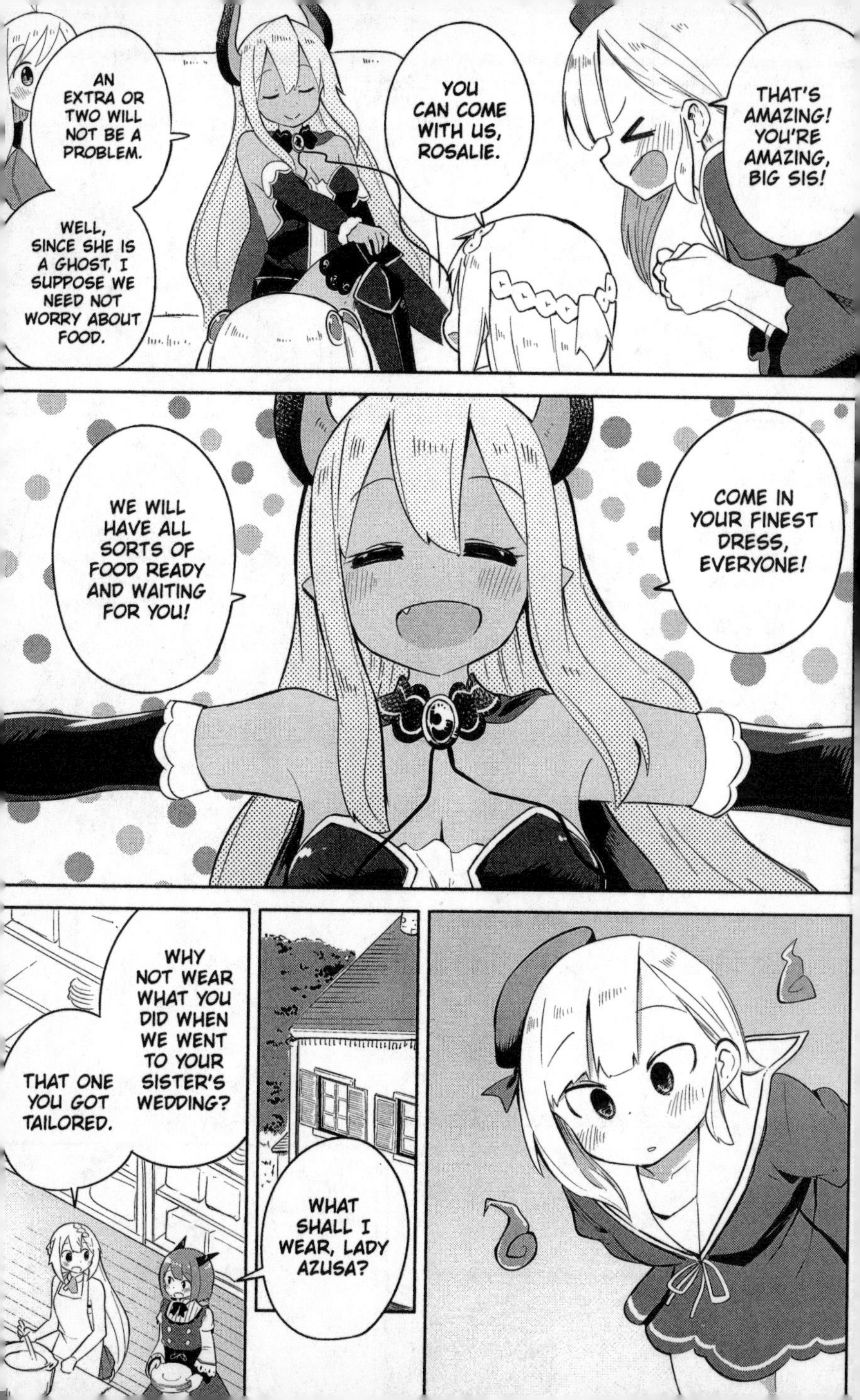
THAT'S AMAZING! YOU'RE AMAZING, BIG SIS!
YOU CAN COME WITH US, ROSALIE.
AN EXTRA OR TWO WILL NOT BE A PROBLEM.
WELL, SINCE SHE IS A GHOST, I SUPPOSE WE NEED NOT WORRY ABOUT FOOD.
COME IN YOUR FINEST DRESS, EVERYONE!
WE WILL HAVE ALL SORTS OF FOOD READY AND WAITING FOR YOU!
WHAT SHALL I WEAR, LADY AZUSA?
WHY NOT WEAR WHAT YOU DID WHEN WE WENT TO YOUR SISTER'S WEDDING?
THAT ONE YOU GOT TAILORED.

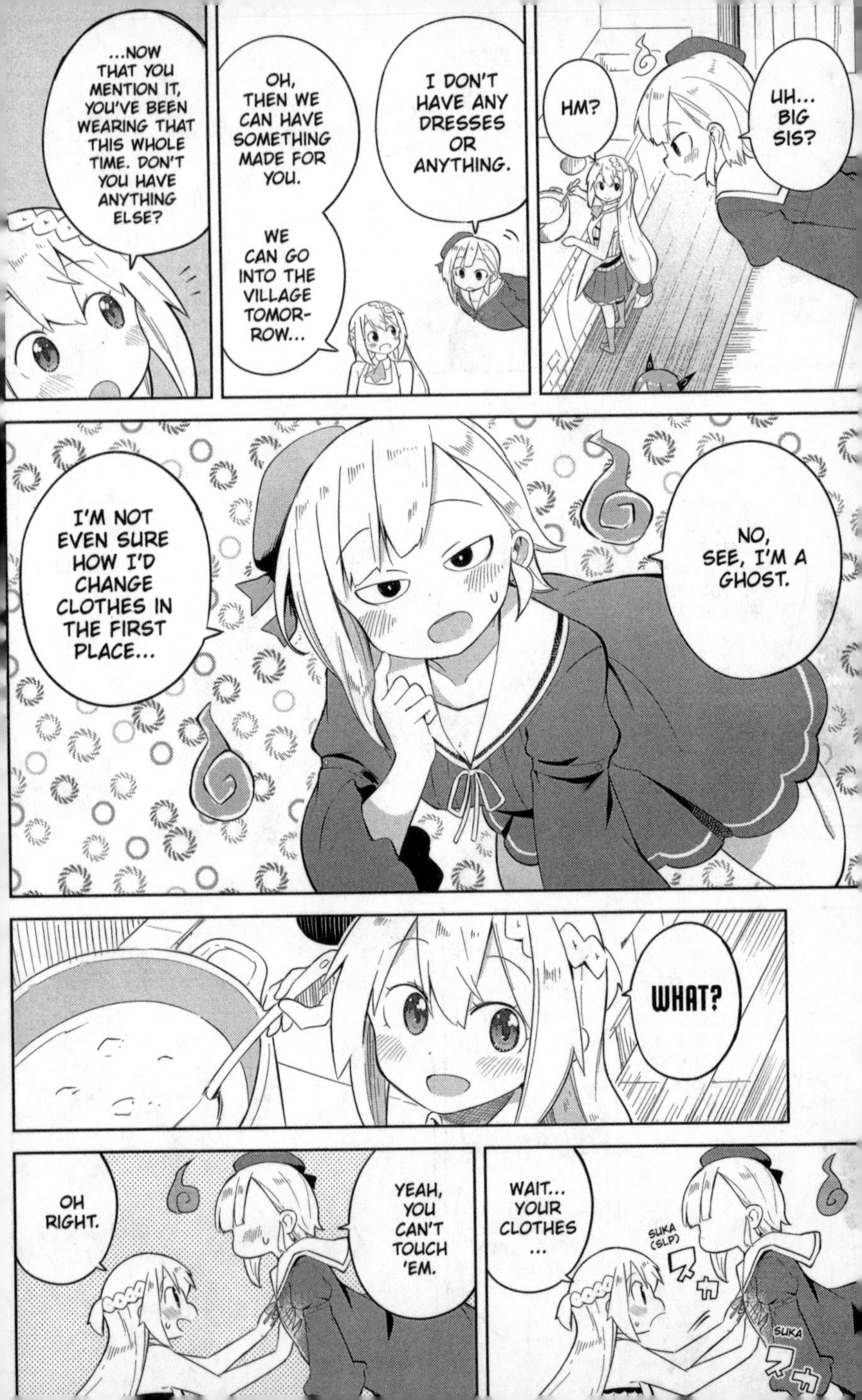
UH... BIG SIS?
HM?
I DON'T HAVE ANY DRESSES OR ANYTHING.
OH, THEN WE CAN HAVE SOMETHING MADE FOR YOU.
WE CAN GO INTO THE VILLAGE TOMOR-ROW...
...NOW THAT YOU MENTION IT, YOU'VE BEEN WEARING THAT THIS WHOLE TIME. DON'T YOU HAVE ANYTHING ELSE?
NO, SEE, I'M A GHOST.
I'M NOT EVEN SURE HOW I'D CHANGE CLOTHES IN THE FIRST PLACE...
WHAT?
WAIT... YOUR CLOTHES ...
SUKA (SLP)
SUKA
YEAH, YOU CAN'T TOUCH 'EM.
OH RIGHT.

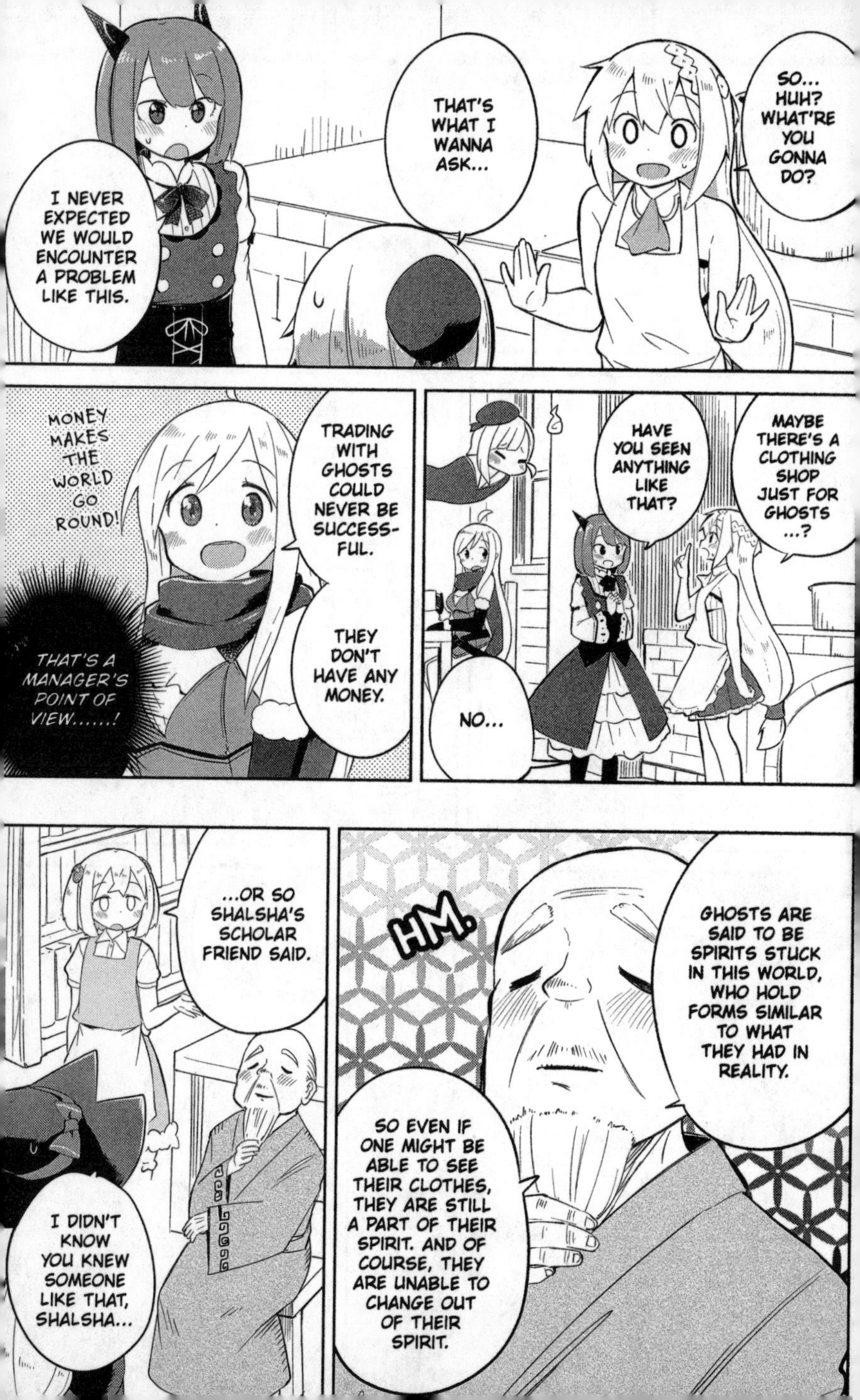
SO... HUH? WHAT'RE YOU GONNA DO?
THAT'S WHAT I WANNA ASK...
I NEVER EXPECTED WE WOULD ENCOUNTER A PROBLEM LIKE THIS.
MAYBE THERE'S A CLOTHING SHOP JUST FOR GHOSTS ...?
HAVE YOU SEEN ANYTHING LIKE THAT?
NO...
TRADING WITH GHOSTS COULD NEVER BE SUCCESS-FUL.
THEY DON'T HAVE ANY MONEY.
MONEY MAKES THE WORLD GO ROUND!
THAT'S A MANAGER'S POINT OF VIEW......!
GHOSTS ARE SAID TO BE SPIRITS STUCK IN THIS WORLD, WHO HOLD FORMS SIMILAR TO WHAT THEY HAD IN REALITY.
HM.
SO EVEN IF ONE MIGHT BE ABLE TO SEE THEIR CLOTHES, THEY ARE STILL A PART OF THEIR SPIRIT. AND OF COURSE, THEY ARE UNABLE TO CHANGE OUT OF THEIR SPIRIT.
...OR SO SHALSHA'S SCHOLAR FRIEND SAID.
I DIDN'T KNOW YOU KNEW SOMEONE LIKE THAT, SHALSHA...

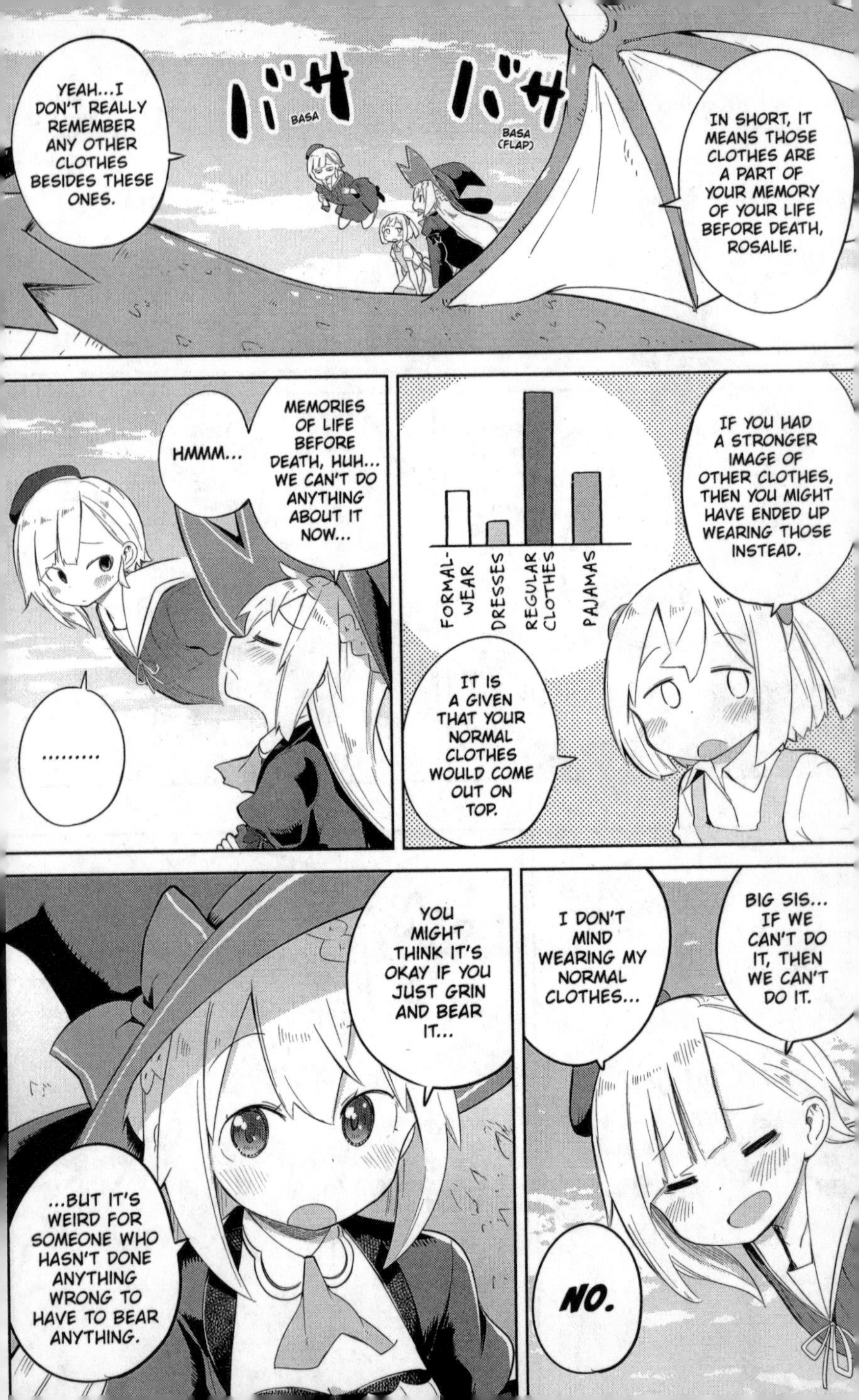
IN SHORT, IT MEANS THOSE CLOTHES ARE A PART OF YOUR MEMORY OF YOUR LIFE BEFORE DEATH, ROSALIE.
バサ
BASA (FLAP)
バサ
BASA
YEAH...I DON'T REALLY REMEMBER ANY OTHER CLOTHES BESIDES THESE ONES.
IF YOU HAD A STRONGER IMAGE OF OTHER CLOTHES, THEN YOU MIGHT HAVE ENDED UP WEARING THOSE INSTEAD.
FORMAL-WEAR
DRESSES
REGULAR CLOTHES
PAJAMAS
IT IS A GIVEN THAT YOUR NORMAL CLOTHES WOULD COME OUT ON TOP.
MEMORIES OF LIFE BEFORE DEATH, HUH... WE CAN'T DO ANYTHING ABOUT IT NOW...
HMMM...
....
BIG SIS... IF WE CAN'T DO IT, THEN WE CAN'T DO IT.
I DON'T MIND WEARING MY NORMAL CLOTHES...
NO.
YOU MIGHT THINK IT'S OKAY IF YOU JUST GRIN AND BEAR IT...
...BUT IT'S WEIRD FOR SOMEONE WHO HASN'T DONE ANYTHING WRONG TO HAVE TO BEAR ANYTHING.

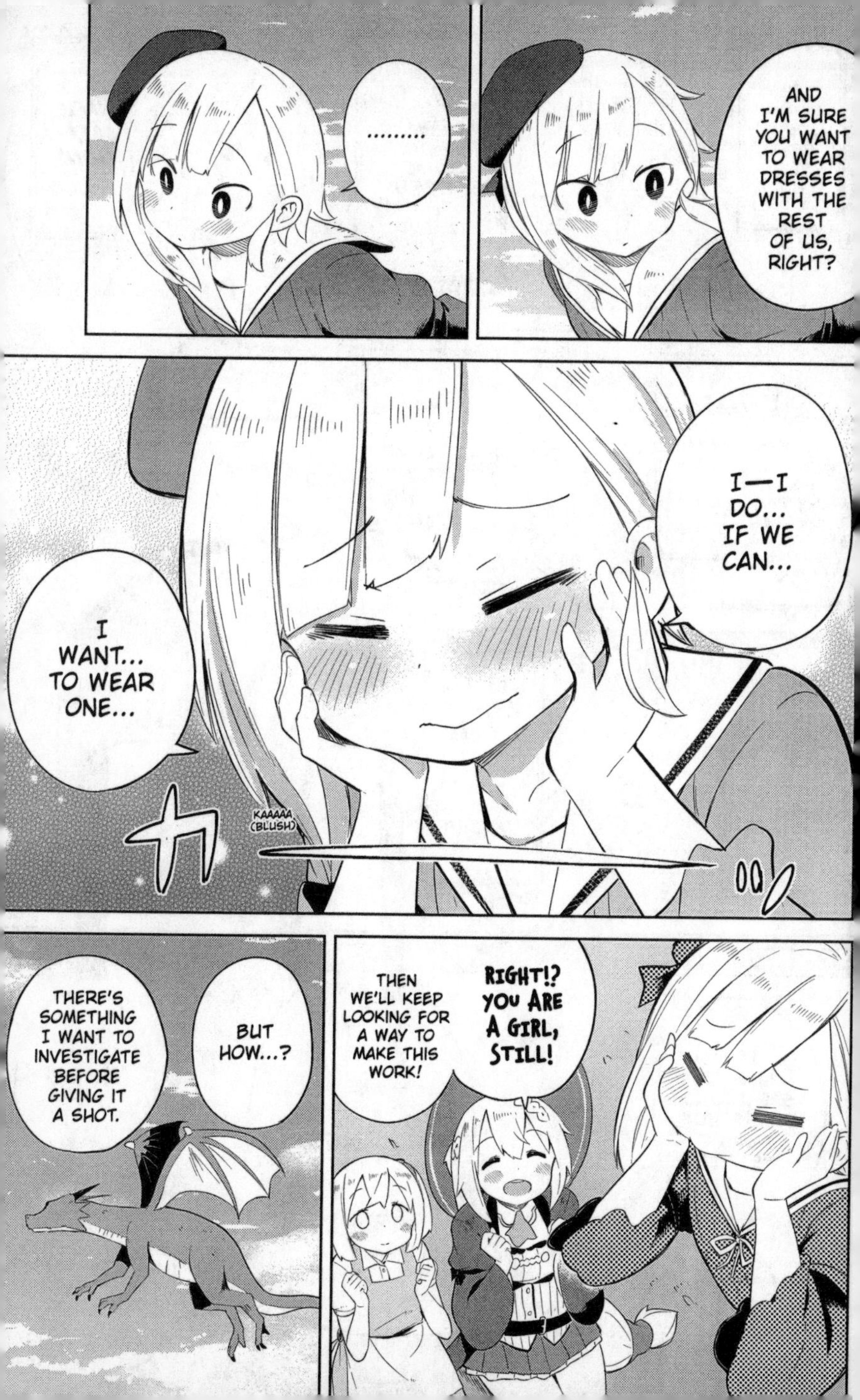
AND I'M SURE YOU WANT TO WEAR DRESSES WITH THE REST OF US, RIGHT?
....
I—I DO... IF WE CAN...
I WANT... TO WEAR ONE...
KAAAAA (BLUSH)
RIGHT!? YOU ARE A GIRL, STILL!
THEN WE'LL KEEP LOOKING FOR A WAY TO MAKE THIS WORK!
BUT HOW...?
THERE'S SOMETHING I WANT TO INVESTIGATE BEFORE GIVING IT A SHOT.

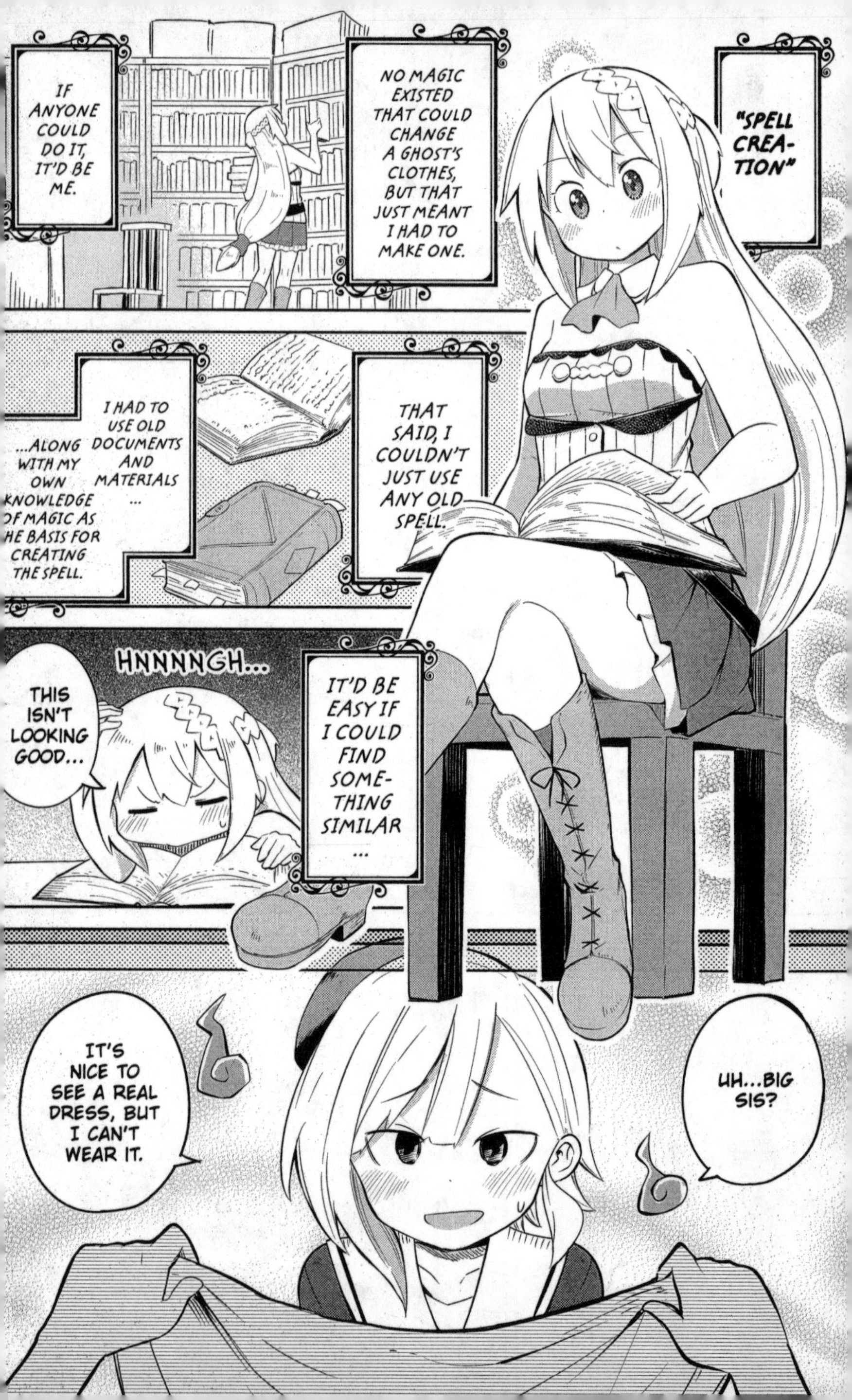
"SPELL CREATION"
NO MAGIC EXISTED THAT COULD CHANGE A GHOST'S CLOTHES, BUT THAT JUST MEANT I HAD TO MAKE ONE.
IF ANYONE COULD DO IT, IT'D BE ME.
THAT SAID, I COULDN'T JUST USE ANY OLD SPELL.
I HAD TO USE OLD DOCUMENTS AND MATERIALS...
...ALONG WITH MY OWN KNOWLEDGE OF MAGIC AS THE BASIS FOR CREATING THE SPELL.
IT'D BE EASY IF I COULD FIND SOMETHING SIMILAR...
HNNNNGH...
THIS ISN'T LOOKING GOOD...
UH...BIG SIS?
IT'S NICE TO SEE A REAL DRESS, BUT I CAN'T WEAR IT.

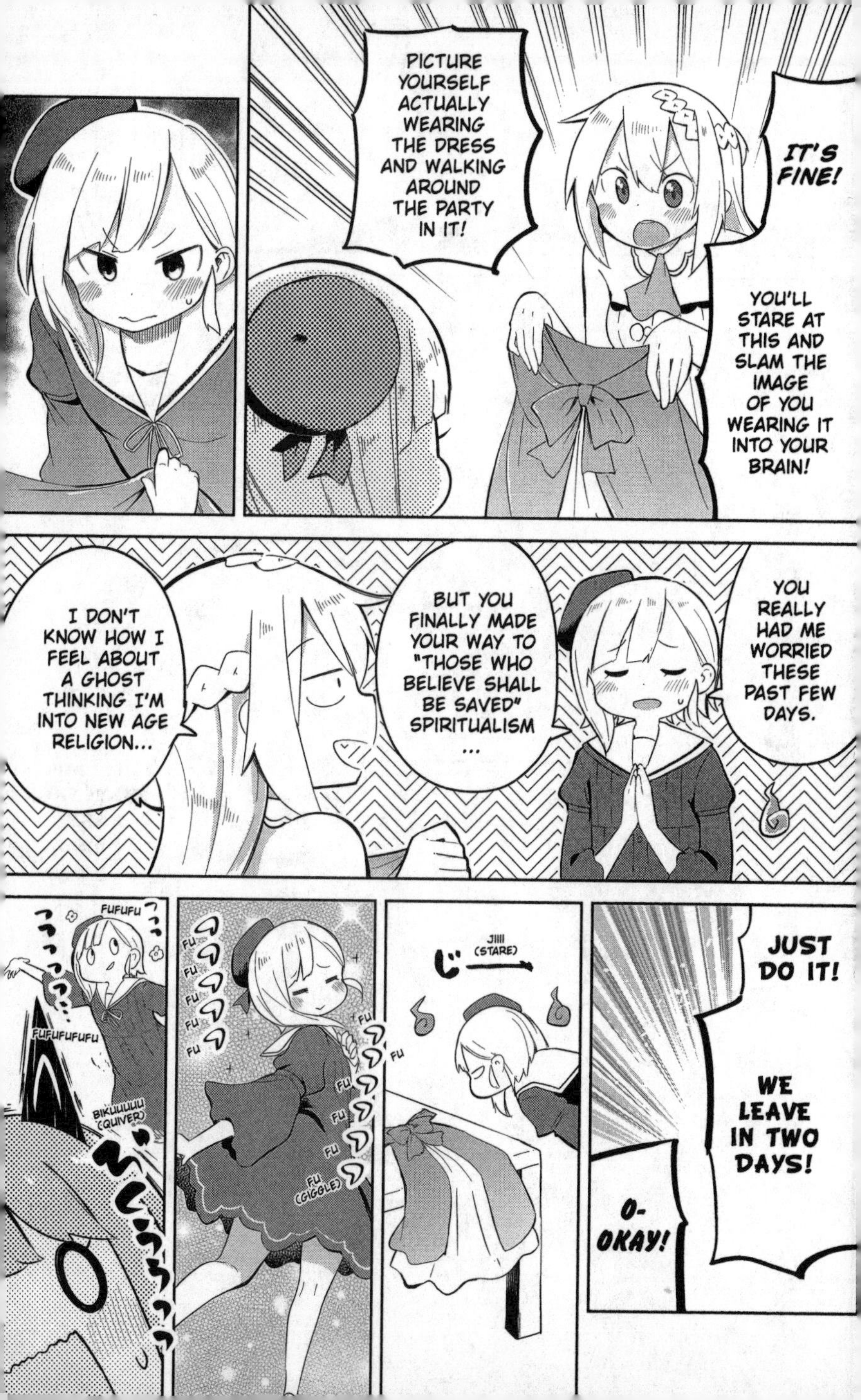
IT'S FINE!
YOU'LL STARE AT THIS AND SLAM THE IMAGE OF YOU WEARING IT INTO YOUR BRAIN!
PICTURE YOURSELF ACTUALLY WEARING THE DRESS AND WALKING AROUND THE PARTY IN IT!
YOU REALLY HAD ME WORRIED THESE PAST FEW DAYS.
BUT YOU FINALLY MADE YOUR WAY TO "THOSE WHO BELIEVE SHALL BE SAVED" SPIRITUALISM ...
I DON'T KNOW HOW I FEEL ABOUT A GHOST THINKING I'M INTO NEW AGE RELIGION...
JUST DO IT!
WE LEAVE IN TWO DAYS!
O-OKAY!
じー
JIIII (STARE)
FU FU FU FU FU
FU FU FU FU FU (GIGGLE)
FUFUFU
FUFUFUFUFU
BIKUUUUU (QUIVER)

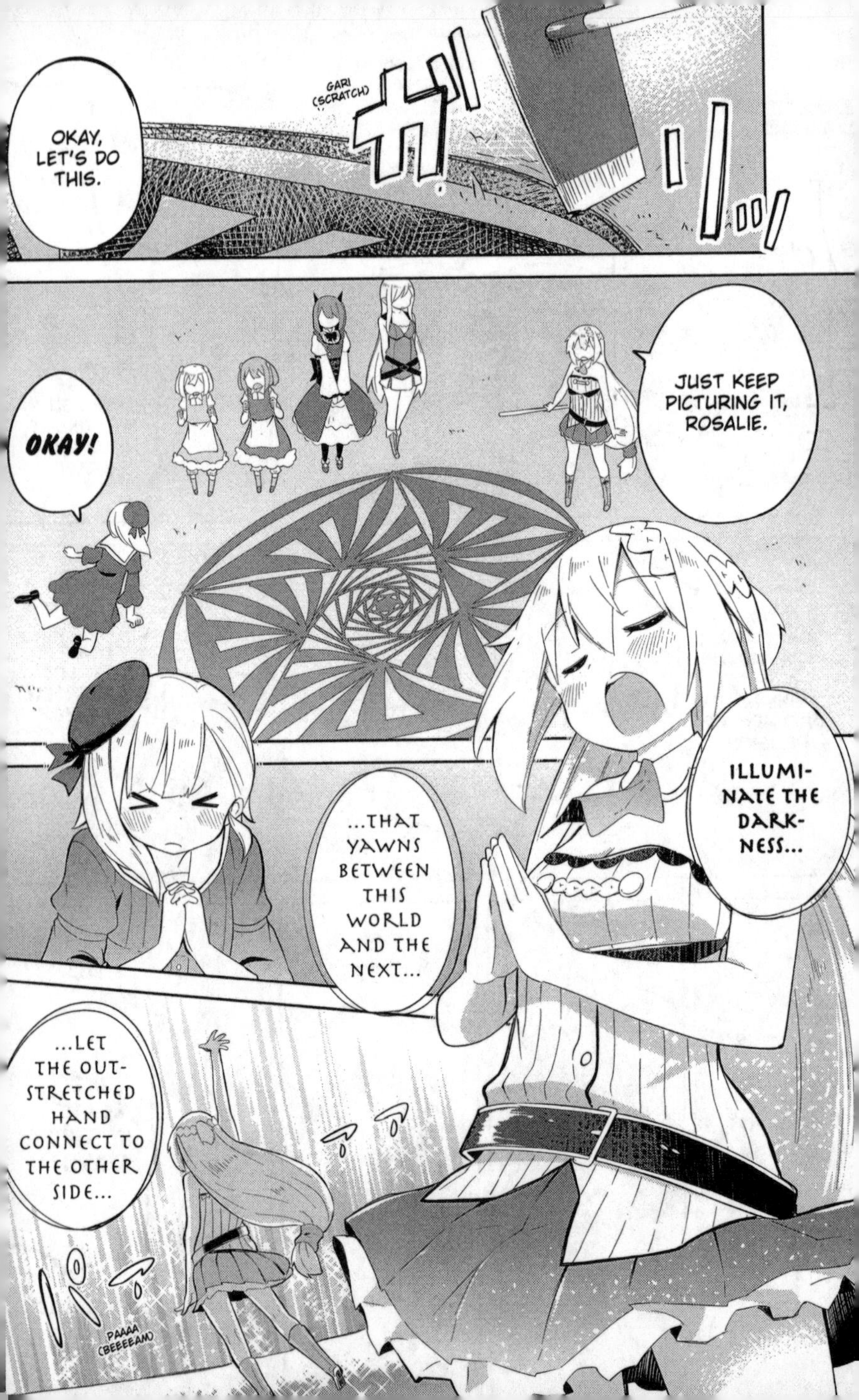
GARI (SCRATCH)
OKAY, LET'S DO THIS.
JUST KEEP PICTURING IT, ROSALIE.
OKAY!
ILLUMI-NATE THE DARK-NESS...
...THAT YAWNS BETWEEN THIS WORLD AND THE NEXT...
...LET THE OUT-STRETCHED HAND CONNECT TO THE OTHER SIDE...
PAAAA (BEEEEAM)

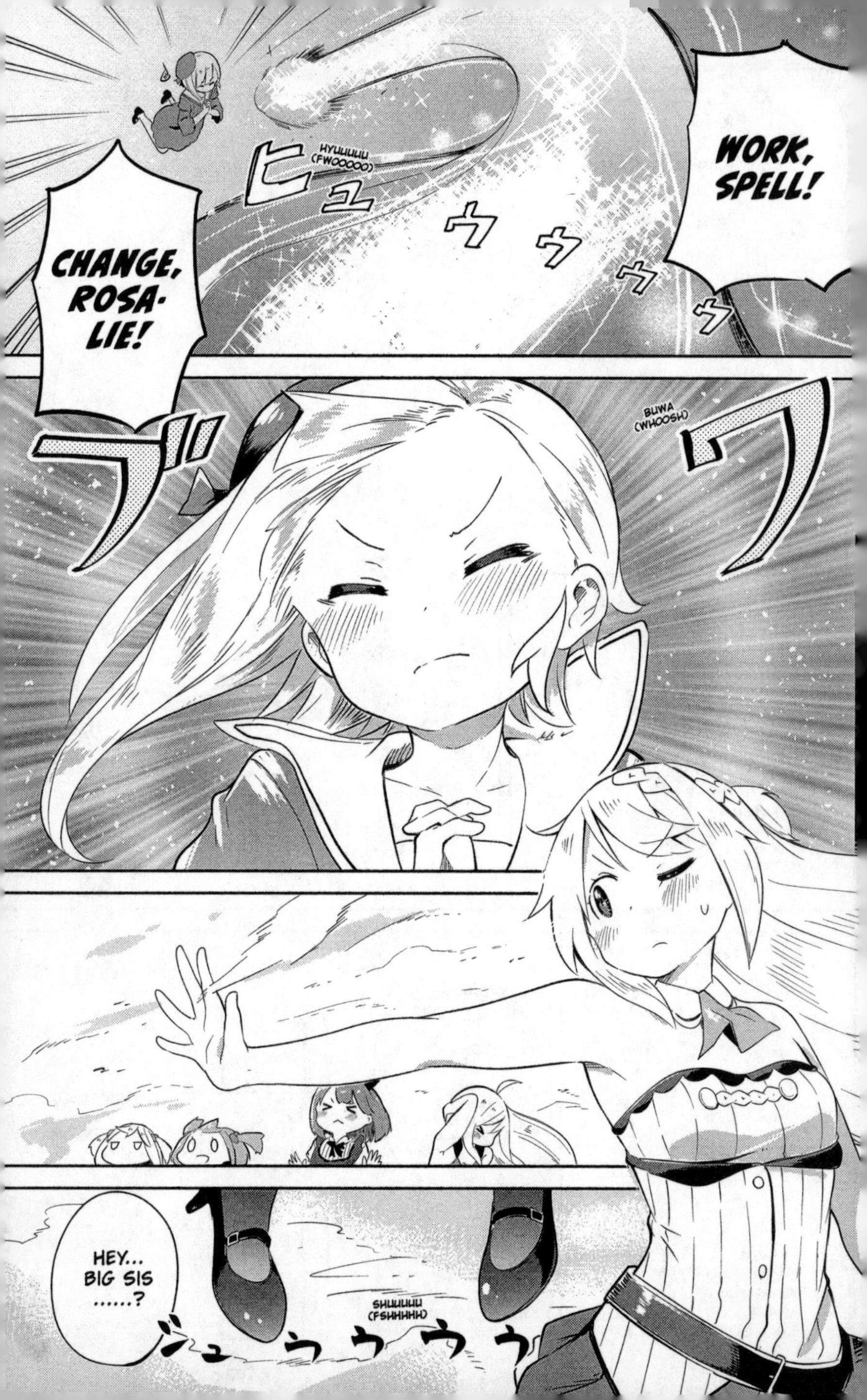
WORK, SPELL!
HYUUUUU (FWOOOOO)
CHANGE, ROSA-LIE!
BUWA (WHOOSH)
SHUUUUU (FSHHHHH)
HEY... BIG SIS ......?

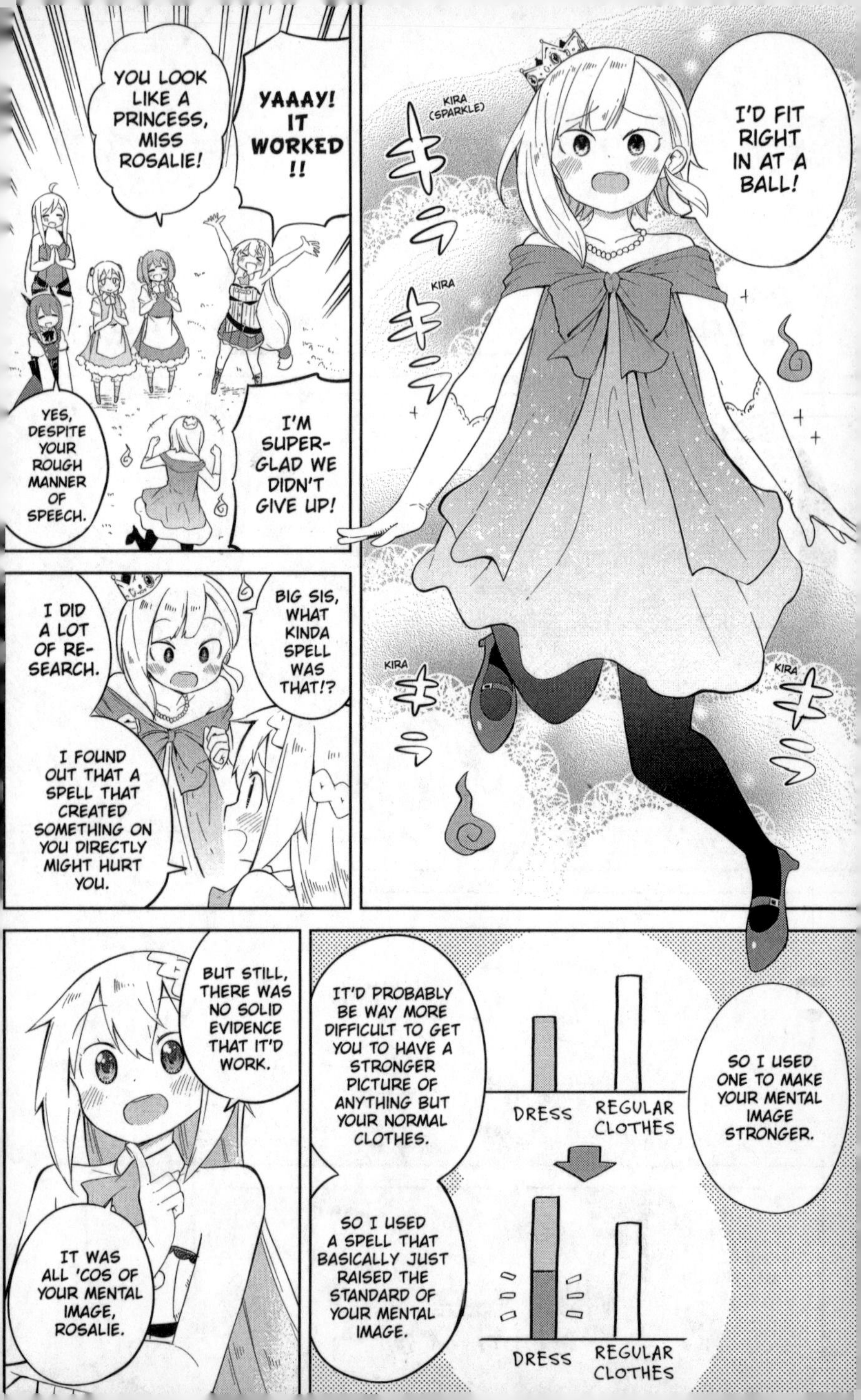
I'D FIT RIGHT IN AT A BALL!
KIRA (SPARKLE)
KIRA
KIRA
KIRA
YAAAY! IT WORKED!!
YOU LOOK LIKE A PRINCESS, MISS ROSALIE!
I'M SUPER-GLAD WE DIDN'T GIVE UP!
YES, DESPITE YOUR ROUGH MANNER OF SPEECH.
BIG SIS, WHAT KINDA SPELL WAS THAT!?
I DID A LOT OF RE-SEARCH.
I FOUND OUT THAT A SPELL THAT CREATED SOMETHING ON YOU DIRECTLY MIGHT HURT YOU.
SO I USED ONE TO MAKE YOUR MENTAL IMAGE STRONGER.
IT'D PROBABLY BE WAY MORE DIFFICULT TO GET YOU TO HAVE A STRONGER PICTURE OF ANYTHING BUT YOUR NORMAL CLOTHES.
DRESS
REGULAR CLOTHES
SO I USED A SPELL THAT BASICALLY JUST RAISED THE STANDARD OF YOUR MENTAL IMAGE.
DRESS
REGULAR CLOTHES
BUT STILL, THERE WAS NO SOLID EVIDENCE THAT IT'D WORK.
IT WAS ALL 'COS OF YOUR MENTAL IMAGE, ROSALIE.

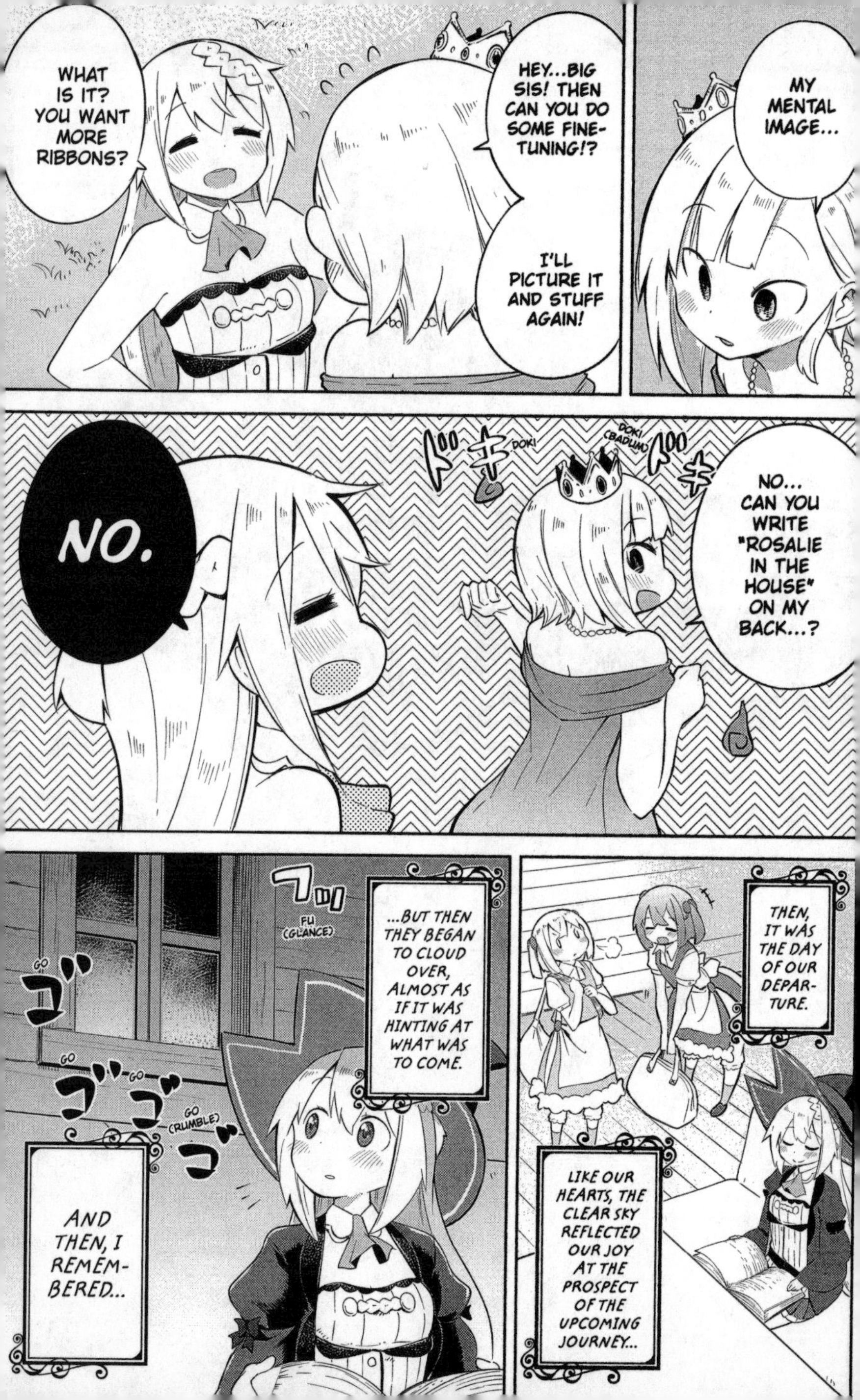
MY MENTAL IMAGE...
HEY...BIG SIS! THEN CAN YOU DO SOME FINE-TUNING!?
I'LL PICTURE IT AND STUFF AGAIN!
WHAT IS IT? YOU WANT MORE RIBBONS?
DOKI (BADUMP)
DOKI
NO... CAN YOU WRITE "ROSALIE IN THE HOUSE" ON MY BACK...?
NO.
THEN, IT WAS THE DAY OF OUR DEPARTURE.
LIKE OUR HEARTS, THE CLEAR SKY REFLECTED OUR JOY AT THE PROSPECT OF THE UPCOMING JOURNEY...
FU (GLANCE)
...BUT THEN THEY BEGAN TO CLOUD OVER, ALMOST AS IF IT WAS HINTING AT WHAT WAS TO COME.
GO
GO
GO
GO (RUMBLE)
AND THEN, I REMEMBERED...

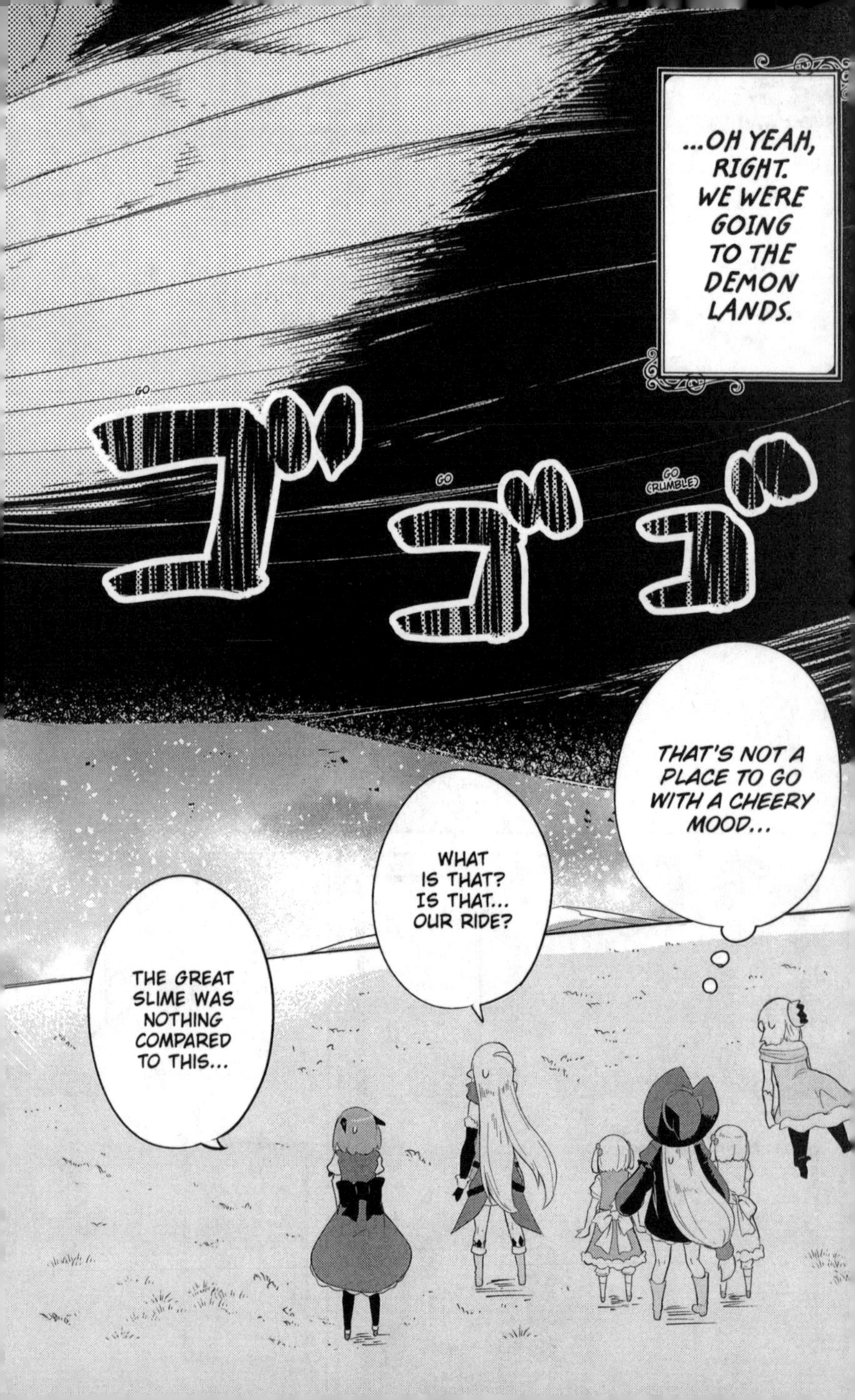
...OH YEAH, RIGHT. WE WERE GOING TO THE DEMON LANDS.
GO (RUMBLE)
GO
GO
THAT'S NOT A PLACE TO GO WITH A CHEERY MOOD...
WHAT IS THAT? IS THAT... OUR RIDE?
THE GREAT SLIME WAS NOTHING COMPARED TO THIS...

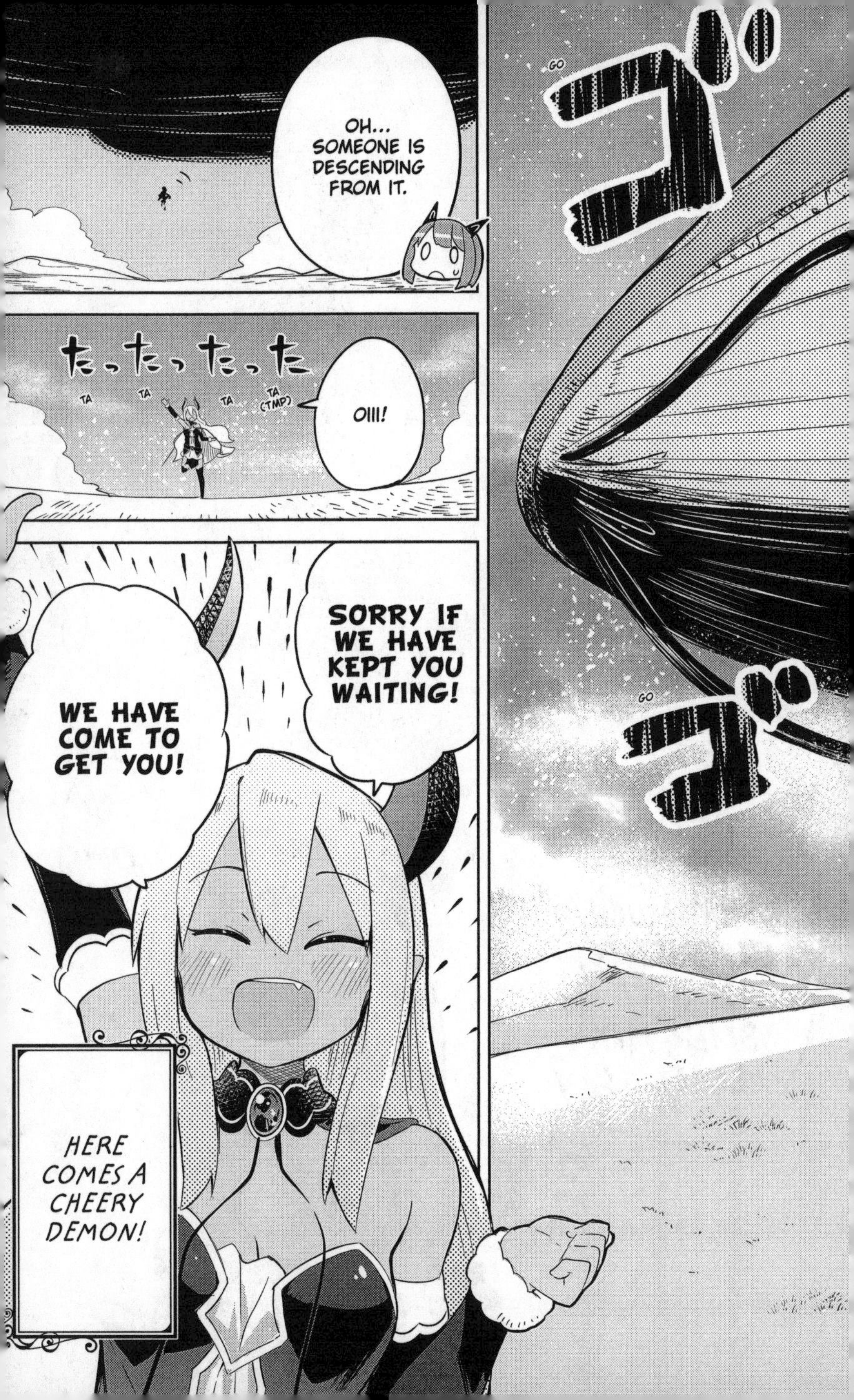
ゴ
GO
ゴ
GO
OH... SOMEONE IS DESCENDING FROM IT.
たったったった
TA TA TA TA (TMP)
OIII!
SORRY IF WE HAVE KEPT YOU WAITING!
WE HAVE COME TO GET YOU!
HERE COMES A CHEERY DEMON!

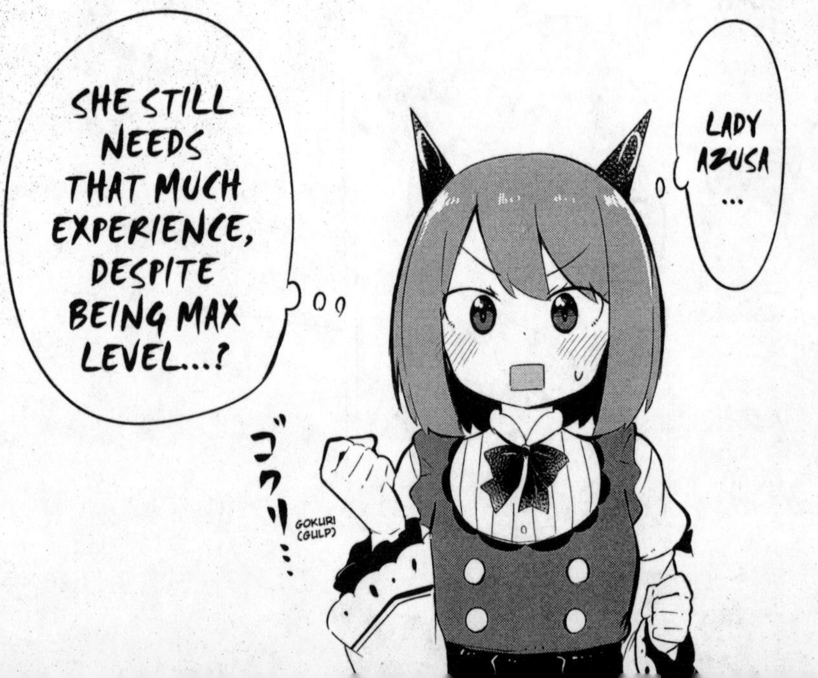
LADY AZUSA ...
SHE STILL NEEDS THAT MUCH EXPERIENCE, DESPITE BEING MAX LEVEL...?
ゴクリ…
GOKURI (GULP)

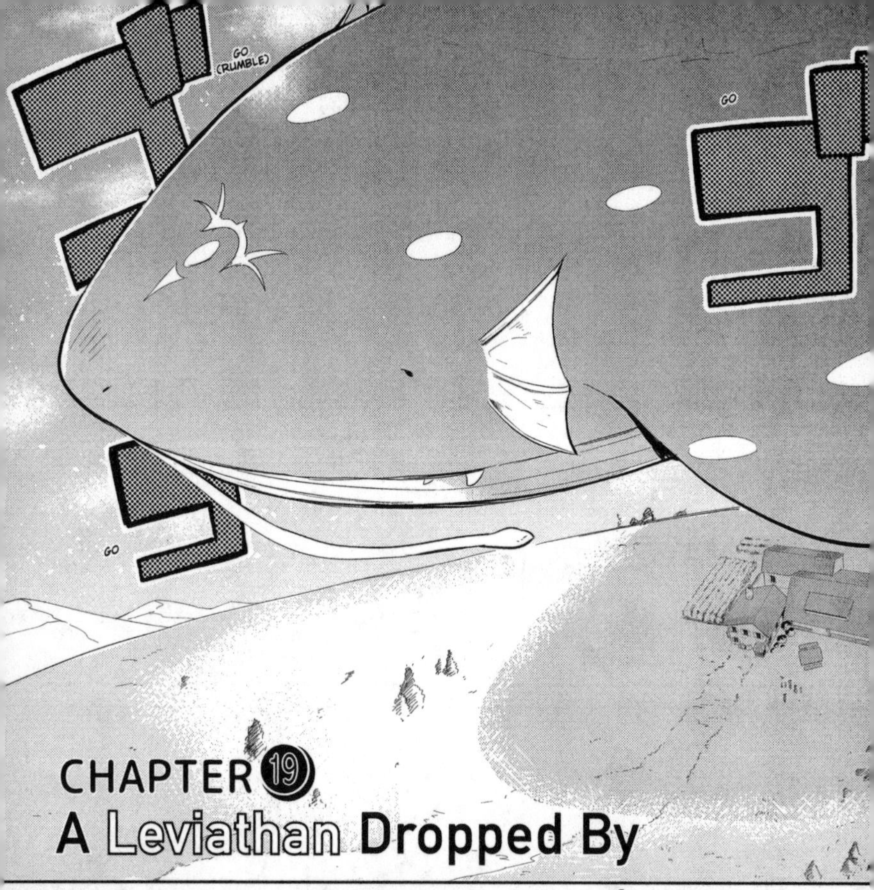
GO (RUMBLE)
GO
GO

CHAPTER 19
A Leviathan Dropped By

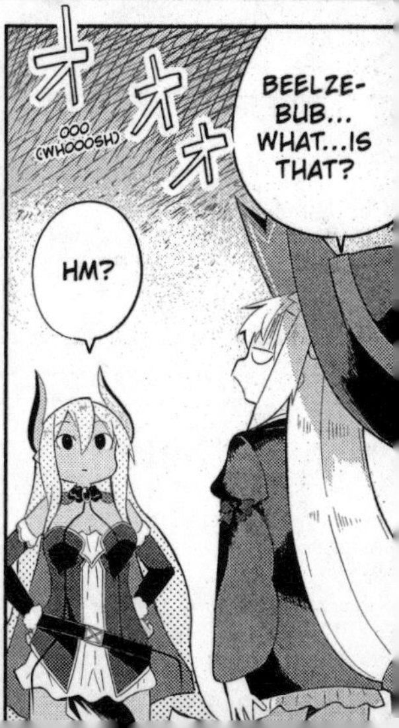
OOO (WHOOOSH)
BEELZE-BUB... WHAT...IS THAT?
HM?

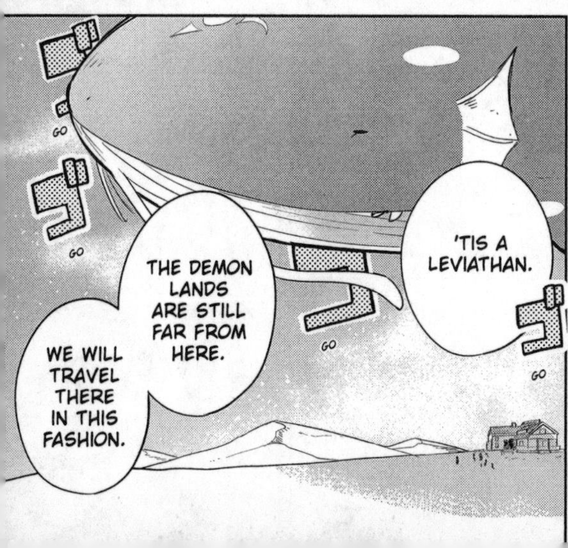
GO
GO
'TIS A LEVIATHAN.
THE DEMON LANDS ARE STILL FAR FROM HERE.
WE WILL TRAVEL THERE IN THIS FASHION.
GO
GO

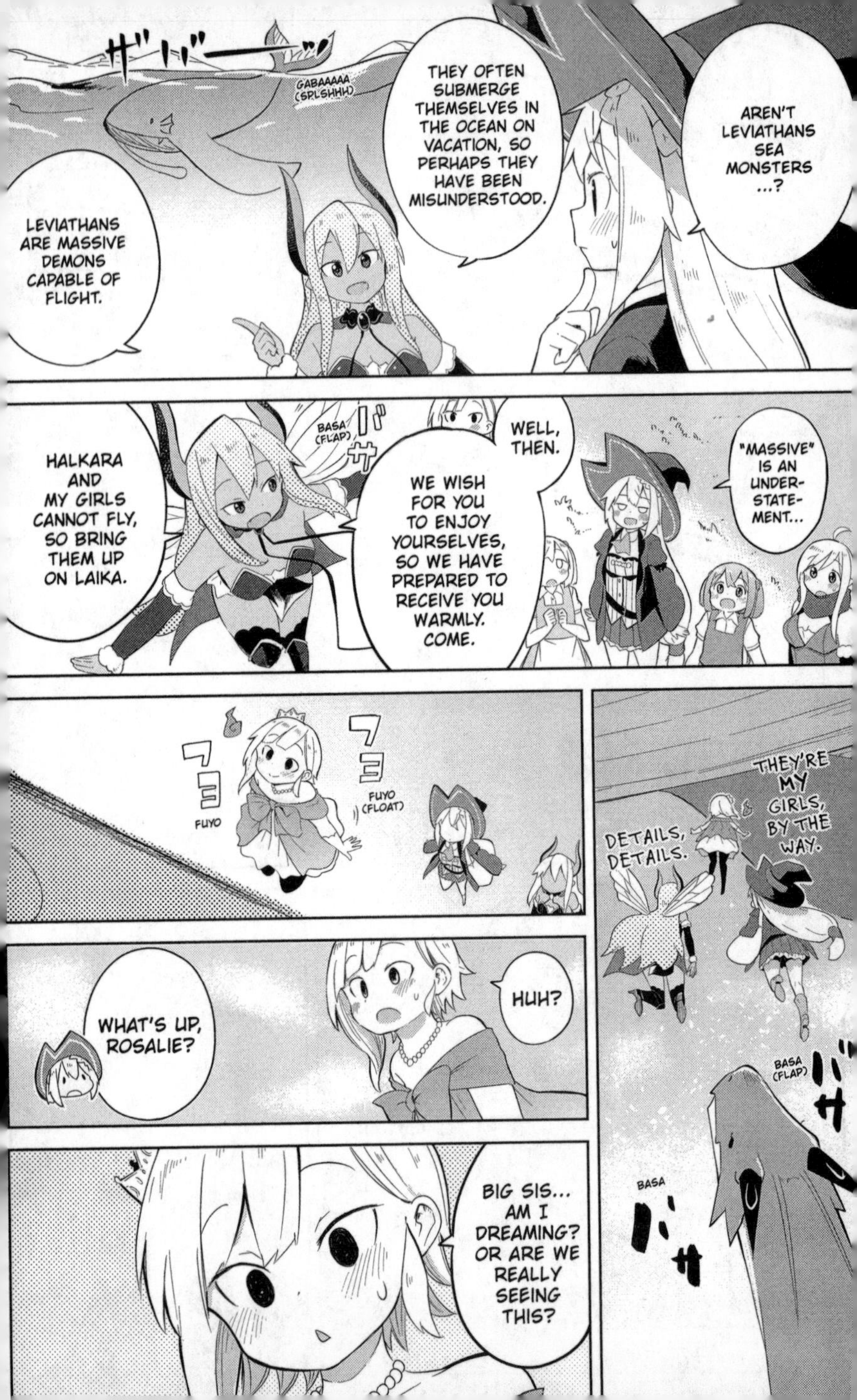
GABAAAAA (SPLSHHH)
AREN'T LEVIATHANS SEA MONSTERS ...?
THEY OFTEN SUBMERGE THEMSELVES IN THE OCEAN ON VACATION, SO PERHAPS THEY HAVE BEEN MISUNDERSTOOD.
LEVIATHANS ARE MASSIVE DEMONS CAPABLE OF FLIGHT.
"MASSIVE" IS AN UNDER-STATE-MENT...
WELL, THEN.
WE WISH FOR YOU TO ENJOY YOURSELVES, SO WE HAVE PREPARED TO RECEIVE YOU WARMLY. COME.
BASA (FLAP)
HALKARA AND MY GIRLS CANNOT FLY, SO BRING THEM UP ON LAIKA.
THEY'RE MY GIRLS, BY THE WAY.
DETAILS, DETAILS.
BASA (FLAP)
BASA
FUYO (FLOAT)
FUYO
HUH?
WHAT'S UP, ROSALIE?
BIG SIS... AM I DREAMING? OR ARE WE REALLY SEEING THIS?

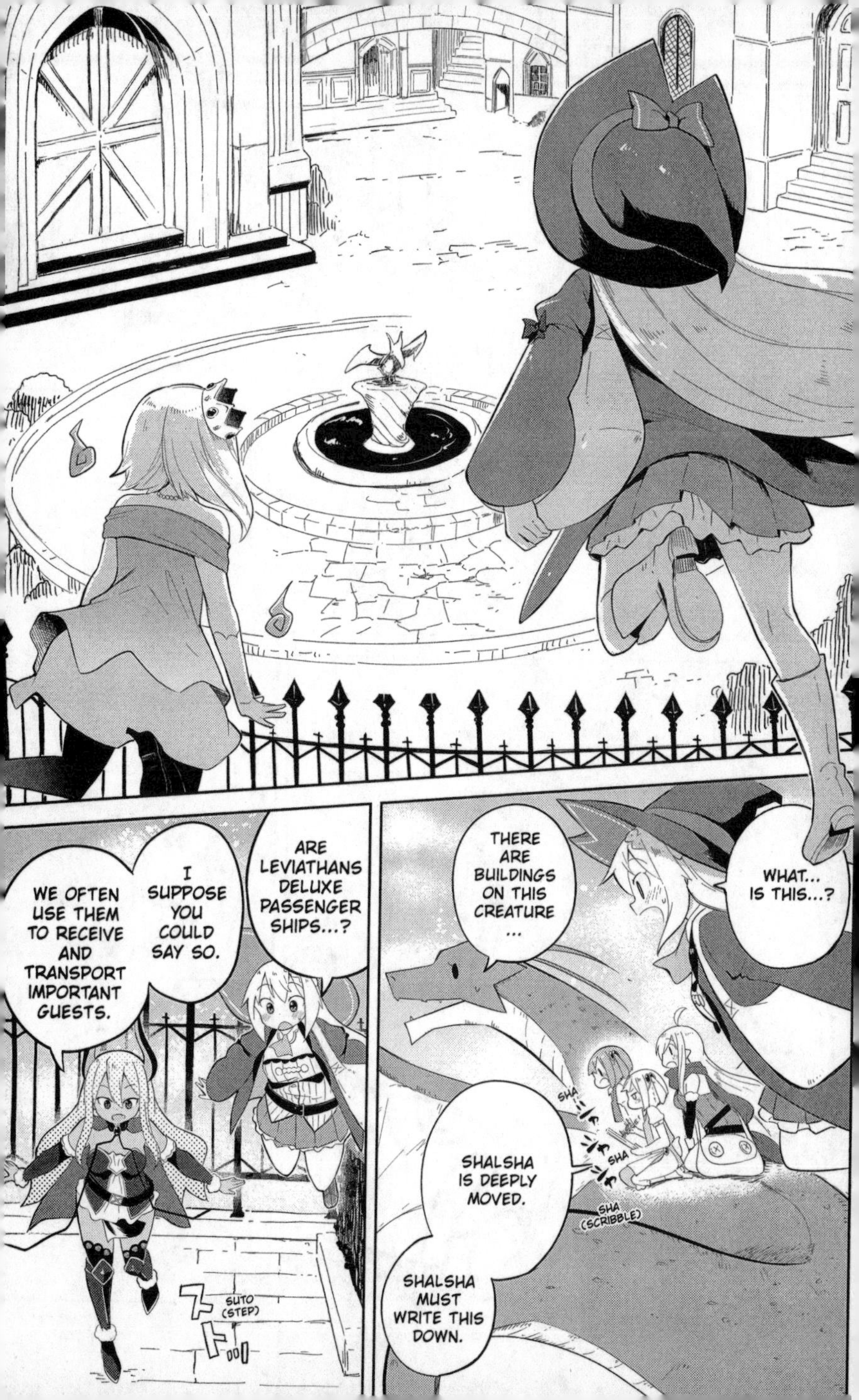
WHAT... IS THIS...?
THERE ARE BUILDINGS ON THIS CREATURE...
SHA SHA SHA (SCRIBBLE)
SHALSHA IS DEEPLY MOVED.
SHALSHA MUST WRITE THIS DOWN.
ARE LEVIATHANS DELUXE PASSENGER SHIPS...?
I SUPPOSE YOU COULD SAY SO.
WE OFTEN USE THEM TO RECEIVE AND TRANSPORT IMPORTANT GUESTS.
SUTO (STEP)

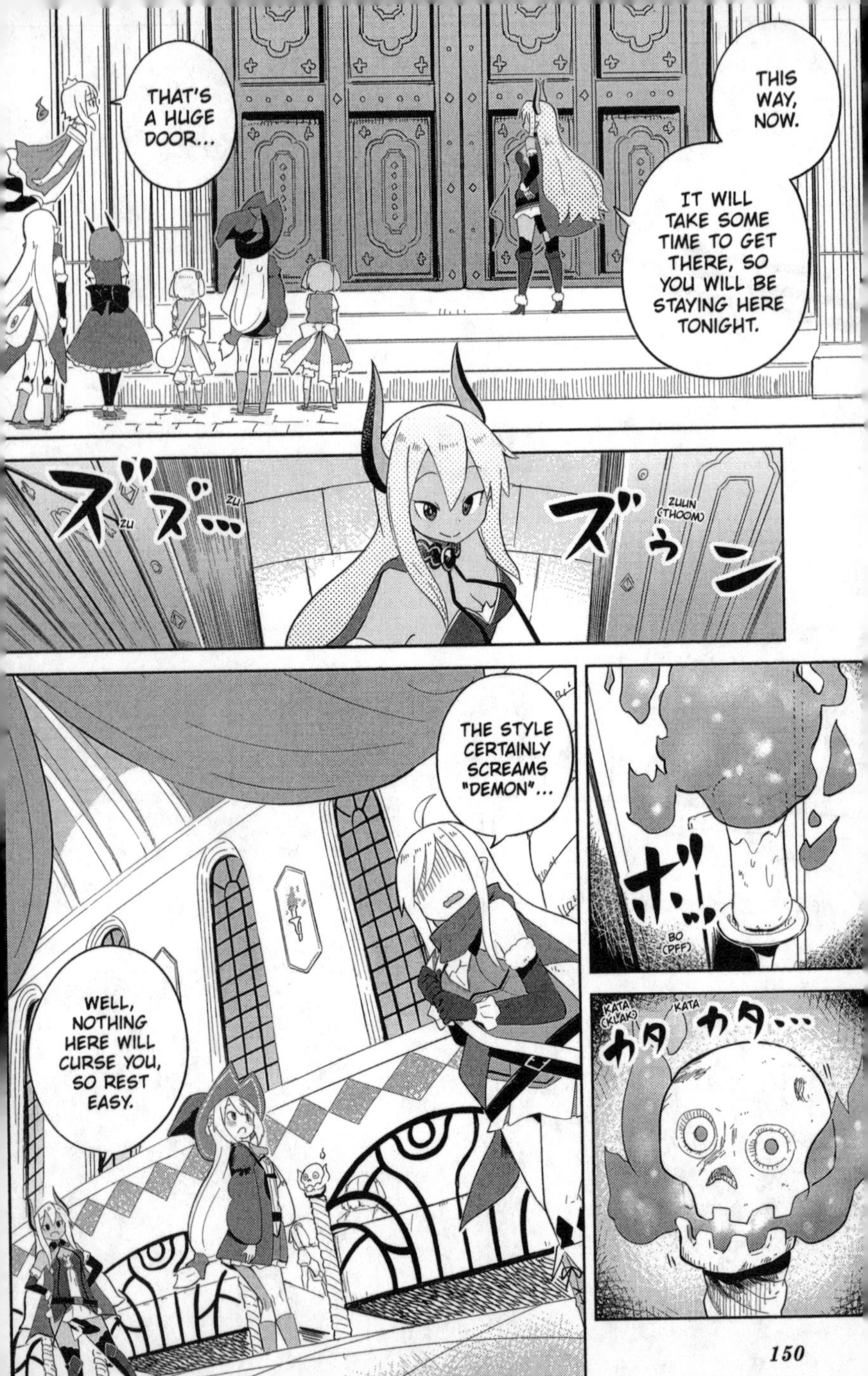
THIS WAY, NOW.
IT WILL TAKE SOME TIME TO GET THERE, SO YOU WILL BE STAYING HERE TONIGHT.
THAT'S A HUGE DOOR...
ZUUN (THOOM)
ZU ZU
BO (PFF)
KATA (KLAK) KATA
THE STYLE CERTAINLY SCREAMS "DEMON"...
WELL, NOTHING HERE WILL CURSE YOU, SO REST EASY.

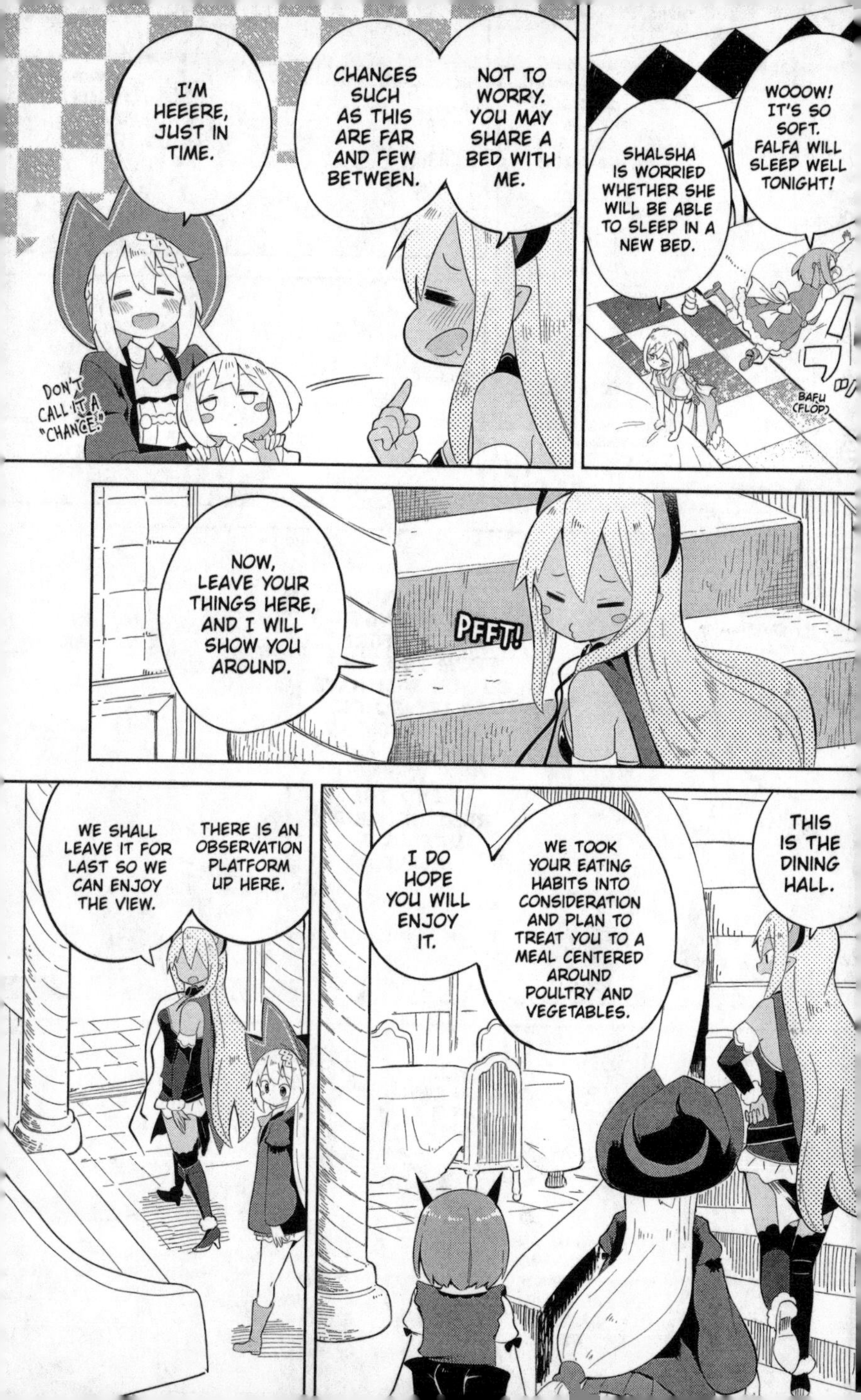
WOOOW! IT'S SO SOFT. FALFA WILL SLEEP WELL TONIGHT!
SHALSHA IS WORRIED WHETHER SHE WILL BE ABLE TO SLEEP IN A NEW BED.
BAFU (FLOP)
NOT TO WORRY. YOU MAY SHARE A BED WITH ME.
CHANCES SUCH AS THIS ARE FAR AND FEW BETWEEN.
I'M HEEERE, JUST IN TIME.
DON'T CALL IT A "CHANCE."
NOW, LEAVE YOUR THINGS HERE, AND I WILL SHOW YOU AROUND.
PFFT!
THIS IS THE DINING HALL.
WE TOOK YOUR EATING HABITS INTO CONSIDERATION AND PLAN TO TREAT YOU TO A MEAL CENTERED AROUND POULTRY AND VEGETABLES.
I DO HOPE YOU WILL ENJOY IT.
THERE IS AN OBSERVATION PLATFORM UP HERE.
WE SHALL LEAVE IT FOR LAST SO WE CAN ENJOY THE VIEW.

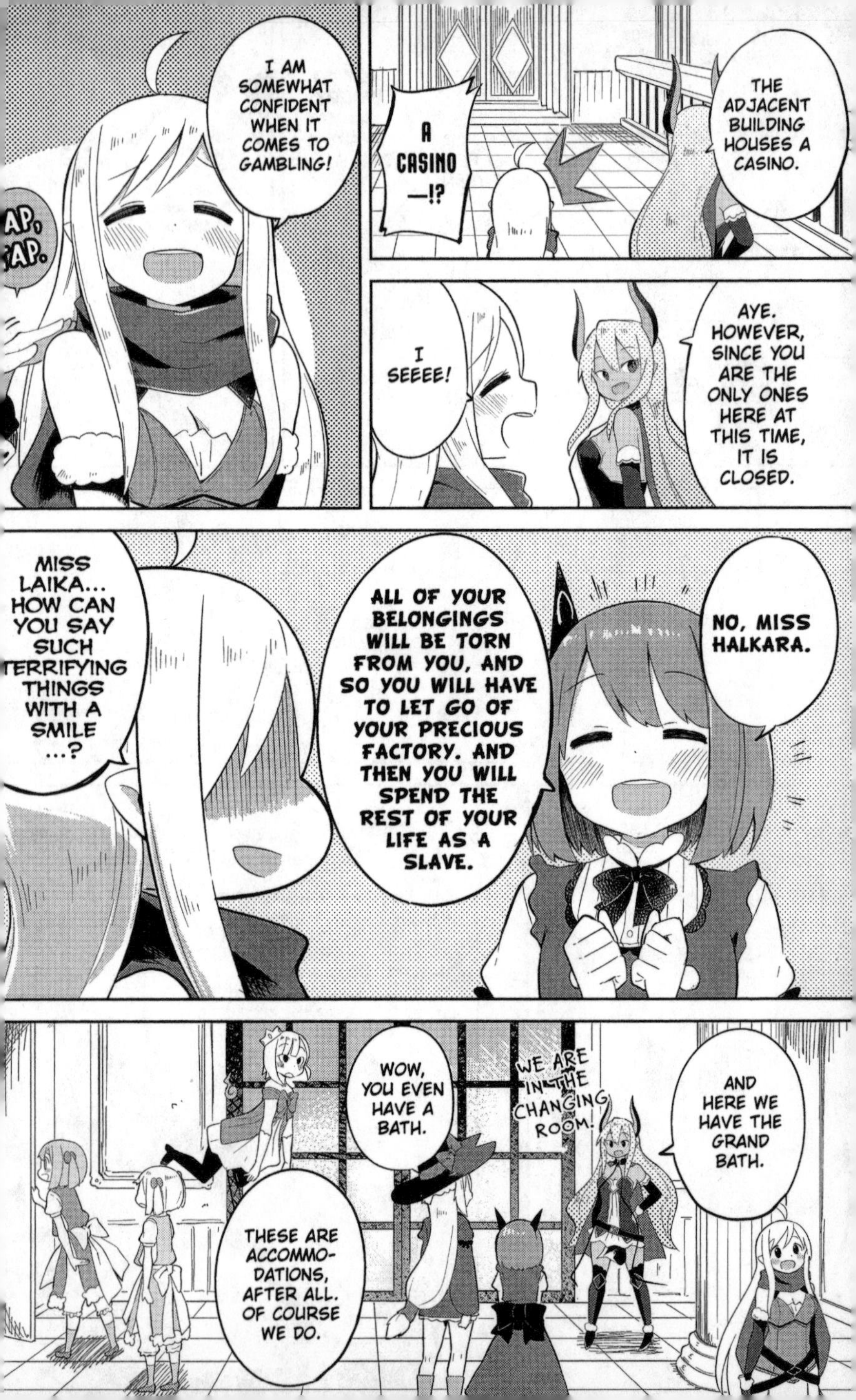

THE ADJACENT BUILDING HOUSES A CASINO.
A CASINO—!?
AYE. HOWEVER, SINCE YOU ARE THE ONLY ONES HERE AT THIS TIME, IT IS CLOSED.
I SEEEE!
I AM SOMEWHAT CONFIDENT WHEN IT COMES TO GAMBLING!
AP, AP.
NO, MISS HALKARA.
ALL OF YOUR BELONGINGS WILL BE TORN FROM YOU, AND SO YOU WILL HAVE TO LET GO OF YOUR PRECIOUS FACTORY. AND THEN YOU WILL SPEND THE REST OF YOUR LIFE AS A SLAVE.
MISS LAIKA... HOW CAN YOU SAY SUCH TERRIFYING THINGS WITH A SMILE ...?
AND HERE WE HAVE THE GRAND BATH.
WE ARE IN THE CHANGING ROOM.
WOW, YOU EVEN HAVE A BATH.
THESE ARE ACCOMMODATIONS, AFTER ALL. OF COURSE WE DO.

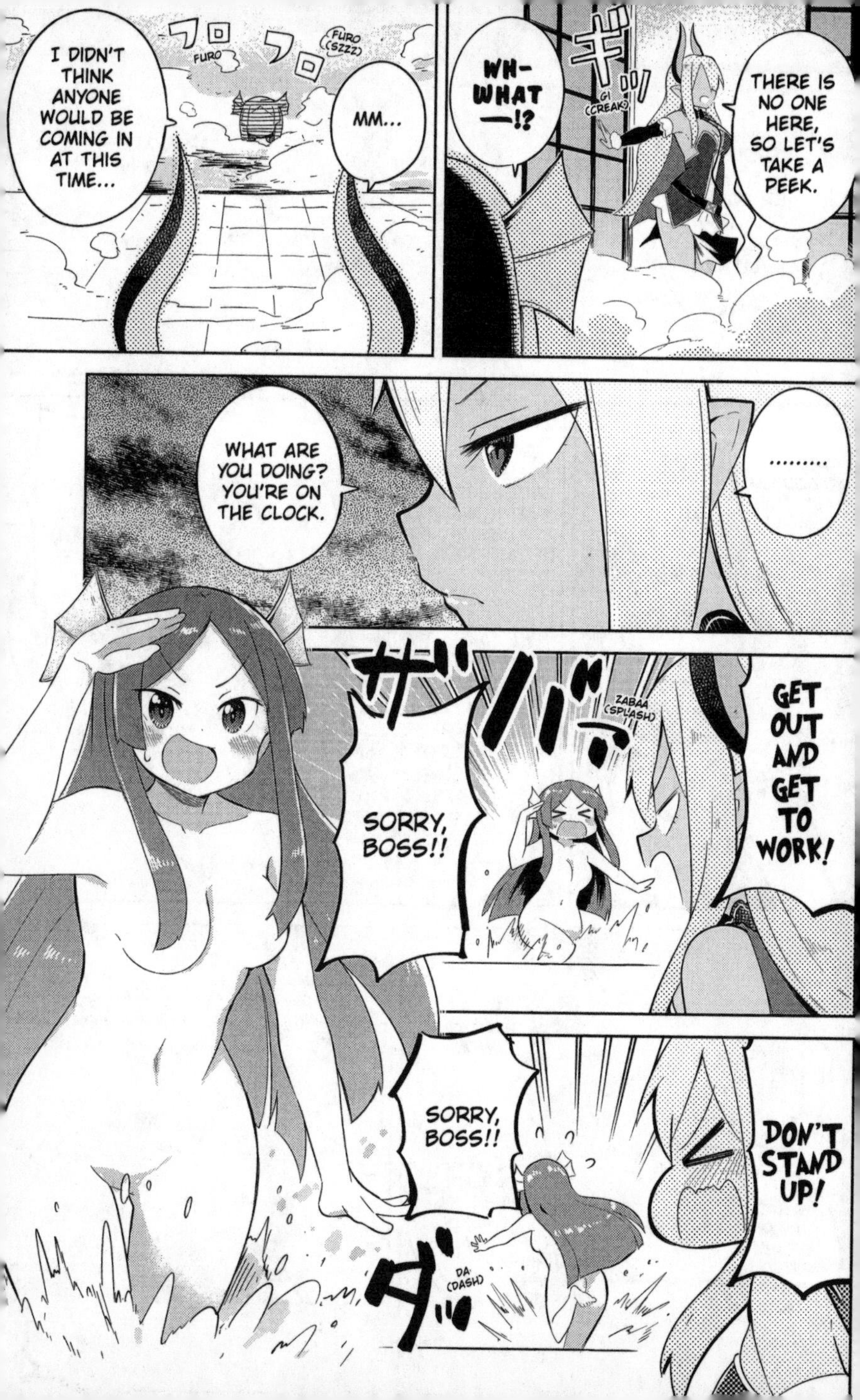
THERE IS NO ONE HERE, SO LET'S TAKE A PEEK.
GI (CREAK)
WH-WHAT—!?
FURO (SZZZ)
MM...
FURO
I DIDN'T THINK ANYONE WOULD BE COMING IN AT THIS TIME...
....
WHAT ARE YOU DOING? YOU'RE ON THE CLOCK.
GET OUT AND GET TO WORK!
ZABAA (SPLASH)
SORRY, BOSS!!
DON'T STAND UP!
SORRY, BOSS!!
DA (DASH)

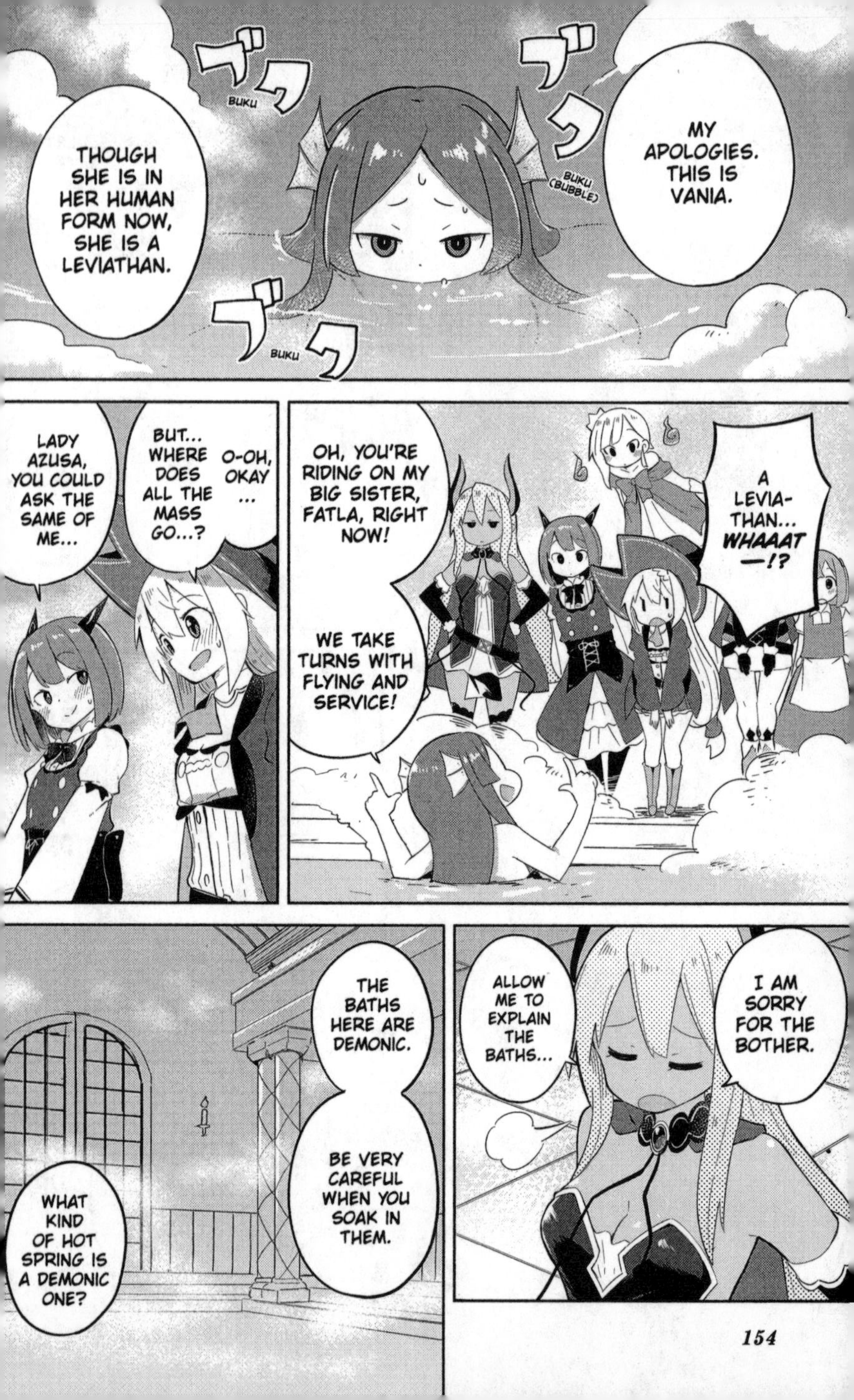
BUKU
BUKU (BUBBLE)
MY APOLOGIES. THIS IS VANIA.
THOUGH SHE IS IN HER HUMAN FORM NOW, SHE IS A LEVIATHAN.
BUKU
A LEVIA-THAN... *WHAAAT*—!?
OH, YOU'RE RIDING ON MY BIG SISTER, FATLA, RIGHT NOW!
WE TAKE TURNS WITH FLYING AND SERVICE!
O-OH, OKAY...
BUT... WHERE DOES ALL THE MASS GO...?
LADY AZUSA, YOU COULD ASK THE SAME OF ME...
I AM SORRY FOR THE BOTHER.
ALLOW ME TO EXPLAIN THE BATHS...
THE BATHS HERE ARE DEMONIC.
BE VERY CAREFUL WHEN YOU SOAK IN THEM.
WHAT KIND OF HOT SPRING IS A DEMONIC ONE?

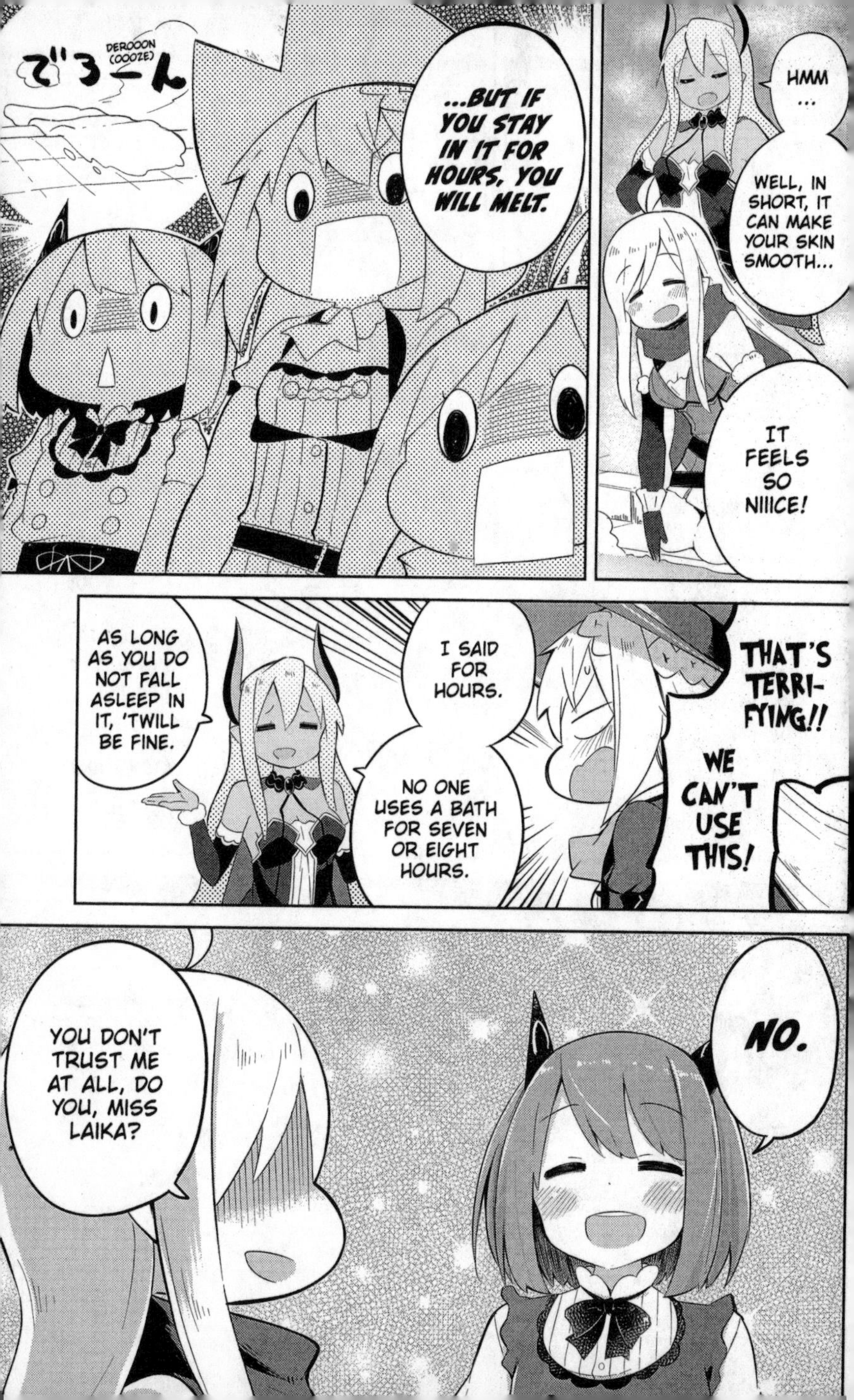
HMM ...
WELL, IN SHORT, IT CAN MAKE YOUR SKIN SMOOTH...
IT FEELS SO NIIICE!
...BUT IF YOU STAY IN IT FOR HOURS, YOU WILL MELT.
でろーん
DEROOON (OOOZE)
THAT'S TERRI-FYING!!
WE CAN'T USE THIS!
I SAID FOR HOURS.
NO ONE USES A BATH FOR SEVEN OR EIGHT HOURS.
AS LONG AS YOU DO NOT FALL ASLEEP IN IT, 'TWILL BE FINE.
NO.
YOU DON'T TRUST ME AT ALL, DO YOU, MISS LAIKA?

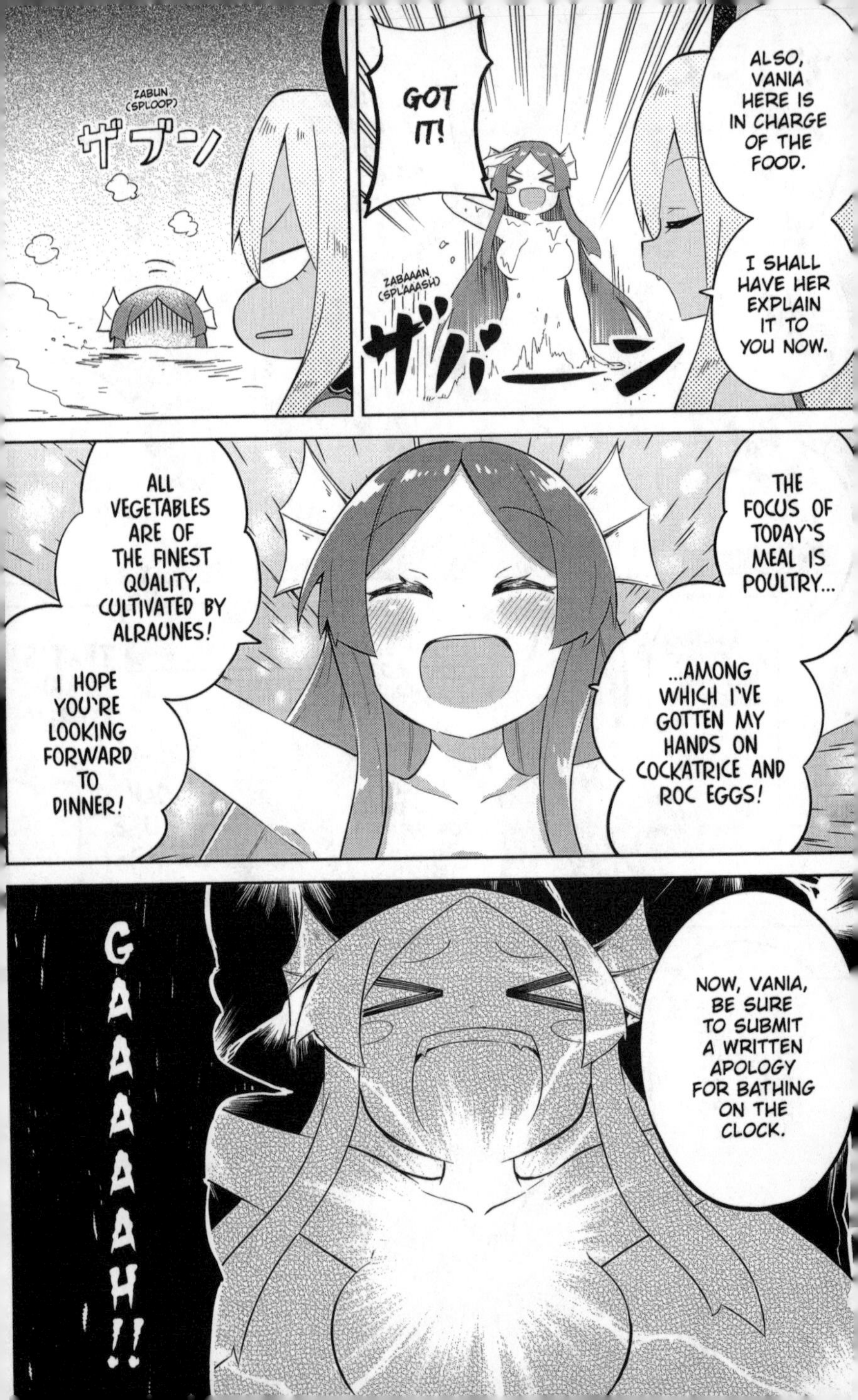
ALSO, VANIA HERE IS IN CHARGE OF THE FOOD.
I SHALL HAVE HER EXPLAIN IT TO YOU NOW.
GOT IT!
ZABAAAN (SPL'AAASH)
ザバーン
ZABUN (SPLOOP)
ザブーン
THE FOCUS OF TODAY'S MEAL IS POULTRY...
...AMONG WHICH I'VE GOTTEN MY HANDS ON COCKATRICE AND ROC EGGS!
ALL VEGETABLES ARE OF THE FINEST QUALITY, CULTIVATED BY ALRAUNES!
I HOPE YOU'RE LOOKING FORWARD TO DINNER!
NOW, VANIA, BE SURE TO SUBMIT A WRITTEN APOLOGY FOR BATHING ON THE CLOCK.
GAAAAAAH!!

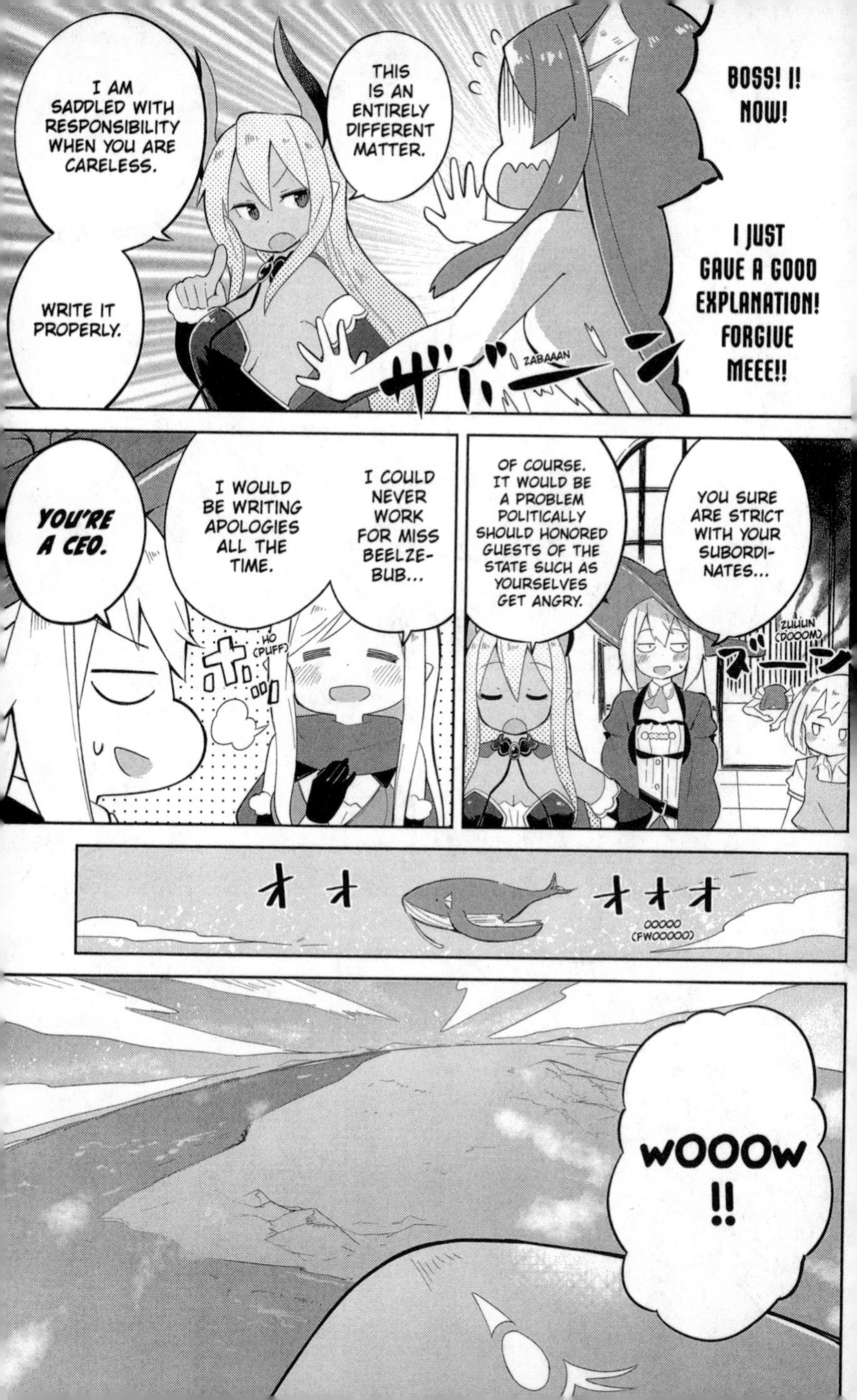
BOSS! I! NOW!
I JUST GAVE A GOOD EXPLANATION! FORGIVE MEEE!!
THIS IS AN ENTIRELY DIFFERENT MATTER.
I AM SADDLED WITH RESPONSIBILITY WHEN YOU ARE CARELESS.
WRITE IT PROPERLY.
ZABAAAN
YOU SURE ARE STRICT WITH YOUR SUBORDINATES...
OF COURSE. IT WOULD BE A PROBLEM POLITICALLY SHOULD HONORED GUESTS OF THE STATE SUCH AS YOURSELVES GET ANGRY.
ZUUUN (DOOOM)
I COULD NEVER WORK FOR MISS BEELZEBUB...
I WOULD BE WRITING APOLOGIES ALL THE TIME.
HO (PUFF)
YOU'RE A CEO.
OOOOO (FWOOOOO)
WOOOW !!

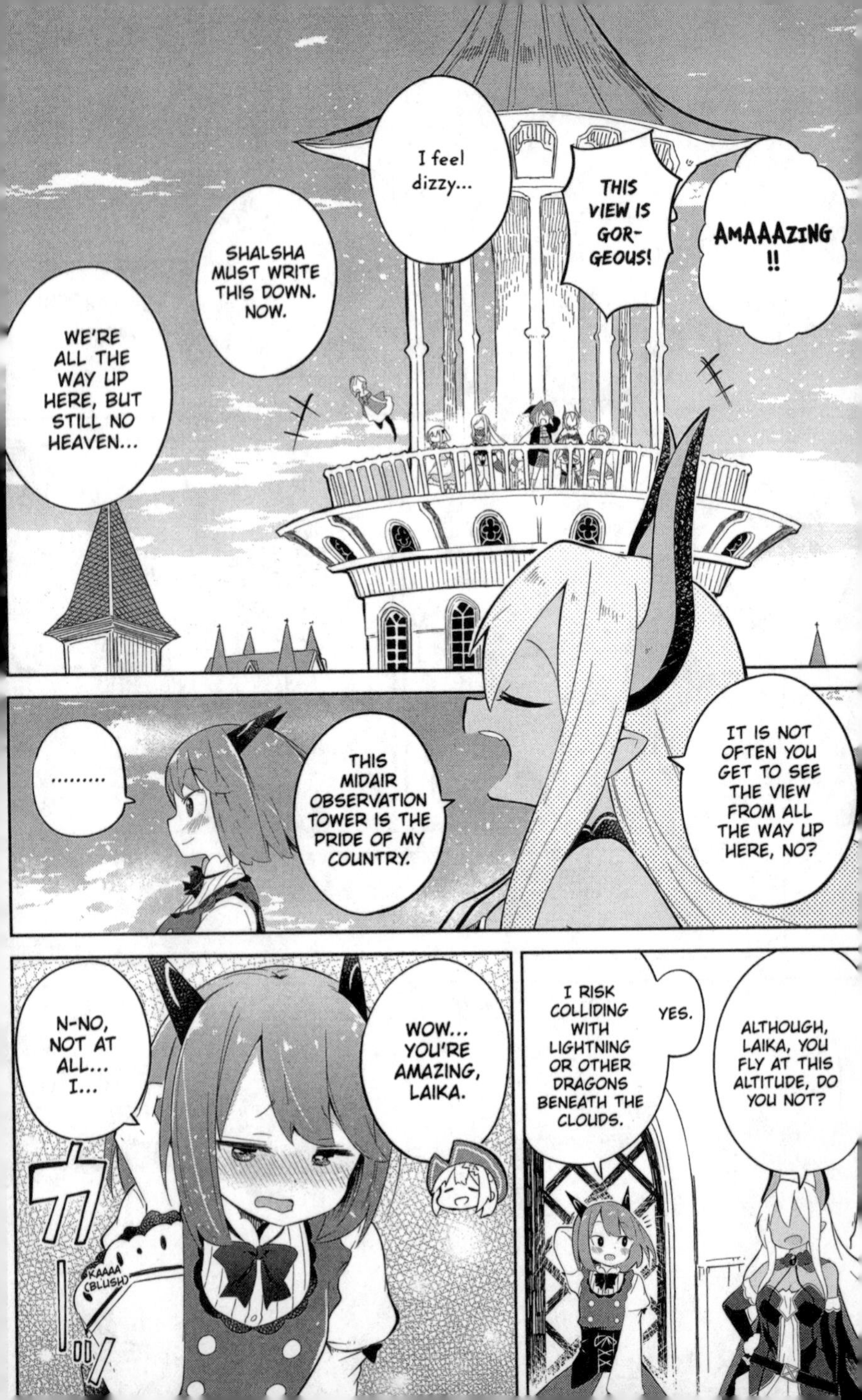
AMAAAZING!!
THIS VIEW IS GORGEOUS!
I feel dizzy...
SHALSHA MUST WRITE THIS DOWN. NOW.
WE'RE ALL THE WAY UP HERE, BUT STILL NO HEAVEN...
IT IS NOT OFTEN YOU GET TO SEE THE VIEW FROM ALL THE WAY UP HERE, NO?
THIS MIDAIR OBSERVATION TOWER IS THE PRIDE OF MY COUNTRY.
....
ALTHOUGH, LAIKA, YOU FLY AT THIS ALTITUDE, DO YOU NOT?
YES.
I RISK COLLIDING WITH LIGHTNING OR OTHER DRAGONS BENEATH THE CLOUDS.
WOW... YOU'RE AMAZING, LAIKA.
N-NO, NOT AT ALL... I...
KAAAA (BLUSH)

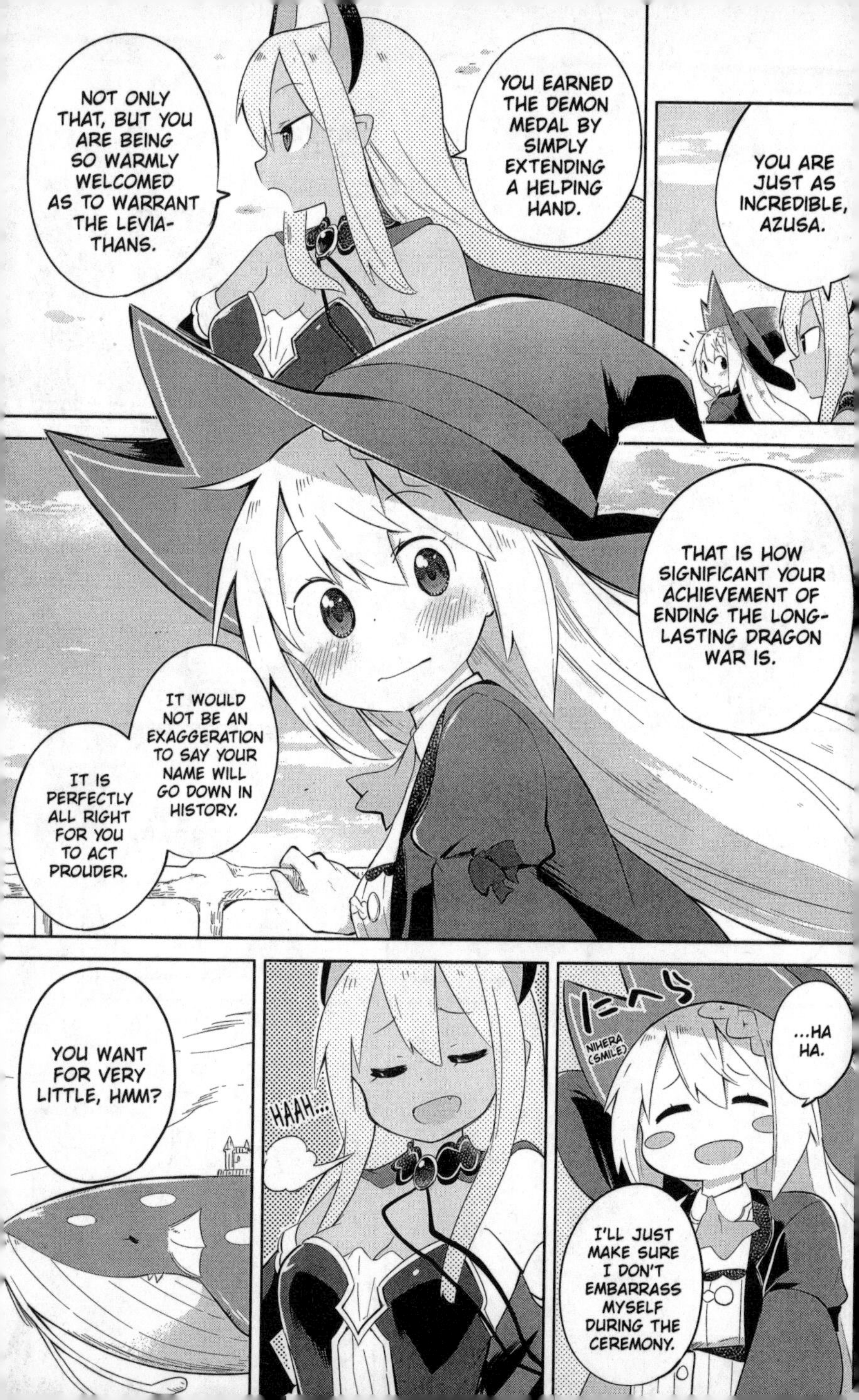
YOU ARE JUST AS INCREDIBLE, AZUSA.
YOU EARNED THE DEMON MEDAL BY SIMPLY EXTENDING A HELPING HAND.
NOT ONLY THAT, BUT YOU ARE BEING SO WARMLY WELCOMED AS TO WARRANT THE LEVIA-THANS.
THAT IS HOW SIGNIFICANT YOUR ACHIEVEMENT OF ENDING THE LONG-LASTING DRAGON WAR IS.
IT WOULD NOT BE AN EXAGGERATION TO SAY YOUR NAME WILL GO DOWN IN HISTORY.
IT IS PERFECTLY ALL RIGHT FOR YOU TO ACT PROUDER.
...HA HA.
NIHERA (SMILE)
I'LL JUST MAKE SURE I DON'T EMBARRASS MYSELF DURING THE CEREMONY.
HAAH...
YOU WANT FOR VERY LITTLE, HMM?

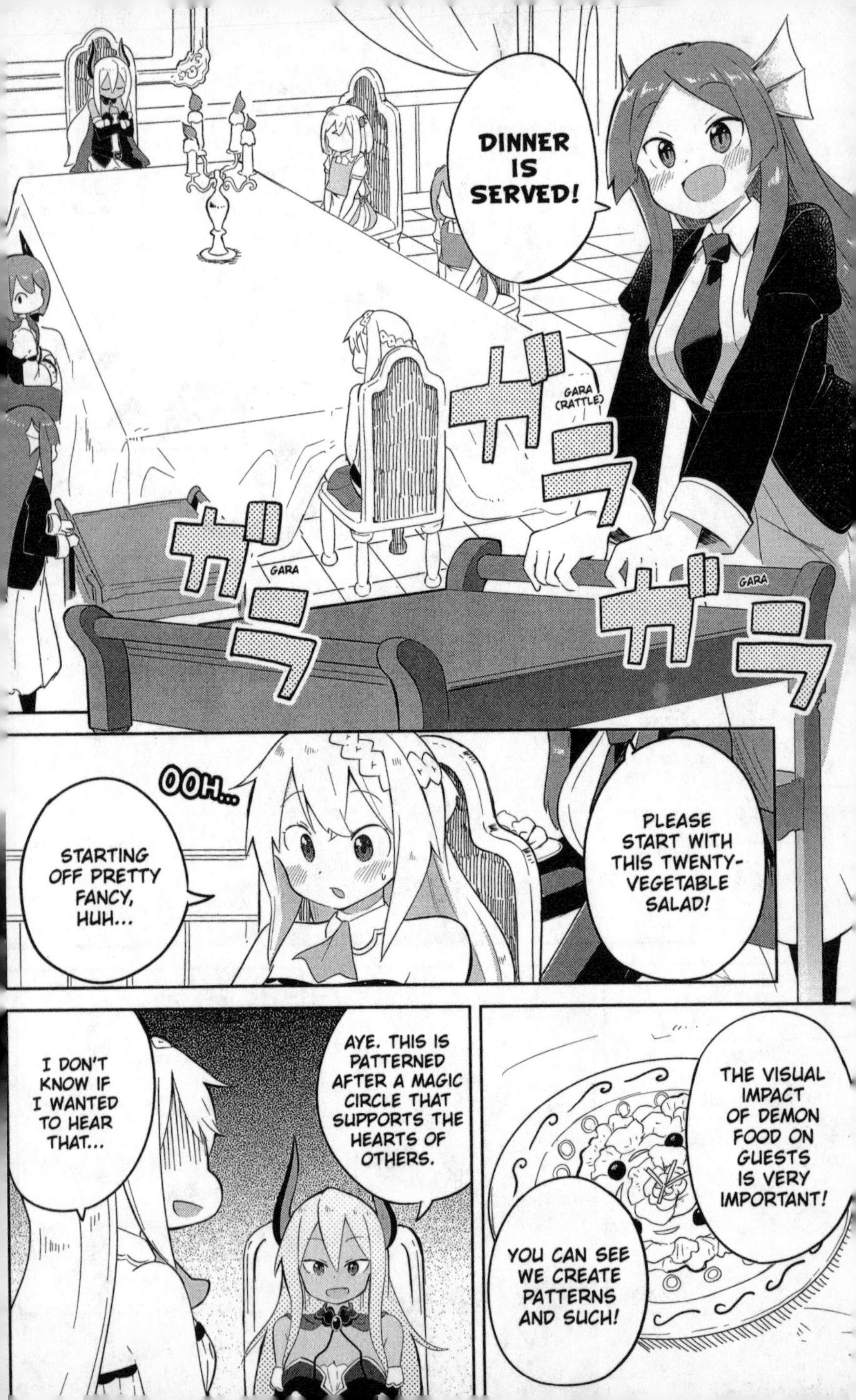
DINNER IS SERVED!
GARA (RATTLE)
GARA
GARA
PLEASE START WITH THIS TWENTY-VEGETABLE SALAD!
OOH...
STARTING OFF PRETTY FANCY, HUH...
THE VISUAL IMPACT OF DEMON FOOD ON GUESTS IS VERY IMPORTANT!
YOU CAN SEE WE CREATE PATTERNS AND SUCH!
AYE. THIS IS PATTERNED AFTER A MAGIC CIRCLE THAT SUPPORTS THE HEARTS OF OTHERS.
I DON'T KNOW IF I WANTED TO HEAR THAT...

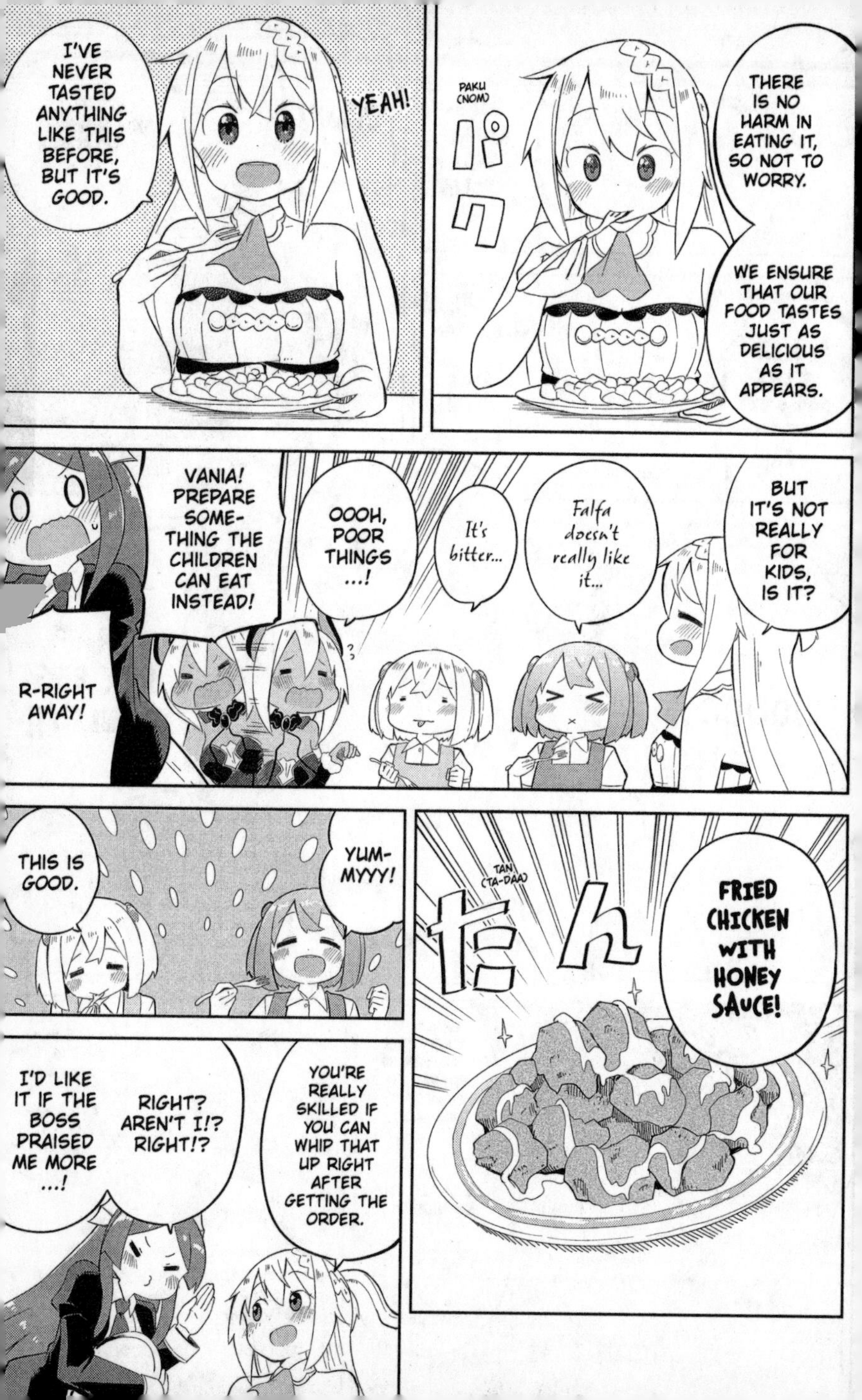
PAKU (NOM)
THERE IS NO HARM IN EATING IT, SO NOT TO WORRY.
WE ENSURE THAT OUR FOOD TASTES JUST AS DELICIOUS AS IT APPEARS.
I'VE NEVER TASTED ANYTHING LIKE THIS BEFORE, BUT IT'S GOOD.
YEAH!
BUT IT'S NOT REALLY FOR KIDS, IS IT?
Falfa doesn't really like it...
It's bitter...
OOOH, POOR THINGS...!
VANIA! PREPARE SOME-THING THE CHILDREN CAN EAT INSTEAD!
R-RIGHT AWAY!
TAN (TA-DAA)
FRIED CHICKEN WITH HONEY SAUCE!
YUM-MYYY!
THIS IS GOOD.
YOU'RE REALLY SKILLED IF YOU CAN WHIP THAT UP RIGHT AFTER GETTING THE ORDER.
RIGHT? AREN'T I!? RIGHT!?
I'D LIKE IT IF THE BOSS PRAISED ME MORE...!

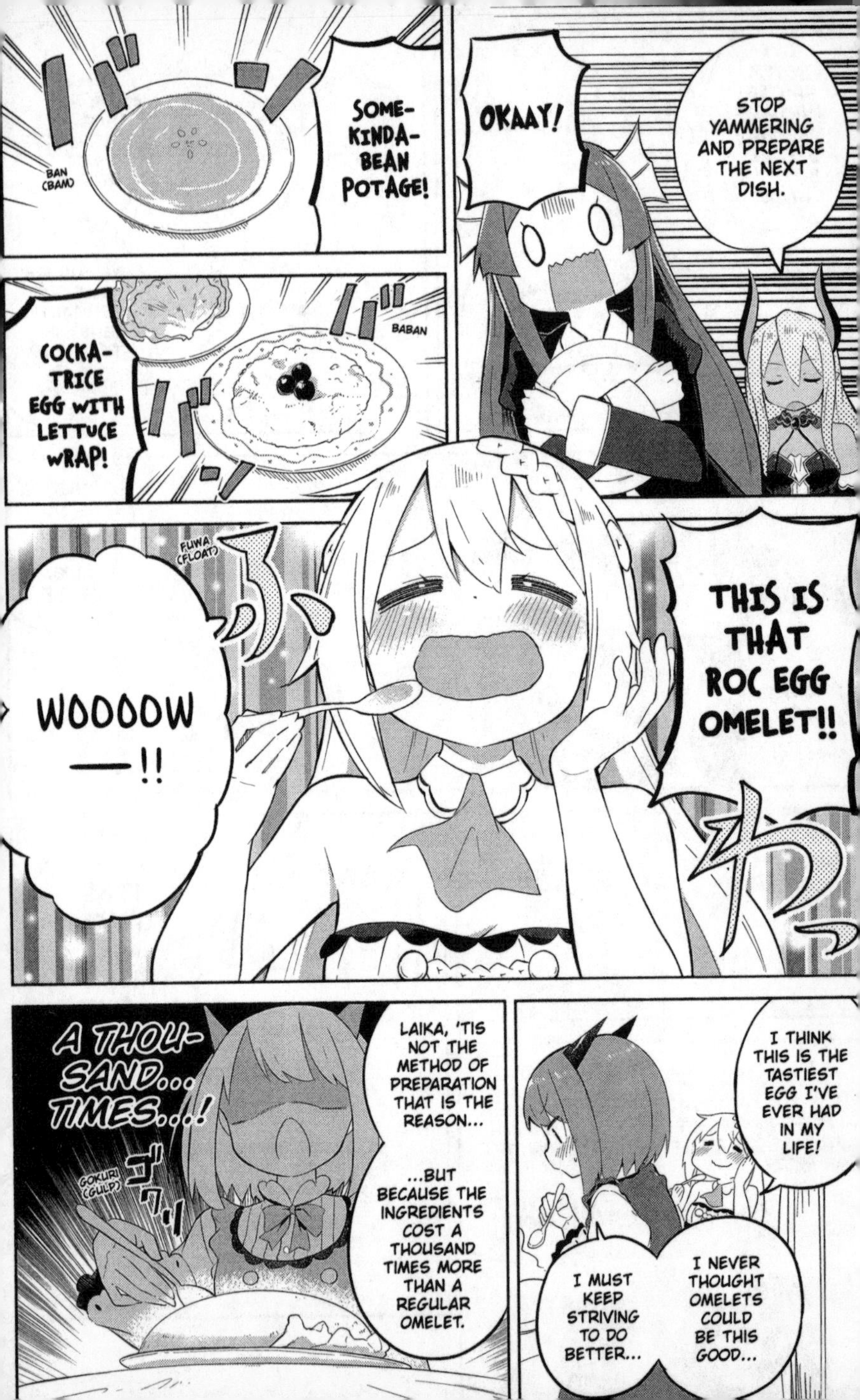
STOP YAMMERING AND PREPARE THE NEXT DISH.
OKAAY!
SOME-KINDA-BEAN POTAGE!
BAN (BAM)
BABAN
COCKATRICE EGG WITH LETTUCE WRAP!
THIS IS THAT ROC EGG OMELET!!
FUWA (FLOAT)
WOOOOW—!!
I THINK THIS IS THE TASTIEST EGG I'VE EVER HAD IN MY LIFE!
I NEVER THOUGHT OMELETS COULD BE THIS GOOD...
I MUST KEEP STRIVING TO DO BETTER...
LAIKA, 'TIS NOT THE METHOD OF PREPARATION THAT IS THE REASON...
...BUT BECAUSE THE INGREDIENTS COST A THOUSAND TIMES MORE THAN A REGULAR OMELET.
A THOUSAND... TIMES...!
GOKURI (GULP)

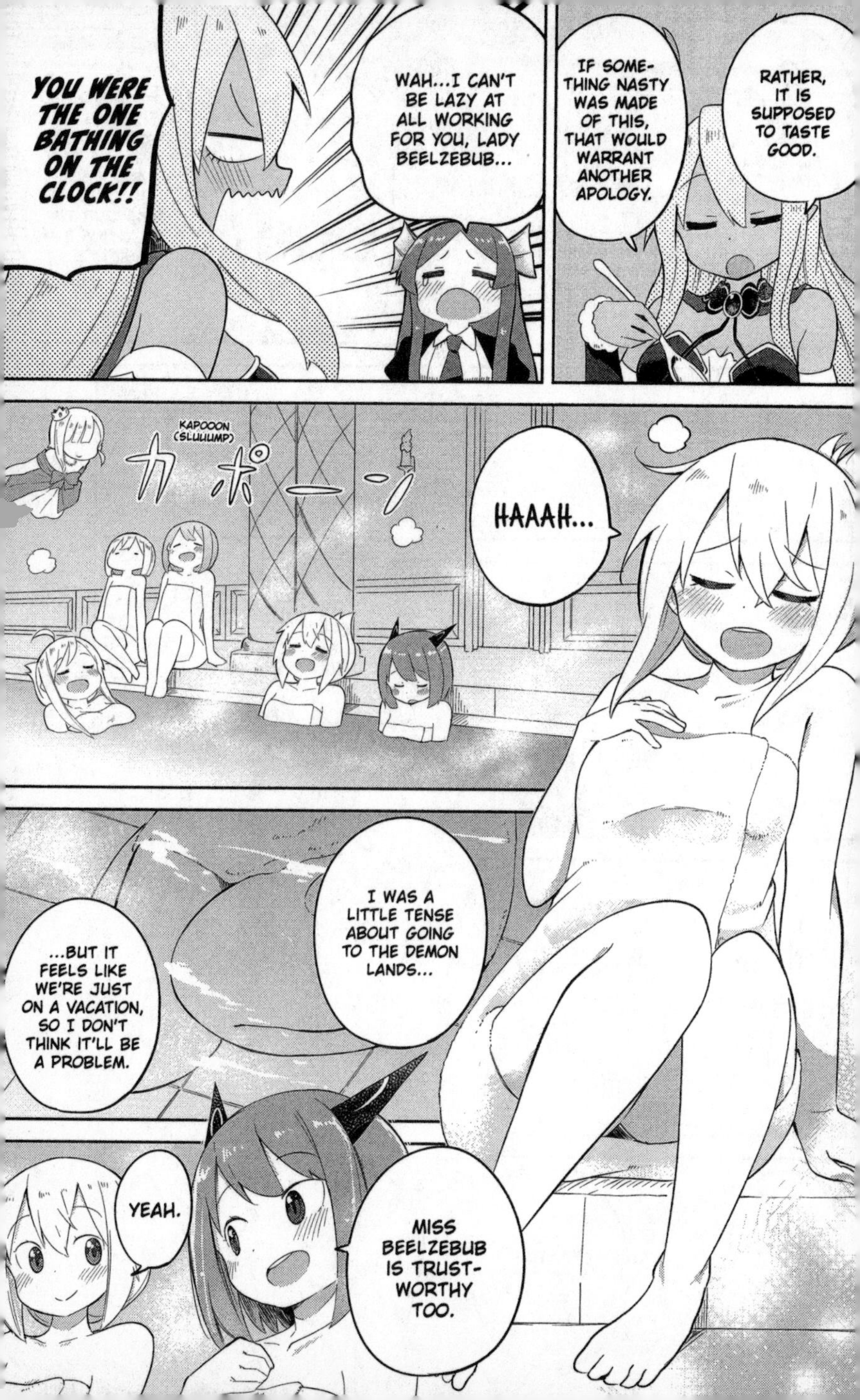
RATHER, IT IS SUPPOSED TO TASTE GOOD.
IF SOMETHING NASTY WAS MADE OF THIS, THAT WOULD WARRANT ANOTHER APOLOGY.
WAH...I CAN'T BE LAZY AT ALL WORKING FOR YOU, LADY BEELZEBUB...
YOU WERE THE ONE BATHING ON THE CLOCK!!
HAAAH...
カポーン
KAPOOON (SLUUUMP)
I WAS A LITTLE TENSE ABOUT GOING TO THE DEMON LANDS...
...BUT IT FEELS LIKE WE'RE JUST ON A VACATION, SO I DON'T THINK IT'LL BE A PROBLEM.
MISS BEELZEBUB IS TRUST-WORTHY TOO.
YEAH.

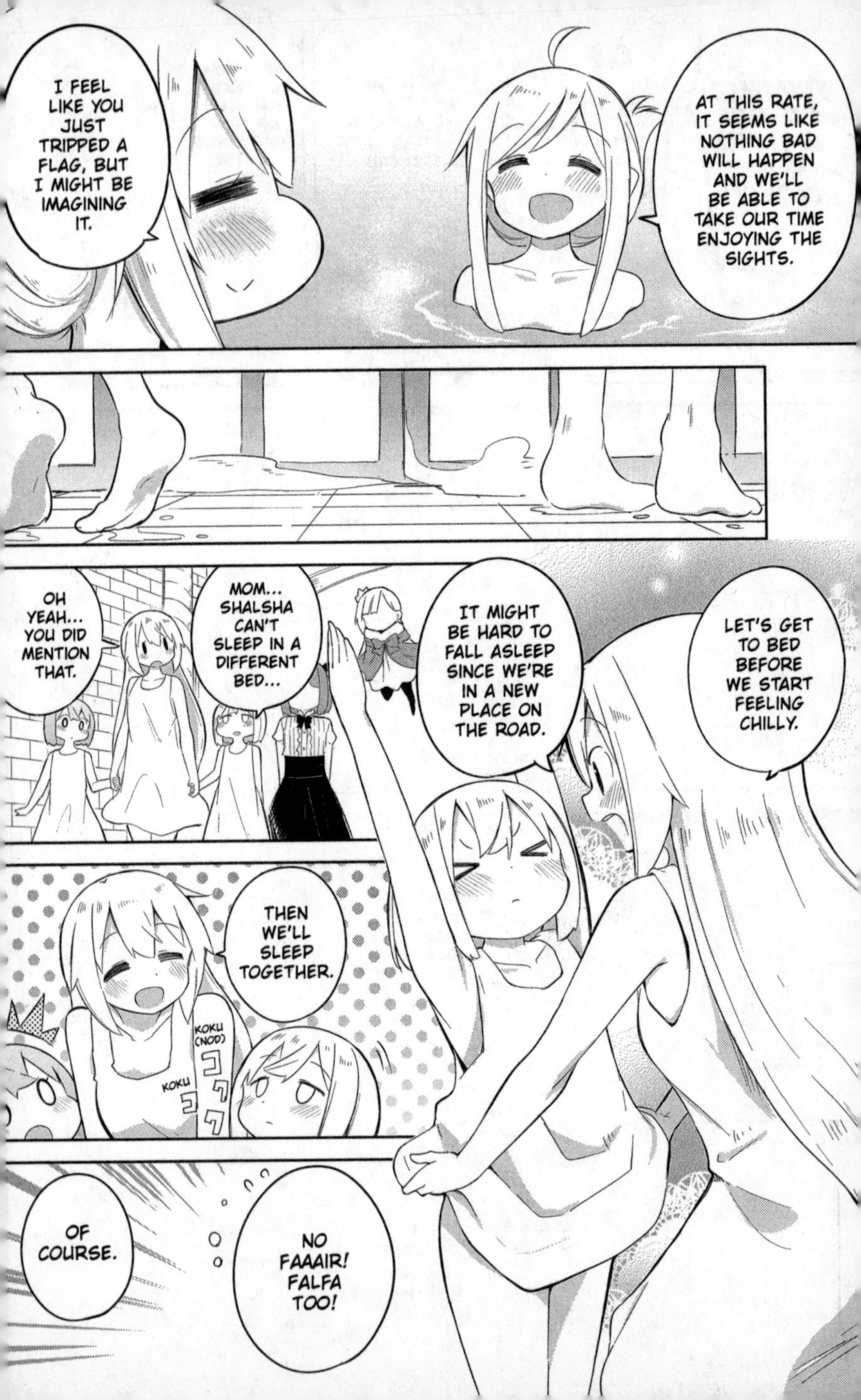
AT THIS RATE, IT SEEMS LIKE NOTHING BAD WILL HAPPEN AND WE'LL BE ABLE TO TAKE OUR TIME ENJOYING THE SIGHTS.
I FEEL LIKE YOU JUST TRIPPED A FLAG, BUT I MIGHT BE IMAGINING IT.
LET'S GET TO BED BEFORE WE START FEELING CHILLY.
IT MIGHT BE HARD TO FALL ASLEEP SINCE WE'RE IN A NEW PLACE ON THE ROAD.
MOM... SHALSHA CAN'T SLEEP IN A DIFFERENT BED...
OH YEAH... YOU DID MENTION THAT.
THEN WE'LL SLEEP TOGETHER.
KOKU (NOD)
KOKU
NO FAAAIR! FALFA TOO!
OF COURSE.

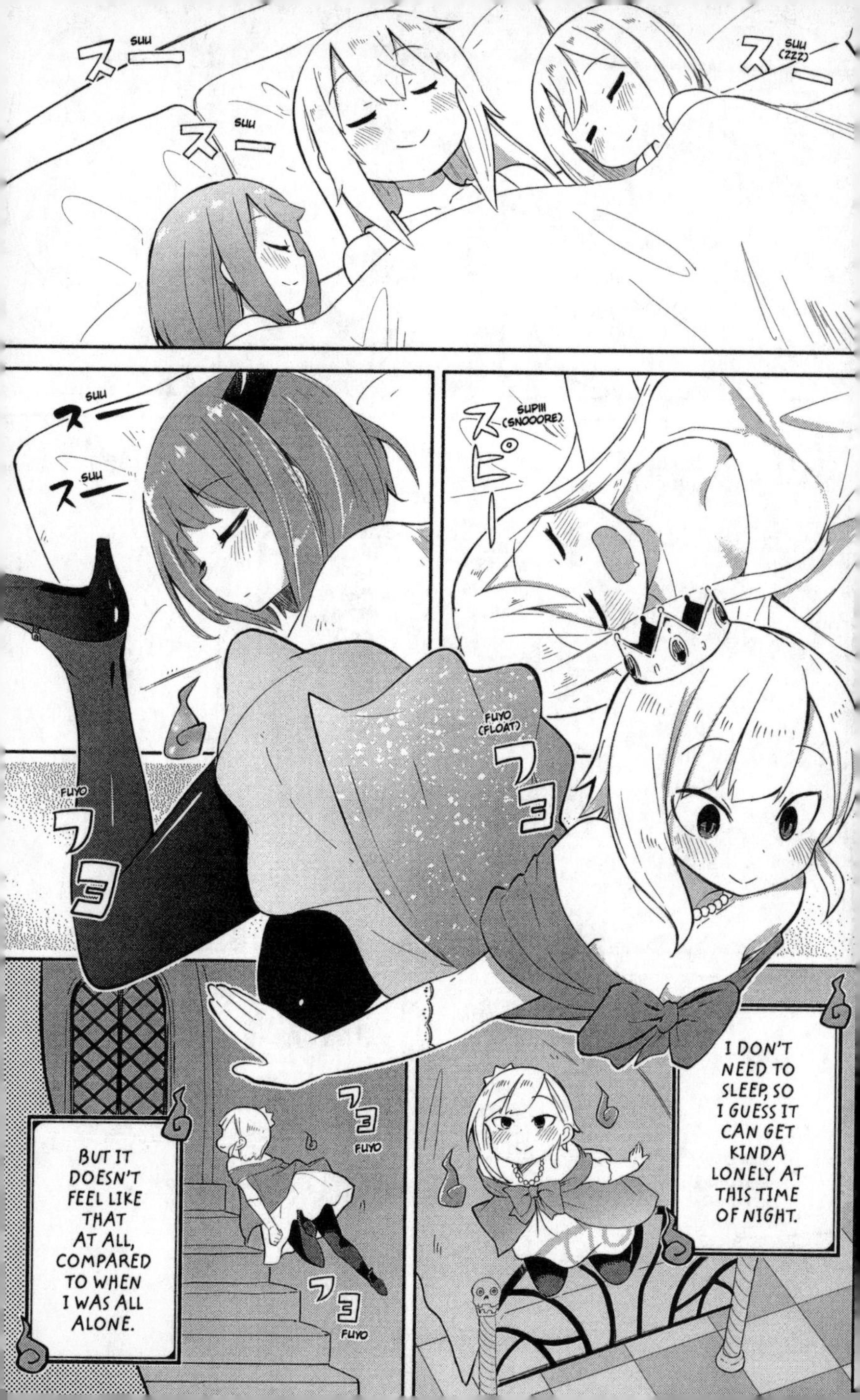
スー
SUU (ZZZ)
スー
SUU
スー
SUU
スピー
SUPIII (SNOOORE)
スー
SUU
スー
SUU
フヨ
FUYO (FLOAT)
フヨ
FUYO
I DON'T NEED TO SLEEP, SO I GUESS IT CAN GET KINDA LONELY AT THIS TIME OF NIGHT.
フヨ
FUYO
フヨ
FUYO
BUT IT DOESN'T FEEL LIKE THAT AT ALL, COMPARED TO WHEN I WAS ALL ALONE.

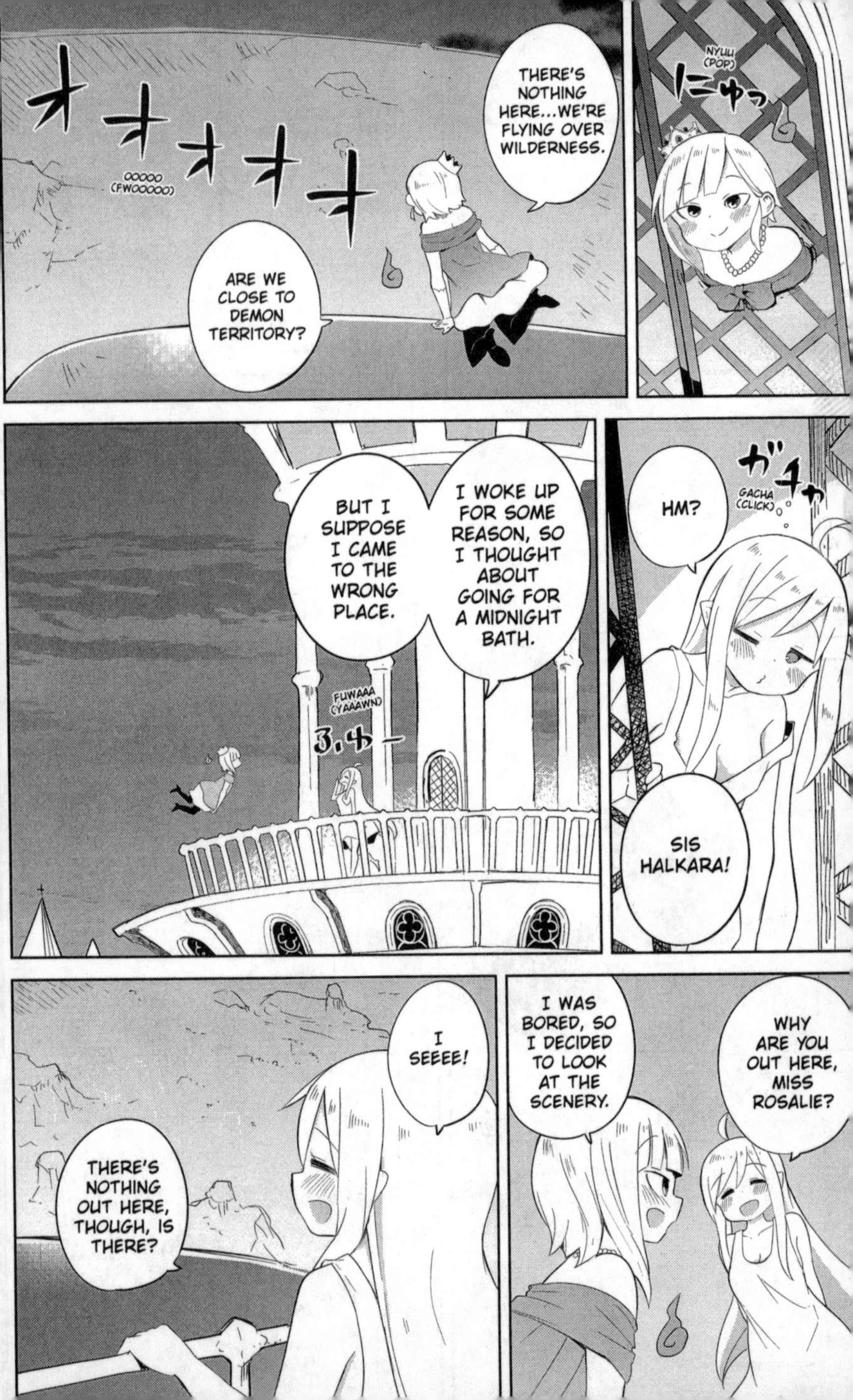
NYUU (POP)
にゅっ
THERE'S NOTHING HERE...WE'RE FLYING OVER WILDERNESS.
オオオオオ
OOOOO (FWOOOOO)
ARE WE CLOSE TO DEMON TERRITORY?
ガチャ
GACHA (CLICK)
HM?
SIS HALKARA!
I WOKE UP FOR SOME REASON, SO I THOUGHT ABOUT GOING FOR A MIDNIGHT BATH.
BUT I SUPPOSE I CAME TO THE WRONG PLACE.
FUWAAA (YAAAWN)
ふぁー
WHY ARE YOU OUT HERE, MISS ROSALIE?
I WAS BORED, SO I DECIDED TO LOOK AT THE SCENERY.
I SEEEE!
THERE'S NOTHING OUT HERE, THOUGH, IS THERE?

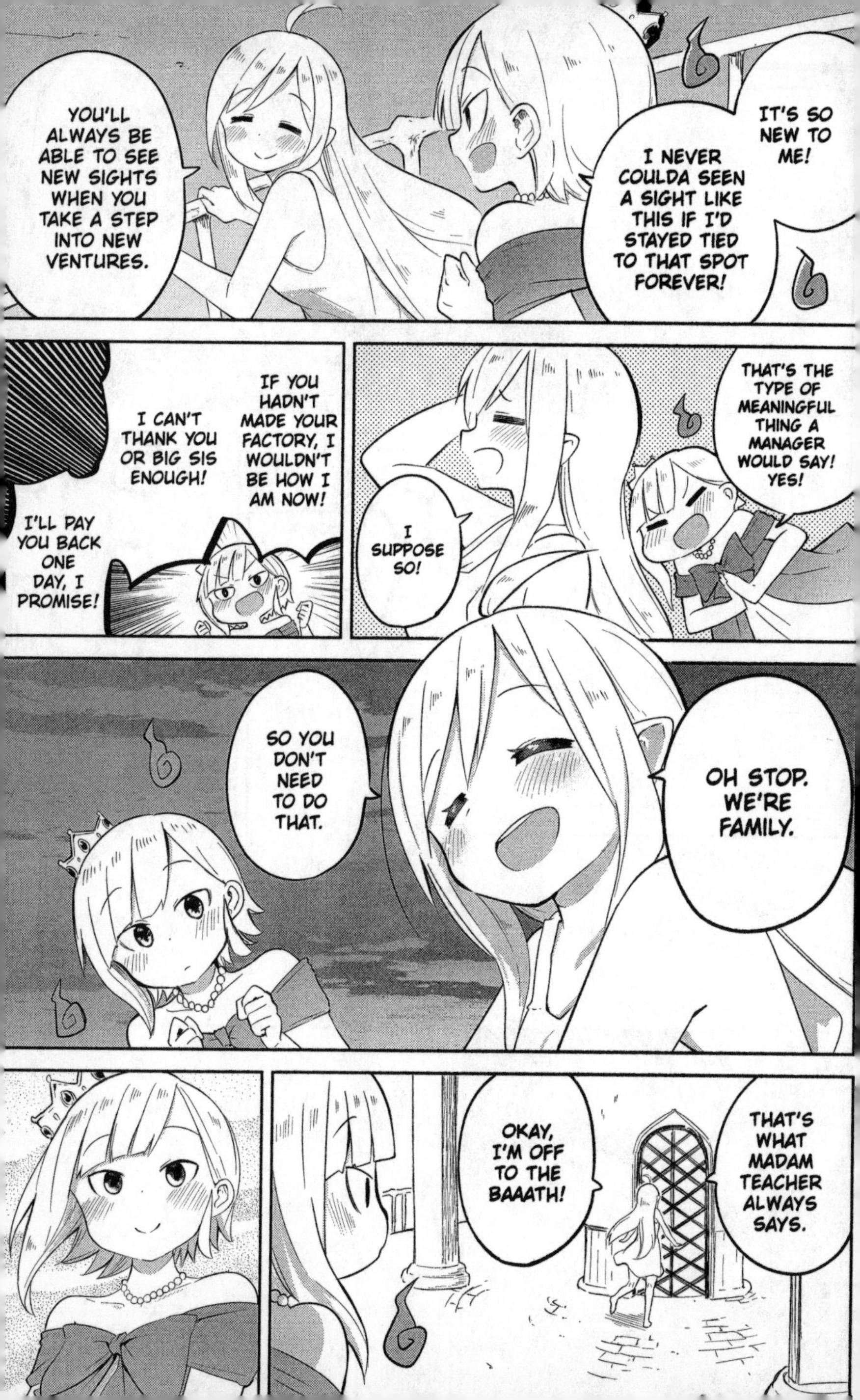
IT'S SO NEW TO ME!
I NEVER COULDA SEEN A SIGHT LIKE THIS IF I'D STAYED TIED TO THAT SPOT FOREVER!
YOU'LL ALWAYS BE ABLE TO SEE NEW SIGHTS WHEN YOU TAKE A STEP INTO NEW VENTURES.
THAT'S THE TYPE OF MEANINGFUL THING A MANAGER WOULD SAY! YES!
I SUPPOSE SO!
IF YOU HADN'T MADE YOUR FACTORY, I WOULDN'T BE HOW I AM NOW!
I CAN'T THANK YOU OR BIG SIS ENOUGH!
I'LL PAY YOU BACK ONE DAY, I PROMISE!
OH STOP. WE'RE FAMILY.
SO YOU DON'T NEED TO DO THAT.
THAT'S WHAT MADAM TEACHER ALWAYS SAYS.
OKAY, I'M OFF TO THE BAAATH!

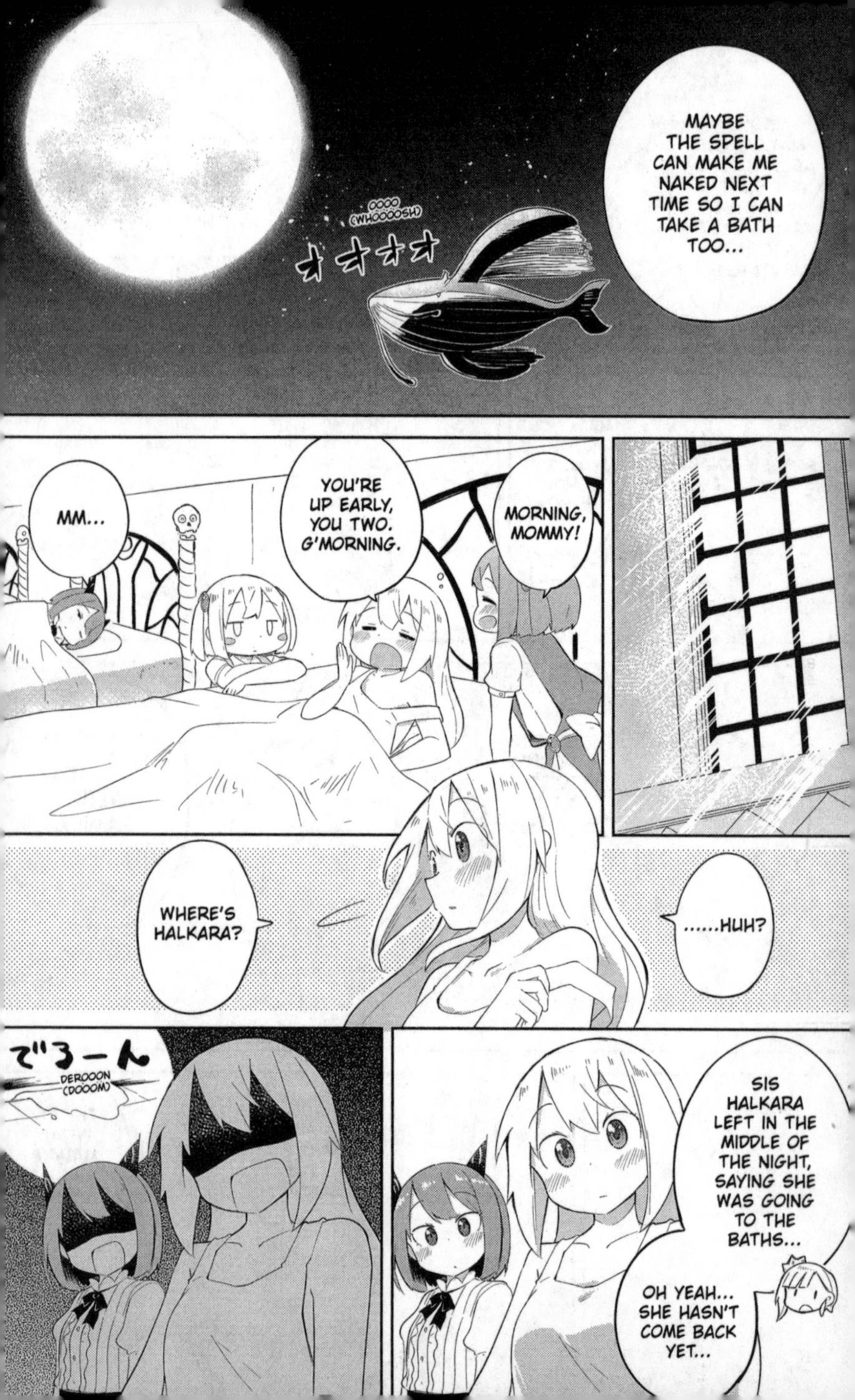
MAYBE THE SPELL CAN MAKE ME NAKED NEXT TIME SO I CAN TAKE A BATH TOO...
オオオオ
OOOO (WHOOOOSH)
MORNING, MOMMY!
YOU'RE UP EARLY, YOU TWO. G'MORNING.
MM...
......HUH?
WHERE'S HALKARA?
SIS HALKARA LEFT IN THE MIDDLE OF THE NIGHT, SAYING SHE WAS GOING TO THE BATHS...
OH YEAH... SHE HASN'T COME BACK YET...
でろーん
DEROOON (DOOOM)

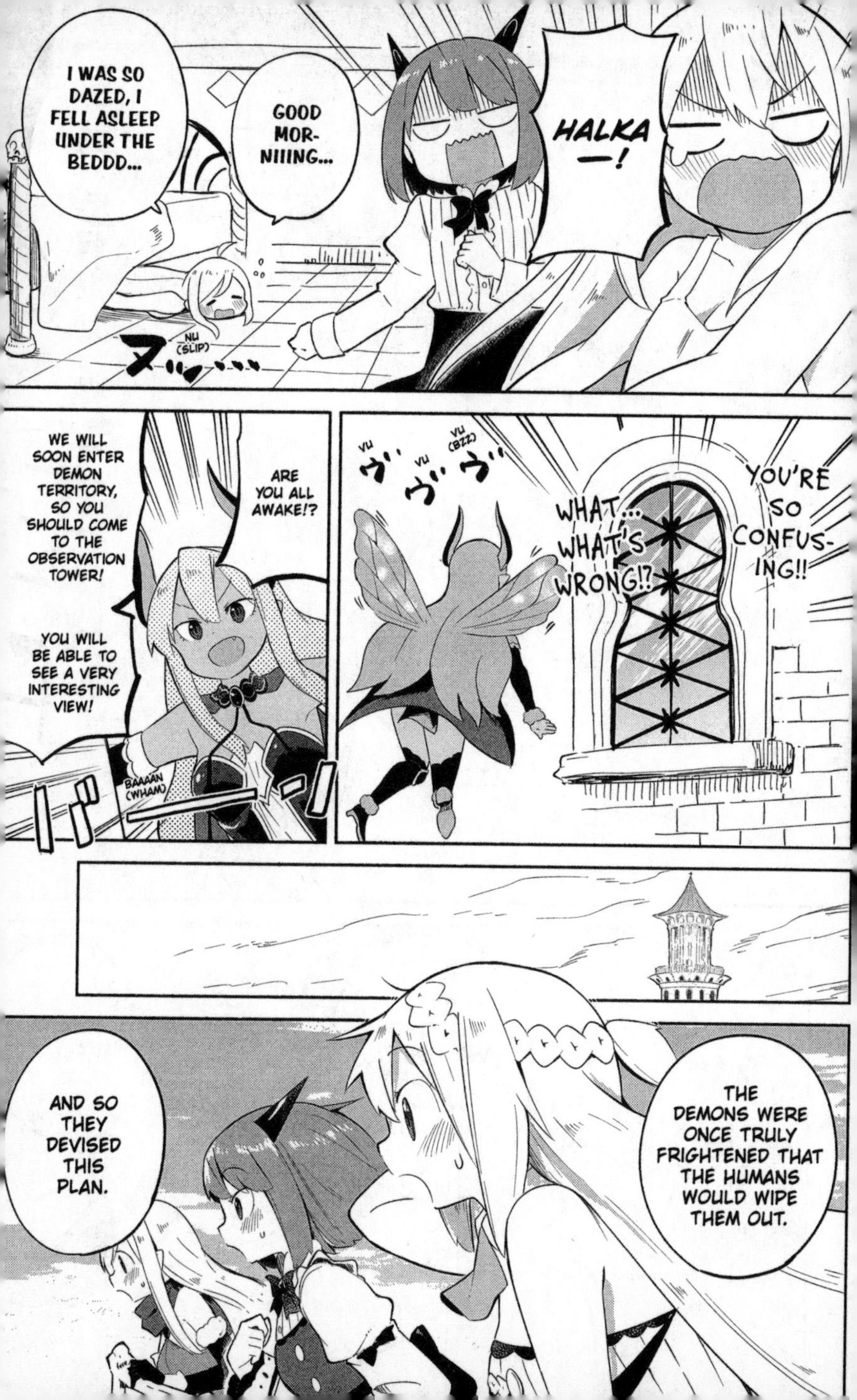
HALKA—!
GOOD MOR-NIIING...
I WAS SO DAZED, I FELL ASLEEP UNDER THE BEDDD...
NU (SLIP)
YOU'RE SO CONFUS-ING!!
WHAT... WHAT'S WRONG!?
VU VU VU (BZZ)
ARE YOU ALL AWAKE!?
WE WILL SOON ENTER DEMON TERRITORY, SO YOU SHOULD COME TO THE OBSERVATION TOWER!
YOU WILL BE ABLE TO SEE A VERY INTERESTING VIEW!
BAAAAN (WHAM)
THE DEMONS WERE ONCE TRULY FRIGHTENED THAT THE HUMANS WOULD WIPE THEM OUT.
AND SO THEY DEVISED THIS PLAN.

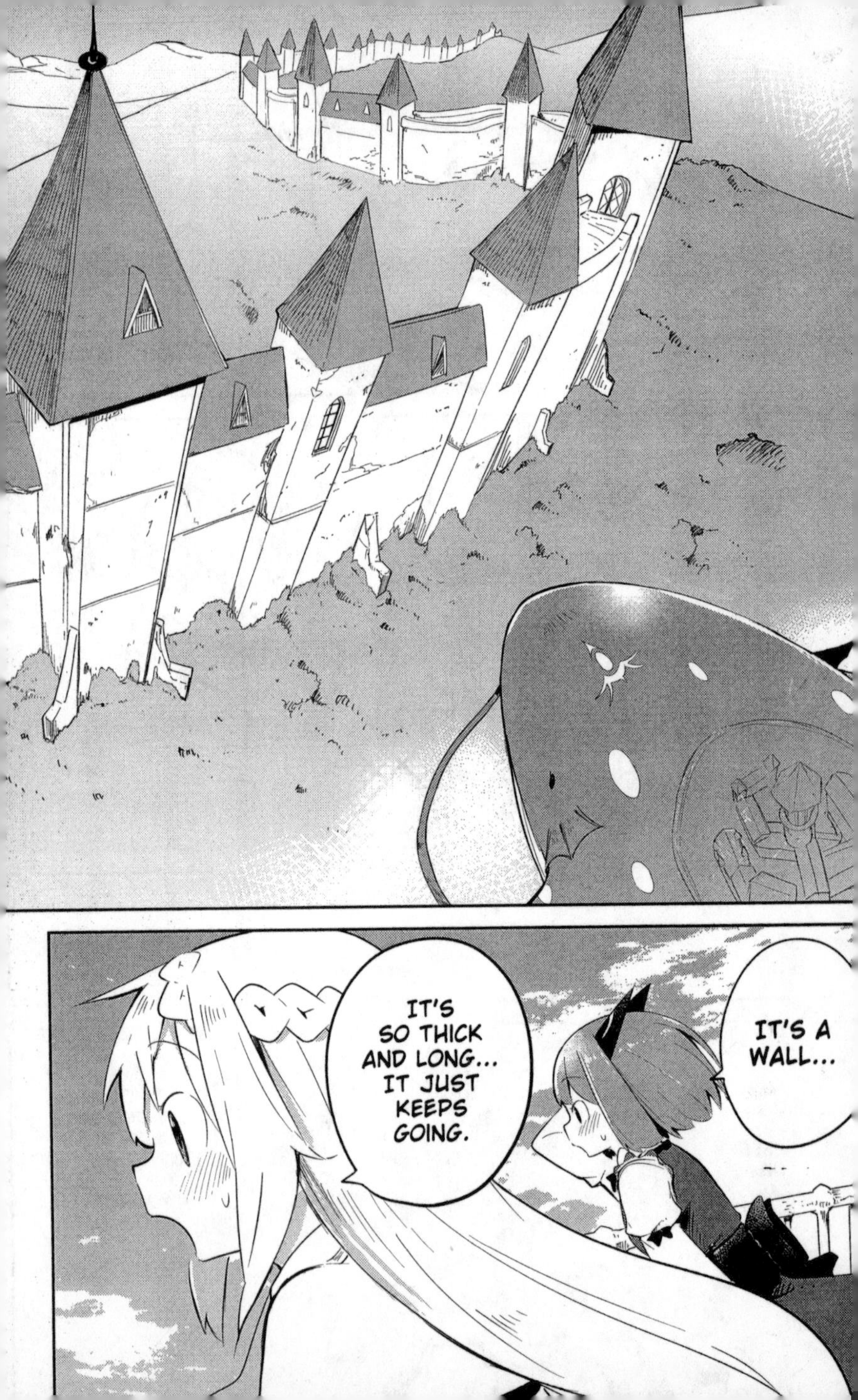
IT'S A WALL...
IT'S SO THICK AND LONG... IT JUST KEEPS GOING.

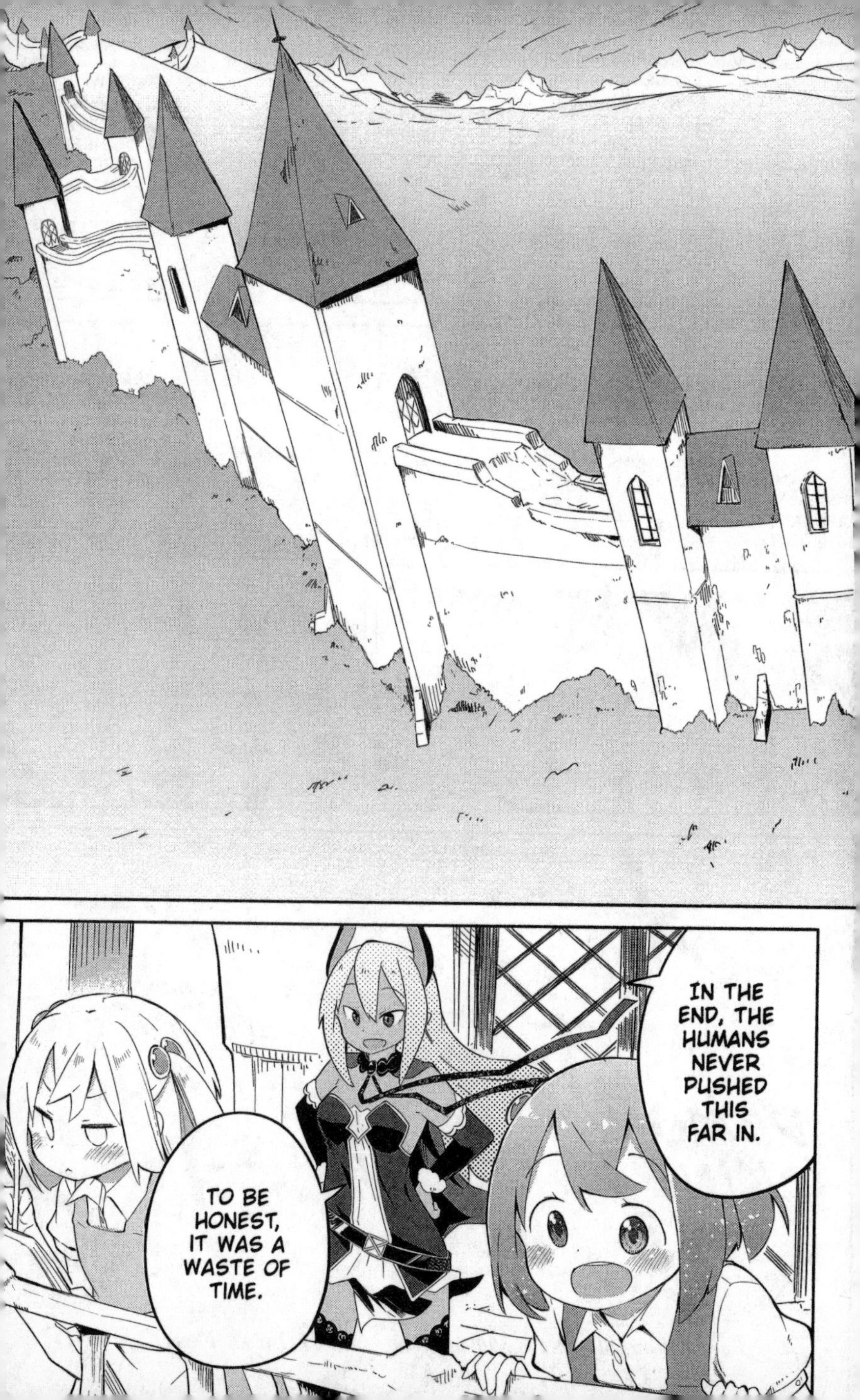
IN THE END, THE HUMANS NEVER PUSHED THIS FAR IN.
TO BE HONEST, IT WAS A WASTE OF TIME.

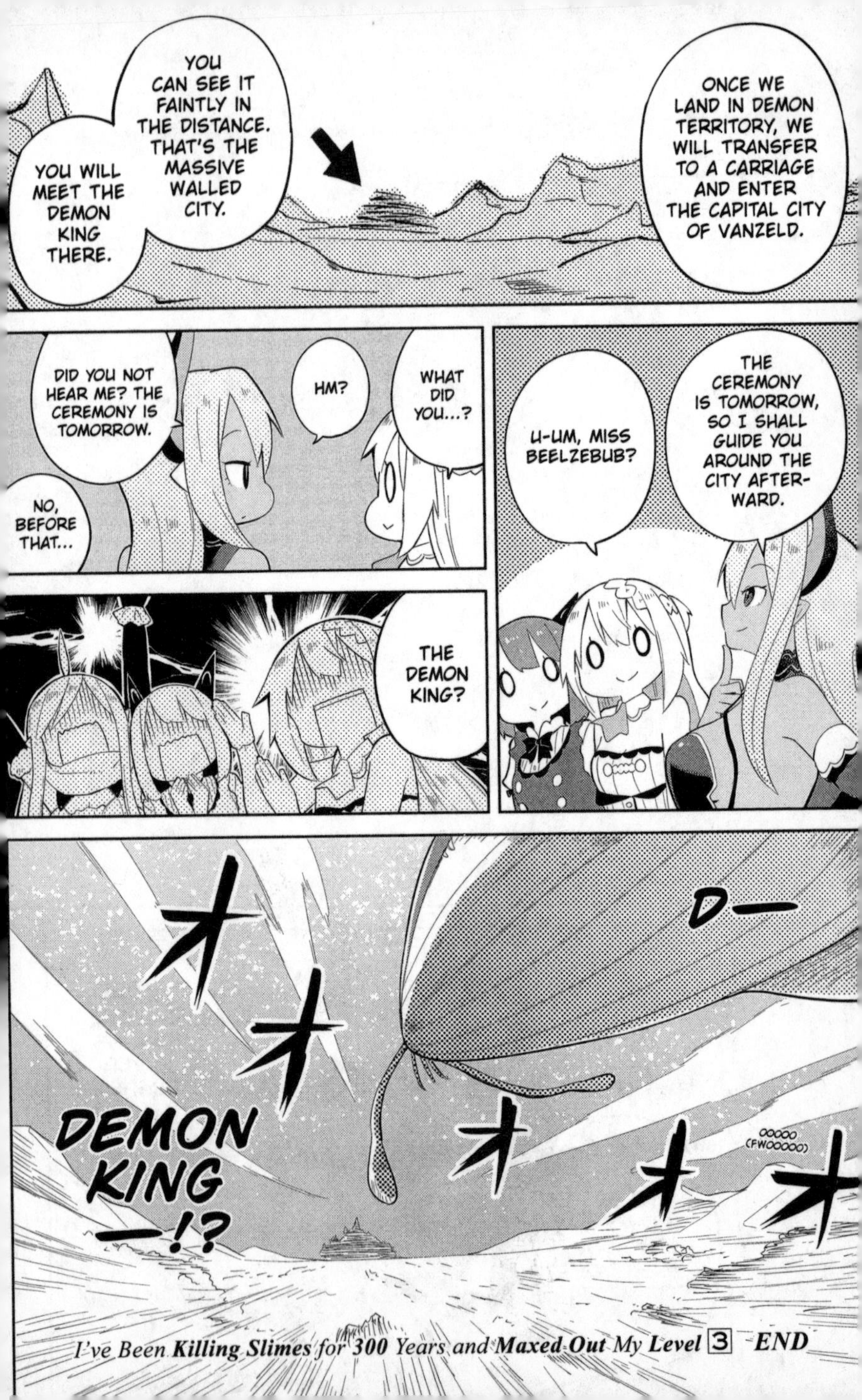
ONCE WE LAND IN DEMON TERRITORY, WE WILL TRANSFER TO A CARRIAGE AND ENTER THE CAPITAL CITY OF VANZELD.
YOU CAN SEE IT FAINTLY IN THE DISTANCE. THAT'S THE MASSIVE WALLED CITY.
YOU WILL MEET THE DEMON KING THERE.
THE CEREMONY IS TOMORROW, SO I SHALL GUIDE YOU AROUND THE CITY AFTER-WARD.
U-UM, MISS BEELZEBUB?
WHAT DID YOU...?
HM?
DID YOU NOT HEAR ME? THE CEREMONY IS TOMORROW.
NO, BEFORE THAT...
THE DEMON KING?
D—
オ
オ
オ
オ
オ
OOOOO (FWOOOOO)
DEMON KING—!?
I've Been Killing Slimes for 300 Years and Maxed Out My Level 3 END

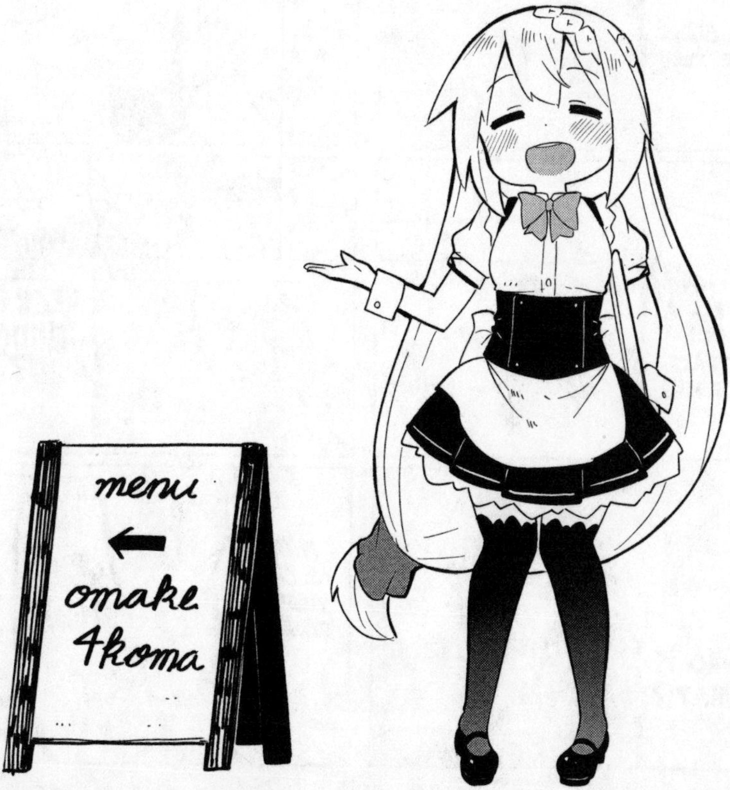
menu
omake
4koma

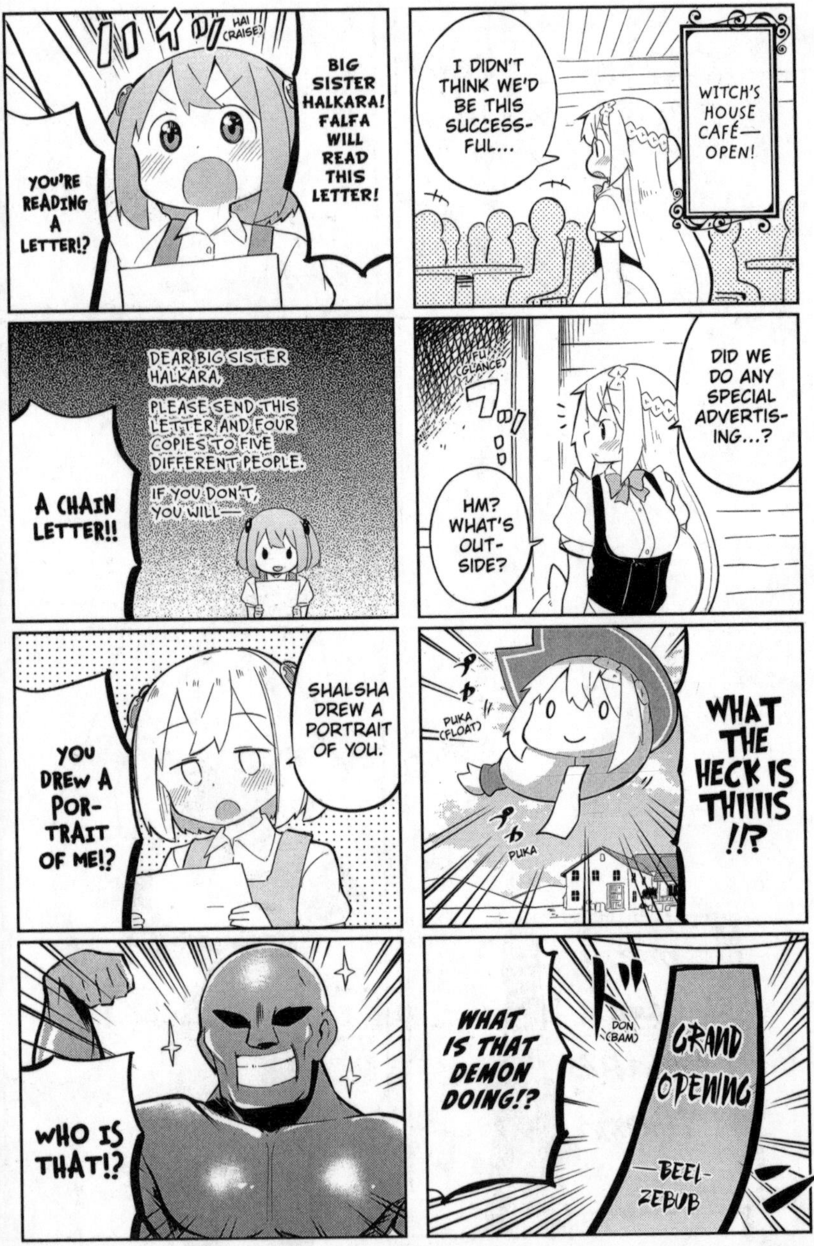
WITCH'S HOUSE CAFÉ—OPEN!
I DIDN'T THINK WE'D BE THIS SUCCESS-FUL...
DID WE DO ANY SPECIAL ADVERTIS-ING...?
FU (GLANCE)
HM? WHAT'S OUT-SIDE?
WHAT THE HECK IS THIIIIS!!?
PUKA (FLOAT)
PUKA
GRAND OPENING —BEEL-ZEBUB
DON (BAM)
WHAT IS THAT DEMON DOING!?
HAI (RAISE)
BIG SISTER HALKARA! FALFA WILL READ THIS LETTER!
YOU'RE READING A LETTER!?
DEAR BIG SISTER HALKARA,
PLEASE SEND THIS LETTER AND FOUR COPIES TO FIVE DIFFERENT PEOPLE.
IF YOU DON'T, YOU WILL—
A CHAIN LETTER!!
SHALSHA DREW A PORTRAIT OF YOU.
YOU DREW A POR-TRAIT OF ME!?
WHO IS THAT!?

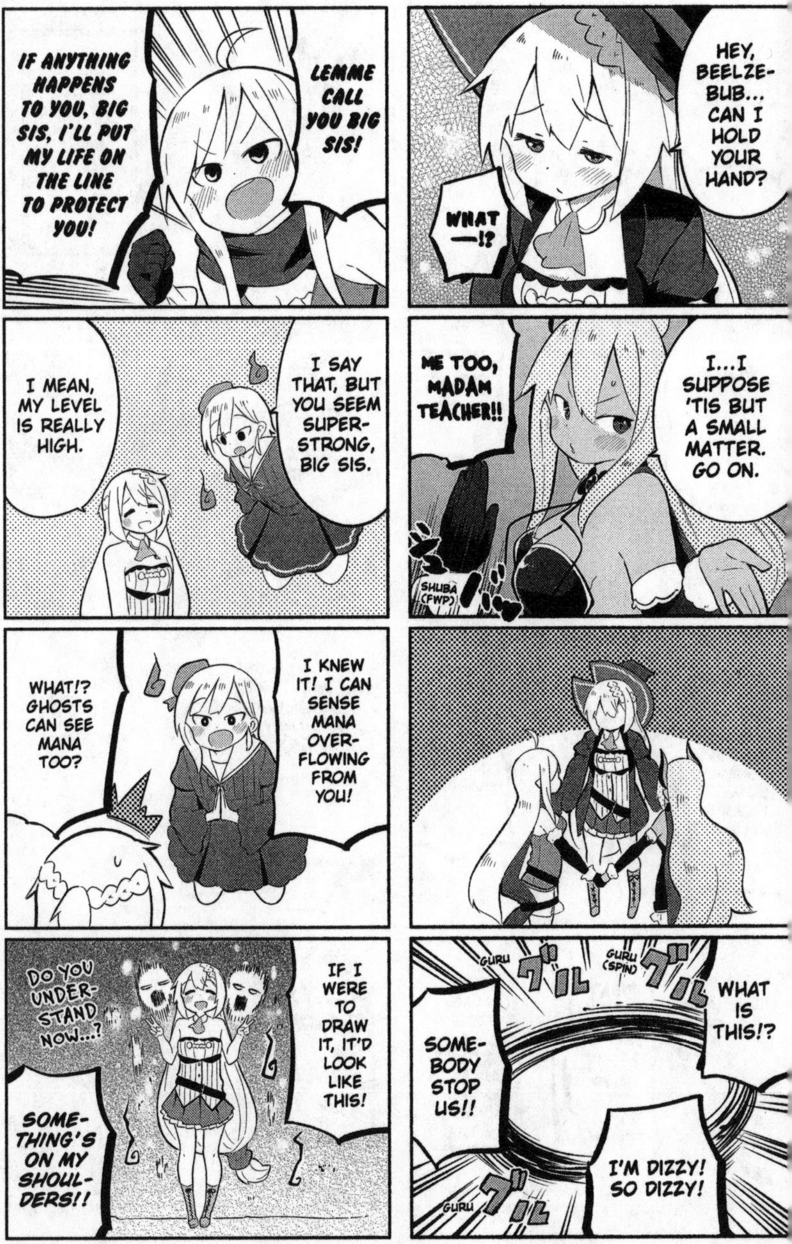
HEY, BEELZEBUB... CAN I HOLD YOUR HAND?
WHAT—!?
LEMME CALL YOU BIG SIS!
IF ANYTHING HAPPENS TO YOU, BIG SIS, I'LL PUT MY LIFE ON THE LINE TO PROTECT YOU!
I...I SUPPOSE 'TIS BUT A SMALL MATTER. GO ON.
ME TOO, MADAM TEACHER!!
SHUBA (FWP)
I SAY THAT, BUT YOU SEEM SUPER-STRONG, BIG SIS.
I MEAN, MY LEVEL IS REALLY HIGH.
I KNEW IT! I CAN SENSE MANA OVERFLOWING FROM YOU!
WHAT!? GHOSTS CAN SEE MANA TOO?
GURU (SPIN)
GURU
WHAT IS THIS!?
SOMEBODY STOP US!!
I'M DIZZY! SO DIZZY!
GURU
IF I WERE TO DRAW IT, IT'D LOOK LIKE THIS!
DO YOU UNDERSTAND NOW...?
SOMETHING'S ON MY SHOULDERS!!

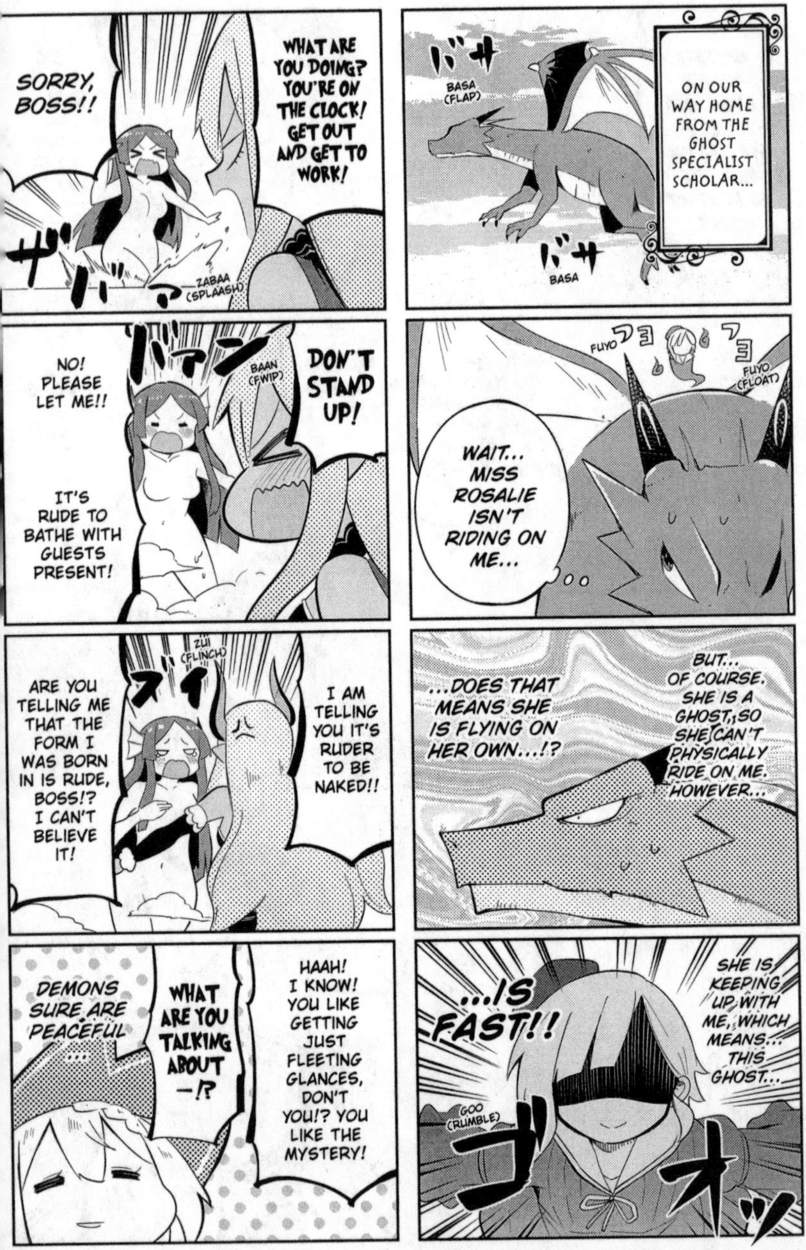
ON OUR WAY HOME FROM THE GHOST SPECIALIST SCHOLAR...
BASA (FLAP)
BASA
FUYO (FLOAT)
FUYO
WAIT... MISS ROSALIE ISN'T RIDING ON ME...
BUT... OF COURSE. SHE IS A GHOST, SO SHE CAN'T PHYSICALLY RIDE ON ME. HOWEVER...
...DOES THAT MEANS SHE IS FLYING ON HER OWN...!?
SHE IS KEEPING UP WITH ME, WHICH MEANS... THIS GHOST...
...IS FAST!!
GOO (RUMBLE)
WHAT ARE YOU DOING? YOU'RE ON THE CLOCK! GET OUT AND GET TO WORK!
SORRY, BOSS!!
ZABAA (SPLAASH)
DON'T STAND UP!
BAAN (FWIP)
NO! PLEASE LET ME!!
IT'S RUDE TO BATHE WITH GUESTS PRESENT!
I AM TELLING YOU IT'S RUDER TO BE NAKED!!
ZUI (FLINCH)
ARE YOU TELLING ME THAT THE FORM I WAS BORN IN IS RUDE, BOSS!? I CAN'T BELIEVE IT!
HAAH! I KNOW! YOU LIKE GETTING JUST FLEETING GLANCES, DON'T YOU!? YOU LIKE THE MYSTERY!
WHAT ARE YOU TALKING ABOUT—!?
DEMONS SURE ARE PEACEFUL...

AFTERWORD

THANK YOU FOR READING VOLUME 3 OF THE COMIC ADAPTATION OF I'VE BEEN KILLING SLIMES. I'M YUSUKE SHIBA.

IT'S GOTTEN EVEN LIVELIER WITH EVEN MORE FAMILY MEMBERS AND OTHER CHARACTERS IN THIS VOLUME. AND I'M SURE IT WILL EXPAND EVEN MORE NEXT TIME! I BELIEVE THOSE WHO READ THE ORIGINAL NOVELS ALREADY KNOW THIS, BUT THERE WILL BE MORE AND MORE. THEY MULTIPLY LIKE SLIMES.

PLEASE DO READ THE ORIGINAL STORY AND TRY TO IMAGINE HOW THESE NEW CHARACTERS WILL TURN OUT IN THE COMIC ADAPTATION AS YOU CONTINUE TO FOLLOW THE STORY HERE—THEN YOU'LL BE ABLE TO ENJOY IT TWICE. THERE ARE A LOT OF CHARACTERS I'M EXCITED TO DRAW, SO I CAN'T WAIT FOR THE FUTURE.

シバユウスケ

YUSUKE SHIBA

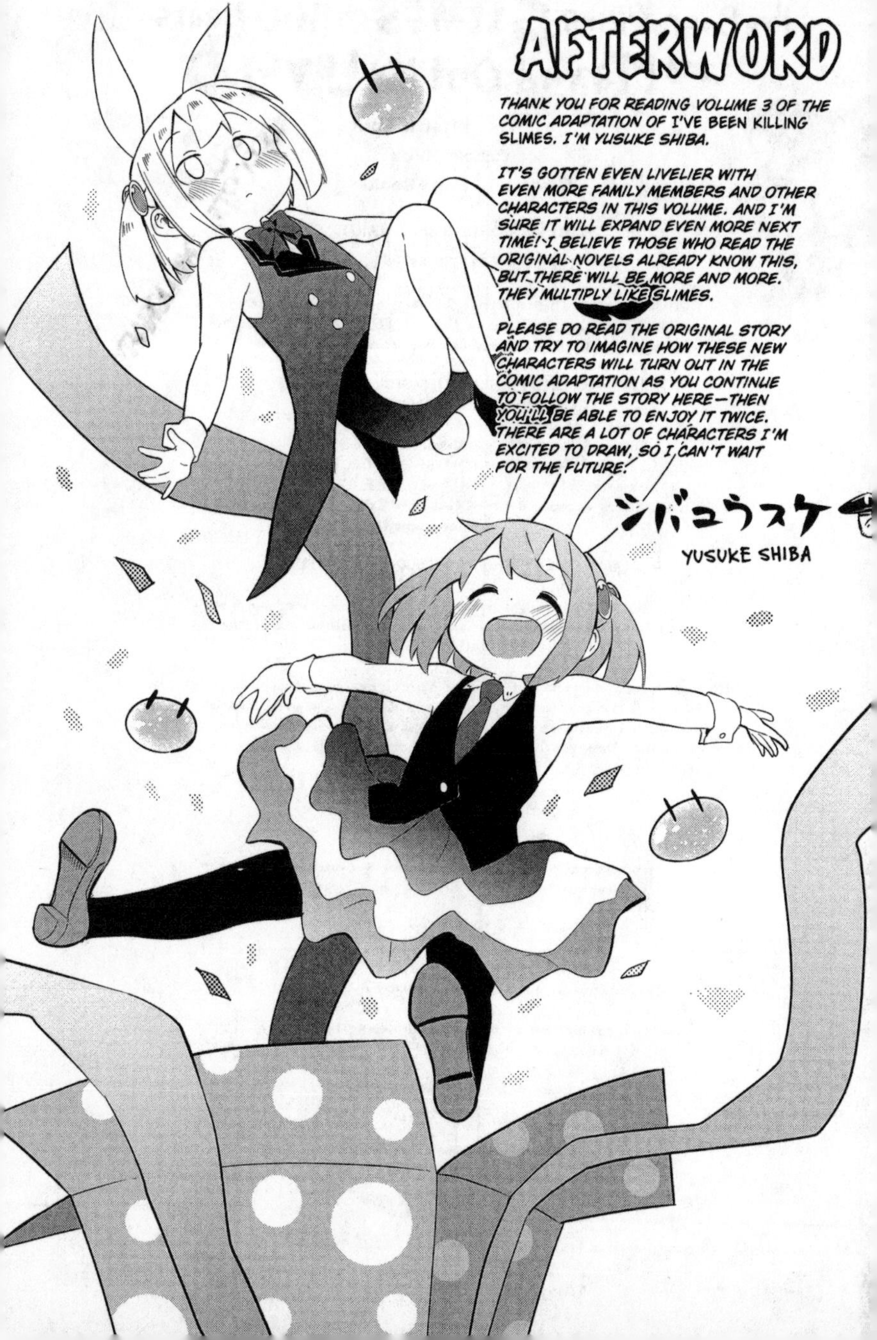

I've Been Killing SLIMES for 300 Years and Maxed Out My Level 3

Original Story **Kisetsu Morita**

Art **Yusuke Shiba**

Character Design **Benio**

Translation: JASMINE BERNHARDT

Lettering: KATIE BLAKESLEE

SLIME TAOSHITE SANBYAKUNEN, SHIRANAIUCHINI
LEVEL MAX NI NATTEMASHITA vol. 3
©Kisetsu Morita / SB Creative Corp.
Original Character Designs: ©Benio / SB Creative Corp.
©2018 Yusuke Shiba / SQUARE ENIX CO., LTD.
First published in Japan in 2018 by SQUARE ENIX CO., LTD.
English translation rights arranged with SQUARE ENIX CO., LTD. and Yen Press, LLC through Tuttle-Mori Agency, Inc.

English translation © 2020 by SQUARE ENIX CO., LTD.

Yen Press
150 West 30th Street, 19th Floor
New York, NY 10001

Visit us at yenpress.com ★ facebook.com/yenpress ★ twitter.com/yenpress ★ yenpress.tumblr.com ★ instagram.com/yenpress

First Yen Press Edition: September 2020

Yen Press is an imprint of Yen Press, LLC.
The Yen Press name and logo are trademarks of Yen Press, LLC.

The publisher is not responsible for websites (or their content) that are not owned by the publisher.

Library of Congress Control Number:
2019953620

ISBNs: 978-1-9753-0919-0 (paperback)
978-1-9753-0920-6 (ebook)

10 9 8 7 6 5 4 3 2 1

BVG

Printed in the United States of America